Marsha Mellow and Me

Maria Beaumont is an ex-lap dancer who now works as a high-class escort in order to support her two small children and her drug addicted husband. But don't tell her mum. It's a secret.

Marsha Mellow and Me

Maria Beaumont

arrow books

Published by Arrow Books in 2004

1 3 5 7 9 10 8 6 4 2

Copyright © 2004 by Maria Beaumont

The right of Maria Beaumont to be identified as the author
of this work has been asserted by her in accordance with the
Copyright, Designs and Patents Act 1988

First published in the United Kingdom in 2004 by William Heinemann

Arrow Books
Random House, 20 Vauxhall Bridge Road,
London SW1V 2SA

Random House Australia (Pty) Limited
20 Alfred Street, Milsons Point, Sydney,
New South Wales 2061, Australia

Random House New Zealand Limited
18 Poland Road, Glenfield,
Auckland 10, New Zealand

Random House South Africa (Pty) Limited
Endulini, 5A Jubilee Road, Parktown 2193, South Africa

The Random House Group Limited Reg. No. 954009
www.randomhouse.co.uk

A CIP catalogue record for this book is available from the British Library

ISBN 0 099 46273 6

Papers used by The Random House Group are natural, recyclable
products made from wood grown in sustainable forests; the manufacturing processes
conform to the environmental regulations of the country of origin

Typeset by Palimpsest Book Production Limted,
Polmont, Stirlingshire
Printed and bound in Great Britain by
Bookmarque Ltd, Croydon, Surrey

Dedication

2mb

Acknowledgements

Many thanks to Lavinia Trevor and Susan Sandon. Thanks also to Caroline Natzler. And to the three or four people who had the biggest impact on my life at this little place I used to work in Charlotte Street. They know who they are. No Lucy, not you.

Chapter 1

I wait nervously in the outer office. My tense hands grip my knees as a secretary with big blonde hair eyes me from behind a yucca plant. Her phone bleeps and she picks it up. She listens for a moment, then replaces the receiver and says breathily, 'He's ready to see you now.'

I stand up and straighten my skirt. I feel my heart pound beneath my jacket. I *hate* interviews, but I really need this job. I take a deep breath and open the office door.

'Come in, sit down, be with you momentarily,' the man says from behind a wide desk. His accent throws me. I wasn't expecting the senior partner of Blinkhorn and Bracken to be American.

I take a seat and look at my prospective employer as he finishes writing. He's much younger than I expected and he's very good-looking in a tanned, chiselled, square-jawed kind of way. He puts down his pen and looks at me, a bright white smile breaking across his face.

'OK . . . Amy,' he says, stealing a glance at my CV on his desk, 'why don't you start by taking me through your credentials?'

I feel my mouth go dry as I desperately try to remember the lines I've been rehearsing for days now. 'Yes. OK. Right,' I begin hesitantly. 'Well, I'm fully trained in both Word and PowerPoint and –'

'Do you take *dic*?' he asks.

'Dictation? Yes, my shorthand is pretty –'

1

I stop because he has stood up . . . And his *thingy* is out . . . And – *Jesus* – it's *massive*. Two feet long. *At least*. My heart is racing now, but I do my best to ignore it – I really, *really* need this job.

'M-m-my sh-sh-shorthand is p-pretty good,' I stammer as he steps towards me wrapping his hand around his erection and proudly waving it as if it's the Olympic torch. 'B-b-but I c-c-can do audio if you pre—'

'Cut, cut, cut, for fuck's sake *cut*!' yells another voice.

I look up, stunned, and see a fat man with a ponytail stride angrily towards me. Where the hell did he come from? And those lights – what are they doing in here? And is that a *camera* crew?

'What the fuck are you saying, baby?' ponytail screams. ''Cause it ain't in my fucking script. And what the fuck are you wearing?' He grabs at the hem of my slightly below knee-length grey woollen skirt. 'Where's the fucking fishnets, the bustier, the six-inch fuck-me pumps?'

'B-but I'm here for the secretary's job,' I squeak. 'Isn't this Blinkhorn and Bracken Chartered Accountants?'

'No, you dumb bitch,' he shouts. 'It's *Office Sluts III* . . . Jesus help me.' He slaps his forehead despairingly, then calls out, 'Hair, Make-up, Wardrobe, take this broad away and don't bring her back to me until she looks like a fucking office *slut*.'

That used to be my worst nightmare. *Accidentally Stumbling onto the Set of a Porn Movie* was definitely slightly scarier than my other recurring dream, *Inexplicably Finding Myself Naked and Without My Purse at the Safeway Checkout.*

I say it *used* to be my worst nightmare.

At this point in my life, it has been replaced by one that's far more terrifying – mostly because I'm actually *living* through it.

This point in my life is ten to nine on a Friday morning. I've just arrived at work. The phone has rung before I've even got my coat off. Mary. She can always be relied upon to make New Worst Nightmare erupt like a bad zit (a fat, crimson one on the tip of my nose on the very day I'm due to represent Great Britain in the final of Miss World – not that I ever would, but I can imagine.)

'Are you still there?' Mary asks after a few minutes of lopsided conversation – her ranting, me mute. As she waits for an answer, I watch Lewis stride into the open-plan office. *Bugger*. I don't want to have this conversation at all, let alone share it with my boss.

'You can't hide from this, Amy,' she goes on. 'Like it or not, the *Mail* is running the story tomorrow. One of their hacks is keeping a vigil on my doorstep. She has a big flask of hot tea and she has sworn not to move until she has prised your name out of me.'

'You're not going to give it to her, are you?' I ask angrily. Lewis's arrival means I can't raise my voice, and the words come out as a strangled hiss.

'Give *what* to *whom*?' Mary says.

'*My* name to *that* journalist.' I add extra hiss to key words.

'Who do you think I am? Some silly trollop who shags a celeb and gets straight on the phone to Max Clifford?'

'OK, I get the point,' I hiss some more.

'And why are you hissing?' she asks.

'I'm *not*,' I hiss.

By now Lewis is only a few feet away, leafing through the post in the in-tray – I *have* to end the call. 'Gotta go, Mary. My other line's ringing.'

I hang up and tell myself to act normal. I force my hands to stop trembling, peel the lid off my cappuccino and blow on the froth. *Shit*, too hard. Fat dollops of foam splatter my keyboard. Mental note: never attempt casual behaviour in vicinity of hot beverages.

I look up at Lewis. We're the only people here, but he doesn't even notice me. He's far more interested in the post. Nothing new, then. Why should he pay any attention to me? I am - after the spotty sixteen-year-old who keeps the copiers topped up with toner - the second least important person in the office while Lewis is . . . *the Editor*.

We're employed by *Working Girl*, which sounds as if it should be the preferred read of escorts, streetwalkers and lap dancers, all the more so because our offices are in Soho. I wish it were the hookers' weekly, because it would be a heap more interesting than the truth. *Working Girl* is one of those recruitment mags that are handed out free at tube stations and are full of ads that try to make toiling for some dreary accountant in WC1 seem as glamorous as being PA to George Clooney.

Working Girl isn't doing too well – they can't even *give* it away. Lewis has only been here a few weeks. He's the new broom who's going to turn things around . . . Or the one who's going to fire everybody when it all goes belly up. Either way he seems to be tough enough for the job. He doesn't say much – he's a narrow-eyed-glare-speaks-a-thousand-words kind of guy. Scary, to put it bluntly.

And, I have to admit, sexy. If you squint he's a tiny bit George Clooney (*ER/Ocean's 11* version – not the goofy hillbilly he played in that film no one I know went to see). And if you *really* squint there's maybe a weeny hint of Brad in there too.

Bugger my hormones. I have a history of being attracted to scary and inappropriate men. It's because of a scary and inappropriate man that I'm in my current mess.

However, given that Lewis hasn't said a word to me in all the time he's worked here and probably doesn't even know my name, I think I'm safe on this occasion.

'Who were you hissing at, Amy?'

'Excuse me?' I'm in shock. Lewis is speaking to *me*. He knows my name. And how much of my bloody conversation did he overhear?

'I said who were you hissing at?' he repeats, still without looking up.

'Er . . . No one. Just my sister,' I lie – I can't exactly tell him the truth, can I? That Mary is my agent. Why on earth would the second least important person in the office have an agent?

'Mary – that's a nice old-fashioned name,' he says without a hint of warmth. 'I hope you didn't hang up on my account.'

Shit, how much did he hear?

'No, no,' I bluster, 'we'd . . . er . . . finished. Definitely . . . Finished.'

'Good, because I want to talk to you.'

Why? I look around the office just to make sure that he's talking to me; that there isn't another Amy here I wasn't previously aware of.

Lewis dumps the letters back in the in-tray and walks the short distance to my desk. He sits on the corner, casually stretching his leg across it. I can't help looking at my hole punch, which is making an indentation in his long thigh, and I'm imagining . . .

Jesus, stop it, Amy. This is neither the time nor the place.

His brown eyes – which are surprisingly large and liquid now that he isn't in narrow-eyed glare mode – gaze down at me and he says, 'So, you reckon we can save it?'

'Save what?' I ask stupidly.

'*Working Girl.*'

That is a bloody difficult question. *Working Girl* is rubbish, even rubbisher than all the other rubbish freebie job mags put together. Therefore the only answer is,

5

'Well, Lewis, we'd stand a better chance of saving Private bloody Ryan.' I don't say that, though. No, I say, 'Erm . . . Er . . . I'm not . . . Um . . . Sure,' which comes out as a cretinous mumble.

'That's a shame,' he says, 'because I thought you'd be the ideal person to ask.'

I look around the office again, because he cannot possibly mean *me*.

'You're a secretary, aren't you?' he explains. 'The kind of girl a magazine like this should appeal to . . . Or not.'

He looks at me expectantly, the brown eyes growing bigger and liquider. *Shit*. He wants me to speak. Better say something – preferably something more intelligent than my last incisive remark.

'Er . . . Well . . . I think . . . That . . . Um . . .' This is going brilliantly. '. . . I think it would . . . Er . . .'

'Yes?' he says encouragingly, though with the tiniest hint of impatience. He surely has something more useful he could be getting on with – like polishing the leaves on his cheese plant.

'Well . . . It might help if there was something . . . Um . . . You know . . . To read in it.'

He looks at me blankly – he's probably forgotten his question by now. I have *got* to say something – *anything* – to make me look as if I'm not completely brain-dead. 'It's the articles, Lewis,' I gabble. 'They're . . . Well, they're a bit . . . You know . . . Crap.'

What the hell did I say that for? My face heats up to gas mark five as I remember that being the editor he is the bloke in charge of . . . Um . . . Articles. He glares at me, his eyes narrowing, and says, 'That's a very . . . *challenging* point of view.'

'Is . . . um . . . it?' I ask dumbly, silently cursing myself for managing to slip an *um* between *is* and *it*.

'Yes, it is. Exactly what this place lacks – challenging

points of view . . . Look, there's something I want to ask you . . . Been wanting to ask you this for a while . . .'

He's playing with my stapler and he's not looking at me. Now his bum is shifting around awkwardly – and more than a little sexily – on my desk.

'. . . I'm not very good at this,' he continues, 'so I'll just say it. Would you like to go to –'

He stops.

Go to what? Lunch? Dinner? Hell? . . . *What*? I really want to know because there's something pleading about his eyes that suggests it isn't hell, but he's stopped. Because a *bloody* phone is ringing.

He reaches into his jacket and takes out his mobile. 'Hi . . . Yes . . . Hi, Ros . . .'

Who's Ros?

He slips off my desk and turns away from me. He's talking in a hushed voice making it perfectly bloody obvious who *Ros* is. And there was me thinking he might have been about to ask me out. Dream on, Amy.

'. . . Call me. We'll do it soon,' he says as he turns back towards me. 'Yeah, me too. Looking forward to it.'

He flips his phone shut and smiles at me warmly . . . But it isn't the same. Everything is different now. He's got a Ros.

'Sorry about that,' he says. 'Where were we? I was just about to –'

'Fucking hell, Amy, I know women have chained themselves to railings for the right to a decent bit of foreplay, but I had to drag him up by his ears and sit on the thing. Oral definitely isn't up there with . . . What's it called? . . . Oh, hi, Lewis. Didn't see you there.'

'I think the term you're after is penetrative, Julie,' Lewis says to my workmate as she arrives at the desk opposite mine and slings her jacket over the back of her chair. Then he's gone. I watch his bum as he walks away from my desk for surely the last time – the bum that (in several fantasies) I have already married and had children with.

'Oops,' says Julie. 'Did I interrupt something?'

'No, nothing,' I say – and more's the pity, I think.

'Good 'cause I want to tell you all about Alan,' Julie goes on. It's the morning after First Shag with New Boyfriend. Time for an action replay.

'How was it?' I ask, glad of a change of subject.

'*Mmmm*,' Julie drools, visibly melting into her chair. 'Let me tell you *all* about it. The man's a *machine*. He kept it up for – Are you going to get that?'

My phone is ringing. I'm torn between ignoring it – because it'll be Mary again – and picking it up in order to avoid hearing every detail of Julie's shag right down to the last secretion. I pick up on the fifth ring.

'For God's sake, Mary, give me a break,' I hiss.

'It's not Mary,' says my sister – my real one.

'Sorry, Lisa,' I hiss again.

'Why are you hissing?'

'I am *not* hissing,' I very nearly shout. Then I calm down and say, 'Sorry. I'm having a nightmare day.'

'Shit, me too. We have *got* to talk.'

Unless my baby sister is about to appear on *Jerry Springer* alongside every boyfriend she has ever had, plus all of their wives, Lisa can't possibly be living a nightmare that is worse than mine, but I let it go. 'I'm a bit busy now,' I say. 'Why don't you call me tonight?'

'But, Amy –'

'My other line's going,' I say, this time truthfully. 'Call me later.'

I click to the call that's holding. 'Good morning, *Working Girl*.'

'Well?' It's Mary.

'Hi, I was just about to –'

'I know, you were just about to ring me the moment you got off "the other line",' she says with audible inverted commas. 'Amy, my dear, the *Daily Mail* hack might eventually catch hypothermia and die a fitting death in the gutter, but this problem is *not* going to wither away.'

'Sorry. I'm not handling this very well, am I?'

'The words pig's and ear spring to mind. Marsha Mellow would cope much better. You should take a leaf out of her book.'

The mention of that name makes me switch immediately to hissing mode. 'Jesus, Mary, I am in the middle of an open-plan office surrounded by people. I can't talk about this now.'

'But you *have* to, angel. You're running out of ti—'

'Listen, I'll see you after work,' I say. It isn't what she wants to hear, but it's the best I can offer. 'Come over to mine at eight. See you then.' I hang up quickly.

I've never been that brusque with her. When it comes to rudeness, we don't have an equal opportunities relationship – that's her job.

I sit back and think about what she has just said: 'Marsha Mellow would cope much better.' Marsha *bloody* Mellow. I *hate* that woman. Especially now that she's about to become the subject of a witch-hunt led by the *Daily Mail*, my mum's and dad's window on world affairs.

My mum and dad!

The thought of them reading about Marsha Mellow starts me sweating.

'Anyway, Amy, where was I?' Julie says, breaking into my turmoil. 'That's right. The man's a mach—'

'Sorry, Julie,' I murmur. 'Not now.'

I do not want graphic sex now. Graphic bloody sex got me into this hole . . . So to speak.

'You OK?' she asks.

'No,' I say, as I rise unsteadily to my feet and head for the loo.

*

'Shit, shit, shit, shit, shit!'

'Whatever works for you, sweetie,' replies an unknown voice from the next cubicle. Whoever she is, she brings me to my senses. I hadn't realised that I was thinking out loud. I hadn't realised, either, that I've been sitting on the lavatory for so long that I've lost all feeling in my legs.

I'm not wasting my time in here. I've been trying to work out how things have got so out of hand. I began by looking for a starting point. Not easy. Think about it. Take any event in your life and backtrack to where it began. Say you met your other half at work. The beginning wasn't the day your eyes met across the fax machine. It wasn't even the day you started at that particular company. What made you choose that employer, handing yourself the opportunity of meeting him/her? And, before that, what made you choose that particular career path? Everything can be traced back and back. Everything starts with the accident of one particular sperm out of millions bumping into one particular egg to produce *you*. In fact, once you embark on this line of enquiry, you end up going back to what led to your parents pairing up, the sperms and eggs that made them, their parents etc. etc. Before you know it you're at the dawn of bloody creation and the miraculous coincidence of circumstances that led to the first amoeba.

Now *that's* where it all started.

I feel ready to strangle the microscopic sod – just let that single-cell fucker have the nerve to show itself.

When I finally get back to my desk it's Julie's turn to be in a flap.

'Where the fuck have you been, Amy? I'm having a crisis here.'

Her too?

'What is it?' I ask.

10

'Alan phoned. He's blown me out for tonight. *OhmyGod*, I'm being dumped, aren't I? I haven't even made it to the second date.'

Weird. To Julie second dates normally represent a scary level of commitment. Most of her boyfriends don't last beyond a couple of drags on their first post-coital fag before she's out of the door with a breezy 'Don't call me . . .' But Alan, I have worked out, is *different*. He's a footballer. He plays for Arsenal. Apparently he's a wing back. Means nothing to me – makes him sound like a sanitary towel. According to Julie he's brilliant, but he can't get into the team because he doesn't speak French, which makes no sense. I'd always assumed that footballers didn't need GCSEs in anything, let alone mod. langs. But I haven't said a word – I don't want to look stupid.

'I don't know what's gone wrong,' she goes on. 'He says he has to do extra training. That *must* be bollocks. Footballers don't train at night.'

'Maybe he's got French vocab,' I suggest.

This is intended to be helpful, but Julie just sneers at me as if I don't understand anything. I don't care though – I've got an e-mail.

Amy – fascinating chat. I'd like you to define 'crap'.
Stop by my office at the end of the day.

This is not good. Either Lewis wants to bollock me for criticising his editorial skills or he wants to pick my brain. Well, he definitely doesn't want to ask me out – he's got a Ros, hasn't he? I hope it's not the brain-picking. With all the stress it's under, picking is the last thing my brain needs.

'Tell us your real name and we'll let you go.'

Even from the cold stone slab to which they've strapped

me, the editor of the *Mail* looks disturbingly sexy in tight black leather. He stays at the back of the dark cellar, while his reporter steps towards me, fumbling in her handbag.

'Just your name, that's all we want to know. Then you can go home, take a bath, watch *Emmerdale*, whatever,' the editor goes on calmly. 'Best to co-operate, eh? Look at poor Mary. Where did her obstinacy get her?'

I twist my head to one side and gaze at the corpse on the slab beside mine. I look at the stumps where Mary's fingers once were, then at her liver, which has been laid out alongside her. I strain my neck to peer at the reporter as she lifts an object from her bag. It's black, cylindrical and maybe a foot long. It looks a little like a set of curling tongs.

'She's very good with that, you know,' says the editor. 'We sent her all the way to Iraq to learn how to use it from the masters.' Nothing to do with haircare, then. 'Why don't you show her, Imelda?'

The reporter smiles a tight, cruel smile and flicks a small button on the side of the cylinder. A thin steel rod shoots from one end and an array of gleaming blades fan out like an umbrella. They start to spin like a Catherine Wheel, making the wicked high-pitched whine of a dentist's drill. The reporter takes another step towards me and –

Daydreaming. *Again*. I've had dozens today. The latest has been one of the more pleasant ones. It's six o'clock now. Julie shuts down her PC and says, 'Fancy a drink? You look like you could do with one.' She's at a loose end thanks to New Boyfriend's no-show. 'Hey, we could go to the Pitcher and Piano. Those guys from that ad agency might be there.'

Julie getting over a dumping the only way she knows how.

'I can't,' I say, grabbing a strip of lank hair and holding it up by way of demonstration – it does need a wash, actually.

'I suppose I'll just have to go home, then. Have an *early night*,' she says as if it's some foul-tasting medicine.

'You'll get over him,' I tell her.

'No, I'll fucking *kill* him. Then I'll get over him.'

I watch her walk out and wonder what the big hair, nail extensions and Gucci sunglasses (indoors, winter?) are all about. I'm getting a real *Footballers' Wives* vibe here. I'm about to follow her when I remember Lewis. Damn. I didn't reply to his e-mail and I've hidden behind my PC every time he emerged from his office. Now I have to walk past him in order to escape.

Nothing else for it, Amy. You'll just have to go for it.

Right. OK. Here goes. I stand up, put my jacket on and stride purposefully towards the lifts. I stop when I draw level with his office. Maybe he isn't in there, but maybe he is and I'm not going to risk him spotting me through the window in his door. Not caring what I might look like to the few stragglers still at work, I drop to my knees and set off on a crawl. I'm almost safe when I hear the door open.

I freeze.

'You all right down there?' Lewis asks.

'Er . . . Fine thanks . . . Just lost one of my stupid contacts.'

This is a lie. Of course I haven't lost a contact lens. How could I have? I don't wear them.

'Let me help you,' he says, dropping onto all fours beside me. A few of my daydreams have involved Lewis being on his knees, but, funnily enough, never in this particular situation.

'Ah . . . There it is,' I say. I prod an index finger at a carpet tile in the manner I've seen from countless contact wearers and then lift it up, carefully balancing the non-existent lens on the tip.

'I don't know how the hell you spotted it,' Lewis says. 'I can't even see it now you've found it.'

'Practice,' I say. 'This happens *all* the time.'

I tilt my head back and peel my eyelids apart with my left hand. Then I bring my finger slowly to my face . . . and dab.

'Ouch!' I yelp as my fingernail scrapes my cornea. I clasp my hands over my now streaming eye.

'Let me take a look,' Lewis says, shuffling towards me on his knees.

'Really, I'm OK,' I say, pulling away from him.

We haul ourselves to our feet and I look at him awkwardly. His eyes flash me a momentary glint of warmth. 'Would you like . . .' he begins and I can't help slipping into the fantasy where he asks me into his office to suggest a holiday on a deserted tropical island – or at least dinner, with maybe the island holiday after a suitable getting-to-know-each-other period – '. . . a tissue for that mascara? It's a bit smudged.'

Get a life, Amy. Like he could ever fancy me anyway. And how could I forget his Ros?

'Were you coming to see me?' he asks, handing me a tissue.

'Er . . . Yes . . . No . . . *Yes* . . . I was coming to see you to tell you that I . . . Um . . . Can't see you tonight.'

'Pity,' he says. 'I've been waiting to hear your thoughts.'

'Sorry. I've got to go home. Mary's coming round.'

'Your sister?'

'No . . . *Yes*,' I splutter, remembering this morning's lie. 'She's having a bit of a crisis.'

This is true. Mary is having a crisis. Being my agent, she's on fifteen per cent. As far as I'm concerned, that means fifteen per cent of *everything* including my crises.

Chapter 2

I sit opposite my therapist, nervously sucking on a cigarette.

'The solutions to your problems don't lie in the present. Going back is the only way forward,' he says calmly. 'We have to find the thing that triggered everything else. What do you think it was, Amy?'

'Perhaps it was . . . the very first amoeba at the dawn of creation?' I suggest hopefully.

'What the fuck is it with the amoeba shit?' he explodes.

Blimey, he sounds a bit like Tony Soprano . . . Hang on, he *is* Tony Soprano. I thought he was *in* therapy, not doing it. Maybe he quit the day job – probably a good thing, because running the New Jersey mob while trying to cope with the trials of family life is a pretty stressful existence.

He rubs his temples in an attempt to recover his composure. 'Look, doll, I'm sorry. But fuck the amoeba, huh? And never mind all the *I'm attracted to my boss as a father substitute* Freudian shit . . . I wanna talk about your mother.'

'Do we have to?'

'Uh-huh. This is therapy. Moms is what we do.'

'OK, so what do I do about her?'

'You explore the patterns of behaviour that she set in train during the very first days of your life. You deconstruct your relationship in order to . . . Aw, fuck this. Here's what you do. You clip the cunt.'

'Excuse me?'

'You *off* her . . . *Whack* her . . . Take it from a guy that's been there. Moms fuck with your head. It's payback time. Face it, your old lady wouldn't be the first to end up in a dumpster with a slug in her head.'

'Fair enough,' I say, deciding to go with the flow for a moment. 'Can you tell me where I could get a . . . you know, a *piece*?'

'Sorry,' he says, slipping back into therapist mode. 'Our time is up.'

I open my eyes to find that I'm on my sofa, a cigarette wedged between my fingers. That's what woke me – it has burnt down almost to my knuckles. I look around my front room. Definitely no Tony Soprano. I check the clock on the video. Mary should be here any minute. I have a stretch. I feel a little more relaxed after my nap – after my dream.

But why did he have to bring up my mum? Bloody stupid, fat gangster – he has no business doing therapy.

The phone rings. It's my sister.

'This isn't a great time,' I say. 'Mary's about to –'

'But you promised,' Lisa protests. '"Call me tonight," you said.'

I could do without this. Here I am burning in my own living hell, and, as usual, my sister is trying to upstage me with a version of her own.

But I *did* tell her to call.

'What is it?' I ask, trying (though not too hard) to sound concerned.

'It's . . . I . . . God, it's awful. It's me and Dan.'

'I thought you two were fine. He hasn't dumped you, has he?'

'No, it's worse. I can't tell you on the phone. Can I come round?'

'No, Mary is –'

'*Please*? It's doing my head in.'

'I don't know if I'd be much use right now.'

'I'm having the worst crisis of my life,' she says with more than a hint of irritation. 'I thought you might have spared me a few minutes. I'm always helping you out.'

It's my turn to be annoyed now. 'No, Lisa, you are always landing me in it.'

'Oh, for God's sake change the bloody record,' she snaps. 'Just for once take responsibility for your own problems.'

'That's exactly what I'm trying to do. Why do you think Mary's coming round? Anyway, what makes you want to talk about Dan all of a sudden? He's been the invisible boyfriend for the last two years. Whenever I've asked about him you've changed the subject. Now you want to spend the bloody evening discussing him.'

'Ha, you're hardly little Miss Candid, are you? You're always the first one to bury your head in the –'

Buzz, buzz, buzzzzzzz!

Saved by the bell – I've been dreading Mary's arrival, but now I'm thanking God for delivering her to me.

'I've got to go, Lisa. Mary's here.'

'Oh, you go. Don't worry about me, will you?' my sister snaps before slamming down the phone.

Still seething, I buzz Mary into my flat. At least, I think it's her – she bursts through my front door wearing a headscarf and sunglasses, a combination I've never seen her in. It makes her look like Audrey Hepburn in one of those sixties romantic comedies – though you have to imagine Audrey fattened up for the part like Renée Zellwegger as Bridget Jones. Only about fifteen stone more than that. Mary is *big*.

'Hi, Mary, come –'

'Shhh!'

She pushes past me, creeps over to the window and peers out. Then she draws the curtains and finally removes the scarf and shades.

'I think I lost her,' she announces triumphantly.

'Lost who?'

'Whom, darling, *whom*,' she corrects annoyingly. 'The *Mail* hack, of course. Did you imagine that she wasn't going to follow me? I tried this trick with the cab that I once read in a Len Deighton – marvellous writer, terribly underrated. It was a *night*mare trying to explain the intricacies of spy craft to a minicab driver who barely speaks a word of English, but we got there in the end. I think we shook her off in Camden.'

I'm surprised that she doesn't now sweep my flat for bugs, but she just plonks herself on the sofa. I flop down in the armchair opposite her.

'Before you even start, I'm not going to come clean,' I announce.

'The *Mail* won't give up easily. You know what these tabloids are like. Getting them off a juicy story is like trying to prise a hormonal terrier off one's leg, my dear – futile and invariably messy.'

She has only been here a few moments, but already I feel hemmed in. I show it by adopting the foetal position.

'Face facts, Amy. Tomorrow morning the *Daily Mail* is going to pronounce Marsha Mellow Public Enemy Number One. Their only problem is that they don't know who she is, and they won't rest until they can put her pretty face on their front page – *your* pretty face.'

By now I'm clutching my legs so tightly to my chest that I'm in serious danger of cracking a rib. I hope she's finished.

She hasn't.

'You know the only sensible course of action, don't you? Announce it. Take control by doing it at a time and place of your choosing. Wouldn't you sooner out your-self with dignity than get caught *in flagrante*? Remember poor George Michael in that grubby public loo.'

Silence.

'Amy, *Amy*, you know it makes sense.'

I uncurl my legs and light up my third cigarette since her arrival. Then I change the subject. 'What I'd like to know is which bastard has been talking to the *Mail*,' I spit.

'Don't look at me like that, sweetie. You know that on this subject my lips have been welded shut. Anyway, I should be outraged too. How the hell did the *Mail* find out I'm your agent? Clearly someone's mouth has been flapping, but now isn't the time for an inquest. We need to focus.'

'I can't do it. I can't get up and say, "Hey, world, it was me." And you agreed to the secrecy plan.'

'I did indeed, but I did it for you. Besides, that was aeons ago. A lot has changed since then.'

'I can't do it,' I repeat. 'My mum would kill me.' I mean this literally.

'She can't be that bad. She's your *mother*. She *loves* you . . . *unconditionally*.'

'You don't know my mother. She does *nothing* uncon-ditionally.'

'Let me tell you two of life's immutable truths, Amy. Nothing is ever as bad as you think it's going to be and no one ever reacts how you'd expect.'

I know – have known all along – that virtually every-thing Mary has said is right, but I'm also certain that I'm incapable of following her advice. That's because she's wrong on one crucial point: I know exactly how my mother will react (see murder remark above).

For the first time in my life those stupid sayings about rocks and hard places, and devils and deep blue seas make perfect sense. I'm starting to panic and I need to do something. I revert to trusty plan B.

'Mary,' I announce as if I've reached a decision.

'Yes, my dear?' she replies expectantly, shifting her bulk dangerously close to the edge of her seat.

'I'm going to the loo.'

Ten minutes later she's banging on my bathroom door. 'You've got to come out,' she orders.

'I won't do it, Mary. I'm not calling a bloody press conference.'

'It's not that, angel. There's someone at the front door.'

I emerge from the bathroom and head for the window. I open a chink in the curtains and peer down at the street.

'Shit,' I say. Then for good measure, '*Shit, shit, SHIT!*'

'It's not the *Mail* reporter, is it? I was sure I'd lost her.'

It isn't the *Mail* reporter. It's much worse than that. 'It's my mother.'

'Wonderful,' she exclaims. 'I've been dying to meet the remarkable woman that gave birth to my star client.'

'Mary, you haven't been listening. You can't possibly meet her,' I screech, not even attempting to mask my panic. 'You'll have to hide.'

'Angel, correct me if I'm wrong, but I thought we were in Crouch End, not some ridiculous Whitehall farce. Besides, how on earth are you going to hide me?'

She's right – it would be like trying to conceal an elephant in the boot of a mini. She is *big*.

'OK,' I say, 'I'll introduce you, but don't think you're hanging about. You'll have to leave . . . And not a bloody word. About *anything*.'

'Would I?'

I raise a sceptical eyebrow, but my options, unlike Mary, are slim. I head for the entryphone.

'Mum, what are you doing here?'

Fair question. She *never* turns up unannounced.

'Sorry, darling, but I'm having a crisis . . .'

Jesus, her as well?

'. . . I had to talk to someone.'

'Can't you talk to Dad?'

'It's about your father.'

The thought of my dad inducing any kind of crisis is ridiculous.

'You'd better come up,' I say.

I buzz the front door open and then plunge headfirst into another panic. I grab a cushion and flap it madly in the air.

'What are you doing?' Mary yelps as she hops out of the way.

'It stinks of fags in here.'

'So?'

'She doesn't know I smoke.'

'Good grief, is there anything the woman does know about you?'

I stop mid-flail and feel my eyes well up.

Mary steps towards me and puts an arm round my shoulders. She steers me towards the sofa and sits me down. 'Don't worry, angel, let me handle this,' she soothes. She picks up my cigarettes from the coffee table and puts them into her bag. Then she heads for my front door and opens it. 'Mrs Bickerstaff, how charming to meet you. Amy has said such wonderful things about you.'

My mother stands on the *Welcome* mat and stares at her. She looks strange. Different.

Not having met her before, Mary can't know this, but she seems to sense something is amiss. 'My God, where are my manners?' she gushes. 'I'm Mary McKenzie. I'm Amy's . . .'

Amy's what? I'm dreading what she's going to say next, but I haven't had a chance to prepare a fib of my own and I can't step in.

21

'. . . neighbour. Thirty-six A downstairs. Your daughter's an absolute sweetie. She lets me pop up for a puff,' Mary continues, flashing my fags at Mum. 'My boyfriend's a bit of a tobacco Nazi.'

I have to say it's a brilliant piece of improvisation.

My mum, who'd be the first to slip on a swastika armband if it would help to stamp out cigarettes, curls up her nostrils, but then remembers her own manners. She offers her hand and says, 'Very nice to meet you, too . . . I do hope I'm not interrupting anything.'

'Not at all,' Mary says, slipping too easily into the role of hostess and ushering Mum into the room. 'We were just –'

'Saying goodbye,' I interrupt, pulling myself together at last and rising from the sofa. '*Weren't we*, Mary?'

'My God, look at the time,' Mary squeals, getting the hint. 'My haddock and pasta bake will be a crisp by now.' With that she bowls past Mum and out of the door, calling out, 'Amy, ring me later about that *thingy*,' from the stairs.

My mother and I are alone now. I look at her properly. *My God*, what is she wearing?

Mum is a Tory. Her allegiance runs much deeper than mere party membership. If she were the tattoo type she'd have one of Norman Tebbitt on her upper thigh. (And don't forget Maggie – she would be inked proudly on her forearm.) Because displaying her loyalty via body art would be plain silly, she does so with her dress. After the decline of Lord Tebbitt she shifted to the Ann Widdecombe wing of the party and styled herself accordingly. She wears frocks – the only word for them – that, in the words of my best friend Ant, make her look like 'a hundredweight of Maris Pipers in a billowy chintz sack'. I'd love to be able to put it more kindly . . . But I can't.

Tonight, though, something has changed. The make-up

22

for a start is just a little more out there than usual. And the outfit. A tailored jacket and skirt. Bright yellow with black piping. And – *my God* – her knees. Nothing wrong with them. What's odd is that I can't remember ever having seen them before. I stand back and look her up and down. The freshly coiffed hair, the suit, the hemline, the heels – she's gone a little bit Edwina Currie.

I've no idea what this means. Some subtle shift in politics no doubt – maybe there's a leadership contest I'm not aware of. Whatever, I find it unsettling. Damn. Unsettling is precisely what I do not need in my life right now.

'You look great, Mum,' I say.

'Well, I feel absolutely dreadful,' she replies.

'What's happened?'

'What an awful woman,' she exclaims, as she marches to the window, flings open the curtains and forces the sash open to its widest extent. 'When did she move in? I thought you had those weird rave types in the flat downstairs.'

'Er . . . Yeah, they went a couple of weeks ago.'

'There's something not right about her, Amy. I can't put my finger on it, but –'

Right on cue a pumping bass line kicks in and forces its way up through the floorboards.

'I knew there was something odd about her,' Mum says. 'The rave lot played that dreadful beat-boop, too.'

(Not, by the way, a new branch of trance or garage or whatever – beat-boop is Mum's term for any music more modern than Elgar.)

'Never mind Mary,' I say, desperate to move the conversation on and get her out of my flat. 'What about you? What's going on with Dad?'

Mum looks at me and her bottom lip starts to tremble. Then she takes a deep breath and says, 'Amy, please try not to be too upset but . . . Your father is having an affair.'

I start to laugh. For the first time in . . . oh, ages I throw back my head and guffaw. I can't help myself. And it feels wonderful. A massive release of pressure and tension. The idea of my father having an affair with anybody is the funniest –

'Amy, this isn't funny,' Mum pouts before bursting into tears.

I move swiftly to her side, grabbing a handful of tissues on the way. 'I'm sorry, Mum, but Dad . . . An affair . . . Come on.'

'He *is*,' she sniffs. 'He's got another . . . *woman*.'

'How do you know? Have you caught him? Did he tell you?'

'No, but he's behaving very oddly. He's out all hours and he never tells me where he is any more.'

'Have you tried asking him?'

'Yes . . . He just says it's work.'

'Well, it probably is.'

My father has always retreated into work. He's big in coat hangers. He has a factory that manufactures them by the thousand. Not the sturdy wooden ones that you steal from smart hotels (everyone does, don't they?), but the flimsy wire sort that wilt at the sight of a thick coat. I never understood how anybody could be that busy making coat hangers until I worked out it was a Mum-avoidance tactic. Some people turn to drink to escape reality. Others obsess over PlayStation. At least one bends wire into hangers. He also avoids her when he's at home, where he holes himself up in his garage. I don't know exactly what he does in there, but I suspect it involves tools. And wood. I say this because he occasionally emerges with something wooden that vaguely resembles . . . erm . . . something made of wood.

'You know what he's like,' I continue. 'He's probably on the verge of a technological breakthrough – a revolutionary unbendable hanger or something.'

'It's not work,' Mum insists. 'He's *different*. Distant. Irritable.'

This doesn't sound like Dad. Distant, yes – his Black & Decker Workmate might as well have been a lunar landing craft that took him off on moon trips for all the contact Lisa and I had with him as kids – but not irritable. Irritability is my mum's department.

'You should try to talk to him about it,' I say.

'I can't. I'm frightened of what he might say.'

My mum *frightened*? Very freaky.

'Do you want me to have a word with him?' I suggest.

'He's hardly going to confess to you, is he?'

'No, but I very much doubt he's having an affair, Mum. It must be something else. Perhaps he's as scared of bringing it up as you are.' I'm on very solid ground here. I know all there is to know about being scared of bringing *things* up with Mum.

She gazes at me through watery eyes. 'Would you talk to him, dear?' she says in a pathetic little voice I haven't heard from her before.

'Yes, of course,' I reply soothingly, as if I haven't got enough problems of my own to deal with. As if The Biggest Secret In The World Ever – well, at least since *Who shot JR?* – isn't really sitting inside my head, threatening to blow the top of my bloody skull clean off.

As I head for the kitchen to make coffee Mary's words return to me: 'She can't be that bad. She's your *mother*. She *loves* you *unconditionally*.' It strikes me now that maybe she was right. No, she's not right. My mum *is* that bad. But at this moment she's also pathetic and vulnerable. Surely it's the perfect time to tell her. While she's blubbing on my sofa, why not slip in my own little confession? I mean, add

My daughter is a sleazy corrupter of public morals to *My husband is a despicable adulterer* and it doesn't sound that much worse. OK, I'll be accused of kicking the poor woman when she's down, but when she's up she's bloody dangerous. I have to put my own safety first.

Yes, I'm going to do it.

I pour water into the mugs and quietly rehearse my opening. 'Mum, you're going to read about me in the *Mail* tomorrow, though it won't actually mention my name. I want you to know that whatever they print I never set out to hurt you. No, I wanted to make you *proud* of me . . .' I like that. It sounds as if I'm putting her feelings first even though I'm not.

I head back to the living room, put the mugs on the table and plunge straight in – there's no other way; dither and I'll be doomed. Dealing with Mum is like pulling off a plaster. You have to ignore the flesh-ripping agony and get it over with.

'Mum, you're going to read something in the *Mail* tomorrow, and –'

'That awful woman,' she exclaims, ignoring me. 'Why on earth do you let her come up here and smoke? Your flat is like an ashtray.' She has a couple of cigarette butts in her hand – she must have been fishing down the back of the sofa cushion.

Jesus, what possessed me to imagine I could tell her The Biggest Secret In The World Ever when I can't even confess to smoking?

The blubbing wreck of a few moments ago has gone. Now her teeth are gritted and her beady eyes dart around the room looking for trouble. She's Mum again, which is unnerving enough by itself, but seeing her post-makeover is bloody spooky. It's like I'm hosting an episode of *Stars in Their Eyes* in my very own flat – '*Tonight, Matthew, I'm going to be Edwina Currie.*' I can't figure out this new look at all. If it's to win back my supposedly stray-ing father, Edwina C. isn't going to cut it – he hides behind a cushion every time she comes on the telly.

'Anyway, Amy,' Mum says, tossing the fag ends into the waste bin, 'what were you saying about the *Mail*?'

'Oh, nothing . . . I think there's an interview with Andrew Lloyd Webber.'

While she hates anything more modern than Elgar, she makes an exception for Lloyd Webber. He writes Proper Tunes about Nice Things – like pussycats and Jesus . . . and hideously disfigured ghosts. And, of course, he's a Conservative.

'Good,' she says, 'something to look forward to when your father's ignoring me at breakfast . . . That's if he bothers to come home at all.'

'He stays out all night?' I gasp.

'No . . . But it's only a matter of time.'

'Mum, don't worry. I'll talk to him.'

The doorbell rings, making both of us jump.

'Who on earth is that?' Mum demands, horrified that I could have a visitor at this hour – nine fifteen – and probably imagining it's the local Hell's Angel chapter come to do a spot of rape and pillage.

I'm alarmed as well, but only because I'm sure it's that bloody *Mail* reporter. I inch to the open window and peek outside.

What the hell is he doing here?

'He' is Ant, whom I haven't seen for over two years. Of course I'm thrilled and delighted, but what the hell is he doing here? He's supposed to be in New York. Now he's standing on my front steps with a holdall, looking tired, dishevelled and – thanks to a pair of tight leather jeans, what appears to be a sprayed-on white T-shirt and a brand-new (to me at least) moustache – exceedingly gay.

Shit. Along with smoking and The Biggest Secret In The World Ever, that's something else I haven't told Mum: Anthony Hubbard – my best friend since age six – is a homosexual. Since she can barely handle the fact that he's a Roman Catholic, how could I?

His timing could be a whole heap better.

'Who is it?' Mum asks.

'Anthony,' I reply.

'I thought he was in America, taking holy orders?'

Two and a half years ago when Ant emigrated and Mum asked what he'd be doing in New York, I didn't reply with 'Oh, most probably any guy he can get the trousers off'. No, I said, 'He's going to the Seminary.' It was the truth – Ant does work at the Seminary. Just not the whole truth – the Seminary is a gay nightclub.

Mum was always deeply mistrustful of our friendship. Partly because she still thinks the Catholics are plotting to overthrow the queen and replace her with the king of Spain. The main reason, though, is that she couldn't conceive of a boy being mates with a girl without him having *thoughts* and at some point being compelled by biology to act upon them. I could cope with her worrying that every time we disappeared upstairs to listen to CDs I'd come back down pregnant, but only because it was preferable to her imagining I'd come down with AIDS (which, as she'll tell anyone who'll listen, can be caught simply by sharing a postcode with a homosexual).

So I never told her that Ant *went against nature*. He helped by not being in the least overt about his sexuality. He did have moments when he made Julian Clary seem like a macho sergeant in an elite SAS team, but never in front of Mum.

*

28

Looking at him now, New York has obviously brought about some changes. Not so much out of the closet as halfway down the catwalk.

'Aren't you going to let him in?' Mum says as I watch him from the window. I go to the entryphone, take a deep breath and pick it up.

'Ant, what are you doing here?'

'Fucking crisis, babe . . .'

What the hell is going on tonight?

'. . . You gotta let me in.'

'Er . . . Come up . . . My mum's here,' I say breezily, hoping to God he'll read between the lines and that on his way up the stairs he'll effect a miraculous wardrobe change. And have a shave.

He does neither.

I open the door and there he is – the long-lost seventh Village Person. He flings his arms about me and squeezes until I'm gasping. 'Am I glad to see you, Amy,' he sighs. Then he looks over my shoulder at my mum and says, 'Hi, Mrs Bickerstaff, how're you doing?'

'Oh, you know, An*th*ony,' she says, pronouncing his name just the way he hates it, 'I struggle on. What about you? Taking a break from God?'

I visibly tense at the question, praying that Ant not only remembers the lie but also still cares for me enough to play along with it.

'One never takes a break from the Lord, Mrs Bickerstaff. I may be three thousand miles from my studies, but He is ever with me.'

I visibly relax.

'And how are your studies?' Mum goes on as she looks askance at his clothes, probably thinking they confirm all her misgivings about Roman Catholics and regretting that Elizabeth the First didn't make a better job of persecuting them to extinction.

'They're going well, thanks,' Ant replies. 'I did my first confession the other day. It was a really juicy one. A paedo—'

'*Mum*,' I yelp, 'look at the time. Don't you have to be home?'

'Well . . . There's no hurry, what with your father *working late* again . . . But I'll leave you two to catch up.'

Thank God – she's usually crap at hints.

I walk her downstairs. As we pass the ground-floor flat she stops, crooking her ear towards the music that's still pumping out of it. I freeze, waiting for her to do her thing – that is, march up to the door, bang on it and demand they take off their dreadful beat-boop immediately and replace it with Vivaldi's *Four Seasons*. I'm terrified, of course, because the door won't be answered by Mary, but by one of the two drugged up clubbers that live there. But Mum doesn't do anything. She merely shakes her head and walks out of the house. A shell of her normal self – only one that's dressed like Edwina Currie.

What the hell is it with the makeover?

'Mum . . .'

'Yes, dear?'

'Your suit.'

'What about it?'

'It's . . . It's . . . Lovely.'

I wimp out – now is not the time for this.

'Thank you, dear. I'm glad someone's noticed. I can't even get your father to look at me any more.'

She throws me one last wounded-puppy look before heading down the steps for her car.

'Hang on, Ant, I'm confused. Who's Fidel?'

'He's the guy who tops up the condom machines at the club.'

'And you think you love him?'

30

'No, no, he was a one-off. I wouldn't even have mentioned him except Alex caught me blowing him in the toilets.'

'And Leon? Another one-off?'

'Uh-huh . . . Well, a two- or three-off.'

'And Alex knows about him?'

'He found his number in my jeans.'

'Jesus, have you got a death wish?'

'How can you work at a place like that and not put it about?' he protests. 'I mean, it may have been a priest school once, but it's called the *Seminary* – the word comes from the same place as semen for fuck's sake.'

'I don't think that defence would stand up in court, but never mind. Which one of them do you think you've fallen in love with?'

'I told you. *Frankie*.'

'The DJ.'

'No, that's Marco. Frankie's the gallery manager. Haven't you been listening to anything?'

'Yes, I have, but your love life is very, very complicated, Ant. I'm not surprised you needed a break from it.'

Keeping up with Ant's daisy chain of lovers has always been like watching one of those films that you have to concentrate on really hard for fear of losing the plot, and even then you're several paces behind the action. Actually, Ant's love life is about as complicated as *Matrix Reloaded*, which I didn't get until two weeks after I'd left the cinema. For the last hour he's been telling me about his latest tangle. To cut a very long story extremely short, Ant lives with Alex, his boyfriend since he moved to America. To complicate things, Ant also works for Alex, a co-owner of the Seminary. As a rule, when your bloke is also your boss, it's best not to cheat on him. Ant had managed to keep a lid on his indiscretions until a few weeks ago when

Alex caught him with – I *think* – Fidel the condom boy. After that it was like tumbling dominoes, with Alex finding out about three other guys. Incredibly, Ant still has a job, though they are having a trial separation. (i.e. they're sleeping at opposite ends of the loft – it is, apparently, generously proportioned). But poor Alex doesn't know the worst of it. Ant thinks he's in love. With Frankie the gallery manager, if I've been paying attention.

'What are you going to do?' I say.

'I was hoping you'd be able to tell me that.'

Oh, thank you very much. Here I am on the eve of being crucified in the *Daily Mail* and all everyone wants to do is dump their problems on me. First Lisa, then Mum and now Ant. I'm surprised that while Mary was round here she didn't chuck in a dead-pet story of her own for good measure. I want to say, 'It's fantastic to see you, Ant, really it is, but if you think I'm going to play Dear Deirdre for you, then you can piss off on the next plane back to Man-bloody-hattan.'

But of course I don't. Mostly because it wouldn't be entirely fair. I have never told Ant – my best friend – my secret and that is something – *another* bloody thing – I feel terrible about.

Instead I say, 'Well, I think it's best if you forget about all the others – Fidel, Leon, Mario –'

'Marco.'

'Whoever. Forget about them, and focus on Alex and Frankie. Work out who you want, and then be completely honest with both of them.'

Ha! Honesty! That's rich coming from me.

'You're right,' Ant sighs. 'That's why I ran away. I had to get some distance . . . Get my head together. I'm sorry to land on you like this.'

'Don't be stupid. That's what friends are for. It's fantastic to see you. I've missed you.'

'Me too,' he says, leaning across the sofa to hug me. 'Anyway, enough of my shit. How the hell have you been?'

Now, surely, is the moment to tell him. After all, the excuse I've made for not doing so is that he's been away and The Biggest Secret In The World Ever isn't the kind of thing you drop into a phone call. But here we are, together again, rebonding on my sofa. So my next line should be something like, 'Ant, I'm going to be in the *Mail* tomorrow.' He, of course, will be amazed and astonished, and the rest will just pour out.

But I just. Can't. Do. It.

'Oh, you don't want to know about me,' I mumble. 'Just the same old boring rubbish.'

Chapter 3

I stumble blindly onto the stage – not because of the photographers' flashbulbs, though I can hear them popping, but because I have a paper bag over my head. A fleshy hand – I think it's Mary's – grabs mine and leads me to a chair. I silently curse Mary for making me do this press conference, and at the same time thank her for being here. She calls the room to order, saying, 'One at a time, please. . . . Let's start with you in the ghastly check coat.'

'Helen Fry, the *Daily Express*: Can you tell us how much of your own experience you put into your work?'

'Er . . . very little.' I quaver, feeling myself blush beneath the protective brown paper.

'So, are you saying that when it comes to sex you don't actually know what you're talking about?'

'That's not fair. I've had some exper—'

'Bob Davies, *Sunday Sport*: Can you tell our readers whether you swallow?'

'Gill Franks, the *Star*: S&M: mistress or slave?'

'Kelly Kershaw, the *Mirror*: Vaginal or anal?'

Shit, they're bloody animals, these hacks.

'Petronella Blomquist, *Vogue*: Can you tell us about the paper bag? Is it a Shilling?'

At last, something I can answer without dying a thousand deaths. 'No, it's a Safeway,' I reply.

'Imelda Pearson, the *Mail*: Why don't you take it off and let us see who you are?'

'I . . . Erm –'

'Yes, why don't you take it off, *Amy Bickerstaff*,' echoes a shrill voice.

'Eject that woman,' Mary booms. 'She doesn't have a press card.'

'I don't need one,' screams the voice, 'I'm her *mother*.'

My eyes spring open and blink in the darkness. That was a new nightmare – a variation on the one where I'm appearing on *Parkinson* (naked apart from the paper bag on my head) and Mum stands up in the audience and unleashes a hail of hot lead spreading poor old Parkie's guts across the studio like . . .

It really doesn't bear repeating.

I sit up and look at the clock: just after five. I wonder why I'm over to one side of my double bed rather than in the middle as per usual. Then I remember that Ant joined me last night. Not for *that* – he's gay. It's the first time I've had a man in my bed since . . . *Him*. I'm being silly. It's been long enough and I can say his name now without falling apart. *Jake Bedford*. There, said it. Jake, Jake, Jakey, Jake . . .

Hang on, if Ant came to bed with me, where is he now?

I get up, slip on my dressing gown and go to the living room.

Ant is on the sofa reading. He puts his book on his lap and looks up at me. 'Hi. Body clock's fucked. I couldn't sleep,' he says. 'I didn't wake you, did I?'

'No, my mum did.'

He looks puzzled.

'Nightmare,' I explain. I sit in the armchair and ask, 'What are you reading?'

'This book I found in my seat pocket on the plane. It's all about this girl who shags anything that moves . . .'

My body tenses.

'. . . I wouldn't normally be interested in hetero filth, but this has me hooked. I can't believe it. The girl in the story is *me*.'

I hope he can't hear the alarm bells clanging in my head.

'OK, she's got a pussy but she's *me*,' he continues. 'She does loads of things I've done. Remember me picking up that bloke on the Harrods escalator and giving him a BJ by the goods entrance? It's in here.'

The alarm bells have turned into wailing sirens, the sort that would announce a full-scale nuclear attack.

'There's tons of other stuff too. It's incredible. Whole chunks of my life in a straight book. I know it's a wild coincidence, but it's freaky, huh?'

I nod – all I can manage because my larynx is paralysed along with the rest of me.

'Never heard of the writer.' He closes the book and looks at the cover. 'Marsha Mellow . . . You know her?'

'Yes,' I whisper.

Ant looks at me. 'You all right, Amy? You look as if you're about to throw up.'

'It's me,' I mouth soundlessly.

'You what?'

'It's me,' I repeat a little louder.

'What are you talking about? Who's you?'

'Marsha Mellow.'

'You're not making sense.'

'I'm Marsha Mellow.'

'Don't be silly. You're Amy.'

God, how many more times do I have to say it?

'I'm Marsha Mellow, Ant. *I wrote that book*,' I shout.

He looks at me, dumbfounded.

'Shit . . . *Fuck* . . .' Ant says. 'You're not kidding, are you?'

36

No, I'm not kidding. I've written a book that 'pits fresh-faced girly wit against sweaty pelvis-pounding eroticism' (*Cosmopolitan*), 'subverts the chick-lit genre with a coruscating shock of raw, hard sex' (*Time Out*) and 'disgusts this reviewer to the very core of his being' (*Daily Telegraph*).

'Why? . . . When? . . . How?' Ant asks in a daze.

'It's a long story, Ant.'

'Well, I think you'd better tell me it. When did you write it?'

'Two years ago. Just after Jake dumped me.'

Jake was my first grown-up boyfriend. Very grown-up – thirty-nine to my twenty-three. I met him when I was working at the *North London Journal*. I was the literary and feature editor's PA. He used to get loads of invitations to book launches, most of which he didn't attend, and they'd be left lying around the office. One evening Lisa met me after work. She was sitting on my desk when she found it.

'Hey, let's crash this party,' she said, running her fingers over the embossed lettering of the invitation. 'It's just up the road from here.'

'We can't do that . . . Who's it for anyway?'

'Never heard of him. Some bloke who wrote a book . . . Jake Bedford.'

I'd never heard of him either and if I'd binned the invitation before Lisa saw it – *like I bloody well should have* – I would never have met him. I blame my sister for a lot. Making me meet Jake is the least of her crimes.

He writes science fiction. Working for the literary editor, I should have known, but I rarely look at a book unless it's aimed squarely at me – i.e. pretty pastel cover that screams *Girly Story*. Jake's covers are black and lurid purple, and show exploding planets and disembowelled androids.

Really it should have been Lisa who went out with him. My younger sister is gorgeous. If the idea weren't completely dumb (and didn't also involve time travel), I'd swear she's the product of a fling my mum had with Jude Law. Though the whole of Jake's party was thronging around him, he didn't take long to spot her. She's a professional flirt and he would have felt the draught from her eyelashes across the room. They were soon locked in conversation while I stood in a corner making polite chit-chat with some vol-au-vents. They made a fabulous couple – matching cheekbones – and Jake on his own was pretty gorgeous. Even at thirty-nine his knee-weakening smile alone would have got him to the final twenty on *Pop Stars*. After a while she dragged him over and made me pretend that I'd read his new book too and loved it just as much as she did. Then she disappeared to the loo to make running repairs to her wind-damaged eyelashes and five minutes later he had my number.

It took me some time to fathom his interest because Lisa got the looks in our family. But I did get something she didn't – breasts. With my mousy hair and plain face, they're my only stand-out features. I'm an additive-free double D and have been since age fourteen. I always hated my surname, and I especially loathed it at school where Bickerstaff became Biggertits. Ant has always said that, beyond their possible use for famine relief, he can't see the point of my boobs. But he isn't Jake. Jake Bedford is what's technically known as a tit man.

'You wrote it to prove you could do it as well as him?' Ant says now.

'No, it had nothing to do with actual *writing* and I

didn't want to prove anything to anyone – well, only to myself,' I reply.

I wanted to prove that I could be as uninhibited as he wanted me to be – at least on paper. It's not fair to say that Jake was just a tit man. He was interested in sex in all its many and varied . . . No, scrub that. Far too polite. He was a rampant bloody sex monster. Any time, any place, any bloody where. A few weeks before I met him I saw an episode of *ER* where a bloke came into the hospital sporting an erection he couldn't get rid of – a round-the-clock hard-on. It had a medical name – chronic stiffy-itis or something technical like that – but I thought they'd made it up. It just seemed a bit silly . . . But then I met Jake.

I didn't see this side of him straight away. It took me until our fourth date. It . . . er . . . wasn't a good night. Suffice it to say it involved a pair of handcuffs and something I later found out was a popper. Call me a prude, but I did feel that handcuffs should wait until at least the tenth date – or, actually, the tenth year of marriage – and the popper gave me my first ever full-on panic attack. (Top tip: panic attacks do not endear a girl to her boyfriend, especially if she has one when he's in the throes of trying to come.)

I really should have bailed out then. But I was besotted. More than that, for the first time in my life I was in love.

Bloody stupid love.

In my defence there was a lot more to him than the boy band smile and permanent horn. He wrote books, for God's sake – ones that were published, even if they were about exploding androids and disembowelled planets. Though I spent our entire relationship feigning interest in warp drives and wormholes in space-time (or whatever), I was as turned on by his intelligence as he was by my boobs. He was all the things I wasn't – worldly, assertive and confident. As for him, he liked the fact that I was an innocent. If I'd rolled over on that fourth date and said, 'Handcuffs are for wimps. Haven't you got some *proper* chains?' I'm sure he'd have moved on. He saw himself as part of my education. I enrolled on his crash course in posh restaurants, wormholes and increasingly . . . er . . . *exotic* sex and I lasted for just over four months.

I flunked out the night he popped the question. I remember the setting vividly – girls do apparently. We were eating at his favourite Italian in Highgate. They liked him as well, because they'd hung his photo on the wall (between Wayne Sleep and someone from *The Bill*). He asked the question over the main course. No, he didn't want me to marry him – I could possibly have handled that. The question was, 'Amy, how would you feel about going to a swingers' party?'

'I'm not sure, Jake,' I said with a mouthful of fettuccini. 'To be honest I'm not a very fancy dress sort of person.'

God, did he *laugh*.

Well, I'm *sorry*, but when he said *swingers'* I immediately pictured Austin Powers driving around swinging London in an open-topped car. I thought he wanted me to put on white boots, a psychedelic miniskirt and a Cher wig, while he wore purple velvet loons and half a ton of love beads.

I felt like a prat when he explained, but I also felt disgusted.

'Let me get this straight,' I said. 'You want me to go to a party and have sex with people I've only just said "Pleased to meet you" to?'

'More or less.'

'While you do the same?'

'Uh-huh.'

'No way. *Ever.*'

I meant it as well. I hated to be a spoilsport, but it didn't seem unreasonable to rule out any form of shagging that involved an audience.

'It was just a thought,' he said, before changing the subject.

I didn't stop thinking about it, though. The way he'd brought it up as if it was a perfectly natural progression in a relationship – romantic dinners, long strolls across the heath, sweaty deviant sex with multiple bug-eyed perverts – made me question my initial 'no'. I hadn't had that many boyfriends, so who was I to say what standard practice was? Perhaps everyone was doing it. The elderly couple on the next table? Posh, Becks and all their showbiz friends? My parents? Why the hell not?

I pictured my mum standing in her front porch dressed in a PVC dress and a frilly apron . . . 'Come in, make yourselves at home. The buffet's in the kitchen – nothing fancy, just sausage rolls and cheesy snips. Feel free to mingle before you swing. And, Amy, do say hello to Reverend Swinton. You'll find him on all fours by the aspidistra – swapped his regular dog collar for the real thing, bless him. Now where's your father got to? I'll try the "Punishment Block" – that's your old bedroom by the way.'

Jake can't have stopped thinking about it either because he brought it up again when our sweets arrived. 'Think about it, Amy. Consider it a learning experience.' (See? All part of my education.) 'It'll be fun. And you don't have to join in. But if you do, well, that's fine, too.'

Now, where had I heard those words before? Mum cajoling me into going to Brownie camp. Except that I don't think she was envisaging Brown Owl leading a juvenile lesbian orgy.

'They are life-enhancing experiences, you know,' Jake went on.

'Hang on,' I said, 'You've been to one of these before?'

'A few.'

Up till then I'd naively thought that this would be a new thing for him as well – something we'd take the plunge into together.

'How many is "a few"?' I asked.

'I don't know. Does it matter? . . . Look, if you don't want to come, don't come,' he said.

'What do you mean, "don't come"?' I spluttered. I'd thought this party was hypothetical.

'It's on Saturday night. I'll be there whether you are or not . . . Excuse me, can I have the bill, please?' he said over the thunk of my jaw hitting the table.

We didn't speak for a week after that. I couldn't call him because I was basically catatonic. That didn't stop me waiting by the phone in the dumb girly hope that he'd phone to apologise. But when he rang it was to dump me. He gave me an assortment of reasons: he was under pressure from his publisher and couldn't handle the distraction of a relationship; he was thirty-nine and needed to 'audit' his life; he was an utter bastard whose monstrous depravity was so overwhelming that it made him oblivious to the feelings of a vulnerable young woman. No, he didn't give me the last one, but that was pretty much the truth.

I wasn't big on self-esteem before I met Jake, but whatever little I had was shot after he left. It took a few weeks before hurt turned to anger, but when it finally did I got really mad . . . And that was when I got writing.

'It was pure fucking revenge,' Ant says. 'A woman spurned and all that.'

'It was not,' I say indignantly. 'If I'd wanted revenge,

wouldn't I have gone public at the outset and rubbed it in his face?'

'I suppose.'

But Ant isn't entirely wrong. I was furious with Jake and I had to hit back. I flailed around for about a month trying to figure out how and then it struck me: if you can't beat them, join them.

(Stupid expression, actually. After September 11th George Bush didn't address the nation with, 'My fellow Americans, these fundamentalists are pretty tough cookies. Frankly, we don't stand a chance, so stick on these false beards and after me, everyone, "Praise Allah! Death to the infidel pigs!"')

OK, I thought, I'll sit down and write a book. After all, everyone has a book in them, don't they? (Mary never tires of saying, 'Sadly, everyone does indeed have a book in them and most of the boring bloody horrors land in an unsolicited heap on my doorstep.')

The idea came at four thirty one night. When I got up the next morning I fully expected to think, 'Write a book? *Duh*!' That's what usually happens after a sleep-induced brainwave – your 4 a.m. plan to learn Portuguese and open a nail bar on the Copacabana Beach never seems quite so brilliant – or feasible – over the 8 a.m. cup of coffee.

But it didn't happen. The more I thought about it, the more it seemed like the finest idea I'd ever, ever had. This was my logic. Every dumped woman dreams of a gesture that will show the ex they're just fine, thanks, they haven't been humiliated and they definitely *don't* feel like crawling into a damp, dark hole and never coming out. In most cases this gesture involves the spurned woman slapping on an extra layer of Boots No. 7 and something in Lycra before heading for a venue where she'll be spotted, if not

43

by ex, then at least by his mates. She then proceeds to have the time of her life. On the inside she might feel like jumping under the wheels of a truck but, looking at her dance, flirt and snog her way through the evening, you'd never know it.

But you could have stuck a gun to my temple and threatened to spread my brains on the wallpaper and I still couldn't have gone out and partied like that. Especially not in Lycra.

Flagrant partying simply isn't me – wasn't then, isn't now.

Writing a novel, on the other hand, is.

OK, so I'd never given the notion a moment's consideration before. However, now that I did, it seemed so very, very *me*. It's a solitary undertaking. And you don't have to tell a soul what you're up to. Having a mother like mine had made me excellent at secrecy. It wasn't as if I was fantasising about being published in a blaze of up-yours-Jake publicity. In fact, I wasn't thinking about publication at all. I saw it as therapy. I'd just write. It would be a load of rubbish, but so what? I'd feel better. Job done.

'So, where did you start?' Ant asks. 'I mean, writing a whole novel . . . Wow!'

'It was easy,' I reply sheepishly.

And much to my surprise it was. Not exactly a doddle, but not nearly as daunting as I'd imagined. I was only familiar with one kind of book. The chick-lit kind – 'Pink squirly type, *Wedding* in the title,' is how Mary describes them. I still love those stories. I usually have three on the go at once. This means the plots tend to intermingle, but that doesn't matter because they're all much the same: single girl in big city looks for love . . .

and finds it on page 260 (just in time for the nuptials on page 280).

That being what I knew, that's what I wrote. I came home from work one night, opened the laptop that my dad had bought me (a present when I decided on a glitzy media career – *North London Journal* followed by *Working Girl* – ha!) and started typing.

> Donna Sanderson was late for work. As she sprinted through the subway and across the platform in a desperate bid to make it through the closing carriage doors, she felt a moist glob begin its journey down her thigh.

I had no idea where this was going (the story, not the glob), but I carried on regardless.

> She made the train by thrusting her arm into the door and waiting for it to reopen just wide enough for her to force her way on board. Then she found the one remaining strap to cling to in the seething carriage. As the train lurched into the tunnel, she felt the glob slither down until it was only just above the hem of her skirt. She wondered if she could stop it descending any further by simply clamping her thighs together or whether she'd have to involve a tissue. Did she even have a tissue? She also wondered whether the glob belonged to Greg or Vaughn.
>
> It had been one of those nights and this was one of those mornings after.

And so it continued. Three hundred and fifty-seven pages of full-on shagging. I couldn't believe what I'd done – how could I have written those things? It was very chick-lit, I suppose: single girl in big city looks for love . . . and finds it . . . several times over. 'Pink squirly type, *Fucking* in the title,' was how Mary put it.

Donna was a promiscuous girl – the Indiana Jones of shagging – and since I'd never been in the least bit like her I borrowed from someone who is. Ant. I've watched his every move since we were four and Donna was Ant after the sex change. I didn't feel bad about ransacking his life because I wasn't writing for publication. As far as I was concerned nobody else was ever going to read it. But now that they have I feel terrible.

'I can't believe you put me in a book and didn't tell me,' he says.

'No one was ever supposed to read it,' I say meekly.

'How could you not say anything? I'm your oldest friend. I told you I was gay the moment I knew.'

How could I forget? We were fourteen and he announced he fancied my boyfriend. We didn't speak for weeks because of the resulting tiff.

'I've always told you everything,' he goes on. 'I might not have fucking bothered if I'd known it was a one-way street. Two years you've kept this from me.'

'I feel awful, Ant.'

'You should.'

'I'm so, so sorry. I don't suppose you'll ever forgive me.'

'Forgive you? I should fucking sue you. I'm going for a shower.'

He gets up and stomps off to my bathroom.

He re-emerges twenty minutes later, thankfully free of the moustache. I haven't been idle during his absence. A tray of breakfast sits on the coffee table. It's five thirty and perhaps a bit early, but I am desperate for forgiveness.

'Peace offering,' I say.

He doesn't reply. Instead he picks up a bacon sandwich and takes a big bite. He chews in silence . . . And then opens his mouth . . . to take another bite. God, I wish he'd say something.

'Ant, I'm truly, truly, *truly* sorry,' I gush. 'I should've told you, but everything happened so quickly and –'

'You've had *two* years.'

'I know,' I say pathetically. 'A day hasn't gone by when I haven't thought about picking up the phone, but the longer it's gone on, the harder it's seemed . . . You must hate me,' I tail off pathetically.

'If you must know I'm really proud of you,' he says quietly. 'I can't believe you've written a book. Don't get me wrong, I can believe you've done it – I've always known you were smart enough. I just can't believe you had the nerve to get it published.'

'I didn't . . . Thank Lisa for that.'

When I'd finished Donna's story (it didn't have a title – not being intended for publication it didn't need one) I forgot about her. The therapy had worked. Jake Bedford was out of my system. I only experienced occasional pangs, mostly when I wandered into a bookshop and saw a paperback with an exploding/disembowelled android/ planet on the cover.

That really would have been that if it hadn't been for Lisa. After a night out she came back to mine, couldn't sleep, found my laptop and then found Donna. The course of my life changed in that instant.

'It's amazing, Amy. Funny, clever . . . *Bloody* filthy,' she gushed the next morning. 'I don't know how you did it. I get writer's block doing my shopping list. You've got to send it off to some publishers.'

'I'm doing no such thing,' I said. 'It's rubbish.'

'It is not. It's the best thing since . . . er . . . since *The Catcher in the Rye*.'

47

'Have you ever read *The Catcher in the Rye*?'

'What's that got to do with it? Everyone who has says it's a great novel. *Yours* is a great novel, too. End of story.'

'Correct, end of story. I'm not showing it to anyone, so you can forget it.'

She wouldn't, though. She nagged for weeks until I finally lost my temper and trashed the entire document.

Over.

Done with.

Finito.

Or it would have been if Lisa hadn't already e-mailed it to her own PC, printed it off and sent it to half a dozen literary agents. Of course, she didn't tell me, nor would she have if she'd received six rejections. But she only got five. The sixth agent was very keen to meet Marsha Mellow, Lisa's new name for me. ('It's to protect your anonymity. Brilliant, isn't it? I came up with it when I was stuffing my face with Tunnock's Tea Cakes.')

I don't often raise my voice, but Lisa was nearly vaporised in the blast. She was shocked. She'd actually thought I'd be pleased. And I'd committed myself so far along the path of righteous outrage that I couldn't possibly let her see that in the deepest depths of the inner recesses of my hidden soul I was . . . er . . . jumping for joy.

Because for all my protestations that Donna's story was personal, strictly not for public consumption, how could I not be delighted that someone – a *literary* agent – liked it enough to take it on? Bridget Jones had a literary agent! . . . Well, the woman who invented her had, anyway. But then something else struck me. The Bridget Jones woman had had the good sense *not* to write three hundred and fifty-seven pages of relentless, wanton, dirty shagging. That was my stupid idea. That's when I felt the first pangs of stomach-churning embarrassment at the filth I'd written. Anger, secret excitement, squirmy shame. My head was a mess.

48

I eventually calmed down enough to meet Mary McKenzie – 'Just out of curiosity, Lisa. One meeting and this goes no further. Understand?'

'Absolutely, Amy. One meeting and then we'll never ever mention it again, I swear.'

Two days later I had an agent. Ten weeks after that I had a publisher and an advance of £5000. And nearly two years on here I sit, bacon sarnie in hand, about to appear in the *Daily Mail*.

I wouldn't normally be quite so alarmed about the prospect. Donna's story has had a few reviews and I coped with those – reading them was a strange mixture of nausea and exhilaration. But tomorrow is different. The *Mail* has got a story. A couple of days ago the headmistress of a posh secondary school in Cirencester walked into the changing room and found eight naked girls. Nothing odd there – it was the girls' changing room after all – except they were accompanied by seven naked boys. Apparently they were going at it like . . . well, like they'd just got invites to Jake's swingers' party and they desperately needed the practice. In the midst of the sweaty heap of teenagers was a paperback. It had a lavender cover containing an illustration of a slightly kooky-looking girl with small, pointy breasts. Its title – in pink squirly type – was *Rings on Her Fingers*. The author, of course, was Marsha Mellow. The book was open at the chapter where Donna goes to her first orgy.

'Un-fucking-believable,' Ant says, wiping the bacon grease off his chops.

'It's a bloody nightmare, Ant.'

'Don't be silly. It's just the *Mail* doing what the *Mail* does best. It'll be lining the bottom of hamster cages by Sunday morning. Why worry?'

'I wish I could feel so relaxed.'

'Don't be so uptight. *Enjoy*. I know I would.'

I don't feel comforted and I obviously don't look it because he leans across the sofa and wraps his arms round me. '*Incredible*. My pal, the author,' he sighs into my neck. Then he pulls away. 'Don't get me wrong, I'm still mad as *fuck* with you. You should have fucking told me.'

'I know. I'm sorry.'

'I could get used to the idea, though.'

'Of me being a writer?'

'No, of me being in a book. I'm a heterosexual role model – never thought I'd see the day. Can't wait to tell my mates.'

'You can't tell *anyone*,' I very nearly scream.

'Shit, forgot, The Biggest Secret In The World Ever.' After a pause he adds, 'You know, that is such a shame. If I were you, I'd be milking this for all it's worth. I don't know what's holding you back.'

'Mum. Remember her?'

'You won't be able to keep it from her for much longer, you know. After the *Mail* has lit the blue touch paper every prick with a press card will want to be the one that fingers you.'

'But you just said it'll be forgotten by Sunday,' I squeak.

'I was trying to make you feel better. I know how you panic. Look, you're going to have to deal with it. We'll have to talk about it. Not now, though. I've got a book to finish. Fuck off and make us another coffee.'

As I head for the kitchen he asks, 'By the way, why's it called *Rings on Her Fingers*? Bit Mills & Boon, isn't it?'

'Another of Lisa's bright ideas. It'll make sense when you get to chapter twenty-two.'

'Explain.'

'It's where Donna . . .' I feel myself blush. 'It's where she puts her . . . God, I can't say this out loud.'

'I don't believe you,' he says through laughter. 'You're embarrassed by your own filth.'

'OK. Right,' I say firmly. Definitely not embarrassed. At all. Deep breath. 'It's where one of her boyfriends wants her to shove her finger up his –'

'Say no more, darling. Guess you couldn't write an entire book about a poof like me and not mention arseholes at some point.'

Chapter 4

'Your wicked deeds have brought shame upon the family,' my father declares in an uncannily authentic Pakistani accent. 'You are to be married immediately. Asif from the video shop has a brother-in-law whose nephew is a tax clerk in Rawalpindi. Your mother and I had hoped for a doctor, but beggars cannot be choosers. We must be grateful to Allah for the few blessings that remain.'

Behind my father and his wagging finger stands my mother. At least I think it's her – her face is covered by a burka and it's hard to tell.

'Asif assures me that your husband-to-be is a forgiving man – he is prepared to accept a wife who has been besmirched by blasphemy and carnality . . . if the price is right. It is most fortunate that we have been saving for such an event. We have enough for the dowry and a single ticket to Islamabad. You leave tomorrow.'

Hang on. I can't possibly go to Pakistan. How am I going to write my steamy, sexy novels out there? It's time to stand up for myself.

'I'm not going,' I say firmly – and, much to my surprise, in an uncannily authentic Pakistani accent.

'Do you defy your own father?' my dad thunders. 'You may be twenty-six, but you're not too old to feel my belt across your behind.'

'You lay one finger on me and I'll tell the whole world

about the shame that you have brought upon this family.'

'How dare you? I work all hours in the factory to put food on the table and clothes on your back and this is how you repay me?'

'According to mother you are not *working* all hours. You have taken . . . *another woman.*'

Mum lets out a glass-shattering wail from beneath her veil and Dad explodes. He pushes me to the floor and stands over me as he unbuckles his belt. Through his yelled incantations to Allah, my mum's screams and my own terrified sobs I hear a phone ring.

'Isn't anyone going to get that?' I manage to ask as the first lash stings my back.

I open my eyes. No abusive dad or hysterical mum. The phone is ringing, though. I stumble through to the living room and pick it up.

'Did I just wake you? It's gone twelve,' Lisa says.

'Ant came last night and we got talking. I hardly slept,' I mumble.

'Oh, so it's OK for Ant to drop by, but you haven't got a spare minute for me.'

'I wasn't expecting him . . . And he did fly three thousand miles.'

I look around the room. There's no sign of him.

'Whatever, I've got to see you,' Lisa says. 'Did you know you were going to be in the *Mail* this morning?'

Shit. My life is flooding back to me.

'What did they write?' I ask, not wanting to hear the answer.

'Oh, it's brilliant. They've put a big colour shot of *Rings* on the front. It's like a giant ad.'

And there was me praying they'd bury it on page 17.

'What's it say?' I ask frantically.

53

'The headline is THE TEEN SEX TEXTBOOK. Then there's some rubbish about these stuck-up kids using *Rings* as an instruction manual.'

My knees buckle as I listen to the paper rustle down the phone.

'This bit's good,' she continues. 'It says one of the girls brought a twenty-four inch altar candle to school in her rucksack. Doesn't Donna use one of those in –'

'Yes, chapter eleven,' I say in a rush. 'What else, for God's sake?'

'There's a graph on page four.'

It goes on to page 4?

'It shows the rise in sales of *Rings* next to a line showing the increase in teenage pregnancies. It's brilliant.'

'Jesus, Lisa, how can you say that?'

'Of course it is. You'll sell loads more books now. Anyway, who cares what the stupid *Mail* writes?'

'Mum, for starters. It's her bible. Now she's going to hold me personally responsible for gymslip mums. I might as well have been caught going round playgrounds with a turkey baster.'

'Listen to you. You get a massive bit of PR in a national newspaper and you're acting like it's the end of the world.'

'It fucking well is, Lisa.'

'You're such a bloody drama queen. I didn't even phone you about the *Mail*. I've got to talk to you about Dan.'

Somehow I'd forgotten about him.

'It's doing my head in,' she goes on. 'Please come and meet me.'

'Where are you?'

'In the West End.'

I should have known. When Lisa is upset she shops.

'OK, I'll see what Ant's up to and –'

'See you at two – the caff in DKNY.'

Things must be bad. When Lisa is having a mild-to-

54

middling crisis she'll burn up her credit cards in French Connection or Morgan. Anything worse and she heads straight for Bond Street.

I hang up and spot the note on the dining table.

Hi Marsha (Love that name!!)

Hope you managed to get a decent sleep. Finished the book. It's fucking amazing, though you could have given me bigger tits. Lisa was right. Best thing since *Catcher* (which isn't all it's cracked up to be if you ask me). Anyway, I'm popping out to see some mates – lots of catching up to do. Back around six. Fancy dinner?

Ant

xxxxx

PS – A woman phoned around ten. Wouldn't give her name. She told me to tell you she wants to talk to you about the 'thingy' in the 'whatsit'. I assume she's your agent. Tell her that if she ever wants to be the secret kind of agent not to bother. She's crap.

I think about calling Mary back. But she can wait. I go to my bedroom and dress.

Forty-five minutes later I'm sitting on a bus. I didn't feel like stepping outside the relative safety of my flat today, but Lisa sounded desperate. She's been known to do stupid things when desperate and armed with a credit card. Like buy the same jumper in two sizes and five colours because she was alone and paralysed by indecision. It's best she has a chaperone.

When I passed the newsagent on my way to the bus stop I averted my gaze. I didn't want to see the *Mail*. There's no avoiding it now, though. The woman across the aisle is reading it. I turn my collar up and swivel my body towards the window, as if it's only a matter of

55

moments before she looks up and shouts, 'Here, you're that filthy Marsha Mellow whore!'

What feels like the *Riverdance* chorus line has started doing their stompy Celtic rubbish in my stomach. Got to think about something else. My mind turns to Lisa. What's going on with Dan? Has he got her pregnant? Maybe he wants to marry her. I try to picture them at the altar . . . But I can't because in the almost two years that Dan has been her boyfriend I've never met him.

The secrecy is weird and so not Lisa. She's unlike me in every respect and she's never hidden anything. While Dad and I have always been introverted and acquiescent (OK, doormats), my sister is like Mum – outspoken and confrontational. For her men are a weapon, most effective when rubbed in Mum's face. As soon as we hit puberty our mother made it clear that she saw it as her duty to vet every boy we dated. Lisa decided pretty quickly that two could play at that game. So while Mum was checking CVs, Lisa was pre-selecting blokes on the following criteria:

1 Rock star and/or biker dress sense.
2 Pallid complexion, dead eyes and sniffiness indicative of possible drug problems.
3 Alternatively, dark complexion indicating traces of 'tar brush'.
4 Membership of the Socialist Workers' Party.

Any one of the above was enough for Lisa to start a relationship. If she found a guy with two or more, she was gone – hopelessly in love. Mum, of course, would hit the ceiling. As soon as Lisa discovered the effect she could have, she knew she had found her life's mission: the search for Mr Wrong. It's hard to pick out her worst, but personally I'll never forget the Russian amphetamine addict who put his hand up my skirt at Sunday lunch. I don't suppose Mum will either since he left his used syringe impaled in the head of her Victorian doll toilet-roll holder.

When Lisa got a job and left home she cleaned up her act a little. She didn't mind layabout-junkie-biker heart-throbs cluttering up Mum's front room, but she was less willing to have them messing up her own sofa. But she still chose men who'd be more likely to end up on remand than the *Sunday Times* Rich List. And she never stopped dragging them in front of Mum purely for the hell of it.

Not the case with Dan, though. Nearly two years into the relationship and all we know about him is that he has his own business and he's a dealer. This could mean anything: antiques, property, shares, cars. My money is on the obvious. He wouldn't be her first drug dealer – the Russian junkie tried to sell me something that definitely wasn't icing sugar. Whatever, the fact that Dan hasn't been allowed near us can only mean there's something so wrong with him – as in thirty-years-with-no-chance-of-remission wrong – that even Lisa can't bring herself to foist him on Mum and Dad.

Now that she's gagging to talk about him, I'm nervous. I can only imagine the worst . . . Hang on. I've just had a thought. Maybe Dan doesn't exist. Maybe he's like the imaginary friend Lisa had when she was a kid. He was called Winston. Jamaican. Even at eight Lisa had an extremely acute sense of what it took to piss Mum off.

'It's two hundred and fifty pounds, Lisa . . . For a T-shirt.'

'Two hundred and forty-nine, ninety-nine, actually. And it's gorgeous. I'm getting it.'

We're in a glitzy little boutique on South Molton Street. Lisa is an unashamed label tart – I once caught her unpicking the embroidered Chloe tag in the neck of a top so she could restitch it to the *out*side. Even her career decisions have been label-led. She works on the designer floor in Selfridges. A perfectly good company, but her choice had nothing to do with trivial stuff like quality of training, prospects of promotion and pension plans. After her interview she told me the clincher: 'They offer the best staff discounts by a mile and on my way out I spotted an *amazing* pair of Joseph trousers.'

We're weighed down with carrier bags. All of them are Lisa's except for the one that contains my new tracksuit bottoms. Ironic or what? Lisa has got through enough money to keep Elton John in flowers for a month, while I have spent twenty-two quid. Lisa is perpetually ducking missiles from the credit card companies, while I have enough in the bank to keep Elton John in flowers for . . . Ooh, at least two months.

The £5000 Mary got me for *Rings on Her Fingers* was more money than I'd ever seen in one go, even after she'd taken her cut. I was thrilled and at the same time terrified. I was too scared to spend it, convinced that Mum would immediately spot the conspicuous consumption and have me down as an escort or – worse – an author of pornographic fiction.

When the book came out a year ago it was to a chorus of indifference. It may have been given a chick-lit cover, but the few copies that made it into bookshops were buried in erotic fiction and it sold so slowly that there was little danger it would ever earn back the advance. Despite the unsettling probability that it was only being bought furtively by blokes who wanted to read it with a box of Kleenex handy, this was reassuring. As long as it remained hidden away my secret was safe. My dabble in dirty books would be short-lived and life would soon return to safe, boring normality.

But about six months ago something strange happened. *Rings* started to sell. Not that quickly, but enough to have Mary phoning me with gleeful sales updates.

'What's happening?' I asked her.

'Is the term hot cakes, as in selling like, too technical for you?' she replied. 'Actually, that's overclaim, but it's leaving bookshops at a steady trickle. W. H. Smith has put in a healthy reorder, and they're going to move it from smut to general fiction. Just think, angel, you'll be nestling alongside Marian Keyes and Tony Parsons. Your worse than useless publisher would have me believe that it's all down to his cunningly crafted marketing strategy. Platinum-plated bollocks, darling. Our little book is getting what publishers regularly sell their grandmothers for. Word of mouth. No other explanation for it. Seems the chick-lit-loving hordes are tiring of stories of trips up the aisle and have latched on to the appeal of a book containing some *spunk* – in both its splendid senses.'

Sales continued to climb, a process that was helped by the belated reviews. Even so, the figures were nothing to give Marian Keyes or Tony Parsons sleepless nights. Or me for that matter. At least not until a week ago. That's when I got my first royalty cheque: £36,543.

Thirty-six and a half grand!

It scared the shit out of me. So much so that I put on a tea cosy hat and dark glasses when I banked it.

We're at the counter now. Lisa is clutching the T-shirt to her bosom. With her spare hand she reaches into her purse and pulls out her Barclaycard.

'Don't,' I say, putting my hand on hers. 'If that gets swiped again today it'll melt. I'll buy it for you.'

'I can't let you do that. It's two hundred and fifty pounds.'

'Two hundred and forty-nine, ninety-nine. Anyway, it

could be two grand and I wouldn't notice. Please let me get it.'

'OK, just this once . . . And I'll pay you back.'

'Don't be ridiculous.'

Lisa has been borrowing money from me since the days when Blackjacks were two for a penny. To date she has repaid less than a fiver.

We stagger out of the boutique like a couple of Gucci-laden pack mules. Lisa somehow manages to link an arm through mine. 'Thanks,' she says. 'I *love* this T-shirt . . . You fancy a coffee?'

We've been shopping for nearly two hours, during which time Dan hasn't been mentioned. I sense that the credit card abuse (aka therapy) is over and she's now ready.

'Hong Kong?' I gasp as our coffees arrive.

'That's right. Hong Kong,' Lisa replies.

'Hong *Kong*!'

'Yes, Hong bloody Kong. Other side of the bloody world. Main language Canto-bloody-nese. Staple bloody diet, bloody jellyfish.'

'Jellyfish?'

'It's true. I read it on the Net.'

'He can't take you there, Lisa. You can't go. *You can't leave me.*'

'I don't want to go . . . But I don't want to lose him either.'

'Tell him to stay, then. If he loves you he'll –'

'He can't stay.'

'I knew it. What's he done?'

'What are you talking about?'

'Coke dealing? Armed robbery? . . . God, has he *killed* someone?'

Lisa looks at me incredulously.

'I knew it! He's on the run. He's one of those Triads, isn't he? You didn't tell me he's Chinese.'

'Don't be stupid. He's not Chinese and he can't stay because his business has been taken over by these people in Hong Kong and they want him to go there . . . Triad? *Duh.*'

'Well, you have got some previous. So what's this *business* involve?'

'It's really complicated. He deals in these . . . *things* . . . Not bloody drugs, all right? I don't know what they are, but it's nothing illegal. *Honestly.*'

I don't believe her and she knows it.

'C'mon. What is it? . . . Got it. He's married, isn't he?'

'He is *so* not married.'

'What then? Does he worship Satan? . . . Go train-spotting? . . . Eat babies? . . . Or his own bogies?'

'I saw a woman reading *Rings* on the tube. She was at least sixty and she had a moustache. Didn't look the type to read a dirty book.'

'Do I look the type to have written one? Stop changing the subject. Dan – *tell me*!'

'I've told you.'

'You've told me nothing, apart from that he wants to take you halfway round the planet probably to make you swallow condoms full of heroin so you'll end up in the Bangkok Hilton like poor Nicole Kidman. Anyway, do you really think Mum will let you bugger off to Hong Kong with a guy she's never met?'

'Who says I'm going? And sod Mum. I'll do what I like.'

'OK, then, do you think *I'll* let you go with a guy *I've* never met? What's so bad about him that you're even hiding him from me? Stop holding back.'

'I'm not.' Then after a very long pause: 'Tell you what. We'll do a deal. I'll let you meet Dan – then you can help

61

me decide whether Hong Kong is the stupidest idea ever . . . But only if you tell Mum about Marsha.'

'Call that a deal?'

'You've got to tell her, you know.'

'I've managed fine without saying anything so far.'

'It's different now. You're all over the *Mail*. It'll only get worse.'

'God, it's nearly five o'clock,' I say as the Riverdance chorus returns to my stomach for an encore. 'I'm supposed to be meeting Ant for –'

'Stop it, Amy. You have *got* to sort this out.'

I stare at her, too scared to speak.

'I know! You can tell her at lunch tomorrow.'

Sunday lunch at *chez Mum* is a sacred ritual. It takes place on the first Sabbath of every month. To go is torture, but to miss it is as good as signing your own death warrant.

'Come on, Amy, we can do this. It'll be like getting your bikini line waxed. Absolute agony, but pure bliss once they slap the baby lotion on.'

I know she's right. I've known for ages, if I'm honest – a bloody rarity these days. I have to come out of my closet because it's suffocating in here.

'OK,' I say slowly, 'I'll think about it . . . But you have to cop for your share.'

'No way. I can't write to save my life. I couldn't possibly take any credit.'

'You know what I'm talking about.'

And judging by the terrified look on her face I think she does.

Chapter 5

Hell must be a four-bedroom semi with a maroon Rover and mature hydrangeas out front. This thought crosses my mind as I walk along Ripon Drive in North Finchley towards the house where I spent the first twenty-two years of my life. The scene couldn't be more serene. The sky is a bland grey, a couple of pigeons are scratching around by the kerb and another is pooing on the roof of my dad's car. Clearly the devil is trying to lull me into a false sense of security, but I'm not having any of it.

Before I left my flat I pleaded with Ant to come with me.

'I'd love to, Amy, but I'd only make things worse. You know I can't spend more than five minutes with your mum since you told her I'm joining the priesthood.'

'*Please*,' I begged.

'My Bible knowledge isn't up to it. She'll ask me a question about Matthew, Mark, Luke and John and I'll blow it by giving her their phone numbers and cock sizes.'

As he helped me on with my coat he said, 'Good luck. You are so doing the right thing . . . Incidentally, "My Way" or "Candle in the Wind"?'

'You what?'

'Just wondering which one you want at your funeral.'

*

I slip my key into the lock and open the front door.

'Hi,' I call out breezily, though breezy is the last thing I feel.

'In the kitchen,' my mum calls back. 'Just getting the greens on.'

That means we won't be sitting down to eat for at least another hour. As far as Mum is concerned, vegetables cannot be pronounced cooked until they can more easily be sucked through a straw than balanced on a fork. Greens that go 'crunch' are fit only for those lower even than homosexuals, the IRA and, probably, writers of porny books – Continentals.

This thought makes me feel marginally better. At least my confession won't begin with 'Mum . . . I'm French.'

'Haven't you been to church today?' I say as I walk into the kitchen.

'Of course. Why do you ask?'

'It's your dress. It's a bit –'

'What's wrong with it?'

Where do I start? It's pink and shiny and tight and very . . . Lisa, actually. If Mum wore it to church it's probable grounds for a public stoning.

'It's gorgeous.' (First lie of the day.) 'Really suits you.' (Second.) 'Where's Dad?' (Rapid change of subject before I dig a hole too deep to climb out of.)

'Disappeared into the garage as soon as we got back from the service. He can't bear to be near me any more,' she says with a heavy sigh.

It's hard to believe that when the sixties were at their swingiest my parents were younger than I am now. If I hadn't seen the proof with my own eyes – alarming photographs of Mum with a beehive and Mary Quant eyelashes, and Dad with bushy sideburns that came well below his ears – I'd be convinced that they've always been what they are now: fifty-something. Actually, I'm sure they spent the Summer of Love holding the fabric of society together while the rest of their contemporaries smoked dope and threw rocks at policemen. Well, somebody had to keep things on track, and you can bet that the hippies were glad of my dad's hangers when they finally hung up their afghan coats in the mid-seventies.

I look at him now bent over his Workmate. He's younger than Mick Jagger – always has been, though it's hard to credit. I try to picture him frisking onto a stage and yelling out, 'Hello, Los Angeles, are you ready for some ROCK 'N' ROLL?' . . . But, no. At least not in that cardie.

'Hi,' I call out.

'Hello, Amy,' he says, turning to face me.

As I look at him it's obvious where I got my looks from. I'm not bald and grey – yet – but I've got several of his other features. I got the big boob gene from him as well – both his sisters are stacked like saggy Dolly Partons, something that makes me even more depressed than having his slightly too long nose.

'What are you making?' I ask, looking at the lump of wood he's hacking at with . . . um . . . a tool of some description.

'Oh, it's a thingummyjig to go in the whatsit.'

'Another one? Anyway, how have you been?'

'Oh, you know . . .'

I don't, actually. I remember the mission that I signed up for a couple of nights ago. I only agreed to talk to Dad to make Mum shut up. It's not as if he could possibly be having an affair. I try to picture him backstage after the LA gig, a couple of leather-clad groupies on his lap . . . Utterly ridiculous. No way is my father doing anything with a woman who isn't my mother – highly improbable he's doing anything with the one that is, come to think of it. Not in that cardie, anyway.

But I've got to say something. At least go through the motions.

'Mum says she hasn't seen much of you lately.'

'Oh, I've been tremendously busy. The business seems to be getting its second wind,' he says with a sudden burst of energy. 'There's all this talk of a global slowdown, but people will always need somewhere to hang their shirts.'

'That's if they haven't lost them,' I say.

'Excuse me?'

'You lose your shirt . . . in a recession,' I explain lamely.

'Oh . . . Very droll. Here, you'll like these,' he says diving into a big cardboard box. He pulls out an armful of hangers. 'These are my next big thing. Plastic coated hangers that let you colour code your wardrobe. Blue for workwear, pink for informal, yellow for . . . Oh, whatever. Take some.'

I knew it, I think as he stuffs the hangers into a carrier bag and gives them to me. Far from wining and dining some short-skirted hussy, he's been burning the midnight oil to perfect the colour-coded coat hanger. Mankind will never again confuse the business suit with the slobbing-around-the-house sweat pants, and monuments will be erected in my father's honour. Mum couldn't have been more wrong.

'Thanks, Dad,' I say with a smile. 'Shall we see if lunch is ready?'

Mum and Dad are in the kitchen loading the dishwasher while Lisa and I sit at the mahogany table in the dining room that gets used one Sunday a month. We've got through the starter and main course without a mention of Marsha Mellow and her horrid book.

'*Chicken*,' Lisa says. 'I knew you wouldn't go through with it.'

'I'm waiting for the right moment,' I reply.

'*Ha*. I've been counting and there've been seventeen lulls in the conversation. You could've dropped it into any one of them. You'll never do it. Look at you – almost twenty-six and they don't even know you smoke.'

'OK, I'll tell them that as well. Just you watch,' I say defiantly. I am *so* going to tell them.

Mum arrives with crumble. Dad follows with custard. No time like the present, I think, strike while the iron's hot – I'm going to do it. Right now. *Definitely.*

'Mum, Dad,' I say, 'I've got something I want to tell you. I'm –'

'Reverend Swinton gave a marvellous sermon this morning, didn't he, Brian?' says Mum, ignoring me.

Don't you just hate it when that happens? You're about to hit your parents with the devastating news of your pregnancy/drug habit/shoplifting arrest and they're not even paying attention.

I look at Lisa, who must feel as frustrated as I do because she's rolling her eyes to the ceiling. I give her a well-I-can't-possibly-do-it-now shrug and she kicks me under the table.

'Yes, excellent sermon,' Dad agrees, ignoring my pained wince.

'He was inspired by the story that was in yesterday's paper,' Mum continues and I hope to hell she's referring to KYLIE'S BRAND NEW BUM that was on the front of the *Sun*. 'The one about the appalling sex orgy at the private school.'

Shit, she wasn't. Hello, *Riverdance* chorus. Back for another encore?

'He made the quite brilliant point that, awful though it was, it demonstrates the remarkable power of the written word, and that if schools put more emphasis on reading the Gospels then perhaps youngsters would –'

'Mum, Amy's got something she wants to tell you,' Lisa interrupts.

'No, I have not.'

There is no way in a million years that I can tell her now.

'Yes, you have. Or would you rather I did it?' She narrows her eyes to convey utter seriousness.

'What is it, Amy?' Mum says, narrowing her own eyes – she's sniffed trouble.

So has Dad. He's gripping the table and his knuckles are bleached – he's been here before and he can sense the imminent arrival of a Difficult Subject. Maybe he'll do what he usually does at times like this? I give him my pleading kitten look.

'Did anyone see that wildlife documentary the other night?' he asks, taking the hint. After years of practice, he's discovered that the best way to deflect the Bickerstaffs from a Difficult Subject is to come out with something so spectacularly off the point that it stuns Mum and Lisa into puzzled silence. It isn't always effective, but I can only pray.

'All about the elephant,' he continues. 'Remarkable beast. The only mammal with four knees, yet it can't jump.'

'Shush, Brian,' Mum says. 'Amy has something to tell us.'

Well, at least he tried.

I look at Lisa again. Her expression makes it clear that there's no turning back. And she's right. I should have done this ages ago. It's going to be hell, but it can be no other way.

'It's actually brilliant news,' I say, taking the final plunge. 'In fact, it's amazing, incredible, out of this world . . .'

Dad perks up.

'. . . But you might be a bit shocked at first.'

Dad's face drops again.

I decide to kill two birds with one stone. I reach into my pocket and pull a B&H from the pack. I toy with it as I take one final look at Mum. This is the last time she'll ever see me as her one obedient, respectful daughter.

'Look, there's no easy way to tell you this,' I say, forcing myself to keep my eyes on my mother, 'so I think I'd better just say it. I –'

As I'm about to do it the sun breaks out from behind a cloud and shines directly through the bay window, back-lighting Mum with its warm glow. She seems to merge with the stained-glass panes running through its centre and she's no longer my mother. She has become a heavenly vision – Saint Charlotte of Finchley.

Thanks a lot, God. Perfect bloody timing.

'Come on, spit it out Amy,' she says.

'I . . . I . . . I was just going to say that . . . It's Lisa who should be telling you really.'

'What?' my sister exclaims.

'That you might be going to Hong Kong with Dan . . . Who's a Triad.'

Lisa nearly chokes on a mouthful of crumble, Dad claps his hands over his eyes and Saint Charlotte glares at me and says, 'Amy Bickerstaff, please tell me that is *not* a cigarette in your mouth.'

Chapter 6

George Michael walks past, stopping briefly to look down at me. 'So beautiful,' he whispers carelessly.

He's right too – I have never looked better than I do lying here in my open coffin. Mental note: to look sensational forget diets, botox and a Harvey Nicks store card – simply visit an undertaker.

He wipes a tear from his eye and continues walking until he reaches the special stage beside the altar. He picks up the microphone and summons up the courage to get him through this, the most difficult performance of his career. The packed congregation in the cathedral, the thousands watching on giant screens outside and the global TV audience of billions waiting on tenterhooks to hear the song that he has spent sleepless nights rewriting. Not to be outdone by his close friend Sir Elton, who is deservedly famous for his ability to recraft lyrics to reflect perfectly the grief felt by a nation, George has lovingly penned a heart-rending tribute to me. Finally ready, he launches into the opening bars of –

'Amy!'

I look up across the crowded tube carriage and see a bag-laden Julie pushing her way towards me.

'I've been calling your name for ages,' she says as she reaches my seat and dumps the biggest holdall I've ever seen onto the floor beside me. 'You were bloody miles away.'

Damn! For once, a daydream worth having and she's walked in on the climax – I *love* 'Club Tropicana'.

'I didn't recognise you at first. What's with the shades?' Julie asks.

'Oh, my eyes are sore,' I lie.

'Heavy weekend?'

'You could say that.'

Yesterday was a total disaster. After I'd broken Lisa's exciting news for her all hell broke loose. It created the diversion I needed to escape, but I don't suppose my sister will forgive me in a hurry. At least I achieved something. Mum knows now that I smoke. One secret blown . . . God knows how many left. While Mum and Lisa were shattering the peace, I fled – if I hadn't I'm pretty certain the funeral would have been more than a daydream (though I'm not sure George would bother turning up to sing at a tiny family do at Golders Green crematorium). Once I got back to my flat I unplugged the phone and thanked my lucky stars that Ant had gone out and I didn't have to tell him what an idiot I'd been.

I've needed to hide this morning as well. I'm everywhere. At least Marsha is. It seems that every paper has picked up where the *Mail* left off. Even *The Times* has me on the bottom of page one: BISHOP ALARMED BY ALTAR CANDLE THEFTS. All the others have debauchery in private schools stories. I haven't dared read them, but surely I can't be behind all of it – I mean, I definitely haven't sold any dope to the sixth formers at Harrow. The scariest is the *Mail*. They've followed up Saturday's scoop with CAN ANYONE NAME & SHAME THIS WOMAN? over a silhouette of a head. It's obviously not me, but . . . *she has my fucking hairstyle*.

When I spotted it on my way to the tube I ducked into a chemist and bought a pair of cheap sunglasses. I feel like Victoria Beckham trying to avoid being recognised when she pops into Tesco for baby wipes. Didn't stop Julie spotting me across the carriage, though.

'I didn't know you caught the Piccadilly Line,' I say to Julie as the train stops at Finsbury Park. She takes the vacated seat beside mine and it's now that I notice the holdall on the floor is a Louis, to match the open hand-bag on her lap, which goes with the purse, make-up bag and key ring holder inside. There's an awful lot of Louis going on.

'This is my line now. I moved to Arnos Grove at the weekend.'

'I thought you hated north London.'

'I did,' she says with a smirk, 'but that was before I met Alan. We're living together.'

'Hang on,' I splutter, 'you only met him last Tuesday. You only went out with him for the first time on . . . When was it?'

'Thursday.'

'And on Friday morning you considered yourself dumped.'

'He wasn't dumping me,' she pouts. 'He was running away from his feelings. He's very sensitive . . . for a foot-baller.'

'I'm surprised you haven't gone the whole hog. You know, got en—'

She flashes a huge diamond at me, big enough to act as a knuckleduster deterrent to anyone who might be considering mugging her for it.

'Don't worry. We're not going to rush into it,' she reassures me. 'Alan says he needs to establish himself in the squad. *Hello!* won't be interested in doing the wedding pictures if he's not in the first team.' As she fills me in on Alan's career plan, the abundance of Louis makes

72

sudden sense. *Footballers' Wives* here we go, here we go, here we go . . .

I've barely sat down at my desk when the phone rings. It's Mary. Had to be her. I've managed to get through the entire weekend without speaking to her, but it couldn't last.

'Isn't it marvellous, darling?' she exclaims. 'I want to invite the editor of the *Mail* on a hot date and shower his sweet behind with butterfly kisses.'

'How can you say that?'

'Because, my angel, he has done us an unimaginable favour. He has performed what is technically known as a Mike Read.'

'A what?'

'Mercifully before your time. He was an irritating DJ in the days when I still listened to the hit parade and dared on occasion to slither into a boob tube. He foolishly used the airwaves to condemn a record by an obscure bunch of scally queens. Said song went on to spend an entire summer at number one. *Relax, don't do it, when you wanna suck it to it,*' she sings raucously.

'What's this got to do with me?'

'Do I have to spell it out? If I were you I'd take a serious look at Cayman Island tax shelters. You'll be needing somewhere to salt away your squillions when sales go ballistic. Now, let's get down to matters at hand. Have you told your charming mother yet?'

'Er, nearly,' I say, getting a word in edgeways at last.

'You'll have to do better than "nearly", darling, because I really think she should know what her daughter does for a living before said daughter embarks upon her second novel.'

'But. *Shit*. What?' I gabble nonsensically.

'Now, I knew you'd say that, but hear me out. If your incompetent publisher possesses even an ounce of gump-

73

tion, the moment he's finished ordering the reprints he'll be on the phone with an offer for the next Mellow. Now, it would be highly remiss of me if I didn't tell you to put on your thinking cap and start mulling over storylines. Far be it from me to tread on your creative pinkies, but I think a sequel might be in order. The way you left Donna gagging at the end of *Rings* suggests there's more to come. I can just picture the little minx becoming a hardcore Harry Potter. Look, I'm sure you have work to do. We'll talk anon. Think sexy thoughts.'

With that she's gone.

Leaving me flapping my mouth at the dead receiver.

'You look like you've swallowed a haddock.' Julie observes. 'What was that all about?'

'Oh, nothing . . . Just family stuff.'

'God, you and your family. You're like the Waltons on Mogadon,' she says through a feigned yawn.

I don't respond because I'm looking at an e-mail.

Why the shades? Ongoing contact lens problems or a clumsy attempt to avoid me? I'd still like to learn your views on our 'crap' magazine. Brainstorm on Ways Forward – my office, 9.30. Please attend as the no-bullshit voice of the reader.

Bugger. I haven't even seen Lewis this morning, but he's obviously spotted me. I glance up, looking for *Big Brother* style surveillance cameras, but see nothing other than cracked ceiling tiles. I'd forgotten I was still wearing the dark glasses. It dawns on me now that the reason celebs wear shades isn't to avoid detection at all. It's their way of saying, 'Hey, look at me. I wear shades in dingy nightclubs and, therefore, must be (a) famous or (b) a prat.' I'm definitely (b). I take them off and toss them into the bin.

*

'No, Elizabeth,' I say firmly, 'I will not use my influence to get you an invitation to the glittering gala reception for Ben and J-Lo, Hollywood's most ravishingly perfect couple.' Annoyed, I put the phone down. It's the fourth time Liz Hurley has called this morning. Doesn't she realise some of us have proper jobs? I look up at the mob of people gathered around my expansive teak desk, anxiously awaiting decisions. *Right, let's go to work.*

'OK, listen up,' I announce. 'Deedee, I want you to cover the Russell Crowe press conference – and this time try and get a shot of him actually landing a punch. . . . Chris, I've read your "On set with Gwyneth" piece and we can't run it. Bring it back when it's less gushy – this isn't *Hello!*. . . . Fiona, I need you to scout locations for my interview with George Clooney. Nowhere too boudoirish – I don't want him getting ideas.'

As I watch them scurry off I spend a moment reflecting on the remarkable transformation in the fortunes of *Working Girl*. Immediately after Lewis invited me to his editorial brainstorming and heard my incisive no-bullshit views, he promoted me to deputy editor, and . . . Well, read the circulation figures and weep bloody buckets, *Cosmo*.

Lewis's office door swings open now and the great man strides towards me. As he nears my expansive oak desk, I register the beads of sweat on his normally pristine brow. Clearly something is seriously wrong. I immediately ring reception and order them to hold my calls. 'Even Madonna?' queries the breathless telephonist. '*Especially* her,' I snap.

Lewis reaches my expansive mahogany desk and slumps over it. 'Oh, Amy, I can't go on like this any longer. It's driving me insane.'

'What is it, Lewis?'

'It's you.'

'But I thought I was doing OK,' I gasp, shocked.

'You are. You're doing brilliantly, amazingly, stupendously. You're a *goddamn* genius and this two-bit job rag would be deader than a flattened duck without you. But don't you see that's the problem? All the time I've been exploiting your incredible talents I've been burying my *true* feelings. But I can't ignore them any longer . . . Amy . . . I . . . *love* you.'

I look into his huge brown eyes, which are now moist with tears.

'I've blown it, haven't I?' he sighs. 'I'll understand if you want to leave now and take the job at *Vanity Fair*. I'm such a lovesick fool.'

My heart is pounding. I want to follow its urging and rise up and melt into his arms . . . But, damnit, I can't – I'm a professional.

'For God's sake stop this torture and say something,' he pleads. 'What are you thinking?'

'C'mon, Amy, what are you thinking?' Lewis asks, his eyes narrowing.

I snap out of my daydream and look at the group assembled around the table in his office. There's Fiona, the entertainment editor, who doesn't actually get to see anything entertaining but cobbles together reviews based on what other magazines have written. There's Chris, another journalist who writes . . . Not sure what, actually – probably working on his CV.

And there's Deedee, Lewis's PA.

She's taking notes, but eyeing me suspiciously – she treats Lewis as her personal property and when I stepped into his office she made me feel as if I should be shot for trespassing. Being at the top of the secretarial ladder, she thinks she's my boss. No, she thinks she's everyone's boss.

The meeting has been running for twenty minutes and

so far I haven't voiced a single point of view, bullshit-free or otherwise. Instead I slipped into my ridiculous fantasy. At least it took my mind off the can of yucky worms that Mary opened on the phone.

But now Lewis wants to know what I'm thinking.

About what?

I wasn't paying attention, was I?

'I think . . . er . . . It's quite . . . good,' I say, hoping he'll move on.

'So, you'd readily pick up a magazine if it contained a feature on street dance workshops? Funny, I didn't have you down as a body popper,' he says, not moving on an inch.

I blush deeply and Deedee looks at me with a sly smirk – no doubt feeling vindicated in her view that the second least important person in the office (after the spotty sixteen-year-old copier topper upper) has no business attending a top-level brainstorming. And, though it pains me to say she's right about anything, she's right about this. What the hell am I doing here? Surely Lewis is thinking the same.

'Look, everyone,' he snaps, 'Amy is clearly bored out of her skull . . .'

I feel myself redden even more – a beef tomato in a mousy wig.

'. . . and I can't say I blame her. I'm bored rigid as well. We can do better than this. Let's see if we can find some inspiration in the papers.'

Oh, please, not those.

Oblivious to my silent plea he reaches over to his desk, grabs the pile of newspapers and dumps them onto the table. *Bugger.* The bloody *Mail* would have to be on top.

'God, she's everywhere,' Fiona exclaims, pointing at the silhouette of the woman on the front page with *my fucking hairstyle.*

'Well, sex always shifts copies,' Lewis says, 'even, ironically, when you're in the *Mail*'s business of condemning it. Obviously this woman has touched a raw nerve. Who's read her book?'

Why is everyone looking at me? This cannot be happening, surely – it must be another implausible daydream. I know this is real, though, because the *Riverdance* crew are joined in my gut by a bevy of high-kicking Vegas girls and a drunken conga line of refugees from a Benidorm package holiday. They might be having a great time in there, but I'm having difficulty breathing.

No one answers Lewis's question so he says, 'Well, I picked up my sister's copy a couple of weekends ago . . .'

OhmybloodyGod, this *so* cannot be happening. Someone please tell me that Starbucks slipped a tab of acid into my cappuccino this morning.

'. . . and for all its chick-lit fripperies it's surprisingly good.'

At this point I'm torn between fleeing to a new life in the Outer Hebrides and dancing on the table because . . . *Lewis likes my book*.

'Anyway, what I think is beside the point. Clearly Marsha Mellow has tapped into the Zeitgeist . . .'

No idea what that is so not sure I should be pleased he thinks I've tapped into it.

'. . . Maybe it's a bandwagon we should be jumping on. Any ideas?'

'I think one of the more interesting things about Marsha Mellow is that no one knows who she is,' says Chris tentatively.

'Go on,' Lewis prods.

No, stop right there, I plead.

'Well, she could be anyone. I dunno . . . A Soho lap dancer or a retired headmistress in Tunbridge Wells or just a boring old secretary – no offence, Deedee,' he apologises, ignoring me, the most boring old secretary in the room. 'How about we commission a shrink to read the book and write a psych profile? . . . Or we could just do the gung-ho tabloid thing and offer a reward for someone to grass her up.'

'Not sure budgets will stretch to rewards, but good thinking, Chris,' Lewis says as I shrivel down in my seat, attempting to slide unobtrusively beneath the table. 'Amy, you're maintaining your silence over there. Any thoughts on the Mellow phenomenon?'

Shit, I'm a bloody phenomenon now. I freeze midslither, my bum half on, half off my chair.

'Um . . . Er . . .' Bloody hell, what are my thoughts, apart, that is, from wishing the whole sodding Mellow phenomenon would piss off and die? '. . . Um . . .' And why is it that every time I open my mouth in front of Lewis nothing comes out other than a series of incoherent mumbles? '. . . Er . . .' I have *got* to say something that contains a subject and a verb – or at least a *word*. '. . . Ah . . . I prefer . . . um . . . *Bridget* . . . er . . . *Jones*.'

'Oh, terrific,' Lewis says, though I suspect he doesn't actually mean *terrific* – I detect a teeny note of sarcasm. 'Let's just dump the idea of Marsha Mellow then. You're right, she's far too topical for a *weekly* magazine.'

Yes, definitely sarcasm. I smile weakly . . . Though obviously all I want to do is to burst into tears.

'If only you'd told me,' Lewis says tearfully. 'But of course how could you?'

He gently strokes my hand from his seat beside my hospital bed.

'I blame myself,' he continues. 'If I'd taken my mind off my own pathetic problems for just one second I'd have seen immediately that you're suffering from the incredibly

79

rare and invariably fatal condition known as Hofflinger's Babble Syndrome which inflicts upon its victims not only severe pain, but also the terrible indignity of being able to communicate only by means of incoherent mumbles.'

I peel the oxygen mask from my face and say, 'Um, er, ah, um, um.'

'No, Amy, I am not worthy of your forgiveness,' Lewis protests.

'Er, erm, um, ungh.'

'Oh, my sweet, how I've longed to hear you say that. I love you, too.'

He leans into me and as I pucker my lips for a kiss he whispers –

'Can I clear this away, or what?'

I look up at the sullen waitress and nod my head. As she takes my plate, I remind myself to stop having pointless daydreams about Lewis who not only must think I'm a complete idiot, but also, let's not forget, has his very own Ros. I check my watch: two forty-five. I'm late. I don't care, though. I've been stretching this lunch hour to its limit, not wanting to return to work – to Lewis's contempt and Deedee's smirks and Julie's celebrity sex life, not to mention the threat of phone calls from an angry Lisa or, worse, an overexcited Mary. But I can't stay in this sandwich bar for ever. I leave some money on the table and slip my coat on.

Outside in Wardour Street I hear a mobile ring. It takes me a moment to realise it's mine. The only person who ever rings it is Lisa – which could have something to do with the fact that I haven't given anyone else the number. I wonder what she wants, but not for long – she wants to kill me of course. I pull the phone from my bag.

'Hi, Lisa,' I say.

'It's me, Amy,' says my mum.

How the hell did she get my number? Lisa obviously, and if my sister has told her that, then what the hell else has she said?

'Mum, hi. You OK?' I say, trying to quell the panic.

'No, I am not. Yesterday was dreadful.'

'I know . . . Lisa's news. Shocking.'

'Never mind that. Did you talk to your father?'

'Yes, we had a long chat.'

Believe me, five minutes in the garage represents a profoundly long conversation with my dad.

'And?'

'Mum, he is not having an affair. Honestly.'

'Did you ask him?'

'Not as such . . . But I can tell. He's really busy at work. He's come up with these amazing colour-coded –'

'He left the house wearing aftershave this morning.'

'So?'

'He *never* wears aftershave. And he's gone to Birmingham. Looking at new machines for the factory – or so he says.'

'Mum, a trip to Birmingham wouldn't stand up in court as evidence of an affair. Maybe it is business.'

'I know your father, Amy. Something's going on.'

'I know him too, Mum. You've got to get it into your head that he is not seeing another . . .'

I stop abruptly because I've seen something through the window of a bar that makes speech physically impossible.

'Hello . . . Amy, *hello*.'

'I've got to go, Mum,' I manage to say. 'I'm in a meeting.'

'No you're not. I can hear traff—'

'I'll call you later. Bye.'

I snap the phone shut and peer into the bar.

What the hell is Dad doing in Soho? For a start he's supposed to be in Birmingham. Secondly, I doubt he could even find Soho on a map.

And more to the point, what's he doing in a trendy bar called . . . I look up at the sign . . . Cuba Libre?

With a woman young enough to be my older sister?

They are sitting at a table locked in animated conversation – my father in *animated* conversation! I squint into the gloom. She's blonde – of course – and quite pretty . . . in that Other Woman Ripping A Family Apart At The Seams kind of way. Don't know why I notice this, but she's wearing strappy high-heeled sandals that display her cerise toenails. Dad is in his best suit – the one that only comes out at weddings, funerals and Tory Party conferences – and I can almost smell the Old Spice from here.

I feel sick. I have to get away and I turn round and run. My legs are pumping and I haven't moved this quick since I had to compete in the relay in year ten. This is far more excruciating – in year ten at least I had the slight advantage of being equipped with a sports bra. I turn a corner and slam into a six-foot wall of flesh dressed in black. The next thing I know I'm on my backside on the pavement.

'Amy?' says a familiar voice.

I look up and see . . .

I have spent my entire bloody life listening to people start conversations with, 'You'll never guess who I bumped into in the West End today.' At first it would amaze me that in a city of millions anyone could ever bump into one of the relatively small handful of people they knew. After a while, though, it simply depressed me. In twenty-six years I have never – not once – bumped into anyone I know in the West End, a fact that has left me feeling sad and unpopular – like maybe I would have bumped into

82

hundreds of acquaintances . . . If only they hadn't hidden in shop doorways the moment they saw me coming.

I'm making up for it now, though, because in the space of less than five minutes my tally has shot from zero to two. But it's an indication of my rotten luck that both of them are people I desperately wish I hadn't come across. Dad with Blonde Bitch Home Wrecker from Hell and now . . .

'Jake?'

Jake Bedford looks down at me – nothing new there – and then reaches out a hand to help me up. I don't want to take it – really I don't – but the pavement is wet, my bum is sore and, most important of all, I must look pretty bloody stupid from his vantage point. I climb unsteadily to my feet and look at him as I rub my behind. He's still lean and handsome. And, no doubt, still an oversexed, manipulative bastard.

'You all right?' he says. 'You went down like a . . .' Mercifully he doesn't say sack of potatoes. 'You must be running late.'

'I am, actually . . . I've got an . . . editorial brain-storming.'

'Oh, where are you now?'

'*Working Girl*,' I say, immediately wishing I hadn't.

He smirks – as I should have known he would – and says, 'Sounds like a trade mag for . . . ah . . . ladies of the night . . . But it's that jobs freebie, isn't it? So, an *editorial* brainstorming. You a journo now?'

'Er . . . Yes . . . Writing bits and pieces,' because it isn't a complete lie, is it?

'Good. Good for you.'

Patronising git.

I give my watch a very meaningful look and say, 'I'd better –'

'Yes, you're late. You'd better go,' he says. 'But fantastic to see you again. We should do it properly. Hey, I'm in Soho for the rest of the afternoon. Why don't we meet up later?'

'I'm not . . . I don't think . . .' I stutter, searching desperately for an appropriate rejection.

'How about the Groucho? You know where it is, don't you?'

Of course I bloody do. It's where he used to take me to show me how many semi-famous media types he was on first-name terms with.

'Six thirty OK?'

Then without even waiting for me to say 'You must be fucking joking', he turns and strides off.

This is just like the first time he asked me out. He was every bit as arrogant, assuming I couldn't be anything less than honoured that he was prepared to make space for me in his diary. Back then I was so thrilled I was on cloud . . . *ooh*, ten or eleven at least.

But this time it's different.

There aren't any wild horses big and strong enough to drag me to a date with Jake Bedford.

Chapter 7

'I'm sorry, Amy, that's never happened before,' Jake whimpers as he rolls his body off mine.

'Don't worry,' I say, not trying too hard to sound sympathetic. 'Probably a touch of nerves, eh?'

I lean over to the bedside table and take two cigarettes from the pack. I light them both and give one to him. It surely doesn't escape his attention that the lighting-two-cigarettes-after-sex thing was always his job when we were going out.

But everything's different now.

I take a drag and look at him lying beside me. Curled up in the satin sheets he seems smaller than I remember. Less imposing. Less *significant*. He's turned away from me, hoping I won't see him crying in the half-light.

'It's OK,' I soothe. 'It's only an erection. No one died.'

'It isn't that,' he says, wiping away a tear.

'What, then?'

'I can't tell you – I'm too ashamed.'

'Yes, you can. I'll understand.'

'It's just that I've . . . I've never slept with someone who has . . . No, I can't say it.'

'It's OK, darling, tell me.'

'Someone who has sold more books than me. It makes me feel –'

'Inadequate?' I suggest gently.

He bites his lower lip as it starts to wobble.

'Emasculated?'

Fresh tears fill his eyes.

'Rather useless and pathetic, and that you might as well jack it all in and get a job teaching English as a foreign language?'

He breaks down into sobs that shake his entire body. I put my arms round him and say, 'It'll be all right, baby. You'll feel better . . . eventually.'

Inconsolable, he tumbles out of bed and pulls his clothes on in a rush. 'I'm sorry, Amy, I should have known it would never work,' he says. 'I can't live in your shadow. You're just too . . . too *brilliant*.'

I try my best to look sad as he walks towards the door.

'Goodbye, Amy,' he says bravely. 'I'll always treasure the memory, no, the *honour* of being allowed to know you and –'

'– Would you like another V&T in there?'

I look up at the barman who has gatecrashed my daydream. Bastard – just when it was getting good. I nod and he takes my empty glass. I sit on the barstool and let unwelcome reality crash back into my head, which tonight arrives in the form of an irritating inner voice.

What the hell are you doing here, Amy? it asks.

Good question.

On a day when I've spotted my dad with his secret floozy and seen my alter ego splattered across every national newspaper, and when my boss has finally had his suspicions confirmed that I'm nothing but *a boring old secretary*, what the hell am I doing in a club waiting for Jake?

Who is, naturally, late.

And what makes you think you can take on a pro like Jake Bedford? Inner Voice continues. *The only place you can handle him is in your dreams. He'll make mincemeat of you just like he always did. Jesus, even his name has a bed in it.*

Though it clearly has a point I say, 'Shut up.'

The barman puts a fresh vodka and tonic on the counter. I take a sip and look around the room. Jake used to call the Groucho Club a media bordello, but he didn't fool me for a second – he loved it. It's a bit B-list tonight, though. There's a man whom I think I've seen reading the news, the camp bloke with the orange face who does the antiques show and a celebrity chef whose name I can't remember, but it isn't Jamie Oliver or the other one who's rude to his customers if they ask for salt.

But my heart skips a beat when *he* walks in. Not Jake. Jason Donovan. OK, he's hardly A-list – he was hardly A-list when he had number ones coming out of his ears (records, I mean, not . . . *Yeuch!*), but I loved him. What can I say? I couldn't help myself. I was *eleven.*

Seeing him now is like stepping back in time . . . To an age when I didn't have anything to worry about. Not even periods, let alone all of today's crap. I bet Jason wouldn't have been as facetious as Lewis was in that meeting. I bet he'd have said, 'Bridget Jones? I adore her too. Let's have dinner at my favourite intimate restaurant and talk about her.'

He sits down on a sofa with a group of friends and I wonder if it would be naff to wander over there and say, 'Sorry to disturb you, but I loved everything you ever did – even that film you made with Kylie that no one except for me bothered to go and see – and would you mind terribly signing this napkin?' What am I thinking? Of course it would be naff. But how naff? Maybe I could get away with it, and I have to kill the time somehow until Jake turns –

Damn. He's here. I watch him stride across the room, and even though he hasn't combined successful acting and singing careers, and he hasn't starred in a single hit West End musical, he still puts Jason in the shade. He is *bloody* gorgeous. He smiles at me and plucks a cigarette from its pack. I used to love the way he smokes. Who says fags aren't hip? In the right hands they're devastating instruments of cool and Jake's broad, strong hands are just about ideal for the job. As he lights up and takes a long drag, his cheekbones display themselves and I feel a long-forgotten tingle in my –

Stop it right now, Inner Voice commands. *Say hello to the man, have a bloody drink and then let's get out of here before you end up with your knickers round your ankles.*

He arrives at the bar and I say, 'Hi, Jake,' in a voice that's as sexy as anything I've ever managed.

Shit, who do you think you are? Mae West?

He leans down and kisses me on the cheek. 'How was the brainstorming?' he asks, taking the stool beside mine.

'Oh . . . You know. Very productive. Tons of good –'

'You look stunning,' he says.

Don't fall for it. You do not look stunning. You're wearing the same outfit you had on when you were flat on your arse on the pavement. Stunning is a word for Cameron Diaz in her Oscar frock, not you in boring old combats and a white T-shirt with tuna mayonnaise on the front.

I look down. Inner Voice is right – my lunchtime sandwich has left its mark on my right boob.

'You look different, actually,' Jake continues. 'It struck me when I saw you this afternoon. What's happened?'

'I split up with you, that's what,' I reply.

Watch it, warns Inner Voice. *Too bitter – don't want him to think he got to you.*

'Not really,' I say, hurriedly taking it back. 'I'm just two years older.'

Good. Nice neutral tone. Keep it up.

He orders me another drink and I ask, 'How are you, then?'

But now they're out, the words sound strange. Jake is one of the tiny number of men to have seen me with my legs pointing towards the ceiling, and here I am doing bland how-are-yous.

'I'm knackered,' he says. 'I've been monumentally busy. *The Venusian Oil Wars* came out last month and I'm still doing bloody publicity. I need a holiday. I know I must look like shit.'

Liar, liar, pants on fire. Obviously fishing. Don't bite.

'No, you look great,' I say, clamping my jaws round the hook.

D'oh!

He offers me a cigarette, leaning forward to light it and cupping the flame with his hand. He doesn't need to do this, since it's hardly blowing a gale in here. In fact, the place suddenly feels airless. I can barely breathe. Just the way he lights my fag sends shivers down my spine. His fingertips brush my hand and I remember how they used to feel on my –

Get a grip, woman, Inner Voice yells - in the nick of time, too.

'So have you booked one yet?' I ask quickly.

'Booked what?'

'A holiday,' I say, sounding like a bad hairdresser.

'I haven't had time to think about it. But I will. I'm exhausted. I don't think I'll be able to write another book for a long time. My publishers have asked me to . . .'

God, I'd forgotten how boringly self-centred this bloke can be.

'. . . but if I agree to that, I'll have to start straight away and I really don't want to . . .'

He just goes on and on and . . .

89

'. . . I said no, of course. I'm not a fucking sausage machine. They didn't like it, but they need me more than I need them . . .'

. . . on and on. About himself. What did you ever see in him?

'. . . and now they're saying I'm one of the few sci-fi authors to rise above cult status and apparently I've transcended . . .'

Just listen to him. He's only a writer, but he's talking as if he's come up with a cure for cancer in between ending world poverty and finding a painless alternative to waxing. Of course, you were always too busy looking at his backside to notice it. There were two people with obsessions in your relationship. You with him, and him with himself.

'. . . but quality is the bottom line and I can't achieve that if I'm not fresh. Hang on, is that Toby Litt over there?'

Toby *who*?

'Excuse me a minute, Amy. I've just got to catch up with him.'

He slides off his stool and I watch him as he disappears through the crowd of drinkers, which parts for him like the Red Sea. He is Moses. Hell, he is God. He is –

Will you pur-lease look at yourself, Amy Bickerstaff. The man is a total prick. There are plenty more fish in the sea, any one of whom would treat you better than he ever did. Jason Donovan, for instance. He's still pretty good-looking, and now he hasn't got packs of squealing teens running after him, you might actually get a look in. Hey, and I bet you anything he definitely isn't into swingers' parties.

The voice in my head isn't going to go away.

But neither is Jake. He reappears after a couple of minutes, casually slipping an arm round my shoulder. I ignore the voice, which is now screaming hysterically, and tell myself he's just getting comfortable.

'I love talking to you, Amy,' he whispers.

'Why, because I never interrupt?'

'No, because you understand me. You're very sensitive.'

His arm gives me a squeeze. I hadn't expected him to flirt so openly and it's hard to resist. He really is the sexiest man I've ever met – except perhaps for Lewis . . . Who just thinks I'm a prat rather than *sensitive* or *understanding* . . . And where does he get off being so sarcastic? Pig. No, Jake is OK. I could easily end up back at his place in a few hours – or minutes. Would that really be such a bad thing?

It'd be a disaster, shrieks Inner Voice. *Remember what Ant said.*

What, be spontaneous, follow your instincts?

No, you nitwit, he said stay away from Jake. He's a user, a shit.

'Oh, go away,' I say out loud.

'You what?' says Jake, whose hand has moved down to my knee.

'Nothing. I was just wondering . . . Are you seeing anyone at the moment?' I ask as casually as I can manage.

I give up, whimpers Inner Voice.

'No one special,' he says with a laugh.

But the voice surrendered too soon because I feel my hackles rise. I wonder if No One Special is at home, missing him like mad and looking forward to seeing him tomorrow? Is No One Special a 38-DD? Or bigger? And does she like swingers' parties?

'What about you? Got a man?' he says, interrupting my unpleasant train of thought (calling at all stations to Terminal Bitterness).

I know Jake. If it's his intention to get me into bed, something as trivial as a boyfriend won't stop him.

He starts to laugh again. 'It's not a hard question, Amy. You haven't changed much, have you?'

'What do you mean?' I snap.

'Look how tense you are.'

I feel my face redden – embarrassment and anger. 'I was feeling perfectly untense, thanks. And you can take your hand off my leg.'

'Sorry, sorry! I forgot what you're like. Come on, I'll get you another drink and see if that does the trick.'

'Which trick would that be? The one where you get me so pissed, I forget what a git you are and go home with you?'

A bit strong but well done, girl. I thought you were a goner for a minute. Inner Voice is back with some moral support.

'What makes you think I want to take you home with me?' he says indignantly.

'Jake, you've been touching me up, sweet-talking me –'

'So? That doesn't mean I want to fuck you. It's called being nice. You know your trouble?'

'Ooh, let me guess - I'm too uptight.'

'Look, forget it. I just thought it would be good to see you again. I thought that maybe you'd like to see me, too. I guess I was wrong.'

He looks angry – an emotion I've never seen in him. He isn't enjoying the fact that I'm not going to tumble into his bed at the click of his fingers. I'm still not so sure that I won't, but he isn't to know that.

'You weren't wrong, Jake,' I say, breaking the silence. 'I was. I thought you might have changed.'

'And you're a whole new person, I take it?'

'I am as it happens. . . . Have you heard of Marsha Mellow?'

Fucking hell! squeaks Inner Voice. *Where are you going with this?*

Actually, I have no idea.

'Can hardly miss her at the moment,' he says wearily, glad of the change of subject. 'Funnily enough, my publisher owes hers a favour and they asked me for a quote for the next edition of her book. I'm trying to find the time to finish it. As if I haven't enough to do. Why do you ask?'

I'm too stunned to answer. Wherever I imagined this going, it wasn't here. I finally manage to speak. 'What's your quote going to say, then?' I ask as nonchalantly as I can.

'What's it to you?'

'I'm just curious.'

'Well, I was expecting the book to be anodyne, fluffy tosh with some sex tossed in to ring the changes, but I've been surprised by what I've read. I think the prose has a really tough, graphic texture.'

'Is that good?' I know it is, but now it's my turn to fish.

'Yes, it's good. Mellow has obviously been targeted at the chick-litters, but she's worthy of better. All the press she's getting just sensationalises the sex, but there's more to her than that. Actually, I say *her* but my editor and I both reckon she's a bloke.'

'Really?' I ask.

'You don't know much about publishing, do you? The book is very clever – it's spotted the niche that *Sex in the City* went for and blown it wide open. The catch is I've never come across a woman capable of being as unapologetically explicit as Mellow is. It takes balls to write like that – literally as well as metaphorically. It's instructive that *Sex in the City* was dreamt up by a guy. No, I'd put money on Mellow being a man hiding behind a woman's name to make the novels more girly friendly.'

The patronising smart-arse! You're not going to take that, are you?

Somehow managing to ignore Inner Voice's screech, I fight off the urge to slap him and say through slightly gritted teeth, 'So women aren't qualified to write about sex? Like they're not in the bed when it happens.'

'No. I'm saying that women can't write about sex without giving in to the urge to mush it up – you know, stick in the scented candles and obligatory I love yous.'

'God, I never fully realised what a chauvinist you are.'

'See what I mean? So uptight. We can't even have a civilised discussion without your defences kicking in. Anyway, whether she's man, woman or beast, Mellow's book is good. You should read it – might help you lighten up. You're a beautiful and clever girl, but you're so held-in that no one ever sees it. Take a risk once in a while. You never know, you might like it.' He sits back, his mouth turning up at the corners in a superior smile.

Never mind the fucking secrecy, girl, tell him everything, yells Inner Voice, abandoning all restraint. *Start with the day he dumped you and bring the condescending git up to date. Let's see how superior he feels when he finds out that you're the babe with Marsha Mellow's balls.*

I don't give in and, holding myself back far more than even Jake thinks possible, I say, 'As it happens I've read her book. It's been a real eye opener.'

'What, you kiss with your mouth open now?' he sneers.

The shit! screams Inner Voice.

'You *shit*!' I chorus, grabbing my coat. 'It's true what they say. Size *is* everything and you are easily the biggest prick I've ever met.'

That was good, says Inner Voice. *Wish I'd thought of it.*

I walk across the room without looking back . . . And see Jason Donovan again. I wonder . . .

If you're thinking of asking for his autograph now,

DON'T. Not cool. Exit stage left . . . VAMOOSE!

Inner Voice is right. Showing complete indifference to Jason as I brush past his table I sweep out of the Groucho Club and into the street.

By the time I climb off the bus in Crouch End I feel terrible. The thrill of victory I felt as I walked out of the Groucho lasted all of five minutes. It has been downhill since then. And I didn't even get Jason's autograph.

As I trudge back to my flat I can't get the image of Dad with Blonde Home Wrecker out of my head. I'm fairly typical in that I have never been able to stomach picturing either of my parents doing . . . *it* . . . but this is worse than anything I've had to deal with before. This makes me feel sad as well as sick. Why couldn't he just be happy with his Workmate? I've seen the ad where it magically morphs into a thousand different configurations like something out of the *Kama Sutra* – isn't that enough to satisfy his cravings?

Part of me wants to believe that it's nothing; that there's a perfectly innocent explanation. But what? 'Amy, I lied to your mum and told her I was on business in Birmingham because she'd never have believed that I was simply going to an outrageously trendy Soho bar to iron out the details of a new overdraft arrangement with my bank manager who just happens to be young, attractive and blonde, and has a taste for exotic Cuban cocktails and strappy footwear.' Case closed, I'm afraid.

As I near my house the front door opens and a figure in shimmering violet flies down the steps. It takes me a moment to realise that it's my mother. Instinctively I throw my body against a cherry tree. I listen to the click-click-click of her heels on the pavement growing louder and thank heaven that my coat is a treetrunky sort of colour – maybe she won't spot me. But, God, why didn't you make me flat-chested? My boobs are jutting out from the side of the tree like inflatable Amy alerts. I wince as she draws level . . . and doesn't see me. She has her head down, lost in thought. She reaches her car and as I watch her drive off the panic I felt at seeing her is replaced by a far worse one. What the hell was she doing in my flat? I look up at my window. The light is on. I assume Ant is home. What has been going on up there? It doesn't bear thinking about, so I don't. Instead I break into my second painful sprint of the day.

When I fall into my living room I see Ant on the sofa. This is worse than I'd feared. His face is white, his hands are trembling and his jaw hangs open at an angle that makes it look dislocated.

'What happened, Ant? What did she do to you? She doesn't know about –'

'No, she doesn't . . . But I know far more about her than I ever thought possible.'

'What are you on about?'

'I just took my first, honest-to-God, *real* confession.'

'Excuse me?'

'She confessed her sins . . . And I absolved her.'

'But you're not a priest.'

'That's not what she thinks, is it?'

'And she's not even a bloody Catholic. She *hates* Catholics.'

'She came to see you and she was really upset. She obviously wanted to talk and –'

'You heard her confession? How could you? That's so deceitful.'

'It was *her* idea. She hardly gave me a choice. Anyway, who started the priest lie? And would you rather I'd said, "Sorry, Mrs B., but I'm not really a man of God. That was just your daughter covering up the fact that I

96

emigrated to New York for a life of twenty-four/seven sodomy"?'

I back off. I know how . . . er . . . *persuasive* Mum can be when she wants something and I can picture the corner that Ant was backed into. 'I don't know how the hell you pulled it off,' I say. 'I mean, when was the last time you went to mass?'

'When I was fifteen. It wasn't easy. I couldn't remember the words to the *in nomine Patri* bit – I think I blessed her in the name of *I Claudius*.'

'So, what did she confess to?'

'I can't tell you that,' he says indignantly. 'It's confidential. Only God is a witness to what is said between she who seeks absolution and her confessor.'

I start to laugh. But he isn't smiling.

'Ant, you're *not* a priest. You haven't taken any vows. What did she tell you?'

'I can't say. I'd be betraying her trust.'

'Stop being ridiculous. Just tell me.'

'Amy, there's no way you'd be able to hide knowing this from her and she'd suss I'd told you. That would be a disaster for all of us.'

'Jesus, what's she done? Nicked from the pick 'n' mix? Murder?'

'Worse than the first one . . . Not quite as bad as the second.'

'Tell me, tell me, *tell* me.'

'I can't, Amy.' Then as I'm about to explode he says, 'Anyway, I don't think your mum is the only one with a confession to make, is she?'

'What are you talking about?'

'Where were you tonight?'

'Working,' I say hurriedly.

'Really?'

'I had to work late. That's not a mortal sin, is it?'

'No, but lying to your best mate is. You've got a message on your answer phone. He rang just as your mother was getting here so I let the machine get it. Amy, what are you playing at, seeing him again? Haven't you got enough shit in your life already?'

I ignore him and press *play* on the answering machine.

'Amy . . . Ah . . . I was really looking forward to seeing you tonight, and I blew it. What can I say? I was out of order . . . And I'm . . . sorry . . .'

What? *Sorry*? The man may have a vocabulary the size of a small planet, but I've never heard him say *that* word before – not even in a mouse-like whisper that I wasn't supposed to hear.

'. . . I'd love to make it up to you . . . If you'll give me the chance. Please call me . . . Even if it's only to tell me what an arse I am.'

The message ends and the silence that follows is so pregnant that it belongs in a labour ward. Then Ant says, 'I've never heard his voice before. He talks like Pierce Brosnan. *The name's Bastard, Jake Bastard.* I hope you're not going to call him.'

'Of course not,' I reply.

And I mean it. All the wild horses in the world put together wouldn't be powerful enough to drag me to a phone.

Chapter 8

'Where are you going?' Julie asks.

'Out,' I say.

'I can see that. Out where?'

'I've got some shopping to do.'

'That's a shame. I wanted you to come and check out this bar with me. It looks wild. I fancy having Alan's and my engagement drinks there. It's called Cuba Libre.'

Aaagh!

'Sorry, I've got to go,' I say, hurriedly pulling on my coat and fleeing the office.

The mention of the place where I saw Dad with That Woman is more than I can take. Dad and That Woman are two of the people I've been trying not to think about this morning. The list is long enough. There's the new and *apologetic* Jake – don't want to go there. There's Lewis, who has reverted to acting as if I don't exist. (Actually, he spent ten minutes in conversation with the spotty sixteen-year-old, so I suppose I'm now officially the least important person in the office.) There's Mum, Ant and that bloody confession. What the hell has she done? There's Lisa as well. Her silence has been deafening – I can only think she's taken out a contract on me. I should call her to apologise . . . But I daren't. Finally, there's Marsha Mellow.

My thought-avoidance tactic has been to throw myself

into work and it was going brilliantly until half an hour ago. That was when Mary called.

Some lunch hours scantily dressed office workers cover every blade of grass in Soho Square. Not today, though. Could have something to do with the fact that it's chucking down. Today there is only me huddled on a soggy bench. I look at my watch. Mary is twenty minutes late. Her office is only two minutes away – above a pizza restaurant on Dean Street – so she'd better have a bloody good excuse. I'm ready to give up and go back to work when I see her bowling towards me like an inflatable Paula Radcliffe.

'Sorry, angel, sorry,' she gushes breathlessly as she collapses onto the bench beside me. 'I had to lose that *Mail* hack. She's still staking me out. I took her via my gym. I saw my psycho Pilates instructor and tipped him the wink to hijack her for his one fifteen. With any luck he'll have given her a major spinal injury by now.'

'I'm soaked, Mary,' I interrupt grumpily. 'Can we get on with this?'

'I'm sorry to drag you out, but it is important. I felt we couldn't do it over the phone, what with you unable to discuss anything other than in a hiss. Now brace yourself for wonderful news.'

I brace myself for the worst – Mary's and my ideas of 'wonderful' reside on separate planets.

'My spies tell me –'

'What spies?' I butt in, panicked.

'You're getting paranoid, darling. It's a figure of speech – like dickie birds and grapevines. Anyway, a *dickie bird* on a *grapevine* tells me that *Rings* will debut on next week's bestseller list.'

I was wrong. That is *wonderful*. Despite all the panic and nausea I feel whenever the subject of Marsha Mellow comes up, the fact that she – no, *I* – I have written a best-seller fills me with a glow that almost makes me forget the rain.

'Fucking marvellous, isn't it?' Mary says, feeling me radiate. 'Bloody well done to you is all I can say. It's not every day I have a bona fide bestseller on my client list. As I predicted, the *Mail* has got our little novel flying off the shelves, and as I also predicted your wholly crappy publisher has been on the phone this morning.'

Mary has never exactly enthused about my publisher. Strange, given that it's her job to sell him to me, her client. But as she said at the time of trying to flog my manuscript, 'No one wants to know Marsha Mellow – rather too much rumpy-pumpy for the sensitive flowers.' I wasn't in a position to be choosy.

All the big publishers and most of the small ones turned down *Rings*. Then one day she asked me, 'Have you ever heard of Smith Jacobson? . . . Of course you haven't. It's a weeny imprint and their list is pretty anorexic. It's still run by one of its founders, Adam Jacobson. Normally I wouldn't go near him. Very touchy-feely, if you get my drift. Anyway, I popped into the newsagent for my *OK!* and Chunky Kit-Kat fix and there he was perusing the top shelf – not the karate mags, in case you were wondering. I had a brainwave right there on the spot. I'd been far too concerned with finding a publisher who'd spot the literary merit in your work. What I actually needed was one who, not to put too fine a point on it, would be captivated by its deluge of bodily fluids. I propositioned him there and then, and since he was clutching a copy of *D-cup Delites*, he was hardly in a position to refuse. Besides, he's not what one would describe as discerning. No disrespect whatsoever to your achievement, my darling, but he'd make an offer for Jordan's grocery list if he thought he could get the hardback out by Christmas.'

Mary has never made Adam Jacobson seem anything other than sleazy and unscrupulous, only one step up from the bloke who used to expose himself to Lisa and me on our way home from school. I have no way of knowing if she's right because I've never met him.

'He wants to meet you,' Mary says as the rain pelts down even harder.

'He can't. I'm a secret,' I squeal.

'Hear me out, angel. He wants to make you an offer and he said he's not prepared to risk – and I quote – "a considerable sum of money" on an author he's never met.'

'He can keep his money. There's no way I'm going to meet him. I don't even want to write another book.'

'What, allow Marsha Mellow to become a literary one-night stand? *Wham, bam, thank you, reader*? That would be a tragedy . . . But it is, of course, entirely your prerogative. However, I suggest that you meet him and hear what he has to say before you decide.'

'I'm not doing it, Mary. *Rings* was a fluke. I couldn't write another book for any amount of . . . What's he going to offer, anyway? Ten or twenty grand?'

'As they used to shriek on *The Price Is Right*, higher, higher.'

'What, thirty grand for something I haven't even written? That's ridiculous.'

'No, my dear, that's publishing. Paying for stuff they have yet to read is what publishers do, and I thank the gods on a more or less daily basis for the fact. And, by the way, if Jacobson wants the next Mellow he'll have to do a damn sight better than thirty.'

'Mary, there isn't going to be a next . . . How much better than thirty? . . . Purely hypothetically because I definitely haven't got another book in me.'

'Oh, this is an extremely silly conversation, Amy,' she snaps. 'I mean if you have no intention of ever again uncapping your pen, I don't see why I should sit here in the teeming rain talking hypothetical *six-figure* advances for non-existent books.'

Damn! She has me hooked now and she bloody well knows it.

'Look, just suppose I did meet him . . . out of courtesy, of course.'

'Of course.'

'What's to stop him blabbing?'

'I've already thought of that,' she says, reaching into her bag. She pulls out an envelope and gives it to me. 'No need to read it now. It's an agreement I had my solicitor draw up yesterday. It forbids Jacobson from so much as hinting at Marsha Mellow's true identity on pain of having his balls chewed off by the Rottweilers in wigs and gowns. I'm sure he'll be amenable to adding his grimy thumbprint to the dotted.'

'Hang on,' I splutter. 'You did this yesterday? You said you didn't speak to Jacobson until this morning.'

'My dear, I don't simply sit on my fat behind for my fifteen per cent. I think ahead – unlike both my author and her publisher.'

I float back to the office on cloud . . . ooh, thirteen or fourteen. *Six figures*. Unless she's counting the decimal point and the pence, that's over a hundred thousand pounds. Well, it could be exactly one hundred thousand, but it's still a bloody fortune. I could do so much with that sort of money. Like pay off my mortgage . . . *Boring*. OK, I could get one of those cute little Audis that look like Barbie-mobiles (have to learn to drive first) or a wooden beach house on stilts in the Maldives (wherever they are) or save some whales (quite a few, I imagine, for a hundred grand). I could buy Lisa's forgiveness with a dozen new wardrobes or –

No you couldn't, says Inner Voice. *Not unless you plan to tell Her.*

Shit. I'd forgotten about Mum. I feel myself deflate, and arrive at work sodden and fed up.

Reality *so* sucks.

Something is different in the office. That's it – flowers. I can't see my desk for them. White lilies cover almost every square inch of the space I share with Julie. It's only because her hair has become so *Footballers' Wives* massive that I can see her squirly ginger ringlets sticking up above them.

'They're gorgeous, Julie,' I say as I sit down. 'Alan must be really gone on you.'

'They're not for me. They're for you.'

'From Alan?'

'They'd better bloody not be. Hurry up and read the note because I've been going through hell waiting to find out who sent them.'

I fumble through the acres of cellophane for the little envelope and peel it open. I pull out the card and read.

Amy – I can't apologise enough for my behaviour. I hope you'll allow me to make up by buying you dinner – Jake xxx

I slump down in my chair, shocked. Flowers and apologies. From Jake. The world's most unapologetic *and* unflowery kind of guy. But I'm thrilled as well as stunned. He even signed off with little kisses – three of them. Though that might mean triple-X, as in porn. No, best not go there . . . *Flowers.* From Jake. *Wow.*

Cut it out, snaps Inner Voice (which, I have to say, is

really beginning to get on my nerves). *He only wants to get into your knickers.*

'Who're they from, then?' Julie asks.

'An old boyfriend.'

'He must be desperate to get back into your knickers.'

What did I tell you? says Inner Voice – so bloody smug.

'I don't know what he's playing at,' I say.

And to be honest I have no idea what Jake's game is. No time to dwell on him, though, because I hear a voice at my shoulder.

'I don't know how you expect to get any work done with your desk looking like the Chelsea Flower Show.'

It's Deedee. *Working Girl* had three different editors before Lewis took the job. Deedee has seen them all off. Lewis's predecessor hated her. Things got so bad that he took her out for a 'clear the air' lunch. Two days later he was clearing his desk. Or as Julie put it: 'Must have told her at lunch, "It's you or me, Deedee." Don't suppose the poor bastard thought it'd turn out to be him.'

'Sorry, Deedee. I was just about to clear them away,' I say.

'Well, when you've done that Lewis wants to see you,' she sniffs.

'Oooh, he must have clocked the flowers,' Julie squeals. 'It's forced his hand and he's got to make his move.'

'I wouldn't get any silly ideas,' Deedee says.

What ideas? The only thought I've got is that he wants to fire me for being such a prat in yesterday's meeting.

'Why wouldn't he want to go out with her?' Julie asks indignantly.

I can think of several thousand reasons, actually.

So too can Deedee, because she switches to her condescending voice. 'Well, Amy is a perfectly *nice* girl. But a man like Lewis is *impossible* to pin down. He sees *dozens* of women, you know. High-powered, *connected* women . . .'

Jesus, she's making him sound like the editor of *The Times*. It's only a bloody freebie.

'. . . And no offence, Amy,' she continues, giving clear warning that she's about to say something deeply offensive, 'but you're neither of those things. You should see who he's meeting tonight. She's stunning. Head-to-toe Prada.' She throws a disapproving glance towards my sodden £29.99 skirt. 'She's from the bank, so it's "work" of course.' The aerial inverted commas gesture makes any further explanation superfluous. What I'm wondering is, has he told his Ros about Miss Head-to-Toe-Prada Bank Manager?

Deedee goes. Off to have a go at some other poor sod about working hours/corporate dress code/unauthorised internet use/correct use of a pen-tidy/not answering a phone in three rings or less . . .

'*Bitch*,' Julie hisses, only just under her breath. Then she turns to me and says, 'I don't see why Lewis wouldn't want to ask you out.'

'Because he's got a Ros?'

'A what?'

'Never mind. If you'd seen me in that brainstorming, you'd know why. I came across like the company retard. There've been redundancy rumours for weeks and I gave him the perfect excuse to make me the first.'

'He won't do that,' she says with a look of genuine worry.

'I couldn't care less if he did,' I say, heaving the flowers onto the floor. 'He's a rude, arrogant pig. I can do without this stupid job.' I don't add, 'because I'm about to be offered a six-figure advance for a book I haven't even written.'

'If you don't give a stuff, why are you checking your face in your computer screen?'

106

'I'm *not*,' I say indignantly, quickly looking away from my computer screen. I look terrible; drowned rats have looked more presentable than this. I stand up and straighten my wet skirt against my thighs. Then I march purposefully – well, kind of – across the office.

By the time I reach Lewis's door any purpose I possessed has evaporated. I don't want to get fired, six-figure advance or not. I peek through the window. He is *so* good-looking. I *especially* don't want to get fired by someone so good-looking. He's at his desk in head-down-scribbling mode. I tap nervously and without looking up he beckons me in.

'Be with you in a minute. Take a seat.'

Take what seat, though? He's got a little sofa against the wall, but it's creamy beige and my wet clothes will leave big damp patches. Don't want to look like I've wee'd myself, especially if he is going to fire me. ('So glad we got rid of that one, Deedee – she was incontinent.') I pull one of the chairs from the meeting table, turn it round and plonk myself down. Damn. The chair is in the middle of the room, about six feet from his desk. I feel exposed, and I *will* be if he happens to look up when I'm crossing my legs. Just have to keep my knees clamped together. And, God, it's hot in here – like a sauna. The muggy warmth is making my wet clothes even clingier. I steal a glance at my damp top. Shit. My bra. Completely bloody visible. He'll think I've spent my lunch hour taking part in a wet T-shirt cont—

'Sorry about that,' he says, not sounding sorry at all. He puts his pen down and looks up – *aagh!* – directly at my bra. 'Anyway, yesterday's meeting was a disaster . . .'

Here we go. Deep breath and try not to cry, Amy.

'. . . A cock-up from start to finish. A waste of everyone's time . . .'

OK, OK, I get the picture.

107

'. . . And, like everything else around here, depressing in its lack of spark and imagination.'

He pauses and glares at me through his slittiest eyes yet. On balance I prefer the liquid-eyed version that I glimpsed on Monday morning, because this is *scary*.

'I'll be honest with you, Amy . . .'

Uh-oh. Not only is he addressing me by name, he's going to be *honest* with me. The *I'm afraid we're going to have to let you go* bit of this conversation can't be far off.

'. . . The publishers have given me two months to turn this place round. If I fail, the magazine closes. There are going to have to be some significant changes . . .'

Yes, yes, changes, cutbacks. *Please* get to the point because this is agony.

'. . . Frankly, though, everything I've seen to date has been so second-rate I don't know where to start.'

You're starting with me, aren't you? Why else am I sitting here?

And why is he so bloody good-looking? And clever? Why can't I get fired by an ugly, stupid pig with a comb-over and dandruff on his collar? I'm sure I could handle that.

'When we spoke the other morning you told me something that no editor particularly wants to hear . . .'

So that's going to be his excuse? The fact that I told him the mag was crap.

'. . . After all the vacuous, self-serving bollocks I've heard spouted,' he continues angrily, 'it was utterly . . .'

God, he'd better hurry up and finish because I can feel my bloody tear ducts twitching, getting ready for the Big One.

'. . . *refreshing*.'

Hang on, that wasn't in the script.

'It was honest and it gave me my first glimmer of hope

108

that we're not completely fucked. Anyway, I really would like to hear more of your views. How about lunch?'

I am flabbergasted. There was me all set to collapse under a deluge of tears, and here he is ruining everything by . . . *what*? What the hell is he doing? Coming on to me? He still looks cross, though. He can't be coming on to me . . . I don't get it.

'Or dinner if you like? Yeah, dinner might be better. How about it then?' he asks, suddenly going saucer-eyed.

Blimey. He *is* coming on to me. And he wants a bloody answer, which should obviously be *'yes'*, because dinner is a *fantastic* idea. But hang on a minute. What about his Ros? Maybe she's now his *ex-Ros* in which case dinner is *still* a fantastic idea. If only there were some clue. Please, God, give me a sign.

'Um . . . Er . . . Um,' I mumble.

Is it just me, or is it really fucking hot in here? Shit, is that steam? My bloody skirt is actually *steaming*. This could not be more embarrassing.

'Up to you, Amy,' he says, picking up his pen impatiently – obviously not prepared to wait the year or two it'll take me to complete a sentence.

'No, no, dinner would be good,' I say, suddenly empowered with the gift of speech. 'I'd really like –'

I stop because there it is. The sign I was asking for has been sitting on his desk all this time. A beautiful wooden picture frame. It's not empty. There's a photo of a woman in it. His Ros? She's . . . My God, she is *stunning* – a bit like whatsername who rolls around on the beach in black and white in the Calvin Klein ads . . . Christy Turlington, that's the one. She's way too young to be his mother. He spots me looking at it and touches it seemingly absent-mindedly, but somehow nudging it just enough so that I can no longer see the picture . . . Definitely not his mum, then. The *bastard*. He's coming on to me and he *hasn't* finished with his Ros. She's still in the frame – literally. He's attached. An attached bastard. And what about Prada Girl bank manager – tonight's *working* dinner? *Jesus*, what is it with men? More to the point, what is it with the ones I meet?

'See Deedee on your way out and get her to find a date,' he suggests, dropping his head and immersing himself in work again – I'm being dismissed.

Mad as I feel, I can't quite bring myself to yell, 'You must be joking, you double-dealing, two-timing love rat,' so instead I mumble, 'OK.'

I peel my wet clothes from the chair and leave in a cloud of steam.

'*Dinner?*' Deedee says with barely concealed disbelief.

I nod dumbly. I have no idea why I'm standing at her desk making a date when I should be trying to get as far away from here as possible. Must be my inbuilt fear of authority – while Lewis may be a womanising shit, he is still my boss. That's me all over. The queen could order my beheading and I'd offer to help by drawing a dotted line around my neck.

'So, when's good for you, then?' Deedee asks.

Never, actually.

'God, is it three o'clock?' I gasp. 'I almost forgot. Supposed to be at the . . . Opticians! . . . Contact lenses. Nightmare.'

Deedee eyes me suspiciously.

'I did mention it, Deedee . . . Last week. Sorry. Gotta go.'

And I haven't moved so fast since the hundred metres in year ten.

Chapter 9

'Let me get this straight, Amy,' Ant says. 'A publisher wants to bung you over a hundred grand, your ex – who in my opinion is a twat, but what the hell do I know? – has bought you enough lilies to qualify him as an honorary queer and your gorgeous, dreamy boss wants to take you on a date.'

I nod.

'And it's been the worst day of your life?'

'Uh-huh.'

He raises a mocking eyebrow.

'You don't understand at all,' I protest. 'It isn't that simple.'

'Oh, I'm sorry. I must have missed something. You'd better take me through it again.'

I refill our glasses from a second bottle of wine – the first was finished in record time (it was very badly needed) – and go back to the beginning again.

'I can't write another book. I don't know how I did *Rings*. It was a complete bloody fluke.'

'You did pretty well to fluke it for three hundred plus pages.'

'I was angry. I was hitting out at Jake. It was a one-off.'

'Come off it. Whatever motivated you, you couldn't have done it if you couldn't write. Look, if you can do it once, you can do it again.'

'Even if I could, Ant, what am I going to do with all that money?'

'Oh, *fuck*, woe is you, darling. Go tell it to the shoe-less bloke flogging the *Big Issue* outside Woolies.'

'Stop being such a smart-arse. You know what I'm talking about.'

'You should tell your mother. She'll survive. God, she might even surprise you.'

'What the hell did she confess to last night, Ant?'

'Don't change the subject.'

'Look, I've tried to tell her . . . But I can't.'

'It won't be as bad as you think. I told my parents I'm gay.'

'Only *just*. Five minutes before you left for New York. "Bye, Mum and Dad. I'll really miss you and by the way I don't fancy girls . . . Ooh, there's my minicab." Incidentally, have you seen them since you arrived?'

'I've been busy.'

It's my turn for the mocking look.

'I *have*,' he protests. 'I'll get round to it.'

'Admit it, Ant. Telling them has completely screwed up your relationship with them.'

'OK, it's not ideal, but believe me it's better than when they didn't know. All that lying did my head in – pretending my reason for liking *Baywatch* was the same as most other blokes' . . . Anyway, enough of that. Why is the prospect of a date with Shag-pants such a nightmare?'

'Which Shag-pants?'

'Your boss – not that git Jake.'

'My God, Ant, his office was like a Turkish bath – so humiliating.'

'Sounds kinda sexy. Anyway, he fancies you, you fancy him. Go out with the poor sod.'

'Look, when it comes to men I'm a bastard magnet. You're right about Jake and Lewis is even worse. God knows how many girlfriends he's got on the go. At least Jake was only a shit to one woman at a time . . . I think.'

'Don't jump to conclusions about him. This woman he's seeing tonight might be a genuine work thing.'

'Rubbish. No one meets their bank manager for *dinner* and I told you about the photo.'

'Did you ask him who she was? Might be his sister.'

'What bloke has a framed picture of his sister on his desk? . . . Unless he's . . . *Yeuch*! That's too disgusting. No, he's involved with someone, which makes him a shit, which means I shouldn't touch him with a very long stick . . . *Ugh*, this is so *depressing*,' I say, emptying my glass and immediately refilling it. 'Why can't I meet a straight version of you . . . No, forget I said that. You're having sex with half of Manhattan – you make Jake and Lewis look celibate. Have you decided what you're going to do about Alex and Freddie yet?'

'It's *Frankie*, and, no, I haven't. I thought it'd be easier being three thousand miles away . . . But it isn't. They just seem to merge into each other. God, this is so *difficult*,' he says emptying his glass. As I refill it with the last of the bottle he adds, 'I'll go to the off-licence and get some more.'

I set the aeroplane on autopilot, strap the parachute to my back and pick up the spare from the floor of the cockpit. Then I walk back to where my two passengers sit nervously in their seats.

'We have a slight technical hitch,' I announce calmly. 'Seems I neglected to refuel the plane. Silly me – I can be such a girly sometimes. Anyway, in a few minutes the engines will stop and we'll crash into the impenetrable jungle. The good news is that we have parachutes. The bad news is that there are only two. Since I've got one of them, perhaps the fairest thing would be to toss the other one out and let you both perish. After all, who will

113

miss a couple of scum-sucking worms like you?'

'Now, h-h-hang on,' stutters Jake. 'I'm an *author*. I have *fans*.'

'Ha. A bunch of nerdy, bearded Trekkies?' I scoff. 'Don't talk to me – a *bestselling* writer, a goddamn publishing phenomenon, "the fearless new voice of female fiction" (*Company*) – about fans. No, if you want to survive, you'll have to give me something better than that.'

Chastened by the brutal truth, Jake cowers in his seat.

'What about you, Lewis?' I continue. 'You're awfully quiet.'

'How many times do I have to explain, Amy?' he says, looking up at me with the big brown eyes. 'She's a face in a photo frame. She means nothing to me. *Nothing*, I tell you. You're the one I love . . . That I've been waiting for my whole life.'

'Huh, bet you say that to all the girls when you're in a plane that's about to plummet into a jungle infested with deadly spiders and grizzly bears, and you're begging for the one remaining parachute.'

'Did you say grizzlies?' Jake asks. 'They don't live in rain forests.'

'Silence,' I snap. 'They're . . . um . . . Amazonian jungle grizzlies. Look, it's my daydream and the bears live where I bloody well choose. And for being such an annoying clever dick you don't get the parachute.'

Jake starts to sob. Next to him Lewis slumps into his seat, relief visibly flooding over his body.

'I wouldn't look so pleased,' I say to him, 'because I'm having two parachutes . . . Unless you can give me a convincing explanation of that photograph – one that doesn't involve wives or girlfriends . . . Or incest.'

'She's . . . She's . . . . your sister.'

'Excuse me?'

'I said hadn't you better phone your *sister*?' Ant repeats, completely destroying my carefully constructed drunken fantasy – we've polished off a third bottle and it's worked a treat.

'Let her stew a bit longer,' I slur.

'The danger with that is she's probably hatching plans for revenge . . . Of course, if you don't mind your mum picking up the *Mail* tomorrow and seeing some blurry holiday snap of you on the front p—'

I've fallen off the sofa and grabbed the phone before he has finished his sentence.

'Lisa, it's me. I'm sorry. No, I'm really, really, *really* sorry.' I gush into the receiver. 'Please don't do it.'

'Don't do what?' Lisa hisses.

'I'm not sure . . . Whatever you might have been thinking of doing.'

'I was thinking of killing you, Amy.'

'I *so* deserve to die. I'm terrible. I don't know what came over me.'

'I do. You're a coward. I'm used to that, but why did you have to drop me in it? Now Mum wants to impound my passport.'

'Well, you don't want to go to Hong Kong anyway . . . Do you?'

'That is not the point. It's up to me to decide, just like I've left it to you decide when you're going to tell her about your stupid book . . . Which you never will. *Pathetic*.'

'Will you ever forgive me?' I whimper.

'Why the hell should I? Anyway, you sound pissed. How much did you have to knock back to get up the nerve to call me?'

'I'm so sorry, Lisa.'

Silence.

I decide to try Dad's tactic – the unexpected change of subject.

'Dad's having an affair,' I say.

'God, you *are* drunk.'

'I'm not making this up. He's cheating on Mum.'

'*Dad*? Come off it.'

'He *is*. I saw her. She's blonde and she wears strappy heels that show off her nail polish and he puts on aftershave for her.'

'I'm coming over right now. Whatever you do, don't pass out.'

'What the hell are we going to do?' I ask.

'Confront him, of course,' Lisa says as if it's obvious.

She's been here for an hour. We've drained a fourth bottle and she's joined me in stupefied disbelief. Ant's been uncharacteristically silent on the subject – which is probably down to the fact that he's been doing most of the drinking. But he speaks now.

'If I were you, I'd leave things be.'

'How can you say that, Ant?' Lisa exclaims. 'This is our *dad*. We can't let him make a complete prat of himself.'

'Of course you can. He's an adult. Who are you to judge him? Anyway, don't you hate it when your parents interfere with your lives – tell you who you can and can't . . . oh, go to Hong Kong with, for instance?'

'That's different,' Lisa says indignantly.

'Yeah, Lisa's right,' I pretend to agree – she's still mad at me, so it's the smart thing to do.

'At least before you wade in and lay down the law, make sure you know the facts,' Ant argues.

'What's there to know?' Lisa says. 'He's shagging a tart in strappy heels.'

'God, listen to you. You sound like an angry medieval mob. *Strappy heels! Burn the witch*! All you know is that the poor bloke had a drink with her,' Ant says.

'Yes, after he'd told Mum he was going to Birmingham

116

to look at coat hanger bending machines. Why did he lie if he's so innocent?' I ask.

'OK, maybe he is having an affair. Even so, you don't know everything,' Ant says cryptically – or maybe he isn't being cryptic, but just sounds it because I'm drunk.

'What do you mean?' Lisa asks.

Ant shrugs.

'Hang on,' I squeak. 'Mum's confession. What did she tell you, Ant?'

'What the hell are you going on about?' Lisa says.

'Mum came round last night while I was out,' I explain. 'She confessed to Father Anthony of Saint Liberace's. He won't tell me what she said, but it must be to do with Dad and Miss Strappy Heels.'

'It had nothing to do with that,' he says. 'And before you ask, Lisa, you could torture me and I wouldn't tell you what she told me.'

She glowers at him, but he ignores her. 'Look, the best thing you can do is to forget about your parents. Let them get on with it. Worry about your own problems . . . Seems you've got plenty.'

'Shut up, Ant,' Lisa snaps. 'You wouldn't be saying that if it were your mum's and dad's marriage going up in flames.'

'Well, what are you going to do about it? Invite a relationship counsellor to Sunday lunch? Hire a private dick?'

I wish he hadn't said that.

Chapter 10

I *really* wish he hadn't said that.

'Why the hell did I agree to do this?' I mutter as I follow Lisa up a decrepit staircase in a crummy old building in Clerkenwell.

'Because it's the right thing,' she replies with absolute certainty.

We reach the top and find ourselves facing a shabby green door. The sign on it reads PARAMO NT IN EST GATIO S (IN ERNATI AL), which might read as a sinister warning in Latin if my mind hadn't already filled in the blanks.

'This couldn't be seedier,' I say. 'Let's leave before it's too late.'

'You can't back out now. Just keep quiet – let me do the talking,' Lisa says, pushing the door open.

'Come in, come in,' booms a rough voice. It comes from a fat, sweaty middle-aged man squashed behind a small desk. This just gets better and better. He has the phone to his ear, one hand covering the mouthpiece. 'Park your pretty behinds,' he continues, gesturing at two plastic chairs.

Lisa and I clear the stacked files from them, sit down and wait for him to finish his call.

'I know it was pitch black, Arthur . . . And, yeah, you were wedged up a tree . . . The dodgy hip, I know all that, but the first thing you should check is whether you've taken off the sodding lens cap . . . Fair dos, Magnum PI

118

didn't take on maritals, but if he had, you can bet he'd've taken off the bollocking lens cap . . . What do I want you to do? I want you to stick to the geezer like shit to a blanket and catch him at it again . . . No, that's the bottom line . . . Well, what do you expect me to show his missus? My holiday snaps? . . . Just sort it . . . *Please* . . . Yeah, love you too.'

He puts the phone down and catches me glaring at Lisa through narrowed eyes. Why the hell did I let her drag me into this?

'Sorry about that, ladies. One of my older operatives. Don't think I'll be using him again,' he explains, looking us up and down – not difficult in Lisa's case because the skirt she's wearing wouldn't cover the knees on a Sindy doll. He hauls himself to his feet and thrusts out a pudgy hand. 'Let's get the formalities out of the way. Colin Mount – CEO and Senior Investigator for Para*mount* Investigations . . . International. Now, how can I help?' he asks Lisa's legs.

She is busy rooting in her handbag for the only photo of Dad that she could find at short notice. It shows him dressed as a reluctant Santa at a Conservative Club Christmas craft sale. His expression suggests he was thinking *Why the hell did I let myself get dragged into this?* Like father like daughter – like mother like other daughter. Lisa pulls the snap from her bag and hands it over. He looks at it and laughs. 'You want me to find him? Didn't anyone explain, sweetheart? He's a fairy story, a figment.' He looks at our blank faces and the chuckles die. 'Sorry . . . Couldn't resist.'

'He's having an affair,' Lisa deadpans.

'Been caught goosing the little helpers?' he says, stifling another giggle. 'Sorry, sorry, forget I said that. It's been one of those mornings. Need some light relief. Having an affair you say? That's not pleasant at all. And which of you princesses is he married to?'

'He's our father,' Lisa says in a tone that suggests she's beginning to realise that flicking open the Yellow Pages and dialling the first private investigator she saw was one of her poorer ideas.

'Your father? There was me thinking he must be barmy to be cheating on a young lovely like either of you two. Now, if you don't mind me blowing my own trumpet, you've come to the right man. Marital's my speciality. There ain't a pants-down scenario I can't get a handle on. You tell me what you know and then we'll talk plans and strategies.'

'*Paramount Investigations*? *Pants-down scenario*?' I splutter as we tumble onto the street. 'Did you hear him? He called us *young lovelies*. And if he'd bent any lower to see up your skirt he'd have been on the floor.'

'It's over, OK?' Lisa snaps. 'I'll deal with him from now on.'

'Yes, but I'll have to pay the sleazy git's bill. I can't believe I just gave him a cheque. *Three hundred quid*.'

'Well, you've been wondering how to spend your cash. This is the right thing to do. We can't confront Dad unless we know exactly what he's up to. And don't whinge about the money. You owe me.'

I do as well. I suppose that if getting back into her good books after the Hong Kong bombshell costs a few hundred pounds, then it'll be money well spent. I only wish I could have bought her a dress rather than have spent it on a detective who makes the man who used to expose himself to us on our way home from school look like a pillar of the community.

I look at my watch. I'm over two hours late for work and I haven't even phoned in.

'You're nearly three hours late,' Deedee says flatly as I arrive at the office.

'Sorry, sorry,' I say. 'My new lenses weren't ready yesterday. Had to go back and collect them this morning.'

'I don't know why you can't make do with glasses,' she says, glaring at me through hers – two glass saucers bolted together.

'I know, pathetic. That's vanity for you,' I say heading for my desk before she can add anything about the steamy disaster in Lewis's office.

'You're Miss Popular this morning,' Julie announces as I sit down. She picks up a message pad and starts reading, 'A woman called. Wouldn't give me her name, but said she wants you to call her about the thingy.'

'The what?'

'That's what she said. The *thingy*.'

It could only be Mary.

'Your mum phoned. Didn't say what she wanted – she sounded a bit desperate. Ant rang as well. He sounds lovely. You sure he's a shirt lifter?'

'Positive.'

'Pity. Anyway, he said he hoped you and your sister hadn't done anything stupid . . .'

Only three hundred quid's worth of stupid.

'. . . And he needs you to call him. He said it's really, *really* urgent. Oh, and someone called Jake called. He sounds *cool*. Flower boy?'

I nod. 'What's he want?'

'Told me to tell you he's on hunger strike until you pick up the phone. He is *gagging*, girl.'

'Well, he can starve because I'm not going to call him. Never in a million years. My life's too bloody complicated already. Anything else?'

'Yeah, Lewis has been hovering like a horny vulture. Doesn't want me. He's just waiting for you to show. What happened in his office yesterday? I guess he didn't fire you.'

'Not exactly,' I reply, hoping she doesn't press me. No

121

chance. Julie wouldn't be Julie if she didn't suck her victims dry of gossip.

'Come on, out with it,' she urges.

'It was nothing. Just boring company stuff.'

'What *company* stuff?'

'It was *nothing*. Boring,' I say. 'End of story. OK?'

'So *not* OK. What was it? . . . I know. He asked you out, didn't he?'

I don't reply.

'I knew it,' she says triumphantly. 'I hope you said yes. If I wasn't mad about Alan, I could spend a few hours sitting on Lewis's –'

'No, I did not say yes. He's a total git and he can rot in –'

I can't finish the sentence because Lewis has stepped out of his office and he's heading my way.

Shit, shit, *shit*. What am I going to say to him? I mean, he *is* a total git, but I can't actually tell him that, can I? Only one thing for it. I dive into my bag and fumble for my address book. I open it at B, grab my phone and dial frantically. Please, please, *please* be home, I think as Lewis draws closer. He picks up on the fourth ring and gives me a gruff 'Yeah?'

'Jake . . . It's me.'

'Amy, hi,' he says, his tone softening like ice cream under a hairdryer. 'I'm glad you phoned . . . I think. You're gonna tell me what a prick I am, yeah?'

Lewis spots that I'm on the phone and halts at a discreet distance – far enough for politeness, but close enough to hear every word I'm saying.

'No . . . Um . . . No, not really, Jake,' I say. 'The other night. I think we both . . . You know. Got off on the wrong foot. Or something.'

What the hell are you saying? splutters Inner Voice. *Why are you letting the shit off the hook?*

Point taken. I'm totally mad. But I've started now . . .

'You're sweet, Amy,' Jake says. 'You didn't have to say that. I was appalling. I'm sorry.'

Wow, the S word again. From Jake Bedford.

Don't fall for it, girl, warns Inner Voice. Too late. I'm going over the parapet.

'Anyway, maybe we could try again, yeah?' he continues. 'Dinner?'

'Yes, dinner. That would be lovely, *Jake*.' I say as I watch Lewis pretend to be fascinated by Deedee's NO BEVERAGES TO BE PLACED ON THE COPIER notice (onto which Julie has graffitied λ *OR BARE SWEATY ARSES*). His ears must be red hot by now.

'OK, what are you doing tomorrow?'

'Um . . . Nothing I don't think.'

Shit, why did I say that? Shouldn't I make myself look booked up? *For ever,* adds Inner Voice.

'OK, tomorrow then,' Jake decides. 'What do you fancy? Italian? French? How about that new –'

'I don't know . . . Anything. Surprise me. Gotta go. I think my boss wants something . . . Bye . . . Oh, and, Jake, thanks for the flowers. They were gorgeous.'

I put the phone down and watch Lewis decide that he doesn't want to see me after all and grab the spotty sixteen-year-old – *Yesss,* it worked. Julie gazes at me in wonder. 'What?' I ask.

'I didn't know you had it in you. You were awesome.'

Awesome? You were bloody insane, laments Inner Voice.

'What do you mean?' I ask.

'Well, you've given Lewis a challenge, haven't you? If he's got any balls, he'll *kill* to get off with you now. Way to go.'

'That wasn't the idea, Julie,' I say feeling genuinely worried. 'I want him to leave me alone.'

'Nah, I've pulled that stunt a million times. You watch.

He'll be all over you like the pox. Anyway, why would you want him to leave you alone?'

'Because he's already going out with someone.'

'So?'

'He's got her picture on his desk. It's obviously serious. He's a rat.'

'All that "other woman" stuff never stopped me,' she says adjusting her Burberry baseball cap (today's addition to yesterday's Tiffany heart) with a shrug. 'But I guess we're different.'

I guess we are, but that's the least of my worries. What if she's right? What if my call to Jake turns Lewis into a slavering sex hound? But God, what if she's wrong and Ant was right and I've got the Ros in the photo frame thing all screwed up? What if Lewis is in his office now sniffing a bottle of Tippex until he feels numb enough to slash his wrists with a letter opener? Either scenario doesn't bear thinking about. But either one is easier to dwell on than the prospect of . . . *OhmyfuckingGod* . . . A date. *Another* date. With Jake Bedford. I must be completely out of my tree.

My phone rings.

I stare at it thinking *please don't be Jake, please don't be Jake* . . .

Julie must be telepathic because she says, 'Want me to get that?'

I nod.

She picks it up and trills, 'Ms Bickerstaff's PA. How can I help?' Then she puts her hand over the mouthpiece and whispers, 'The *thingy* woman. Wanna take it or shall I tell her to stick it up her whatsit?'

I reach for the phone – I think I can handle this.

'Sometimes I feel as in the dark as your poor mother,' Mary complains before I've said a word. 'You didn't tell me you qualified for secretarial assistance.'

124

'Believe me I don't . . . What's that noise?'

It sounded like a prolonged fart. From a very big elephant.

'A passing barge tooting its horn, angel. I'm calling from a payphone on the Embankment.'

'Why?'

'Can't trust my office line any more. Pound to a penny the *Mail* has it bugged. Caught their hackette going through my rubbish last night. Fortunately I was one step ahead. I'd booby-trapped it with some smoked mackerel that had been in my fridge somewhat past its sell-by. Now I can smell the little cow clean across Soho – not sure if that's an advantage. No matter. On to business. There have been developments . . .'

Don't like the sound of that.

'. . . We're meeting Jacobson tomorrow lunchtime . . .'

Definitely don't like the sound of *that*.

'. . . I booked us a suite at the Langham Hilton . . .'

Christ, what are we doing? Lunch or a threesome?

'. . . And please don't imagine it's going to degenerate into some Mellow-esque orgy . . .'

Oh.

'. . . I just knew you'd never agree to anything unless it's behind a locked door and away from prying eyes . . . So, what do you think?'

'Not sure.'

'Why not come along and meet the fellow? Hear him out. Then make up your mind. And no pressure from me to take his money . . . I swear. Entirely your decision. *Entirely*.'

'I really don't know.'

'Angel, you'll never forgive yourself in years to come if you don't meet him.'

'You said no pressure,' I hiss.

'I said I wouldn't press you to take his money. I absolutely think it would be a grave mistake not to meet him. You'll spend the rest of your life wondering what might have been . . . End up clinically depressed. On Prozac by the time you're thirty. One step away from the loony –'

'OK, OK, I'll come.'

'Excellent. Marvellous. Trust me, this is the right thing . . .'

Which is exactly what Lisa said about the private detective.

'. . . Now, if I might be allowed to give you some advice. Dress.'

'What about it?'

'Wear one, my darling. Something with va-va-voom. No disrespect, but I've only ever seen you in jogging pants or admirably sensible skirts. Perhaps if you slipped into something that projected a little of what you write it might help limber up Jacobson's cheque-signing hand. He may deal in the written word, but he's like all men . . . Actually more so than most. How can I put this delicately? He requires a little visual stimulation.'

'Jesus,' I splutter, 'I agree to a simple meeting and now you want me to turn up looking like a lap dancer.'

'Apologies, angel. I've overstepped the mark. I'm coming on like your pimp – which in a funny sort of way I suppose I am. Wear what you like. My fifty pee's almost expired. I'll love you and leave you. See you tomorrow at one. In the lobby. If I'm a little late don't fret – I'll be shaking off my stalker. There go the pips. Toodle-oo.'

She hangs up leaving me reeling.

'You're a dark horse, Amy. Who are you meeting dressed like a lap dancer?' Julie asks. She has, of course, been hanging on every word – it's a good job that Mary did the vast majority of the talking, leaving few fag ends for Julie to pick up.

'No one,' I reply.

'Doesn't sound like no one.'

'It is. Just my . . . Um . . . My bank manager. I want to extend my mortgage.'

'I tried that once,' she says. 'I wore a crop top and hotpants when NatWest dragged me in about my over-draft. Didn't work. The bastards still cut my cash card in half. But you go for it. I'd bung you a hundred grand for those tits.'

She dissolves into giggles, having not the faintest idea of how close to the truth she is.

'Hi, Ant,' I call out as I walk into my flat. 'Sorry I didn't call you back, but I haven't had a spare minute. You will not believe the day I've had. I really need to talk to you . . . Ant? . . . *Ant*!'

I see a letter on the table. Even from a distance it looks too long to be a 'just popped out for milk' note. I pick it up nervously.

Amy

By the time you read this I'll be on a plane. Sorry to run out on you, but I did call to tell you. Explanation: I've made up my mind. Alex phoned me this morning, 4 a.m. his time. Definite sign of keenness! I'm forgiven. Doesn't even want me to join Sexoholics Anonymous or whatever the fuck it's called. We talked for an hour. It was fantastic. He's fantastic. Don't know what I ever saw in Frankie. Thanks for putting me up. I've loved being here. It's been a reminder that friends don't come any better than the ones you make in reception class. We mustn't leave it so long in future. Pop out to New York. Any time. You can't use the pathetic 'I can't afford it' excuse any more. I can't believe what you've become. A famous blah! (Won't write the word in case a spy reads this) I know you're in turmoil

127

about it, but it won't last. One day you'll wake up and see
that this is the most amazing thing you've done. Taxi's here.
I'll phone as soon as Al and I have finished the kissing
part of the making up bit . . . Might be some time. Love
you.
  Ant

I feel like crying. I *need* Ant, but he's on a bloody plane
. . . promising himself he'll be faithful to Alex, but –
knowing him – eyeing up an airline steward while he's at
it. I crash onto my sofa and light a fag. I'm dreading
tomorrow. I close my eyes and picture Jake and Jacobson
circling round me, drooling. God, why has it never struck
me until now? Even their names are too close for comfort
. . . Like they're involved in a conspiracy.

I'm being stupid. I've got to think about this sensibly.
I feel as if I've no choice other than to go through with
the meeting with Jacobson. Mary said I'd never forgive
myself if I don't, but, actually, she's the one who'll never
forgive me. Fine, I can handle him. I'll go in there,
demurely shake his hand, listen to the schmooze and
depart. I can cope with that. And I'll wear my dowdiest
dress – one that Mum (or at least the pre-Edwina Currie
version of her) would approve of.

But what about Jake? As a tactic to get Lewis off my
back the phone call worked a treat. He spent the rest of
the day shut in his office. But now I can't help thinking
that a simple 'Thanks, Lewis, but I don't think dinner is
a good idea' would've had the same effect – with the added
bonus of not landing me with a date with *him* . . .

Which part of me – and this is the real problem –
desperately wants to go on. Not my nagging Inner Voice
part – obviously. (That wouldn't stop telling me what a
complete and utter idiot I am. Luckily, by four o'clock it
had screamed itself hoarse and has now shut up.) No, I'm

talking about the bit of my brain that still fancies Jake –
that always did fancy him, even when he was being a pig
two years ago. And, hey, he did say sorry after all. Maybe
he has changed.

'Yeah, and maybe bears poo in nice clean toilets and
the Pope's a committed Buddhist,' Ant would say . . . If
only he weren't on a bloody aeroplane.

I have got to talk to someone who'll tell me I'm mad
even to think of seeing him again . . .

Lisa.

She knows what a bastard he is.

She watched me go through the hell of being dumped.

She'll talk me out of it.

I pick up the phone and dial.

Chapter 11

The lobby of the Langham Hilton is busy. Smart Europeans mingle with expensively dressed Japanese tourists creating a civilised bustle of activity. They stop as one, however, when the lift doors slide open and *he* steps out. Even glimpsed through a forest of grovelling flunkies he is unmistakable. John Travolta – Hollywood handsome, tanned to the colour of teak and, miraculously, once again as slim as when he wore the tight black T-shirt in the unforgettable finale of *Grease*. He sweeps through the foyer looking neither left nor right until he has almost reached the revolving door and spots the dress . . . Or, I suppose, *me* in the dress.

He freezes, his peripheral vision catching the glint of the jet-black beads on the boned bodice. He turns towards me and takes in the taut fabric as it clings to my body like a new skin; one that has been painstakingly stitched to my every curve by first-rate cosmetic surgeons. Then he struts to where I sit. He stops a few feet short of me and stares – God, does he *stare* – with those eyes that have lost none of their youthful sparkle. He clicks his fingers and one of his entourage immediately breaks from the pack and scurries to his master's side.

'Call Cameron's people and tell them thanks but no thanks,' Travolta commands without averting his gaze from me. 'This is the one . . . *the one that I want*.'

Maintaining my cool I give him a slightly quizzical look.

'I'm sorry,' he says addressing me for the first time. 'I was so captivated by your beauty that I forgot my manners. I've been scouring the world for the woman who'll play opposite me in *Return to Night Fever – the Gangsta Rap Years*. Now, at last, my search is over.'

'But, Mr Travolta –'

'Please, call me John.'

'John, I've never been in front of a camera in my life.'

'Maybe, but you have the elusive . . . *it*. With me at your side I *know* you can do it . . . There is just one question.'

'Yes?'

'In *Return to Night Fever* you'll play my lover. The integrity of the script *demands* that we rise to the very summit of human passion and make poetic love as has *never* before been committed to celluloid. Do you think you could . . . With me?' he asks, nervously fingering the legendary dimple in his mythical chin. 'Or would you rather –'

'– lick the grit from a dirty tramp's flesh wound.'

'Pardon?' I say as Mary collapses into the chair beside mine, making the vision of a slim Travolta evaporate.

'Bloody taxi nightmare. I had the rudest driver. He had the gall to ask for a tip and I told him I'd sooner lick . . . Never mind. Did you see John Travolta just now?'

'The whole lobby did, Mary. I didn't realise this hotel was so posh.'

'Only the best for my star client. My word, hasn't he turned into Mr Tubby Guts? The pair of us nearly jammed up the revolving door. I know I'm hardly one to talk, but an army of personal trainers would struggle to get his midriff back to a twenty-eight. Tragedy . . . Now *that*

131

takes me back. My God, I'm burbling today. Let's away to our suite and await the man with the chequebook.'

As I stand up she looks at me properly for the first time and gasps, 'Amy, good grief, I didn't expect you to take me so literally. You look . . . *remarkable*.'

'I'm suffocating, if you must know.'

I attempt to yank the hem of my dress down to a more respectable level, but the fabric is wrapped so tightly round my thighs that any movement is difficult – I can feel the beginnings of a tingling in my feet on account of the constricted blood flow.

'Well, you look perfectly stunning,' Mary says as I totter behind her towards the reception desk, 'and if Jacobson's tongue lolls at ankle height you'll know why. There was no need to splash out on a new frock, though.'

'I didn't. It's Lisa's.'

I called my sister last night. She didn't share my dread of the J-men. Just the opposite. Where I saw a nightmare in stereo, she spotted a gold-plated opportunity and her first thought was wardrobe.

'If you want to impress your publisher, you have *got* to look like the woman who writes the world's horniest books,' she explained.

'*Book*,' I corrected.

'Oh, you'll write another one,' she said dismissively. 'And what works on your publisher will work on Jake.'

'The last thing I want to do is to *work* on Jake,' I protested.

'That's not what I mean. What you want to do is rub what he's missing in his face. What have you got that's suitable?'

'Erm . . .'

'Thought as much. I'll be round in half an hour.'

She arrived with a bin bag stuffed with sexy cast-offs.

'I can't wear this,' I said as she squeezed my boobs into the beaded and corseted dress. 'Jake and Jacobson will think they're being attacked by torpedoes.'

'Perfect. Blokes only have three obsessions – boobs, football and military hardware. Combine two of them and you can't fail. Now, I've got the perfect shoes,' she said diving back into the bag. 'If you wear them, though, you'll have to watch your head on any low-flying chandeliers.'

I sit on one of the suite's two sofas, slip off Lisa's four-inch heels and rub my agonised feet. The dress is beginning to give me serious breathing difficulties, and I'm tempted to peel it off and put on one of the fluffy white Hilton Hotel dressing gowns in the bathroom – but what the hell would that make Jacobson think?

Why do I go along with my sister's mad ideas? Yesterday's private eye and today's little black number are just the latest examples. A much more significant one is the fact that my book was published at all. If it hadn't been for Lisa . . . Well, I wouldn't be sitting in a five-star hotel running the risk of permanent deformity.

'The word on the street,' Mary announces as she emerges from the bathroom, 'is that the charts will have a new number one next week.'

What? Gareth Gates? S Club Pre-school? Is Robbie's new one out yet? I had no idea she kept up with pop.

'*Rings on Her Fingers* is trouncing all comers.'

OhmyGod, those charts. 'That's incredible . . . Number one?' I manage to say. 'That can't be right.'

'My spy at Waterstone's tells me he hasn't seen anything like it since the last *Potter*. If JKR wants to keep up with you she'll have to have Harry strip off and shake his pimpled little booty.'

'*Number one*,' I repeat in a dazed whisper.

'You, my angel, are the goose that is laying Jacobson twenty-four-carat eggs,' she continues, ignoring my shock. 'He will, of course, pepper your behind with little kisses, my dear – not literally, though seeing you in that dress the thought will cross his mind. Don't let the five-star treatment go to your head because it will be a calculated attempt to soften you up for the money. When he names the figure, he would like nothing more than for you to fall to your knees in gratitude . . . Which under no circumstances must you do.'

'Look, Mary, nothing's changed,' I say pulling myself together. 'I don't want his money. I don't think I could write another book.'

'For crying out loud *don't* tell him that. As far as he is concerned your head is brimming with sexy novels queuing up for word processor time. Got that?'

I nod.

'Now, I want you to try a little exercise,' she continues. 'Look at me as if I've told you that no, you can't have another Cornetto.'

I pull a face that's supposed to communicate disappointment – I think it's what she's after.

'Not bad,' she says. 'That's what I want to see when Jacobson names the figure. I don't care how humungous it is. Look devastated.'

The phone rings and Mary picks it up.

'He's here, my dear,' she says after a moment. 'Now, don't say a word. Just sit back, exude hormones and marvel as Special Agent Mary McKenzie goes to work.'

My publisher isn't the man I've pictured. All of Mary's preparation had given me a mental image of . . . Well, of the bloke who used to expose himself to Lisa and me and whom, much to the frustration of the police, we could never describe in great detail from the waist up. But as I watch Mary embrace Jacobson like a long-lost friend he strikes me as elegant and even dashing – in an old-enough-to-be-my-dad kind of way. He's tall and thin with a lush crop of swept-back white hair – sort of Christopher Lee for once getting to play the good guy in a tweed suit.

Mary peels herself away from him and says with a flourish of her flabby arm, 'Adam, may I present the author of *Rings on Her Fingers*.'

I attempt to stand, but feel a sharp pain in my ribs . . . And was that a crack? I flop back down and wonder if a boned dress has ever killed anyone. Perhaps I'll set a medical precedent.

'At last, I meet the mysterious gem that is captivating the reading public . . . And, my word, what a gem,' he says, doing a bit of the tongue-lolling thing that Mary warned me about and giving me my first glimpse of the inner Jacobson. 'Mary, how could you keep this young lady a secret? She is enchanting – a publicist's dream.'

I start to blush as he mentally undresses me. (Actually, 'undress' is the wrong word – getting me out of this frock would require the help of firemen with specialised cutting equipment.) He steps towards me and takes my hand. God, he's not going to kiss it, is he? But he just holds it and says, 'Marsha Mellow, I cannot tell you how thrilled I am.'

Weird. No one has ever called me Marsha Mellow to my face. It's always seemed like someone else's name – something on the cover of a book. But I suppose that for the next thirty minutes or whatever I am Marsha. I'm playing a role and the ridiculous dress that I've forced myself into is my costume. The last time I played a part was in primary school – Mrs Beaver in *The Lion, the Witch and the Wardrobe*. Now I'm playing . . . Well, I'm not quite sure how to put it, but as Ant would no doubt point out it still involves beaver.

'It's good to meet you too, Adam,' I reply, surprised at how composed my new Marsha Mellow voice sounds.

'Amazing, absolutely amazing,' marvels Jacobson as he sits in the sofa opposite mine. 'You disprove the rule that writers never look . . . How best to put this delicately? . . . That they never look like what they write. Ever wondered why Andy McNab refuses to show himself? Pens SAS yarns by the yard, but he's such a disappointment in the flesh . . . Tell me, Marsha, are you a London girl or do you hail from the provinces?'

'London,' I reply automatically, 'Crouch En—'

Mary kicks me – *hard* – and says, 'Now, now, Adam. You know the score. Marsha isn't here to give you her life story.'

'Of course, Mary,' he smarms. 'You know, before we get down to business I think we should call room service and order champagne. We owe a toast to the author of a remarkable debut . . . And of course to the editor of the *Mail* for drawing her to the nation's attention.'

Mm, I like that. He isn't so bad after all. I sit back and fully relax for the first time since I woke up this morning. Bad move because as he picks up the phone I attempt to cross my legs and hear a couple of stitches ping. I'd better keep my knees clamped together if I don't want to discover the quick way of getting this bloody dress off.

My head is swimming. Two glasses of bubbly and I've slipped into the role. I'm Marsha Mellow, the babe who is 'single-handedly changing the face of popular fiction', the doll who is 'without doubt, the most important young writer in Britain today', the minx whose 'torrid prose is sending a blast of super-heated steam through the fusty corridors of publishing'. Or something like that – I'm too tipsy to remember it word for word. Whatever, Jacobson is laying it on with a jumbo trowel and I'm loving it.

He pops the cork on the second bottle and refills my glass. I am feeling . . . very . . . reee . . . laxed. So much so that my bottom is threatening to slither off the sofa. I hope that by the time he quits telling me how ravishingly wonderful I am and gets down to business I haven't fallen asleep. Mary must be thinking the same because she decides to move things along. 'Now, Adam, delightful though it is to listen to your lucid appraisal of Marsha's work, I'm sure that's not the reason we're here.'

'Quite so, Mary, quite so,' Jacobson replies, actually looking relieved that he can lay off the crawly bum-licking for a moment. 'As you must know, we're delighted that we managed to acquire Marsha's first novel. However, we're interested in developing a long-term relationship. There's nothing more gratifying for a publisher than to see one of his authors mature and grow. With that in mind, we'd like to offer an advance for Marsha's . . .' He pauses and looks at me. 'For *your* next three novels.'

Three! Did he say *three*? I'm not even certain I can write *one*. Must focus. I pull myself upright. Poor idea because the dress doesn't want to move with me. I feel another rib crack and an involuntary '*Ouch*' leaves my mouth. Mary attempts to stifle it by stamping on my already agonised toe. At the same time she asks, 'Did you have a figure in mind, Adam?'

'Indeed. We at Smith Jacobson have enormous faith in you, Marsha, and we believe the offer we have prepared reflects this.'

He takes the hotel notepad from the coffee table, uncaps his pen and writes on it. Then he tears off the sheet, folds it in half and slides it across the table to Mary. I try to peer over her shoulder as she reads it but a couple more stitches ping and I give up before my boobs flop out and the situation turns into *Carry On Publishing*. Mary refolds the paper and passes it to me. I open it out and, as I look at the number written in Jacobson's spidery hand, I start to giggle. Mary stamps on my foot again and I remember her instructions – 'Look devastated.' Given the combination of shock and wooziness that I'm feeling, I don't know how my expression comes out, but it's probably less disappointment and more 'Fuck me, that idiot has just offered me £425,000!'.

That's right, *four hundred and twenty-five thousand pounds*.

To write three books.

About sex.

As I'm trying to absorb it, Mary speaks. 'Thank you, Adam,' she says calmly. 'Clearly a great deal of thought has gone into your proposal. However, I don't think we can accept it.'

Now it's my turn to stamp on her toe. What the hell is she doing? The man has just offered a fortune and she's turning it down. Without even asking me first.

Jacobson sits back in his chair and peers at her over his glasses. His face is impossible to read, though this could be because I'm starting to see two of him.

'Perhaps you'd like to go back, talk to your people and have a little rethink,' Mary concludes gently.

'I can't believe you just did that, Mary,' I rage as soon as Jacobson has left. The alcohol has completely killed my inhibitions. Massacred them brutally, actually – bits of dead inhibition all over the place. The half of my brain that would normally flee in terror at the thought of so much money is slumped in a coma and the bit that's greedy and grasping is wide awake and mad as hell.

'Calm, my dear,' Mary soothes. 'Believe me, if I thought for a second that four hundred and twenty-five thousand pounds was his highest offer, I would have chewed his arm off at the shoulder. You mark my words, just like Arnie he'll be back. Anyway, aren't you through with writing? I thought you didn't want his money.'

'I . . . um . . . I don't. But just say I did . . . *Hypothetically* . . . You might have really screwed things up . . . In theory,' I slur.

'Darling, I have negotiated more book deals than your Donna has had grubby sexual encounters with nameless strangers. I have not screwed anything up,' she says firmly. 'Just leave the agenting to me and you get on with the writing . . . Oh, but I'm forgetting. You've retired, haven't you?'

'Yes . . . No . . . Oh, I don't fucking know, Mary. Three books? That's impossible.'

'Oh, it might not seem so daunting once you've sobered up, angel. Dickens managed a couple of dozen or so.'

'That's stupid. I'm not Charles Dickens.'

'Thank the Lord. Vastly overrated, if you ask me. No, Amy, you're Marsha Mellow and ignoring the oily bullshit heaped on you by Jacobson, you are a very talented author in your own right. If you want to write more books, then you will. That's the key: if you *want* to.'

'I don't know . . . *Four hundred grand*. Jesus . . . It's all too much. I can't think about this now.'

And I can't, because I've just seen the time. It's nearly four o'clock. I've got to somehow hobble back to work in Lisa's shoes, sit at my desk for an hour without slipping into a persistent vegetative state and then teeter off to the second instalment of my day with the J-men.

I'm meeting Jake at a place called the Sanderson.

Which sounds like a good name for a hardware store, but is apparently an extremely hip hotel.

Just the sort of place where writers hang out and agonise about their colossal advances.

God, I feel pissed.

Chapter 12

My head is *killing* me. If there's anything worse than waking up with a hangover it's getting one before you've even gone to bloody bed. And it isn't even seven o'clock yet.

'Bloody Mary, please,' I mumble to the barman.

I've never had one before. I'm not even sure I like tomato juice, let alone all that spicy stuff that goes in it, but it's what people with hangovers drink, isn't it? Hair of the dog . . . Which sounds like . . . a hair . . . of a dog . . . *yeuch*.

I lean on the Sanderson's long bar as I wait for my drink. The place is filling up with scary men in (mostly) black who have raised looking bored and cynical to an art form (just like Jake in other words), and skinny women who wear sexy and revealing far better than I ever could. The way I'm dressed should make me feel at home, but it only makes me more uncomfortable. And my *feet*. Unless I get my weight off them they'll explode right out of Lisa's shoes. Now I know why she calls them her fuck-me stilts – they're stilts all right and they've fucked my feet right up. I attempt to scale a bar stool, but the dress is too tight for me to raise my leg to the foot rail. I'd need a crane to get me up there, but whaddya know, no cranes in tonight. I'll have to grin and bear it until Jake gets here.

And when he does get here you'd better watch your behaviour, Inner Voice chips in – sounding infuriatingly perky and sober. *The first sign of monkey business and I'm out of here.*

'Oh, just . . . bog off,' I mouth grumpily. Do I really look like I'm in the mood for *monkey business*? And why does Inner Voice sound like my mother?

I do not sound like her. And I'm being serious, you know. My bags are packed and ready. I'll go and find someone who takes me seriously.

My Bloody Mary arrives in a slender glass complete with a sharpened stick of celery, which I remove before taking a sip – could have my eye out with that. I raise the drink to my lips and . . . *God*, fuck, *Jesus*, that *burns*. How much spicy rubbish did he put in it? The insides of my mouth are being eaten alive by Tabasco and my eyes are streaming – which means I'll have to check my mascara before Jake arrives.

But now that the drink is going down I can feel it doing something. It's *working*. I'm still in pain on a number of fronts, but I feel somehow better. Only one thing for it. I pinch my nose with one hand, pick up the drink with the other and down it in a single breathless gulp.

Aaaaaaaaaaggggggggggggghhhhhhhhhhhhhhhhhhhhhhh! . . . That feels . . . good. A magical tingle running through my body. Headache fading. I think I'll have another. I order and then remind myself of Lisa's final instructions re. Jake Bedford (handling of). Do not under any circumstances:

1 Let him know that my last boyfriend was . . . er . . . Jake Bedford.
2 Hint that my confidence was eroded, undermined, blown to smithereens or otherwise affected by his leaving me.
3 Go home with him.

She really banged on about number three. And she's absolutely right. However tempting, I mustn't end up back in bed with the bastard. Now that I've revived myself with a Bloody Mary I know I can do it. I'll have a will of iron. I'll be like Jesus on his stint in the wilderness . . . Though Satan only tempted him with a few silly loaves of bread. If he'd magicked up Jesus's idea of a dream date – J-Lo in a baggy cotton smock sort of thing – it might have been a different . . . No, stop it. *I can do this.*

My drink arrives and as I'm about to repeat my down-in-one trick my bag vibrates against my hip. It's my mobile. I fish it out and the barman looks on disapprovingly. *What?* My phone not cool enough for the Sanderson? It does have a pink cover with purple hearts all over it – a bit *Powerpuff Girls* I suppose. As I put it to my ear he says, 'You're supposed to switch them off in here, madam.' Too late because I can hear my mum going, 'Amy . . . Amy, are you there?' They may disapprove of mobiles, but they'll definitely frown on calls from Mum in a place as hip as this. 'Hi, Mum,' I whisper, as if that will somehow make the fact that I've got an illegal pink phone stuck to my ear less obvious.

'Amy, why haven't you called me back?'

'Sorry. I've been really busy. What's the matter?'

I pray that she doesn't want to discuss Dad. Knowing what I know, I don't think I could lie convincingly any more – *Well, Mum, Lisa and I have put a private detective on his tail, but don't worry, I'm sure it's nothing.*

'Actually, it's not you I really need to speak to,' she says awkwardly. 'It's Anthony . . .'

Ant? My God, the confession.

'. . . I've been trying to reach him. Do you know where he is?'

'He's back in New York.'

'Oh,' she says, sounding utterly deflated.

142

'Mum, what's going on? What have you told him?'

'Why? What's he told you?' she asks in a panic.

'He hasn't told me anything, but why are you pouring your heart out to him?'

'Anthony is a deeply spiritual young man,' she says defensively. 'He has a *calling* and his words brought me enormous comfort.'

Pur-lease! Ant? *Spiritual*? If Jesus appeared to him in a vision he'd ask him for his phone number and whether he's sub or dom.

'Mum, Ant is a . . . He's a . . .' What am I going to say here? '. . . He's a Roman Catholic.'

'Don't be such a bigot, Amy. Haven't I taught you tolerance? . . .'

I *so* cannot believe this. Mum? *Tolerant*? Next to her Ian Paisley comes across like a cuddly old liberal.

'. . . Besides, we can learn a lot from the Catholic faith. Their teaching on sex outside of marriage, for instance. Very sensible. I picked up some pamphlets from Saint Mary's . . .'

Mary! She's everywhere today – Saint, bloody, bloody agent . . .

'. . . and I'm thinking of . . . going over.'

'You're going to convert?' I splutter.

Picture all the ayatollahs in Iran suddenly becoming Jews. Imagine Bernard Matthews setting his turkeys free and embracing veganism. Both far more plausible than my mother turning her back on the Church of England. What the hell has Ant done to her?

'I'm only *thinking* about it, dear,' she says. 'No decisions. Anyway, Anthony. I'd really like to talk some things through with him. Does he have a number at the seminary?'

Well, yes, but if you call it you'll be hard pressed to hear him over the pumping techno soundtrack and the general hubbub of men in leather discussing anything but their relationships with God.

'Yeah, he's on the phone, Mum. I don't have his number on me. I'll ring you with it.' I don't add 'never'.

As I end the call and switch off my phone my head is spinning, and not entirely thanks to one and a half Bloody Marys. I think about four hundred grand and the other bloody Mary being convinced that I've got *at least* another three filthy books in me and how much harder it will be to tell my mother if she has embraced Rome and No Abortions and No Condoms and, actually, No Sex Under Any Circumstances Whatsoever.

Thanks a bloody million, An*th*ony.

I sink my head into my hands and I want to sob, but my make-up must look enough of a state already and Jake will be here any . . .

I jump as a hand touches my shoulder. As I land, my left shoe teeters . . . and collapses. A sharp pain shoots up my leg and I reach down and grasp my ankle, feeling another dozen stitches ping in the process.

'Are you OK?'

I look up from my crouch and see Jake viewing me with concern. I mean *real* concern – he's not even taking advantage of a gift-wrapped opportunity to peer down my cleavage.

'Yes, I think so,' I reply hauling myself upright. 'New shoes.'

'*Sexy* new shoes. And your dress . . . *Wow*. Is that what passes for workwear at *Working Girl*?'

Hardly. I got my first proper bollocking from Deedee this afternoon. Mostly because I was so late back from lunch, but in part because as far as she was concerned I'd taken the mag's title literally and dressed accordingly. As I stood in front of her desk receiving her wrath I could see Lewis

144

peering at me through the window in his office door. I had never seen his eyes more narrowed and it was scary.

But he's a *total* bastard and I *so* don't care.

I'm wincing at the pain. Jake places his hands on my waist and lifts me onto the bar stool. No mean feat – the dress may have forced me into the sylphlike form of a slinky model, but, believe me, I am so not sylphy and slinky. My first instinct is to slap him, but my relief at finally sitting down is so intense that I also want to kiss him. He reaches down and gently lifts up my leg. He runs his hand over my ankle . . . *Oooh*, that feels *nice* . . . and says, 'No sprain by the looks of it. Just a very attractive ankle. Shall we go and see if our table's ready?'

I slide off the stool and realise that the shoes make me almost as tall as him – his equal. Hang on, with a four hundred grand advance on offer *more* than his equal. As we set off for the restaurant I slip my arm through his.

Whoa there, shrieks Inner Voice.

But it needn't be alarmed. I can *soooooooooo* handle this.

'You've really changed, Amy,' Jake says as the coffees arrive.

You don't know the half of it, schmatey, I think drunkenly – God, even my thoughts are coming out slurred. Another Bloody Mary and half a bottle of wine have helped me to slip back into the role of Marsha Mellow, literary minx, and Jake has been feeling the benefit over the last three courses. I haven't actually told him that I'm Marsha Mellow, literary minx, but, well, another drink and I just might go the whole way.

'I don't mean how you look either,' he continues. 'It's . . . everything. You seem cooler. More confident. It makes you very attractive.'

145

His hand sets off on a snaky journey across the table. Through the empty glasses and round the salt and pepper until his fingertips touch mine. I don't pull away. In fact, my own hand creeps forward.

This is all starting to go hideously pear-shaped, moans Inner Voice.

But we're only holding hands for crying out loud. It isn't sex.

Yet.

Oh, shut up.

'Thanks, Jake,' I murmur. 'I have changed. A lot has happened in the last couple of years. You wouldn't believe it, actually.'

'Tell me about it.'

'I will . . . Later.'

Ooh, I've never done mysterious before – maybe it's the alcohol, but I think I could be pretty good at it.

Good at it? You're pissed, girl. You're a bloody disaster.

I ignore the voice, mostly because my shoes are giving me even more grief. I ease them off, stretch out my legs and wiggle my toes . . . What's that? *Ugh*! It's hairy. *Damn*. Jake's leg. My right foot has somehow gone up his left trouser leg and a big grin is spreading across his face.

That does it. I'm outta here, snaps Inner Voice. *Have a nice life.*

It was an *accident* . . .

No reply.

Oh well, I'm on my own now. Just have to busk it somehow. I keep my foot where it is, but only because it would look funny if I suddenly pulled it away. Anyway, it's only bloody flirting. It isn't sex.

And so what if it was? I'm not the only one who has changed. Jake is different too. He's light years from the bloke who shoved possibly illegal drugs up my nose while

146

I was handcuffed to his bed and who invited me to a swingers' party like it was a trip to McDonald's for a Happy Meal. He's been in therapy. He's been telling me all about it. He reckons he had a problem empathising (can't disagree with him there): 'That's why it didn't work out with us, Amy. It wasn't you. It was me. I was an island, completely oblivious to how anyone else might have felt.' See? Poor man. He was an *island* for God's sake. How much fun can that be? All to do with his mother apparently. She was too domineering. Or not domineering enough. Can't remember, but it made perfect sense at the time.

One thing hasn't changed about him, though. That grin he's giving me as my big toe strokes a fleshy bit of calf – he may be forty-something but he'd still be first pick in a boy band . . . Wonder if he can sing? Wonder who'd care?

'This is a fabulous hotel,' he says in a sexy hush that I have to lean in really close to catch, which I think is the general idea.

'It's lovely,' I murmur.

'Not just the bar and restaurant. The rooms are stunning. A genuine triumph of minimal postmodernism.'

'Really?'

'Uh-huh. Do you want to check one out?'

'What, now?'

'Yeah . . . They've got these really cool phones and the showers are –'

'OK, then.'

Look, Lisa's point number three said 'don't go home with him' and I am not going home with him.

All right?

'I can't tell you how much I've missed you, Jake. You were such a bastard two years ago, but that never stopped me fancying you like crazy.'

147

I don't say this, of course. I couldn't even if I dared because his mouth is clamped over mine. And if his tongue weren't lunging down my throat looking for the last of my dessert he might just be saying, 'God, yes, I was such an unforgivable bastard, but please give me a chance to make it up to you now.'

OK, probably not.

But I don't care because this is the best kiss I've had since the last time we did this, which was so long ago I've forgotten it so, actually, this is the best kiss *ever*. The lift door slides open and we fall out into the corridor – very nearly literally in my case – and head for our room. Once inside he grabs me round the waist, but I pull away – I've got to be a little bit hard to get. OK, nodding like a noddy dog when bloke makes first suggestion of heading upstairs to check out 'triumph of minimal postmodernism' scores an E-minus in the hard-to-getness exam, but I should put in a tiny bit of effort.

'Cool phone,' I say, looking at the silvery space age blob on the bedside table that could either be the telephone or something left by the previous occupant who has now headed back to Mars.

'Fuck the phone. Come here,' he commands.

I ignore him and walk to the window, where I pretend to be fascinated by the taxis coming and going four floors below. I can feel his eyes boring into my back – or more likely my bum.

'You've changed,' he says – admiringly I think.

He's right. Two years ago I never dared to pull away from him – not even when he was coming at me with the handcuffs.

'I'm not the girl I was,' I reply, almost adding 'I'm a *woman* now', but stopping myself in the nick of time – I may be drunk, but I'd have to be borderline paralytic to say something as corny as that. Instead I say, 'It takes a lot to faze me now . . . An awful lot.'

Shit, that sounded good. I really should try the mysterious thing more often – I'm quite the Kim Bassinger. I turn round and move towards him . . . And teasingly brush past him. I keep on going until I get to the bathroom. I shut the door behind me and collapse against it. I feel sick. For a brief moment out there I thought I was going to throw up on him. That would have killed the moment – you can usually forget moody and mysterious when your dinner is heading for your date.

Deep breaths . . . Iiiin . . . Ouuut . . . Iiiin . . . Ouuut . . . It's going away now. Thank God. Too much to drink and too much to eat. I can feel my waist wanting to explode out of its corset prison and I don't know how many more stitches can go ping on this dress before it's a total write-off. Never mind – it'll be coming off in a minute. Mind you, how the hell am I ever going to get it back on again? Worry about that later.

I head for the sink and fill a glass with water. I gulp it down and then have another. Definitely feel better now. The nausea is passing. I look in the mirror and, though it's gone eleven and I've had more to drink in a day than I usually manage in a month I look pretty damn good . . . Or maybe I only think so because of the amount I've had to drink. Can't figure it out. Whatever, Jake is virtually panting out there.

I reach into my bag and pull out my lipstick and mascara. This is something I've never done before – fix my make-up immediately *before* going to bed – but I want to keep Jake dangling for a minute or two. I can hear him moving about the room. Now I can hear him talking. I hope he's calling room service because I could do with a coffee. I could do with a pee as well, but that's a fifteen-minute operation in this bloody frock and I don't want to keep him waiting that long. I clamp my thighs together and go to work with the lipstick.

I pucker my lips, blow myself a kiss and say, 'You fucking gorgeous number-one bestselling author, you.'

Marsha Mellow is ready for her public.

Jake is on the bed and I head straight for him. I feel confident enough to put a bit of a catwalk wiggle into my hips, but I hear a couple more stitches go and knock that one on the head. I sit down beside him and slide off my shoes – Lisa told me they're the only shoes she leaves on for sex, but sorry, Jake, I'm not keeping them on for a second longer.

'Who were you calling? Room service?' I ask.

'Uh-huh.'

'Good.'

He leans over and kisses me and I let him this time. It's every bit as sexy as it was in the lift . . . But eventually we have to come up for air. While he moves back in and chews on my neck I say, 'You won't believe what I did, Jake.'

'Just now in the bathroom?'

'No, about two years ago.'

'When we . . . er . . . finished?'

'More or less.'

'Tell me.'

'It was amazing. I wrote a . . . *Oooh*, Jesus, Jake, that is *fantastic*.'

No, he hasn't found my G-spot. He found the zip on my dress and he has pulled it down. I can breathe again. *Wow*. Sweet bloody *relief*. If the sex is only half as good . . .

'Go on,' he says, peeling the bodice away from my breasts. 'You wrote a what?'

'Later,' I reply and push him back onto the bed. I yank the dress up my thighs and, finally able to move again, I climb on top of him.

'Fuck, I've missed you,' he says, pulling me down to his level and burying his face in my breasts – to whom the comment was probably addressed . . . But right now I couldn't care less.

There's a knock on the door. Room service. *Damn.* Whose stupid idea was coffee?

'Can't we ignore it?' I murmur.

He unclamps his mouth from a boob and says, 'I'd better get it.'

I roll off him and he stands up. I grab a corner of the bedspread and pull it over my chest as he opens the door. The slender brunette who steps into the room doesn't look like any room service waitress I've ever seen. She's wearing a tight sapphire dress that's even more revealing than the one I've still got half on. Her shoes are toweringly tall and she seems to be far more at home in them than I was in Lisa's. Impressive hotel, dressing their staff up like models . . . But, hang on, where's her tray?

'Amy, I'd like you to meet Kia.'

And why does Jake know her name?

Kia, who I'm beginning to suspect isn't on the payroll here, flashes me a white smile. 'Hi, baby. Jake vas right. You very beautiful,' she says in a heavy East European accent. She sounds like a Bond girl. She *looks* like a bloody Bond girl – if her cheekbones were any higher you'd need oxygen to reach them. What the hell is going on? Instinctively I pull up the bedspread until it's tucked beneath my chin.

Jake sits down on the bed, puts his arm round my shoulder and says, 'Kia has come to help us have the most amazing night of our lives.'

What? Does she sing? Tell jokes? Do magic?

Jake goes to work on my now tense body. While he tries to worm a hand beneath the bedspread and in the general direction of my bottom my eyes are on Kia. She

151

takes off her small jacket and lays it over a chair before turning and slipping the thin straps of her dress from her shoulders as she walks towards the bed.

Hang on just a bloody minute. I know this scene. *Rings on Her Fingers*. Chapter eighteen.

> Donna locked eyes with the hooker's as she peeled off her bra and climbed onto the spongy hotel bed. She moved up it on her hands and knees like a leggy cat until she reached her goal – Paul's cock, which Donna was cradling in her hand, presenting it to her like a . . .

Feeling hurt, angry and incredibly sober all of a sudden I push Jake away. He falls backwards and takes the bedspread with him exposing my tits. Kia – the *hooker* – gasps, 'Vow, Jake, you veren't jocking. She *big* girl.'

Now I am *really* furious. I glare at Jake who looks as if he's beginning to get the feeling that he might just have blown it.

'What the fuck do you think you're playing at?' I yell.

'But I thought . . . You said . . .'

'What? What the hell did I say to make you think this'd be OK?'

'I thought you'd changed. You told me . . . How did you put it? That I'd be amazed by what it takes to faze you.'

'This isn't what I bloody meant, Jake,' I splutter as I clamber off the bed and attempt to fit my boobs back into Lisa's dress. No easy feat when you're hopping mad, slightly blinded by impending tears and standing in front of a bemused audience. Kia is frozen in the middle of the room, unsure what to do with her own exposed breasts. I should think her English is good enough for her to have figured that half of her clientele isn't deliriously happy about her arrival.

152

Jake shuffles across the bed towards me. 'I'm sorry, Amy. I got it all wrong. I'm truly sorry,' he says. 'I'll ask Kia to go and we can start afresh.'

'I thought this whole evening was about starting afresh. All we've done is pick up exactly where we left off a couple of years ago.'

'I'm sorry. Please forg—'

'Oh . . . Piss off, Jake.'

These should be my parting words. I should go now. Walk out of Jake Bedford's life for ever. Slight problem there. However hard I pull I can't get the lower half of my dress below my bum and the top half is covering my boobs only because my hand is holding it in place. Since he unzipped me my stomach has gratefully expanded to its natural state and it's not about to be forced back into its prison.

But I can't stay in this room for another second. I grab my bag and jacket, and spin on my heel. I throw open the door and flounce into the corridor. I reach the lift, finally managing to ease the dress over my bum with one hand while the other clasps my jacket to my bare chest. As I wait for the lift I feel angry and sick . . . something else, too. I feel soft carpet beneath my bare feet . . . *Shit*, Lisa's bloody shoes. I can't go back for them now. But what was it she said? 'One scuff on those and I'll kill you. They're irreplaceable.'

God, she made them sound like a pair of ancient Ming vases.

I can't leave without them.

I turn round and head back to the room. I knock on the door. Hard. Don't want the bastard to think I'm feeling sheepish. After a moment it's opened by Kia, who is fully dressed and jacketed again – not staying as Jake's consolation prize, then. He is sitting on the edge of the bed and he looks up at me, surprised. 'Amy –'

'I want my shoes,' I state flatly.

I push past Kia and walk into the room. Without looking Jake in the eye I bend down and grab the shoes. At the same time I hear a terrifying sound. Not a wailing siren warning of impending nuclear attack. Not the screech of a werewolf leaping from the closet. Something much worse: the sound of an extended rip as Lisa's dress finally gives up the ghost.

I'm on the street trying to hail a taxi. I think it's the sort of hotel where the doorman does that for you, but I can't approach him with my bottom hanging out of my ripped dress. One hand is holding the front of my jacket while the other, the one clutching Lisa's shoes, is behind my back attempting to grip two skimpy flaps of fabric. No wonder I'm crying. At least I didn't follow Lisa's advice and put on a G-string – a *proper* pair of knickers is covering most of my bum. I watch forlornly as to my right the doorman scurries out of the hotel and clicks his fingers to a passing cab. It squeaks to a halt and he opens the door. I'm tempted to dive for it, but before I can pluck up the nerve a vision in sapphire clicks confidently towards it on skyscraper heels.

Kia.

Bitch.

As she climbs in she spots me . . . And gives me a little wave.

Bitch, man.

'Where you live?' she shouts from the open door.

'Er . . . Crouch End. North London.'

'Me also! Archway. We share taxi. Jake pay,' she says, waving a wad of twenties.

Chapter 13

'Lisa,' I say tentatively. 'Would you ever . . . You know . . . Have a threesome?'

'A what?'

Like she doesn't know what I'm talking about.

'You know . . . Sex . . . With a bloke and another woman?'

'Oh, I've done that,' she replies breezily, not seeming to care that we're in a bar packed with post-work drinkers.

'You haven't! When? How? Who with?' I splutter.

'Remember when I went to Corfu with Devon?'

'Which one was he?'

'Looked like Wesley Snipes. Drove a forklift.'

'Oh, I liked him. What's he doing now?'

'Three years, I think. Handling stolen goods. Anyway, we met this German girl in a club. We did it with her.'

'Oh, right, *her*,' I say. 'Who? Tell me about it. *Immediately*!"

She puts her glass down, smiles and leans in closer. 'She was nice, fairly sexy – for a German. We were all off our faces and ended up back at her apartment. We were knocking back her duty frees for a bit. Then we realised Dev had disappeared. Next thing we hear this Barry White voice coming from the bedroom.' She attempts deep and gravely. '"Come on, ladies, let's do it – the three of us." So, me and Geisla – that was her name, I think – we looked at each other and kind of said OK. And that's how it happened.'

'You kind of said *OK*? Simple as that?'

'Pretty much. The funniest thing was that watching two girls was obviously Dev's dream scenario, but he was so pissed he passed out and missed it. Poor lad – he'd probably been preparing for the moment since his first stiffy. Anyway, I didn't like it that much – wasn't for me.'

She stops and has a sip of wine. Story over. She's *rubbish* at including proper details. I always have to wring them out of her.

'You can't stop there, Lisa. What about the sex? Why is it not you?'

'I don't know about you, but the thing I like about sex is the actual *sex* bit . . . You know, the fucking. That's the thing a girl can't do.'

'Let me get this straight. You're saying that in principle it's not that you don't like the idea of sex with a woman. A woman can turn you on—'

'Sure. Haven't you ever been turned on by another girl?'

'Not recently, no.' (My best attempt at casual-hip.) 'But as I was saying, a woman *can* turn you on. So if, for example, a girl had one of those false whatsits –'

'A strap-on?'

'One of those – you'd be up for it?'

'I suppose so. I've never thought of it like that. Anyway, why the sudden interest in threesomes? Research for the next book?'

'No,' I say a little too hurriedly.

'What then? . . . *Shit* . . . Last night. What the hell happened?'

'Nothing.'

'Liar. Tell me.'

'Absolutely nothing happened. I swear.'

'You went home with him, didn't you?'

'I did not,' I reply truthfully.

But she isn't buying it. She raises an eyebrow and I

can't resist her – the police could easily do away with beating confessions out of suspects; all they need do is wheel in Lisa and her eyebrow.

I crack. 'OK, OK. He tried to get me to do it with another girl.'

'You said you didn't go home with him.'

'At the Sanderson.'

'What? In the lobby?'

'We were kind of . . . You know . . . In a room.'

'You went upstairs with him . . . Amy, you *idiot*. What did I tell you?'

'I only went to see the design. He said it was a triumph of modern post-something or other.'

The eyebrow ratchets up another inch.

'All right. I was going to do it with him. But then *she* showed up.'

'Who? His girlfriend?'

'No . . . A call girl.'

'*Jesus.*'

'She was really nice, actually. Polish. She's only been here a few months but her English is excellent.'

'*Fuck* . . . You actually *did* it with her?'

She's white with shock. What's OK for her is clearly way too outrageous for her boring big sister – the one, incidentally, who has written an explicitly porny novel.

'No I did not,' I explain. 'We shared a cab home.'

'*Un*-fucking-believable, girl,' she says. 'You nearly did a stupid thing, but you got out of it. A lucky escape. Put it down to experience. Anyway, sod Jake. What about Jacobson?'

I tell her about the offer.

'Four hundred and twenty-five grand?' she squeals.

'Four ninety. Mary called this afternoon. It went up.'

'That is stunning. Outrageous. You have *got* to say yes.'

'I already said no.'

'Are you mad?'

'Mary's advice. She reckons she can squeeze him for more.'

'*Wow*! You're gonna be rich, girl.'

'I'm not sure, Lisa. I'm not really a writer.'

'Of course you bloody are. You'll say yes,' she says confidently.

And, as it happens, I think I will.

Last night in the cab. Kia. She's a lovely girl. And her English is surprisingly good. I think she wanted the conversation practice because I couldn't shut her up. Between the West End and Archway she gave me the first three chapters of the next Marsha Mellow.

I felt so inspired that this morning I defied my hangover, took my life in my hands and actually started to write it at work. My fingers flew across the keyboard like I was retaking my typing exam. I have never looked so busy. At one point Julie told me to stop before I got the rest of them sacked.

'So my dress worked a treat yesterday,' Lisa says. 'It had Jake gagging and Jacobson bunging you zillions.'

Damn, I was hoping she wouldn't mention the dress. The only reason we've met up tonight was so that I could return it – she needs it for a party at the weekend. I can't bring myself to tell her that I dropped it off at the dry cleaners this morning. I'm hoping their invisible mending has improved since the last time I used them – the wobbly row of stitches on the rip in my favourite trousers was visible from across Crouch End Broadway.

'Where is it?' she asks.

'My God, I forgot it,' I squeal with all the drama I can muster.

'Amy!'

'Sorry.'

'Actually, you've probably done me a favour. Dan really didn't want me to wear it to the party. In fact, we had a bit of a row about it.'

'What, he tells you what you can and can't wear?' I exclaim.

'No, never, but –'

'Please tell me he isn't one of those really possessive blokes who hits the roof when other men look at you,' I gabble, my imagination reaching turbo boost. I'm no longer seeing Dan the Triad – I'm picturing Dan the psycho Yardie. He's holding a gun. And a machete. And he's standing over my terrified sister, about to dismember her for looking vaguely in the general direction of a man that wasn't him. Sounds hysterical, but I've *seen* the guys my sister goes out with. 'Lisa,' I say slowly, 'does he . . . You know . . . Ever . . . *Hit* you?'

'Don't be ridiculous,' she snorts, but she's rubbing her arm through a sleeve. I bet there's a painful bruise under there.

'You should talk about it, you know. Denying abuse is the worst thing you can do. I saw it on *Trisha*.'

'*Amy*, shut up, will you? Dan does *not* hit me. We rowed about the dress because it's a posh party and he didn't think it was suitable . . . OK?'

I'm far from convinced and it shows.

'Oh, believe what you bloody well like,' she says wearily. 'Let's change the subject, shall we? How are you going to hide four ninety grand from Mum? She might start to suspect something when you turn up for Sunday lunch in a Ferrari.'

Hmm . . . Mum. Don't want to think about that one right now.

'She's acting weird at the moment,' I say.

I tell Lisa about the bizarre call I had from her last night.

159

'Mum turning Catholic?' Lisa says. 'That's almost as ridiculous as Dad and Miss Strappy Heels. Talking of which, I had a call from our private dick today . . . No, he hasn't got anything yet. It was just an excuse for the sleazeball to ask me out for a drink. He did give me an interim report, though.'

'Miss Strappy Heels?'

'No sightings. But Dad was tailed to a sandwich bar. He bought a cheese and pickle bap.'

'*OhmyGod*! Not cheese and pickle?'

'Hold on, that's not all.'

'What? You mean he got a Diet Coke too?'

'Piss off, Amy. He had a copy of the *Guardian* under his arm. Unbelievable, huh?'

Lisa sips her wine as the implication sinks in. As far as Mum is concerned our father could commit only one sin worse than sleeping with another woman: voting Labour. Of course, being caught with the *Guardian* wouldn't win a conviction in court for rabid socialism, but it's more than enough evidence for our mum. '*But, darling, it was just the once. I bought it for the cricket report. I swear I didn't look at the political columns. It means nothing to me. You know I could only ever love the* Mail.' The poor bloke could protest his innocence till he's (Tory) blue in the face, but Mum would still have his clothes out of the wardrobe and spread across the front lawn in sixty seconds flat.

I shake my head. Dad is skating on extremely thin ice. But then, which of us isn't? I can't get my mind off Lisa and the Triad-Yardie-woman beater. And she's thinking of disappearing halfway round the world with him so he can sell her into slavery?

'Have you decided what to do about Hong Kong?' I ask nervously.

'Nightmare. He's really putting the pressure on me to make my mind up.'

'I *knew* it. He *is* hitting you.'

'Not that kind of pressure. He just needs a decision and . . .'

She trails off as I'm distracted by a face in the street. I stare over her shoulder towards the plate-glass window at the front of the bar.

'What is it, Amy?'

'Don't look now, but a bloke has got his face pressed up to the window and he's looking this way.'

'What's he like?'

'Thirties. Suit and tie. Specs. Curly hair. A bit tubby. A bit nerdy too . . . God, he's really giving me the stare.'

'Is he on his own?'

'Looks like it . . . And, *shit*, he's coming in . . . He's looking at us . . . He's walking over.'

I watch him bear down on me as if he knows exactly who I am.

'*Fuck*, I bet he's a reporter. What am I going to do?'

She doesn't get a chance to answer, because he has reached our table and he's standing over us. I look up at him as he leans over and . . .

Gives Lisa a kiss – a sloppy, slightly open-mouthed one that isn't really appropriate for someone you've only just clapped eyes on. Outraged, I jump in on her behalf. 'Hey, what the hell . . .'

Lisa puts her hand up and stops me. 'Amy, this is Dan.'

'I could kill you, Lisa,' I spit when he's gone to the bar.

'How did I know it was him? You told me not to turn round. Anyway, I should be mad at you. First you accuse him of beating me and then you call him nerdy.'

'Why didn't you tell me he was coming?' I say, ignoring her entirely reasonable point, which goes to the heart of my embarrassment.

'I thought I'd surprise you. Anyway, he can't stay long

– he's flying off to Chicago in the morning. So, what do you think? Apart from *nerdy*.'

I look at Dan, who is waving a twenty in the fond hope of being served. He seems to be the kind of bloke who turns invisible the moment he tries to buy a drink. I guess that being five foot six can't help.

'He's not exactly what I expected,' I say hesitantly.

Well, he's white for a start and, though my knowledge of criminal gang culture is strictly limited, I'm pretty certain that would disqualify him from both the Triads and the Yardies. Another thing: Lisa has always gone for looks and Dan . . . What can I say? . . . Well, he must have plenty of *inner* beauty. And where are the track marks on his forearms? The inverted crucifix and/or vial of blood around his neck? The Charlie Manson swastika tattoo on his forehead? He doesn't have a single one of the standard Lisa's Bloke trademarks . . . Unless he's *pierced* . . . You know . . . *Down there*. No, he's not the type, not in that suit. He looks too . . . damn . . . *respectable*.

There must be a catch.

'He seems lovely,' I continue, using an adjective I would never have applied to any of her exes. 'And, honestly, he's not nerdy . . . That was just because I couldn't see him properly . . . You know . . . Through the window.'

Dan has finally got a barman's attention – which could have something to do with the fact that he's now the only one at the bar – and he turns to flash us a triumphant and wonky grin . . . And (please, God, forgive me) he looks like such a nerd.

Dan has spent the last half-hour trying to explain how he earns his living. He owns Rushe Forward Investments and they make . . . erm . . . forward investments. You know, *investments* that go *forwards* as opposed to backwards, sideways or diagonally . . . No, I haven't a bloody clue what they are. I feel dumb, but I am slightly consoled when Lisa – who has been going out with him for *two* years – makes a breakthrough and blurts out, 'I get it now . . . So it *doesn't* involve actual *rushing* forward in some way.'

Time to change the subject.

'So, Hong Kong? That's a big move,' I say.

'Six thousand three hundred and seventy-seven nautical miles to be exact,' says Dan, giving me the impression that being '*exact*' is something he's big on. 'I've got something of . . . um . . . a track record in the Asian markets,' he continues, taking off his glasses and fiddling with them. 'They want me over there and, well, they had to buy the company to get me. I just hope I can persuade Lisa to join me.'

'It's a huge step,' I say on my sister's behalf, 'and I'm not sure how she feels about the jellyfish.'

Dan looks puzzled.

'I told you,' says Lisa. 'They eat them over there.'

'They have other things too,' he says. 'Chicken, beef, baby deer, grouper fish, fox, snake, sea slug . . .'

Lisa is turning green. He should have stopped at beef.

'Well, it's a big, big decision for Lisa,' I say.

'I know what she's going through,' Dan replies, putting his hand comfortingly on hers. 'You watched me go through a bit of turmoil, didn't you, sweetheart?'

She shoots him a look through narrowed eyes.

'You know,' he goes on, 'when I had to bite the bullet and resign my – *Ouch!*'

Either he's been stung by a wasp – a big one because he's clutching his shin and there are tears in his eyes – or Lisa has kicked him.

'Don't you have to go home and pack for your flight?' she asks, but it isn't a question – it's an order.

*

163

'What was all that about?' I ask after I've watched the mushy goodbyes.

'All what?'

'You know, the flying drop kick under the table. What did he have to resign?'

'Nothing. Some boring seat on a City committee.'

'Come on, this is *me*. I know you better than anyone. What was it?'

'*Nothing*. I just wanted him to get home – he has to be up at the crack of dawn. Anyway, you don't know me at all. You expected me to be going out with an abusive gangsta.'

She slips into a sullen silence.

I need to get to the bottom of this, because she's hiding something. I'm starting to think that Dan might just be her worst one yet – worse than the crack dealer with two wives, the alcoholic car thief *and* the schizophrenic bookie. Maybe his nerdy exterior is a cover for something dark and truly dangerous.

'What is it with you two? Why the secrecy? He seems like a lovely bloke,' I prod, hoping to lull her into a confession. 'He seems kind, clever, dependable . . . I admit, he's not what I imagined to be your type but –'

'Exactly, Amy,' she exclaims. 'Not my type.'

'I was going to say that's a *good* thing. Anyway, you love him. What else matters?'

'OK, remember that thing I once did in my diary? *My Perfect Fella*.'

I nod. I recall it vividly. A drawing of a man who looked like Tim Roth after a crash course of steroids and a visit to the wall-to-wall tattoo parlour. It was accompanied by a list of professional qualifications. He had to be able to play thrash metal bass, understand the mechanics of Semtex letter bombs (for posting to animal vivisectionists) and have a workable plan for smashing global capitalism.

'Dan doesn't exactly fit the picture, does he?' Lisa says.

'You were fourteen then. You've grown up. Look, you're obviously nuts about him. I shouldn't be saying this because I'll miss you like mad, but you should stop being so pathetic and go to Hong Kong.' I don't mean this at all, but I need to flush the truth out of her. 'You can always come back if you hate it. And take him home to meet Mum. Get it over with. I don't know what you're worried about. She'll love him.'

'That's the trouble,' she mumbles.

'Excuse me?' I exclaim in disbelief. 'Is that your problem? That you've finally fallen for a bloke that Mum will actually like?'

Lisa shrugs, embarrassed. We are talking about the most un-embarrassable person I know. I've never seen her like this. Then she pulls herself together and snaps, 'OK, Amy, I'll tell you, and then I don't want to discuss it any more.'

Shit, here we go. Finally the ugly, black truth. I brace myself.

'*Yes*, Dan is wonderful,' she continues. 'And, *yes*, Mum would love him. Not just because he's so bloody respectable. She'd be all over him because . . .' She trails off.

'Because?'

'The thing he had to resign.'

'What was it. Chairmanship of the Ku Klux Klan?'

'You're not that far off the bloody mark as it happens. He was due to stand for Parliament at the next election. He'd been selected as a candidate for Chingford . . .'

'He's into politics? OK, so it's not exactly rock 'n' roll, but it's not the end of the world.'

'. . . For the fucking Conservative Party.'

Lisa needn't worry because I couldn't discuss it even if I wanted to – I'm laughing too hard.

Chapter 14

Oh, how things can change in a couple of weeks.

A fortnight ago – once I'd got over my hysterics at Lisa's revelation – reality came crashing back with a vengeance. The blast of inspiration I'd felt on meeting Kia and starting a new book had carried me through the day. But it couldn't last and by the time I left the bar I was going out of my mind with worry again. You know, stuff like how to break the news of my secret sordid career to Mum, what to do about Dad's steamy affair, how to get over the fact that both Jake and Lewis belong to the Liars, Bastards and Perverts Club, and how the hell to advise my sister on emigrating halfway round the world with a monster raving Tory.

How trivial it all seems now.

Mary was right. Nothing is ever as bad as you imagine. From the top:

Mum was thrilled about Marsha Mellow. Yes, I told her. Straight. Just like that.

'Mum,' I announced, 'I write hardcore pornographic fiction. How does that make you feel?'

'No golden showers or animals I hope?' she asked nervously.

'No *way*. That's disgusting.'

'Good,' she sighed. 'You have to draw a line. And does it pay?'

'A bloody fortune.'

'Thank heaven for that. I've been worried about you being stuck in that dead-end job of yours. I'm so glad you've found a career that combines financial security with intellectual stimulation,' she said as she ran a Cif wipe over her kitchen worktop.

As for Dad, talk about getting the wrong end of the stick. Miss Strappy Heels turned out to be the older sister I never knew I had. Mum and Dad thought they'd lost her for ever in a tragic hospital blunder – apparently she disappeared from the maternity ward after she was bundled into a laundry basket of cot sheets. They had never been able to bring themselves to mention her to Lisa and me. Then one day Dad met her at an international coat hanger conference at Wembley and, well, he just *knew* instantly who she was. Not only did she have the Bickerstaff boobs, but she was also in the same business as him – as a young girl she'd been irresistibly drawn to wire coat hangers as if they were in her genes – which I suppose they were. Anyway, he finally brought her home to be reunited with her real family and . . . *God* . . . It was *so* emotional. Exactly like something off Cilla's *Surprise, Surprise*, except without the telly cameras. You really had to be there.

Mildred – that's her name, I'm afraid, but she's so totally adorable that it doesn't matter – is one of us now. Tomorrow we're all going on our first family holiday in ages – our first one ever as a complete family, now we've got our Mildred with us. We're off on a Caribbean cruise. Paid for by Jacobson's whopping advance, which has grown to seven hundred grand.

In fact, I worked out that I have enough in the bank to ask the captain to make a slight detour and drop Lisa and Dan off in Hong Kong to start their new life as Mr and Mrs Rushe. It finally hit her how silly she'd been, as I knew it would. She realised that when you truly love someone it simply doesn't matter if he believes in bringing back the birch, keeping Britain out of Europe for ever and ever until the end of time and putting asylum seekers to work in labour camps alongside gays, drug addicts and single mums.

Oh, and guess who else is coming on the cruise with us.

Jason!

That's right. Jason Donovan.

We bumped into each other – literally – on the street in Soho and it was total love at first sight. For *him*, anyway – he'd never clapped eyes on me before (except for that evening in the Groucho when he wasn't really looking properly), whereas I'd been in love with him since 'Too Many Broken Hearts'.

He's been brilliant for me. He's sweet, tender and considerate, and he doesn't endlessly go on and on and on about his pop star past – except for when I ask him to relive those crazy days lip-syncing in shopping arcades. And best of all he's made me completely forget those other two blokes . . . What were their names again? Jack and Louis? Jim and Leroy? Whatever. *Losers*.

Jason does absolutely everything for me. He's just put the dinner on (something incredible with duck and paprika that would make Nigella keel over with jealousy) and while it simmers away he's packing my case for the cruise.

'Jason,' I call out, 'remember to pack my bikini tops. I may write torrid, no-holds-barred porny books, but I don't think I'm ready to go topless in front of my mum.'

As I listen to his laughter ring out from the bedroom (he finds me so funny) I think what a totally brilliant and amazing note to finish a story on.

Because that's it.

The end.

Happily ever after and all that.

Chapter 15

No, really.
    That's it.
    The end.
    Over.
    Amy Bickerstaff has left the building.

Chapter 16

I bloody wish.

All of the foregoing was lies. Wishful thinking. Also known as bollocks. I made it all up. Except for the bit about Jacobson's offer. That stands at seven hundred and three thousand. (Why the three? Like that's really going to swing it his way.) For the past few days he's been phoning Mary with a little bit more. Quite a lot more, actually. And I know I should be thrilled, but it's just another part of the nightmare. Every pound that it ratchets up increases my blood pressure a notch.

Because I cannot tell my mum about it and if I can't do that then my only option will be to skip the country and send her a postcard from tax exile in Monaco and, actually, that's not an option at all because I don't want to live in a place where everyone except for Princess Caroline is over sixty and the poodles drive around in their own Porsches. Call me boring, but I like it in Crouch End.

I can't tell my mum for all the old reasons plus one brand-new one: I think she's going bonkers. She's dumped the freaky Edwina Currie look and gone for even freakier black. I don't mean seductive-little-black-cocktail-dress black or vampy-Gothic black, but the kind of black you see in Mediterranean countries. The black-headscarf-to-black-shoes black worn by old ladies. Whose husbands are dead. Now, I know Dad is a bit on the quiet side for much of the time, but I'm pretty sure he isn't dead yet. And it isn't just the black. There's the constant rattle as she fiddles with the string of wooden rosary beads. And the fat crucifix round her neck. Big? If she swung it around a few times she could take out Arnold Schwarzenegger with it. And if that isn't enough, she rang me up a couple of nights ago:

'Amy, I've just seen the most astonishing thing.'

'What's that?'

'Madonna.'

In boring old Finchley? I thought. Isn't that pushing her supposed love of all things London too far?

'Where?' I asked.

'In a potato . . .'

Blimey. I know she's worn some bizarre things in her time, but a root vegetable?

'. . . I'm holding it now. I was slicing up some spuds to go with the chicken and there she was. The Virgin Mary . . .'

Oh, *that* Madonna.

'. . . Her face was staring out at me from a King Edward. I've wrapped her in clingfilm and popped her in the fridge, but I'm worried about her shrivelling. I'm going to take a few snaps of her, rattle off a quick note and post them to the Vatican. And you must give me An*th*ony's number. He'll be thrilled to hear about this. Fancy that, eh? Our Lady, the *Mother* of Jesus, in a Budgen's potato.'

I rest my case.

And I blame Ant.

Except I can't have a go at him, because it was me that kicked off the whole Father An*th*ony thing.

I'd really like to talk to my dad about her, but he's busy . . .

With Miss Strappy Heels.

And while his behaviour disgusts me I can't say I blame

him. I mean, look what the poor bugger married; a woman who dresses as if he's already dead and buried, and who sees holy visions in root crops. It would have me seeking refuge in the arms of a bottle blonde with cerise toenails.

My dad's behaviour.

That's what I'm about to get the gory details on. Lisa and I are climbing the grubby staircase to the office of Colin Mount, international private investigator. Yesterday he called Lisa to tell her he has a written report and . . . *photographs*.

'You know, I really think we should take Ant's advice,' I say as I lag behind my sister.

'What, walk away now? We might as well see what he's got. We'll have to pay him whether we meet him or not.'

'*I'll* have to pay him. Anyway, what are we going to do with the information? Shouldn't Dad be allowed to screw up his life if he wants to? Like Ant said, he's a grown-up.'

'Typical bloody Amy. You're burying your head in the sand again. You're doing what you've done with the whole Marsha Mellow thing and –'

'Marsha Mellow,' rasps a lecherous voice from behind us. 'Now there's a minx whose number I wouldn't mind having in me Filofax.'

Colin Mount is wheezing his way up the staircase, crimson-faced and topped up with a liquid lunch.

We're trapped.

'You dolls must be feeling devastated. Believe me, I know how difficult this is,' says Colin Mount, doing his best to sound like a bereavement counsellor. 'I mean, what you're looking at is pretty bloody shocking, if you'll pardon le frog.'

What we're looking at is pretty bloody nothingy, actually. Spread before us on the desk is a selection of blurred and grainy black-and-white prints. They were taken at night and they show the back of our dad's little factory in Edmonton. A man that looks sort of like Dad is standing in the tiny car park next to a white van. He's with a woman.

'Is it her?' Lisa asks me.

Well, she's blonde, but it's hard to tell. The pictures were obviously taken from way off and the mesh of a wire fence in the foreground breaks up the view of Dad and the woman. It's like studying those crap photos of UFOs that don't look anything like spaceships and were probably cobbled together in someone's back garden using a bit of string, a Tupperware plate and some sticky-backed plastic.

'I think so,' I reply. It would help if the photos were colour, then perhaps the cerise toenails would shine out and give her away. 'But even if it is her, this doesn't actually prove anything. It just shows that Dad had a chat with a woman in a car park.'

'The same woman he was *drinking* with in Soho,' adds Lisa, like she's Helen Mirren in *Prime Suspect* and she has just spotted the vital piece of evidence that cracks the case.

'She could be anyone, Lisa. She's probably a client. The head of wire hanger purchasing at Sketchley or something.'

'Not unless she's moonlighting, she ain't,' Colin Mount interrupts. 'Her name's Sandra Phillips. Sand to her mates. She's twenty-nine and she works for Premier Catering in Soho.'

'See? Nothing to do with coat hangers,' exclaims DI Tennyson . . . I mean Lisa.

'She lives in Wood Green and goes dancing at the Lite

173

Fandango on the high road,' Colin Mount continues. 'She likes a Southern Comfort and lemonade, and gets her roots done at Kurlz 'n' Tintz. And she's a thirty-four B . . . Though you probably didn't need to know that.'

Lisa sits back and folds her arms – case closed.

'Look,' I argue, 'just because Dad knows a catering professional –'

'A blonde, *tarty* catering professional,' Lisa adds, sounding worryingly like our mother.

'Whatever. Just because he knows her doesn't prove he's sleeping with her. He could be planning some big coat hanger trade fair sort of thing and she's doing the sausage rolls. We shouldn't jump to conclusions.'

'You're doing it again, Amy. Get your head out of the sand and smell the cheap perfume. Face facts. Dad has never planned an event in his life – he's a social disaster. What's he doing with her if he isn't screwing her?'

'I'm afraid your sister's bang on the money,' says Colin Mount. 'You're refined young ladies and I didn't want to have to show you this.'

He reaches into a drawer, pulls out another print and puts it on the desk in front of us. It shows the man who sort of looks like Dad sitting on the back of the open white van, his legs dangling over the edge . . . And it shows the blonde crouching down in front of him. I look at Lisa, who has turned as white as I feel.

'She could be bending down to fasten the buckle on her strappy sandals,' I say very tentatively . . . Though I know damn well that she isn't.

I feel sick as I climb on the tube train that will take me back to work. I feel as if I should be able to cope with this. I'm Marsha Mellow. According to the *Sun* I've written the book with the highest 'bonk count' in the English language (and they showed their exhaustive 'bonkometer' results to prove it), but I can't get my head around seeing a picture of my dad going at it. But who could? I mean *parents* and *sex* . . . It's just . . . too . . . revolting. And upsetting. I *hate* my dad.

I fish a paperback out of my bag and try to forget about him. The book is a porn-free Patricia Cornwell where the only naked bodies are lying on slabs with tags tied to their big toes. But I can't concentrate. I *really* hate my dad . . . And I realise that it's the first time I've ever had a strong feeling about him. I've hated my mum plenty of times – well, she asks for it. But Dad? He's always just been . . . kind of . . . *there*. But now I realise that if I detest him this much I must have really loved him before.

And that doesn't help at all.

It just makes me want to cry.

The train stops at Holborn. Two girls jump on and throw themselves into the seats opposite mine. I look at them briefly before burying my nose in my book, but my eyes won't focus on the words.

'Fucking hell,' screeches one the girls, 'have you read this?'

That gets my attention and I look up. They're reading the *Mail*. The front page headline screams PRICE OF PORN: £1M above the silhouette of the girl with my hairdo – still (thank God) the closest thing they've got to a picture of Marsha Mellow. Where did they get a million from? It's seven hundred grand, actually, not counting the odd three.

'I'd stick my sex life down on paper if I thought someone would pay a million for it,' the girl goes on in a voice so loud it's as if she's taken a loud hailer from her bag. The whole carriage can hear and ears prick up. She carries on, oblivious to the audience. 'Anyway, listen to this. "The advance being offered for Mellow's next three novels is surprising given that many critics have dismissed the secretive author as a sleazy sensation seeker."'

'That's bollocks,' yells her friend, taking a megaphone from her own bag – well, there are people in the next carriage who must be straining to hear. 'Have you read *Rings on Her Whatsit?*'

'Yeah. It's brilliant,' bellows the first girl.

'Fucking filthy more like,' shouts her friend. 'Mind you, I feel sorry for the poor cow. They're making her out as a right criminal. No wonder she wants to stay anonymous. I'd love to know who she is, though.'

'Me too. Here, it's not you, is it?'

I watch them dissolve into noisy giggles as the train pulls into Tottenham Court Road. As the doors slide open I'm through them and galloping up the escalator like a rat up a drainpipe.

I'm walking along Oxford Street on wobbly legs. My jaw is juddering and tears streak my cheeks. No one is coming within ten feet of me and I'm getting strange looks – a mix of fear and good old British embarrassment: *'Ooh-er – she's either one of those care in the community loonies who's forgotten her medication or she's had a row with her boyfriend.'*

Why am I so rubbish at coping? Lisa's right. The first sign of a crisis and I'm haring off in search of the nearest sandpit. *Get out of the bloody way, ostriches, Amy's coming*! But you can't avoid anything for ever, can you? And today it's all going off at once. I've got one parent who's turning into Mother Teresa of Finchley, another who thinks he's Robbie-shagging-Williams and a national newspaper that wants to bring back public flogging, hanging and burning at the stake just for little old me.

I can't go into the office feeling like this . . . Or *looking* like this – I've just caught sight of my reflection in a shop window. My face is blotchy red, my nose is streaming snot and I resemble one of those toddlers you see having screaming fits in supermarket aisles. People are crossing the road to avoid me – risking death beneath the wheels of a double decker rather than a brush with me. I have a flashback to the gorgeous, Christy Turlingtonish Ros in Lewis's photo frame. No *way* can I go back to work. I'm at the top of Dean Street. I wonder if Mary's in. She always has tissues.

'You took an enormous risk coming here,' she says. 'What if that *Mail* hack had been outside? You're lucky to have caught her on her first toilet break in weeks – she must have a bladder like a beach ball.'

She's right. I shouldn't have come. But now I'm inside I feel safe. I've always liked her office. I don't know why because it stinks of pizza from the restaurant below – I think she has the smell piped in. It's also tiny. There's barely enough room for Mary in here, let alone all the rubbish she has accumulated. Pizza boxes mostly. And tons of books. You'd expect those with a literary agent, except that ninety per cent of Mary's are about slimming. I'm sitting on one. Jamie Oliver's *The Pukka Diet* covers a gaping rip in my chair.

We've been talking for an hour. In between blubs I've managed to tell her about my crises and I feel marginally better – at least I think I could step outside again without sending everyone diving for cover.

'Secrets, eh?' she says now. 'Never a good idea. There's you with yours and now your father's sneaking around like a schoolboy behind the bike sheds. And your mother's making secret confessions to your best friend who she thinks is a priest because you're too scared to tell her he's gay. Then there's your dear sister hiding her boyfriend because what? He's wealthy, successful and highly respectable? What is it with you Bickerstaffs? If I was a researcher for Jerry Springer I'd be calling him now to say I had an entire series of material for him.'

I raise a weak smile. If we seem ridiculous it's only because we are.

'Mind you, with your father rediscovering that his willy isn't just for widdling and your mother going doolally, it could be the ideal time to slip your own little missile under the radar. It might just get lost amidst the familial chaos.'

Nice thought . . . But I doubt it.

'Now, I'm glad you've stopped crying,' she continues, 'because we can talk business for a moment. Jacobson phoned not long before you breezed in. Seven hundred and forty thousand.'

'*My God.*'

'Told me he has remortgaged both his house in Blackheath and his *gîte* in the Dordogne to raise the necessary. It wouldn't surprise me if he'd also sold his Filipino wife back to the catalogue from which he bought her. He claims it's his final, *final* offer and I'm inclined to believe him. So I think we should let him sweat for a day or two and then you should acc—'

'Mary,' I interrupt, suddenly feeling tense again, 'where the hell did the *Mail* get that figure of a million?'

'They could just be making it up, sweetie – you authors have nothing on journalists when it comes to feats of fictive imagination. However, I rather suspect that Jacobson leaked it having first inflated it a tad – round numbers make neater headlines. And actually, now I think about it, he's probably the source that put the bloody hack onto me in the first place.'

'The bastard.'

'Much as it pains me to defend him, I have to say he's only doing his job. *Rings* is still at number one and he simply wants to keep it there. And the *Mail* has been performing a stunning marketing job for him.'

'But if he leaked that what else is he planning to let slip?'

'Remember the confidentiality agreement? He knows I'll have his balls for good luck charms if he breaches it. Besides, what else does he really know about you apart from your hair colour and the fact that you can't hold your champagne?'

She's right. Again. I relax.

Then I see the time and feel my stomach churn.

'Shit, Mary, it's nearly five. I've at least got to show my face at work.'

'Heaven preserve us,' she mutters. 'The girl's on the verge of earning squillions and she's worried about keeping her day job.'

As I'm putting on my coat Mary peeks out of the window.

'My stalker's back. Best nip down the fire escape and out via the pizzeria. I'll phone ahead and have them give you an empty box to carry out . . . And I think I'll order myself a *Quattro Staggione* while I'm at it.'

'Amy! Where've you been?' Julie says as I slump into my chair. 'Deedee's going crazy ape. She wants Lewis to give you a written warning.'

'Let her,' I say wearily.

'Anyway, never mind her. You're coming tonight, aren't you?'

'Tonight?'

'My en*gage*ment drink . . .'

Somehow it had completely slipped my mind.

'. . . You've *got* to. Half the Arsenal squad will be there. Except for the French ones. Which is most of them. Snooty bast—'

'Julie, I don't think I can make it.'

'You're kidding,' she wails. 'You can't let me down. I

179

can't get Deedee to do up the zip on my new Versace. *Pleeeeease* come, Amy. There'll be loads of free booze. Lewis is sticking a hundred quid behind the bar.'

Lewis. Aaaagh! I definitely can't go.

'Sorry, but I've got to . . .' I trail off as I try to think of an excuse. '. . . I've got to . . . I just can't come. I'm really sorry.'

Well, I can't tell her I'm going home to run a hot bath and slash my wrists with a Ladyshave, can I? Julie glowers at me . . . Maybe she'll save me the trouble of killing myself. Or if she doesn't, perhaps Deedee will. She's stomping across the office towards me.

My phone rings.

Thank you, God.

She stops in her tracks as I pick it up. It's Lisa.

'Amy, we've got to do it tonight.'

'Do what?'

'Confront Dad. I've been looking at these photos again and it can't wait. We've got to tell him to stop acting like he wants to be Rod Stewart all of a sudden. He's our *dad*, for God's sake.'

'Yes, we've definitely got to do it,' I say, while desperately trying to think of a reason to put it off. 'We've got to get in there . . . Strike while the iron's hot . . . Except . . . I can't. Not tonight.'

'Amy, this is important. Why the hell not?'

Bingo!

'It's Julie's engagement drink . . . You know, my best mate at work. I can't let her down. Who else is going to zip her up? Besides, I'm going to be her maid of honour and there's going to be footballers and everything,' I babble.

Julie is staring at me in shock. Maybe I should've left off the maid of honour bit.

'But, Amy,' Lisa protests.

180

'We'll do it tomorrow. Definitely. Gotta go. Talk later. Bye.'

As I put the phone down Julie says, 'So, are you coming or not?'

'Yes . . . No . . . I don't know.'

But I'm not really concentrating on her because Deedee is bearing down on me again. As she reaches my desk the phone rings once more. She glares at me as I pick it up and announce in my sweetest telephone voice, 'Hello, *Working Girl* magazine, Amy Bickerstaff speaking. How may I help?'

'Are you sure that's you, Amy?' asks a rough and familiar voice. 'Or is it Marsha Mellow?'

My heart stops . . . Really, it stops dead.

'I don't know what you're talking about,' I say weakly.

'Course you do, darling,' says Colin Mount.

'You've got the wrong number.'

'I wouldn't hang up, because the next call I make will be to the *Daily Mail*. I'm sure they'd stump up for what I know.'

Silence.

Deedee is still standing menacingly over me. A bemused Julie is looking alternately from her to me.

'You wanna know how I figured you out?' he asks.

Yes. Desperately. How the *fuck* does he know?

'It's your sister . . .'

Had to be her, didn't it?

'. . . If she hadn't flapped her mouth on my staircase, I wouldn't have a clue. While you two were flicking through the snaps of your dad I had one of my hunches. I figured it was probably nothing, but what the hell – you've got to give these things a whirl, haven't you? Any road, I followed you back to work. Only you didn't go straight there, did you? You popped in for tea with your agent along the way.'

181

Mary! *Fuck*. Her name has been in the *Mail* a dozen times over the past few weeks along with a picture of her wearing her headscarf and shades, and shoving her hand into the photographer's lens.

'Like I said, I could go to the papers,' he goes on. 'But my guess is that a lady as discreet as yourself might be willing to pay to keep her privacy. Seemed only fair to ask first.'

Oh, that's very fucking reasonable, you fat, sleazy shit.

'Truth is I've had a bellyful of shinning up trees to snap randy gits like your old man,' he goes on. 'I've got my eye on a gaff in the Algarve. Property still goes for a song over there, so I'm not asking for much.'

'I . . . er . . . um,' I mumble. I have no idea how to handle this, and even if I did I couldn't do it in front of an audience.

'Now, it's probably a lot to take in straight off, darling, so I suggest we have a chat over a drink – my shout. You can tell me where Marsha gets all her inspiration from, you saucy little –'

I slam the phone down as my heart kicks off again – it's racing, making up for lost time. Julie and Deedee are staring at me.

'Wrong number,' I say. 'Bloody weirdo.'

'We need to talk,' Deedee commands.

'Can't,' I say, my eyes welling up. 'My contacts are about to explode.'

I grab my coat and nearly knock Deedee over in my rush to escape.

Chapter 17

I've been hiding for twenty minutes now. I'm standing by the door that leads from the *Working Girl* building and I'm peeking through the glass. I can't leave. Colin Mount is lurking in a shop doorway opposite. But I can't go back upstairs because I'll only find Deedee waiting with my P45. Obviously I can't stay here all night, but I have no idea what I'm going to do. The only consolation is that as long as I can see the sleazebag I know he isn't on the phone to the *Mail*.

But it's a pretty bloody small consolation, because this is definitely, categorically and utterly the biggest nightmare of my life – so far. On top of everything else I had to go and find myself a blackmailer . . . Or rather Lisa found him for me. In the Yellow bloody Pages.

Thanks a million, sis.

I could kill her.

Because now I think about it – and I haven't been doing anything else for the last twenty minutes – everything is down to her. *Everything.* The fact that she opened her big mouth on Colin Mount's staircase. The fact that my book got published in the first place. The fact that I went to see Jake dressed like Jordan and nearly ended up in bed with a Polish prostitute (who turned out to be really sweet, but that's completely beside the point). The truth is that the Lisa-getting-me-into-shit thing has been going on for years. When I was fourteen who was it that pushed me in front of a camera when Michael Barrymore and his *My Kind of People* show turned up at Brent Cross? *Lisa*, that's who. I only sang one verse of 'The Wind Beneath My Wings' and it was never broadcast, but the memory still brings me out in cold sweats.

But killing Lisa wouldn't be fair, would it? No, I should tie her up and do very painful things to her with kitchen utensils over a number of weeks . . . And then kill her.

'*Amy*, what are you doing?'

I turn round to see the lift doors opening. Julie is piling out with a bunch of girls from the office. She looks . . . *amazing*. More the new Mrs David Beckham than the fiancée of some old substitute no one's ever heard of.

'I thought you'd left already,' she says as she reaches me.

'No,' I reply, spotting my escape, 'I felt bad about not zipping you up.'

I fling myself into the middle of the gaggle as it pours through the door into the street. Julie puts her arm through mine, seemingly pleased that I'm still here. Once we've walked a little way down the road I glance over my shoulder.

Damn.

I've been spotted. Colin Mount is ten yards behind us. He gives me a little wave. I pick up the pace, virtually sweeping Julie off her feet.

'What's the hurry?' she squeals. 'We've got all night.'

My normal tactic at parties is to find a corner and attempt to blend with the wall – I have a number of magnolia woodchip effect party dresses bought specifically for that purpose. But not tonight. Tonight I'm a social butterfly, flitting from group to group, gassing my heart out. I've discussed dwindling advertising revenues in the face of increasing competition with *Working Girl*'s head of sales,

184

timeshares in Florida with a bald bloke whose name I didn't catch and I've listened to about fifty rubbish impressions from the spotty sixteen-year-old who tops up the copiers, I've even been talking to the footballers. Julie's Alan told me what a wing back does and it has absolutely nothing to do with sanitary protection. And a lovely big bloke called Sol who someone said plays for England has explained four-four-two. He was going to do offside as well, but I said, 'Hey, I'm not one of those girly girls who doesn't have a clue about offside and makes you do those stupid demonstrations with salt and pepper pots.'

I'm exhausted.

The only reason I'm keeping this up is that as long as I'm talking to someone, that shitty little blackmailer will leave me alone. He's sitting on a stool at the bar and he hasn't taken his eyes off me all night.

'. . . Nah, I haven't seen a wet proof in donkey's years,' says Vic from production, my current conversational project.

'Really?' I reply, trying my best to look riveted.

'That's right. They died a death when printing turned digital. Everything's in bloody pixels these days. Does my ruddy head in.'

'I bet,' I say, wondering what on earth a pixel is and hoping he isn't going to ask questions later.

'Anyway, sweetheart, do us a favour and look after my bevy while I visit the gents. I'm busting.'

He hands me his bottle and turns away, leaving me in a panic. *No one to talk to.* Colin Mount has seen his chance and is slithering off his stool. My eyes dart frantically round the room looking for someone (*anyone*) to latch onto. Sol looks to be at a loose end, but I haven't got any more football questions and I can't admit that, actually, I haven't the foggiest about offside. I see the spotty sixteen-year-old and decide I can probably feign laughter at his '*Chianti and f-f-f-fava beans*' a fifth time. I quickly push my way through the throng towards him, but I don't make it. Deedee grabs me. I didn't know she was coming, but she must have been here a while because she seems drunk – after a few seconds she's still clinging on to me for support.

'Amy, bloody awful party,' she slurs. She seems to have forgotten that a few hours ago she wanted to fire me.

'Is it?' I say as I glance over her shoulder and check that the sleazebag is safely back on his stool.

'It's full of bloody footballers,' she moans.

'Well, Julie's bloke – it's kind of what he does.'

Now her gaze is fixed on Julie whose body is entwined with Alan's. Looks like his tongue is boldly going where no dentist has gone before. *Lucky bitch*. No cares. No worries. Nothing more stressful to deal with than a big, athletic lump of a guy who can't wait to whip off her £250 La Perla bra.

'God, it'd take a fireman's hose to separate those two,' says Deedee.

Envious as I am, her tone makes me bristle.

'Mind you,' she goes on, 'it won't last. Six months max.'

'At least she's got someone. That's more than you or I can say.'

'Well, I prefer not to hop into bed with every man I meet,' she huffs.

'Maybe if you tried it once in a while, you'd get rid of that big fat chip that's made itself at home on your shoulder,' I snap. My God, did I really just say that? Must be drunk.

Deedee isn't listening, though. Her attention has shifted to the bar, where a tall brunette is waiting to be served. She doesn't need the twenty-pound note she's waving to attract the barman's attention – her lips, cleavage and hosiery model legs are capable of doing that all by themselves. Striking though she is, it isn't her looks that stun me. It's the fact that Lewis is standing next to her.

'That's Lewis's new girl,' Deedee sneers, making me suspect that maybe he's tried it on with her as well.

'Have you met her?'

'She came into the office one evening last week. Lewis says she's the one . . . But I'm not sure. Bit of a cold fish. I don't see her lasting.'

I do. Look at those lips . . . That cleavage . . . Those legs. Jammy cow. Mind you, who'd want to last with a pig like Jake? I mean Dad. I mean *Lewis*. God, I'm stressed. I'm getting my bastards all muddled up.

The brunette's drinks arrive. She hands a glass to Lewis before taking a mobile out of her bag. While she takes her call he comes towards us. I've made a really good job of avoiding him over the last three weeks or so, but it looks as if I'm stuck now – I can't leave Deedee's side because Colin Mount is waiting to pounce like a fat, beery panther.

'Deedee, would you do me a favour?' Lewis says when he reaches us.

'Of course,' she smarms.

'When Ros gets off the phone, take her round to meet everyone. She'd really appreciate it.'

OhmyGod, that's his *Ros*!

In flesh and blood!

Living and breathing!

Before my very eyes!

But this isn't the girl in the photo frame. She must be the *original* Ros who called him the first time he ever spoke to me. Jesus, poor thing. I wonder if she knows about the girl in the picture? He gets through them – he's like Jake on a Viagra power surge. Thank heavens

I didn't go there. Why would I ever want to be with a man who delegates girlfriend introductions to his PA? I've heard of bosses getting their secretaries to buy their women flowers and underwear, but this is outrageous. I wonder if he'll get Deedee to dump her when he's had enough.

'Love to, Lewis,' Deedee gushes and immediately skips over to Ros. She's either dumber or shallower than I thought – both probably.

Lewis and I stand in awkward silence . . . Which he eventually breaks.

'Well, Amy, it seems we're alone at last – apart from fifty or sixty drunken revellers, a bunch of footballers and some bar staff.'

'Er . . . Um . . .'

Listen to me. I've automatically slipped into mumble mode. And I'm staring at him. He does look gorgeous. Those big eyes. And his shirt is really nice – turquoise and shiny and a little bit tight and I bet he's got lovely pecs under –

Stop it, stop it, *stop* it! He's a bastard. With a girl-friend. Probably more than one, actually, if facts (or photo frames) are to be believed.

'Are you all right?' he asks. 'You've been distant lately.'

'Um . . . Yes . . . Er . . . Fine. Just a bit . . . Erm . . . Busy.'

'Only I thought it was me. You know . . . Something I'd done.'

What could you possibly have done, Lewis? I mean, apart from getting me to fancy you in the first place, asking me out while a Christy Turlington lookalike is gazing at you from a frame on your desk, and then turning up at a party with poor, deceived Ros.

'No . . . Um . . . God, no . . . You haven't done anything.'

188

'You sure? I can come over a bit . . .'

Superior? Arrogant? Facetious?

'. . . brusque sometimes . . .'

Brusque will do for now.

'. . . and I don't mean to be,' he says, sounding sweeter than I've ever heard from him – not *that* sweet, but everything is relative. 'That afternoon in my office . . . Maybe you got the wrong imp—'

Forget it, Lewis. It's way too late for you to try to convince me that deep down you're a nice bloke who never cheats on his girlfriends and leaves saucers of milk out for hedgehogs.

'Really, you haven't done anything wrong,' I say a little aggressively.

'Good . . . Good. Anyway, what do you think of her?' he asks, gesturing towards Ros, whom a virtually paralytic Deedee is dragging round by the hand.

Why should you care about my opinion of your girlfriend?

'She seems . . . er . . . *nice*,' I say coldly.

'She is. And I think she'll make my life a whole lot easier.'

Oh, isn't that lovely for you?

'How long have you known her?' I ask, still icy cold.

'I interviewed her last week.'

I can't keep my indignation bottled up and I finally snap. 'You *interviewed* her?' I squeak.

'Yes,' he says, a little taken aback. 'She starts next week.'

'She *starts* next week?' I squeal, outraged now. 'You give your *girlfriends* a *start* date?'

'My girlfriend? She's not my . . . Ros is my new deputy editor.'

My mouth is flapping. Nothing will come out.

189

And – of course – Lewis is laughing. Like a bloody drain.

Normally in a situation like this I'd do the sensible thing and run for my life, but I can't go anywhere without my pet blackmailer following. So I stay put and flap my mouth some more.

He finally pulls himself together. 'So, now that we've established I won't be marrying Ros any day soon, what about you?'

'What about me?' I ask in a virtual whisper, terrified of putting my foot in it again.

'Well, the last time I checked you were on the phone. Making a date. How's that going?'

'Oh . . . It's . . . Er . . . Not. At all.'

'That's a shame. Such lovely flowers he sent you, too. Very, er, vast.'

'He's a bast— It was never going to work.'

'Does that mean that . . . You know . . . Um . . .'

Why has he gone all quiet and mumbly now? I can barely hear him.

'. . . I could . . . Er . . . Resurrect that invitation . . . To dinner?'

Did I hear him right? I think so, and I can feel outrage kicking back in. Because how could we forget the girl in the photo frame? I mean, she could just be the new assistant deputy editor, but I'm fairly certain it's not normal practice to put pictures of employees in pretty frames on your desk.

'Dinner would be lovely, Lewis,' I say in a very formal voice. Now for the punchline. 'Why don't you ask your *girl*friend to come along as well?'

'Who?' he asks, stalling for time – no doubt while he thinks up a smart explanation.

'The one on your desk.'

'Who's on my desk? I'm not with you, Amy,' he says awkwardly.

'In the photo frame,' I snap. 'The one who looks like Christy bloody Turlington.'

He smiles now. No bloody shame at all. Just like Jake. He's probably going to invite me on a disgusting three-some with them.

'She *is* Christy Turlington,' he says. 'I'd love to ask her . . . But you know what? I've lost her number.'

Excuse me? My turn to look confused: (a) how could he possibly be going out with Christy Turlington? And (b) if he is, why would he be so stupid as to lose her number?

'You're really getting it arse about tit tonight, aren't you?' he says. 'That photo frame was a birthday present for my mum . . .'

My mouth. *Damn.* It's doing the flapping thing again.

'. . . I bought it that lunchtime. It still had the picture in it from the shop. You know, the one they put in to show you how gorgeous your plug-ugly relatives will become once you stick them in there.'

Hole, I command you to open up in the floor RIGHT NOW!

'I'm so . . . I feel so . . . God . . . Sorry,' I manage to say.

'You're dying, aren't you?' He smiles, putting a hand on my arm. 'After heart disease and cancer it's the biggest killer.'

'What is?' I ask in a panic – terminal bloody illness on top of everything else.

'Embarrassment.'

'I'm really, really sorry,' I mumble. 'You must think –'

'Actually, what I'm thinking is that we should stop all this pissing about . . .'

He has switched back to his corporate, I'm-the-boss voice and it's getting a bit scary again.

'. . . and go out some time.'

Oh.

'So, how about it?'

The fact is that I'd love to go out with him now that I know he isn't sleeping with Ros or Christy, but especially Christy, and that there might be a chance that deep down he's a really nice bloke.

So I say, 'I'm sorry, Lewis, but . . . Um . . . This isn't a very good time.'

Sorry, Lewis, but this isn't a very good time?

In all the dating manuals I've ever read, even the rubbish ones, that is not the thing to say when Dream Boat asks you out. But why did he have to pick *The Worst Day Of My Life (By Miles)* to reveal that, actually, he's not an unprincipled sex monster and then to ask me out? He looks crestfallen and I can't face him. I need an escape and my eyes flit around the bar . . . And settle on Colin Mount. *Shit*. I'd forgotten about him. He gives me a sickly grin. And he must have had enough of hanging around for a gap in the conversation because he's flopping off his stool . . . *Fuck*, he's coming this way. What the hell do I do now?

Got it . . . Sudden change of tactics on the Lewis front.

'Actually, sod it, Lewis,' I gabble. 'Let's go out, yeah?'

'What?'

Wow, that threw him.

'Now!' I add as I grab his hand and pull him towards the exit. I barge through a mob of six-foot-plus footballers, brushing them aside like they're the under-fourteen netball squad. I look back only to make sure that Lewis is still with me. He is and moments later we're in the street.

'Amy, what are you doing? . . . Where are we going?' he asks nervously, but I'm not listening. I'm looking for a taxi, hoping that for once I'll get lucky and . . . *Phew*! Thank *fuck*. The rattle of a black cab. I thrust out my arm and it squeals to a halt in front of us. I grab the door, fling it open and drag Lewis inside.

'Where to?' asks the cabby.

Shit, hadn't thought that far ahead. I look back towards the bar and see Colin Mount emerge into the fresh air.

'Just drive,' I shriek.

'You've been watching too many movies, sweetheart,' the driver mutters, but he sets off anyway. I turn and look out of the rear window. Colin Mount is standing on the edge of the pavement searching frantically left and right for a cab of his own . . . But for once I did get lucky and he's stranded. I turn back and find my eyes locked on Lewis's. He's staring at me as if I'm completely mad, as if he has no idea whether he has struck gold or hooked up with *Working Girl*'s resident bunny boiler.

'Amy, what's going on?' he asks again.

'I don't know, Lewis,' I reply weakly. 'I really don't know.'

My eyes fill up.

'Is it your contacts?' he asks peering at the tears.

The floodgates open.

'No, not your contacts.' He reaches out, puts an arm round my shoulder and pulls me towards him. 'It's OK,' he soothes.

'No it isn't,' I sob.

'Tell me about it.'

And I'm tempted to, I truly am . . . But – and it's a huge *but* – if any of the dating manuals I've read happened to mention the subject of confessing your secret life as a porn writer/blackmail victim/daughter of a philanderer/ religious nutter on a first date, then I'm pretty sure they concluded that it's a poor idea, one likely to cast a major shadow over any future relationship.

I *wish* that it would all magically go away. That Colin Mount would get bored and give up, Jacobson would discover an author who's even filthier than me and the *Mail* would find something else to preach about, leaving me to lie back in Lewis's embrace and let him kiss me . . .

But of course that's not going to happen and even if it did where would that leave us? We'd still be doomed. Imagine if we went out and had a really good time. Then we'd have to go out again. And again. Next we'd be having sex and if it were any good, we'd do *that* again and again, and we'd probably be getting on so well, we'd end up getting engaged, married and having five or six adorable kids and before we knew it, we'd be surrounded by frolicking grandchildren and celebrating our golden wedding. Finally we'd be sitting on the patio of our dream retirement cottage in Wiltshire or wherever, and we'd get round to playing the stupid game that old people who've been with each other for ever always play: I confess/you confess. I'd be so racked with guilt that I wouldn't be able to refuse. I'd wait nervously as he owned up to something really stupid. Then it would be my turn. 'I was Marsha Mellow,' I'd say tremulously. He'd be devastated. How could I have kept it from him? How could I betray him like that? His love for me lying in shreds, he'd take the antique shotgun down from above the fireplace (because those old cottages in Wiltshire always come with those). He'd point it at me, squeeze the trigger and *blam*! Then he'd place the barrel in his mouth and –

Secrets always tear couples apart. I know – I've seen it time and time again on *EastEnders*.

But so does the truth.

God, we're doomed whichever way I look at it.

'Maybe you'd feel better if you talked about it, Amy,' Lewis prods gently.

'I can't . . . do this,' I reply, yanking myself away from

him. I lean forward and tell the cabby to pull over.
'Amy,' Lewis pleads as I open the door.
I climb out and take one last look at him.
'Sorry,' I say before I turn round and run.

Chapter 18

The back of the van opens and warm, bright sunlight floods in. As my eyes adjust I can make out two people waiting for me: a man and a woman, both in dark-grey suits, both wearing Ray-Bans. The woman looks oddly familiar.

'Welcome to the Witness Protection Programme, ma'am,' the man announces in a deep, drawly Tommy Lee Jones kind of voice.

'Technically she's not a *witness*, sir,' his partner says as I step out into the street.

'Well, what is she, Agent Flugmann?'

She looks down at her clipboard. 'It states here *writer*, sir – *sexually explicit fiction*.'

The man takes the clipboard from his partner and checks it for himself. He slides his shades down his nose in order to scrutinise me better. It's now that I see that he doesn't just have the voice – he *is* Tommy Lee Jones. Nothing surprises me any longer, though.

He looks up from the clipboard and says, 'Are you sure you need federal protection, ma'am?'

'Perhaps she booked onto the writers' summer retreat – it's in the next valley,' suggests Agent Flugmann.

It has only just clicked why she too seems familiar. She's Velma from *Scooby Doo* – all grown up and in the FBI. No, *nothing* surprises me.

'What do we do, sir?' she asks. 'Send her back?'

'I *need* protection,' I gabble. 'I'm on the run . . . From my mother.'

'You're in the right place, then,' Tommy Lee Jones says, gesturing towards the white-painted house that is to be my new home. 'Most of your neighbours are mob informants. We've also got some fugitives from the Colombian cartels and a couple of Russkie spooks – leftovers from commie days, but they can't bring themselves to leave. A pretty good bunch all in all – lots of community spirit . . . Oh, and check out the kid in thirty-seven. He's only fourteen, but you two have something in common. His mom found the stash of *Hustler*s under his mattress and he had to flee home.'

That just about sums it up. No life, no friends, no family. All I have to look forward to is getting to know a bunch of Mafia grasses and retired drug traffickers . . . Oh, yes, and a little boy who's scared of his *mommy*.

I start to cry.

Tommy Lee Jones gives Agent Flugmann – *Velma* – a nod and she jumps to my side, proffering a crisp white FBI issue handkerchief.

'There, there, ma'am,' she soothes stiffly, patting me on the arm. 'Optic fluid ejaculation is a very common reaction to sudden enforced separation from familiar life patterns. You'll adjust in time and –'

'– on behalf of Virgin Atlantic, I'd like to thank you for flying with us and we hope that we'll see you again soon.'

You what? . . . *Shit* . . . Are we there already?

I blink my eyes open and feel my ears pop as the jet sinks into clouds. I've slept through the entire flight to New York and I'm gutted. For the first time in my life I'm in business class and I've missed the lot. The champagne, the massage, the choice of several thousand movies, padding up and down the aisle in my free towelling slippers – probably a floor

197

show, too, involving dancers, jugglers and a leading New York stand-up comedian. *And* the food. Whatever the flight attendants served up, it was surely better than the *Chickenorbeef?* I'm used to from charters to Alicante – at the very least it must have been edible.

I forked out more money than I care to think about for the ticket and all I've got to show for it is a stupid dream featuring Velma from *Scooby Doo*. OK, Tommy Lee Jones as well, but it was still ludicrous. This has been the most expensive sleep I've ever had. I must have needed it.

After fleeing from Lewis last night I went straight home, praying that Colin Mount didn't follow me there. Although I never gave him my address, he's a private detective. He's no Sherlock Holmes, but he did manage to discover pretty much everything about Miss Strappy Heels – including her bra size. Finding out where I live won't be too taxing.

As soon as I'd shut my front door, I got on the phone to the airlines. I discovered that you can go anywhere you like, whenever you like, provided money is no object. Twenty minutes later I had a ticket and I was thinking that I could get used to being stupidly rich. This morning my doorbell rang and I looked out of my window to see my minicab. After a quick check to see that my blackmailer wasn't lurking behind a tree I dashed for the door and was on my way.

I had a couple of calls to make on the ride to Gatwick. First work. I was hoping I'd get her voicemail, but Deedee decided my call would be the one she'd actually answer this month.

'I'm really sorry,' I said, 'but I don't think I'll be in for a few days.'

'Not you as well. Everyone's been phoning in with *tummy bugs* after last night's piss-up.'

198

Damn. I was going to use that one.

'I'm really sick, Deedee. I think it's . . . chickenpox.'

(It was the first disease that sprang into my head. The second, actually – the first had been leprosy, but using that might have been overkill.)

'Oh, yeuch!' screeched Deedee. 'Don't come anywhere near me, then.'

Which was exactly what I'd hoped she'd say.

'Take off as long as you need,' she went on, trying for the sympathetic tone that will always be beyond her. 'I suppose Lewis and I will just have to manage here on our own somehow.'

The mention of him made me flip my phone shut.

Next, I had to call Ant to let him know I was coming. But hadn't he said to drop in? *Any time*. As I dialled his number, I calculated that it would be three in the morning over there. I got his answering machine and heard Alex's voice for the first time. They must have still been at the club. I hung up before the tone. There seemed no point in leaving a message. What the hell would I have said? Better, I figured, just to arrive.

At Gatwick I had second thoughts. What was I doing? Surely running away wasn't the answer. I'd have to come back at some point. And besides, when Colin Mount realised his cash cow had scarpered, wouldn't he simply go for option two and sell me out to the papers? Then I saw a stack of *Daily Mail*s outside W. H. Smith. 'PART-NERS IN GRIME' blared the headline. Beneath it were two pictures. The first was of Jacobson – it must have been old because his hair was black. The second was of Mary. I didn't bother to read the story, but seeing my two accomplices splashed across page one like wanted terrorists clarified matters.

If I'm going to be named and shamed, I reasoned, then I'd much rather it happens while I'm on another continent. Getting as far away as possible was the best idea I'd ever had.

After my first yellow cab ride I'm in a street that runs between Broadway and the Bowery. Apparently this is the Lower East Side, though it could be the Upper Northwest for all the sense compass points make to me. It's midday and I'm outside Ant's apartment building. Ant and Alex will almost certainly be in bed. I stand back and gaze up at the four-storey brick block. It's exactly as Ant has described it: 'If it looks a bit like a shabby old shoe factory that's because it once was. The only way you can tell from the outside that it's been turned into swanky lofts for people with pots of money is from the bullet-proof glass in the front door – keeps the crack-heads out.' I look at the big metal door and see a row of six shallow indentations, each as big as a ten-pence piece. I recall Ant telling me about the boyfriend of a tenant who'd sprayed the entrance with an Uzi after an argument over TV channels.

Shit, I'm in New York. City of Uzis, Busta Rhymes and 'Have a nice day, *muthafucka*'.

I panic. I have to get off the street before I become just another statistic in one of the ten thousand drive-by shootings that take place on a daily basis (which must be true because it said so in the *Mail*). I quickly scan the names on the stack of buzzers until I spot A. RITTER & A. HUBBARD. My finger freezes over the button. What if they're having an orgy in there? After all, isn't that what gays do on a daily basis? (Ditto, the *Mail*.)

What to do?

I'm stuck.

Certain death in a drug-related shooting on the street or the certain shame of being the only guest with breasts at a bring-a-tube-of-KY party.

What to do, *what to do?* . . .

I see a six-foot-plus black guy walking towards me and my mind is made up. He must be over fifty feet away, but I'm sure his long, grey coat is concealing a machine-gun. I plunge my finger down on the buzzer, keeping it there as I pray for Ant's voice on the intercom.

After a few seconds the tiny speaker crackles. 'Who is it?' Ant asks.

The black guy is less than twenty feet away. He's smiling at me – a sure sign that he's about to whip out a gun.

'Ant, it's me, Amy. Lemme in,' I gabble.

'Amy, what the fuck are you –'

'Lemmein*now*!'

I hear a buzz and push open the heavy door. I rush through with my bag and slam it shut behind me. I peer through the small square of bulletproof glass at my would-be killer. He has reached the door and he turns towards me. Still smiling, he opens both sides of his coat to reveal . . . dozens of leather belts hanging from one side of the lining and a wide selection of watches dangling from the other.

That's it – he was going to bludgeon me to death with a fake Rolex.

What sort of idiot am I? And Lisa would have loved one of those. Now he's gone, so I've missed my chance. Still feeling foolish, I head up the stairs to the third floor where Ant is waiting at his door. He's wearing a short silk dressing gown, showing off his wiry legs and bare, bony feet. His hair is an uncombed tangle and his eyes are barely open – two sleep-caked slits in his unshaven face. He looks like shit.

He's also the most welcome sight that I've ever laid eyes on and I fall sobbing into his arms.

Half an hour later we are sitting on towering, vertigo-inducing stools at a stainless-steel island set amidst the biggest expanse of polished wood floor I've seen outside a gym hall. It is so vast that the New York Thingummies could play a game of basketball on it and the Romanian gymnastic squad would still have room to go through their floor routines in the corner. None of that is happening, though. Instead, it's just Ant and me talking in the huge, minimally furnished space that he and Alex call home.

This, then, is a loft. I've always wondered. When London estate agents advertise loft-style living they're referring to a few square feet of floorboards overlooking a rubbish-strewn canal basin in Docklands – in other words, not terribly impressive. This, though, is hugely, massively, *boastfully* impressive.

We're onto our second jug of coffee (mostly for his benefit) and the tears have more or less dried up. I've told Ant everything.

'You think I've made a mistake, don't you?' I say nervously.

'Running away? Yes and no. Your scuzzy blackmailer will almost certainly go to the papers, but at least it'll take care of telling your mum. And this way you don't have to be in the room when it happens . . .'

I smile because this has been my *brilliant* thinking too.

'. . . But, of course, you won't have any control over how bad it sounds – that'll be in the *Mail*'s hands.'

Smile fades.

'You haven't told anyone you're here?' he says. 'Not even Lisa or that agent of yours?'

'Not a soul.'

'Right, here's what you're going to do.'

Oh, *God*, he wants me to *do* something. Having to do something is precisely what I'm fleeing from.

'You're going to relax, have fun and forget about it . . .' he continues.

Hallelujah! Sweet music to my ears.

'. . . At least until you have to go home.'

D'oh!

I hear a noise. Movement from the far end of the loft where a partition separates the area where – I assume – Ant and Alex sleep. Alex must be waking up. It startles me, but my reaction is nothing compared with Ant's. He nearly jumps out of his skin, like it's slipped his mind that he lives with someone.

'You must be starving,' he says in a rush.

'Not really. I didn't eat on the plane, but –'

'Let's go for lunch. There's a diner across the street. Why don't you go now and order something. I'll get dressed and join you in ten.'

'It's OK. I'll wait. I'm really not that hung –'

But Ant has pushed me off my stool and he's bundling me towards the door. What's going on? Why is he so desperate to get me out of the way? Doesn't he want me to meet Alex? Shit, maybe Alex is a *bad* person. With a *gun*. Well, this *is* America.

We reach the door. Ant is about to open it when I hear movement again. I turn, look down the length of the loft and see Alex emerge from behind the partition. I look at Ant, who has frozen. Alex, wearing a dressing gown identical to Ant's, pads towards us. Though it's hard to tell from this distance, he's smaller than I'd imagined. He has shaggily cropped hair and a boyish face – almost elfin . . .

Uh-oh. Just had a thought that might explain the panic. Maybe this isn't Alex. Best check – it pays never to assume with my best friend.

'Is that Alex?' I whisper.

'No . . . He's visiting his folks in Buffalo,' Ant whispers back. 'It's Frankie.'

'*Ant*!' I hiss. 'I thought you'd sorted that out.'

'So did I,' he says dejectedly.

He decides it's probably too late to smuggle me out and we head back into the loft. As Frankie reaches the island he rubs his still sleepy eyes and peers at us suspiciously. He really is *very* elfin – not the sculpted, protein-supplements-for-breakfast type that Ant usually goes for.

'Morning. Any coffee left in the jug?' he calls out.

Hang on. *Fuck*. Did I say *he*?

Because Frankie is definitely *not* a *he*.

'So what's it like, then?' I ask.

'What? Sex with a bird?' Ant says. 'It's not all straight blokes crack it up to be. It's a bit . . . *squidgy*. I kept wanting to flip her over and do her up the –'

'Ant! *Pur*-lease.'

'Anyway, what do you think? Am I completely losing it?'

'*God*, what do I think, Ant? I *think* I'm still in shock.'

After impersonating a talkative tornado as she simultaneously dressed, drank coffee, used her mobile and applied make-up, Frankie has left for work leaving Ant to explain and me feeling dazed and confused. I now have a sense of what he went through when he discovered I was Marsha Mellow. And – though I hate to admit it because I'm not sure I should be experiencing this emotion – I feel betrayed. Like one of those poor women in the problem pages who comes home to find her husband in bed with a bloke from his pub darts team – only I'm not married to Ant and Frankie doesn't seem the darts type.

'Why?' I ask him.

'I don't understand it myself. I just felt drawn to her the moment I saw her and –'

'You told me all that in London. You also told me Frankie was six-two and had a goatee . . . You like her because she's so boyish? . . . Is that it?'

Silence.

'Why didn't you tell me the truth?'

'That's rich coming from you, *Marsha* . . . I couldn't tell you.'

'I've been your best friend since for ever. You've always told me *every*thing. Haven't you?'

'Yes, I have, but I couldn't explain what was happening to myself. How could I explain it to you?'

'You could have just talked about it. Maybe it would have helped.'

'I wanted to, but I was scared.'

'*Scared*? Isn't it supposed to be the other way round, Ant? Aren't you meant to feel that when you tell people you're *gay*?'

'I *am* gay. That's my point. I've always been one of those queers that *hate* bisexuals. Like it's an affectation – a fashion thing – or they're just plain greedy. Now look at me.'

'You can't help your feelings. If you love Frankie, why deny it?'

'I don't love her. I'm pretty sure of that now. I really like her, but I couldn't ever *love* her. I know that now we've had sex.'

'But you've been seeing her for months.'

'Yes, but last night was our first shag. I've been too terrified to do it. *Jesus*, the excuses I've come up with – I've had more fucking headaches than the woman in the Tylenol ad. Anyway, we finally did it and it just didn't work for me. I had to turn the lights off and imagine she had a cock. And the *noise*. You girls don't half *scream*.'

'Not all of us,' I say indignantly. 'It must be a New York thing.'

I am *so* not a screamer. You could hear a pin drop when I have an orgasm – though I have severe difficulty remembering the last time *that* happened.

'Whatever,' Ant says. 'All this time I've been thinking she turned me on and . . . It was just curiosity. I was *straight*-curious.'

'So what are you going to do?'

'Finish it with her I suppose.'

'I feel sorry for her now. She seems really stuck on you. What are you going to tell her?'

'The truth.'

'That you're already involved?'

'She knows that. I mean tell her I'm gay. She thinks Alex is a lingerie model.'

Chapter 19

Two days in New York and I feel like a new woman. Slight exaggeration. It's more as if the old me has been steam cleaned, waxed and valeted. I've taken Ant's advice to heart and have forgotten everything, which isn't so hard in a place like this. Despite seeing it in a thousand films, it's still a shock to the system. It's just so . . . New Yorkish.

I've been to the top of the Empire State Building (didn't see a thing – thick fog), taken a boat ride around the Statue of Liberty (only slightly seasick) and gazed awestruck and fearful at the hole in the skyline that used to be the Twin Towers. And I've overcome my terror of becoming a drive-by/mugging/other unspecified violent crime victim and have even managed to walk across Central Park in the twilight without my heart rate rising significantly.

I've done more than just the obvious sights. I managed to discover what isn't in a single guidebook – the only bar in Manhattan that still allows smoking. I had trouble finding it and when I asked a policeman for directions he looked at me as if I wanted to know how to get to the nearest crack den. They're really down on fags here. It's enough to make me give up, actually. Not the fact that I can't smoke anywhere, but the fact that I *could* in that bar. Every smoker in America was there, a packed huddle of desperate asylum seekers. After one beer my eyes were streaming and my white top was yellower than the filter on my B&H.

I've done shopping as well. I'm no Lisa when it comes to credit card abuse, but you can't fly all the way to New York and not shop, can you? Having said that, I've discovered exactly the same stores selling exactly the same things as in London – everything except for an M&S. Even so, I've managed to fill a quarter of Ant's and Alex's loft (no mean feat) with assorted carriers. I've also splashed out on a huge silver suitcase in which to lug my purchases back home.

Home. Aaaaggggghhhhhh!

I'm going back tomorrow. I've toyed with the idea of staying on for a bit – well, *for ever*, actually – but I can't. I have to face things. Get my head out of the sand. Take responsibility. All that crappy grown-up stuff. God knows what I'll find when I get back. I haven't dared to phone anyone for an update. And, like I said, that's what I've spent the past two days trying to forget. But with departure less than twenty-four hours away, my guts are warming up for some serious churning.

Ant has decided to take my mind off the prospect by taking me out. I'm dressed and ready. It took me all of three minutes to throw on some clothes and smear liner across my lids. Ant, by contrast, has been locked in the bathroom for sixty-seven minutes (and counting). God, sometimes he is just so *gay*.

Not that Frankie ever noticed.

Poor cow. How must she feel now?

Ant finished with her the afternoon I arrived. He went to see her at work, hoping the peace, serenity and super-rich clientele of an upmarket art gallery would minimise her hysteria. It didn't. Now she wants to sue for emotional distress and the gallery is after him for the damage to a Hockney print. I don't see how they can blame him – he was only ducking.

Frankly, though, he deserves everything he gets. I

haven't told him this, of course. I mean *me* lecturing *him* on deceit? Talk about pots and kettles. It would be like Pavarotti telling Placido Domingo to lay off the cream cakes. Ant knows I can't say anything. Though did he really need to point out to me how his experience should teach me something about the havoc that secrets and lies can cause? Smug git.

I can't say I'm happy with him at the moment. He's been tense and awkward ever since I arrived – not that I've seen much of him. With Alex being away he's been 'extra busy' at the club. This may be true, but I suspect it's also an excuse for avoiding me. I feel as if I've done something wrong, but it wasn't my fault I walked in on him and his *girl*friend. Who was it who told me to drop in – *any* bloody *time*?

His attitude is another reason I feel I should leave. Much as I've enjoyed the city, I don't feel very welcome here. Besides, Alex gets back tomorrow and I don't want to be in the way. *In the way*! That's a ridiculous thought. With the amount of space they've got, if I sat quietly in a corner, they wouldn't notice me for weeks.

I feel hurt. I've flown three thousand miles with an epic crisis on my hands and my best friend in the world has virtually blanked me. I'd *never* do that to him. When he came scurrying to London a few weeks ago I was completely at his disposal (except when I had to go to work and/or deal with various crises of my own, which was quite a bit of the time, but even so I was totally bloody *there* for him). I know we're going out now, but I'm sure he's only taking me out of duty – because it's my last night. Well, he needn't bloody bother. I'll go out on my own to my favourite bar and smoke tons of fags. I'll tell him the moment he gets out of the –

Click.

The bathroom door opens. Ant steps out and he looks

. . . *sensational*. He's wearing a tight green lamé shirt with his favourite jeans that look fourth-hand, but which cost him the best part of a month's wages – 'It takes several hundred man hours of highly skilled labour and two designers called Dolce and Gabana to get clothes looking this fucked.' Although my dress is new I feel depressingly dowdy next to him.

'You look great,' I say.

'So do you,' he replies.

'Do not,' I pout.

'Well, I'd fuck you . . . If I was still into that sort of thing.'

I'm not laughing. I am *so* not laughing.

We're in a cab heading uptown. (Uptown, downtown, it's all Greek to me and I just have to take Ant's word for it.)

'Where are we going?' I ask.

'A new restaurant. Starfucker's paradise. Don't ask what I had to do to the maître d' to get us a table,' he says, trying to keep up the light tone he kicked off with at the apartment. But it's not working and we slump into an uncomfortable silence. I stare out of the window at the steaming manhole covers (I'm amazed they actually exist – I thought they were a special effect) while Ant shifts in his seat . . . And takes my hand.

What does he think he's playing at?

'I'm really sorry,' he mumbles.

'So you bloody should be,' I reply. 'You've probably scared Frankie off men for life. And what about Alex? What have you put him –'

'No, I'm sorry for what I've done to you.'

'Me?' I say, turning round to face him. 'You haven't done anything to me. Apart from lying, blanking me for the last two days and leaving me and my credit card to fend for ourselves.'

'Relax, you're loaded now. What are you worried about?'

'I was forgetting. Or trying to, anyway.'

'Do you know why I was scared of telling you about Frankie?'

I shake my head.

'I don't know how to say this because it makes me seem really . . . I dunno . . . Conceited, I suppose. . . . I was worried that if you knew I was seeing a girl, you'd be . . .'

I know exactly where this is going. He was worried I'd be hurt. Feel betrayed. *Jealous.*

Well, I am.

Big time.

And I can't believe I feel like this. Ant and I made friends when we were four, and in twenty-two years I have never, not *once* thought of him in *that* way. Not even when we were playing doctors and nurses and he had my ankles round my ears while he shone a torch up my – Look, we were *kids*. By the time we were teenagers and I might have thought about him in *that* way it was off the agenda because we both liked boys (the same ones usually). The notion of me fancying him has never entered into the reckoning. It's not that I wouldn't – he's clever, funny and attractive even with his clothes off – but why even bother going there?

All that changed a couple of days ago. When I saw that Frankie was a Francesca a single thought came crashing to the surface – one that I've been trying my damnedest to push back down. It was, of course, *What the hell is wrong with me, then, Anthony bastard Hubbard*?

I sit here now and wait for him to finish his sentence, but he doesn't need to. We've been friends for so long that we both know exactly what the other is thinking.

'What was so special about her?' I ask.

'Physically?'

I nod.

'You said it the other day. The first time I saw her, I thought she *was* a boy. I thought she was about fourteen and that was quite appealing.'

'For God's sake tell me you don't do it with fourteen-year-olds.'

'Not since I was fourteen as well . . . Anyway, apart from her East End gangster's name, that's what fooled me into thinking I fancied her – her . . . um . . . lack of obvious *womanliness*. She's the complete opposite of you, Amy. If I remember it right, you needed a trainer bra in pre-school.'

Instinctively I cover my boobs, proving he has a point.

'Haven't you ever wanted to . . . You know?' I ask.

'Once when we were sixteen and you were going out with that guy who played rugby.'

'Jeremy Crane . . . *Yeuch*!'

'That's not what you thought at the time. I walked in on you when you were in the bedroom at Carol Lennon's party.'

'I didn't see you.'

'You were so busy you wouldn't have seen me if I'd been the Changing of the bloody Guard.'

'What were you doing in there?' I ask.

'Looking for somewhere to have a snog with Carol's older brother.'

'I didn't know he was gay.'

'Neither did he, darling. Anyway, that's not the point. When I walked in on you and the prop forward I had this pang that didn't go away for weeks . . . More of a hard-on than a pang, actually. It was just jealousy, though. You were my best friend and I wanted you all to myself.

It bothered the hell out of me that I could never do that with you.'

'You never asked,' I say – whimper pathetically, actually.

'Come on, Amy, look at us. I'm bent as a bloody ninepence piece and you've got a figure that makes Marilyn Monroe look like a diesel dyke. Frankie was a complete fucking brainstorm. I know that now.'

And so do I. Anthony Hubbard is pure, unadulterated, one hundred per cent homosexual. It's strange how reassuring that thought is – at least one thing in my world is as it should be.

'I'm sorry I've been such a git the last few days,' he continues. 'I didn't mean to be, but you've been so pouty –'

'Have not,' I pout.

'– that I just knew I'd upset you. The funny thing is that I feel bad for fucking up Frankie's life, not to mention Alex's – *repeatedly* – but the person I'm most worried about hurting is you . . . You've always been there and I hope you always will be.'

Shit, I'm crying now.

We're walking out of the restaurant and Ant is looking for a taxi. Dinner was . . . Er . . . Did we actually eat? I've seen loads of places in New York that put up signs that say ALL YOU CAN EAT – $9.99. Tonight's wasn't one of them. I burned more calories chewing than were on the plate. And the *chairs*. They were designed for supermodel arses – I've got *two* of those. They were also very shiny and angled slightly downwards, the idea being to deposit the diner on the floor as rapidly as possible, thus maximising the number of sittings – however famous the bum on the seat, there is always a more famous one waiting to sit down.

213

Because – and this was the good bit – it *was* a star-fucker's paradise. It was like stepping into a copy of *Hello!* minus the crap weather girls and minor cast members from *Emmerdale*. Everybody was a somebody, and all of them were craning their necks to check whether anybody was more of a somebody than they were. As I stared inanely at Al Pacino chatting to Susan Sarandon and Tim Robbins in between air-kissing Helen Hunt and Liza Minelli, Ant said, 'Ironic, isn't it? In British terms at least, you're one of the more famous people here, but no one would ever know it.'

We climb into a cab and I ask Ant where we are going.

'There's an opening tonight. Alex and I got invites. You can use his.'

An *opening*.

In *New York* City, which, apparently, is so *good* they named it twice. (Something else that, along with steaming manhole covers and Down-/Up-/Mid-/Sidewaystown baffles the hell out of me.)

Ten minutes later the taxi drops us outside a big stone building. Its entire frontage has been painted with a beautiful mural of peaches, plums and pomegranates.

'What is it, Ant?'

'A shop. It's called Fruit, oddly enough.'

It doesn't look like any greengrocer I've ever seen.

'What's it sell?'

'Wait and see.'

We walk past a TV crew and up to the door, where a gaggle of well-heeled guests are flashing their invitations at the black-suited doormen. We join them and within a couple of minutes we're heading inside to the most glamorous do I've been to since I imagined my perfect launch party for *Rings on Her Fingers* (location: three-hundred-foot yacht moored off Mustique, guest list: Madonna,

214

both Georges – Clooney and Michael – J-Lo and Ben Affleck . . . Oh, you get the gist).

'Ant, this is in*cred*ible,' I gasp.

'It's buzzing, huh?'

I don't know where to look first. At the groups of New York's beautiful people sipping champagne and nibbling canapés? (*Canapés*! I'm starving.) At the fabulously over-stated Gothic interior, all black, blood-red and gold leaf? At the towering pyramid displays of erection-enhancing creams, double-ended dildos and –

Hang on a minute. What the hell is going on here?

'Ant, this is a fucking *sex* shop,' I hiss, as a girl in a bustier so tight it's a miracle she can breathe, let alone walk, totters up to us with a tray of champagne flutes.

'Ten out of ten for observation,' he replies, grabbing two glasses.

'Why the fuck have you brought me here?'

'You might at least say thank you. Now you can put your jaunt down as research for your next book and write off the cost against tax.'

'You're supposed to be my friend, not my bloody accountant. This reminds me of Jake trying to drag me to that swingers' party.'

'Will you please relax? Sex is just sex. We all do it. You more than anybody shouldn't need me to tell you that.'

Ant always has an answer for everything. It's why I like him. And also why he sometimes annoys the hell out of me.

I do as I'm told and try to relax.

I sip my champagne and take a proper look around. If the restaurant was like stepping into *Hello!*, this is like walking into a copy of *Penthouse* – or a novel by Marsha Mellow. Fruit is four floors of sexuality – hetero-, homo-and every shade between. It may be a sex shop but it's

215

about as different from Ann Summers as Fortnum & Mason is from Kosmo's Korner Shop at the end of my road. It's as luxurious as any boutique I've ever seen. Even the mannequins are drop-dead gorgeous and the only way I can tell them from the guests is that the latter aren't wearing baby doll nighties or studded leather bondage gear – well, most of them aren't.

'There's supposed to be loads of movie stars here,' Ant says.

'I think I saw more than my fair share at the restaurant.'

'Not that sort, stoopid, *porn* movies. I read somewhere that there are now more porn stars than carpet fitters in the States and I think most of them will be here tonight.'

Now he mentions it, I think I can spot them. I've never knowingly been in the same room as a porn star, but they've got a look all of their own and you can see them a mile away. Or, rather, you can see their breasts, which arrive several seconds ahead of their owners. For the first time in my life I feel pathetically under-endowed.

Wonderful.

'Now I know why it's called Fruit,' I snigger. 'I haven't seen this many melons outside of Sainsbury's.'

'What is it about big tits?' Ant replies. 'They're just double-D entendres waiting to happen.'

We empty our glasses and grab a couple more. Then we steal a tray of canapés from a passing waitress. After devouring the lot, we head off to mooch around the ground floor. Nothing they're selling is *that* outrageous – nothing among the uniforms, leather and PVC, tapes and DVDs, sex toys and flimsy lingerie would have appeared out of place in *Rings*. There's the pink vibrator described on page 17 and, not far away, a nurse's outfit, complete with surgical gloves, much like the one that saw service in chapter eight. I give myself a pat on the back for having got it so right.

Ant drags me by the hand to the bras.

'This is *you*, Amy,' he squeals, picking up a hanger containing something black, lacy and unspeakably sexy. As he holds it up to my chest I'm accosted by a stunning six-footer whose lips are vying with her boobs for the Most Artificial Additives award.

'That is *sooo* horny, baby,' she drawls, fingering a bra cup. 'Your tits'll be arrested in it. Buy, buy, *buy*.'

She sashays off and I look at Ant whose jaw has hit the floor.

'I thought you'd got over all that straight nonsense,' I say.

'I have, but he's the *hottest* thing in gay cabaret,' he gasps.

'*He?*'

It must be to do with the time difference or something because I've been muddling up my genders ever since I got here.

'I'm buying you that bra,' Ant announces. 'Alex won't believe me when I tell him it's been *touched* by Maxxxi Mantis.'

He's virtually drooling with excitement and he needs another drink. We exchange our empty glasses for full ones, drain them and take a couple more – well, they're free and it would be churlish not to. Then we head for the escalator and the first floor. As we travel upwards, things grow darker, a warning that what we've just seen was merely an appetiser.

'It's like a record shop,' Ant says, as we pass beneath a sign that reads SOFTCORE IS FOR PUSSIES. 'They stick all the top forty crap and greatest hits CDs at the front of the store. If you're serious about music you have to delve a little deeper.'

For those who are serious about sex, then, delving deeper is probably exactly what they have in mind. For them, the first floor and beyond is paradise on earth. S&M, rubber and bondage freaks would feel right at home. If being lashed by a nail-studded whip while dangling from an elaborate harness and wearing a rubber face mask with no discernible air vents appeals, then head straight to Fruit. They have manacles, leg irons, replica NYPD handcuffs, and anti-chafe bondage rope by the yard. We come across enough gynaecological equipment to stock a Harley Street clinic and chastity belts (velvet-trimmed for enhanced comfort) in all sizes up to XXXL. And my favourite: a replica of Old Sparky ('As seen in *The Green Mile*'), a steal at only $2990. The assistant tells us the manufacturer has thoughtfully set the voltage to 'pleasantly stimulate' rather than 'fry, you murdering scumbag'.

But all that is merely the tip of the iceberg. Every fetish is catered for. Does being babied turn you on? Giant Pampers and kingsize wipes, aisle five. Is getting dirty your thing? Head for aisle three and the tubs of genuine Mississippi mud. Are you a balloon burster? Assorted packs just below the clockwork, guaranteed-retrievable Anal Hamsters (as used by Richard Ge— No, better not).

Here I am, 'the Annabel Chong of erotic fiction' (*Time Out*), and I'm gobsmacked.

And pissed.

'I can't *believe* this place,' I slur, as I drain my fifth or sixth or seventh drink. 'I don't know whether to throw up or take notes.'

'Well, they do draw a line,' Ant slurs back. 'I just asked where I could find a rubber bondage suit that would fit a Doberman and the snooty bastard said they didn't work with animals.'

I know it isn't *that* funny, but we giggle like when we

218

were six and Ant had scrawled *poo* on the blackboard. We draw sub-zero looks from some party-goers for whom sex is clearly no laughing matter.

'I think we'd better leave before they throw us out,' Ant says.

By the exit Ant stops by a bin full of small, luminous $6·99 vibrators. 'Souvenir for Lisa?' he asks.

'No, she can make do with the plastic Statue of Liberty I bought.'

I can't repeat what Ant says next.

'Thank you, Ant. I have had the *best* time,' I say in the cab. 'And you know what? I don't think anything will ever shock me again.'

'Really?' he replies. 'How about this? *I know he has never seen anything like it before and the thought spurs me on. I sit astride Deborah's back, riding her like a horse, and I reach for her dangling breasts. Then I grab her hair and yank her head back, before forcing her mouth down on Richard's co—*'

'What are you doing?' I sputter. I'm not the only one who's wondering. The Iranian taxi driver, who wasn't able to speak a word of English when we climbed in, has suddenly developed a working grasp and is craning his neck to hear.

'No, wait, this is the good bit,' says Ant, ignoring my protest. '*Before forcing her mouth down on Richard's cock. I stroke it as Deborah sucks, sensing that he's close. At the point of no return I pull her off him so that he splashes all over her —*'

'Stop it!'

'Listen to you. You wrote it, woman. Why are you so . . . What are you? Ashamed?'

Does he really have to ask?

'I just don't need to be reminded of it right now,' I say. 'Not while I'm having such a good time.'

'Well, call me a party pooper, but tomorrow it's back to reality.'

'You're a fucking party pooper. *God*, I don't want to go home.'

'Well, you don't have to yet. We're going to a club now.'

'The Seminary?' I squeak excitedly – I've been dying to see it.

'The only way you'd get in there is if you check your tits at the door. No, we're going to a place called En Why. It's supposed to be very happening – for a straight place, at least. Alex wants me to check it out.'

I'm not sure about this. I'm a pretty unclubby sort of person, but the idea of going back to the apartment and to bed only makes the thought of home seem even more terrifyingly imminent. I decide to go along with him.

'By the way,' I say. 'How come you know chunks of *Rings* by heart?'

'Oh, my memory was getting terrible – I kept forgetting appointments, my keys . . . my name. I bought an *Improve Your Memory* tape. It's amazing. Now I can recite chapters one to three of your novel and most of the As in the New York phone book. Still forget my fucking keys, though.'

Chapter 20

It has just gone five in the morning and I'm *soooo* happy. Couldn't possibly have anything to do with the fact that in a few short hours I have to fly back to England to face a firing squad made up of my mum, my blackmailer and the editor of the *Daily Mail*. No, it must be the Ecstasy.

I took Ecstasy!

E!

Drugs!

I have never taken a mind-altering substance in my life, apart from when Jake shoved that popper under my nose and then my consent didn't come into it. OK, I drink and smoke, but pills? Never. I get nervous popping an Anadin from its blister pack.

When we were at En Why my usual club phobia was creeping up on me despite the vodkas I was throwing down my neck. Ant spotted the symptoms and tried to drag me onto the dance floor, but I wouldn't budge. That's when he produced a little white tablet from his pocket.

'Try this,' he said.

'It's OK,' I said. 'I'm just a bit tired. I haven't got a headache.'

'It's X. Try it.'

'It's what?' I shouted above the music, which was, now I thought about it, giving me a headache.

'Ecstasy!' he yelled back.

'Fucking hell, Ant,' I yelped, jumping away from him

as if he was proffering a petri dish crawling with anthrax. 'Where did you get that?'

'It's a nightclub, Amy. Look around you. It isn't the booze that's making everyone act like loved-up loonies.'

I scanned the room and everyone did seem a bit mad. And *happy*.

'Go on,' he encouraged. 'It won't turn you into a slavering junkie.'

I thought what the hell; I'm going to die in a few hours anyway. Might as well go with an idiotic grin on my face. I took the pill from him and put it on my tongue. Then I swallowed and . . . Nothing happened. No dizziness, nausea, violent agonising convulsions, adrenalin rush or weird hallucinations where the club turned into the purple interior of an elephant's womb and the clubbers morphed into pixies and trolls or whatever it is that happens in weird hallucinations.

So I shrugged and went to the bar for some drinks. I'm a bit hazy on what happened immediately after that – did I actually get the drinks? The next thing I do remember is throwing myself around the dance floor, my boobs bouncing around my ears like Princess Leia's hair buns. I was being the *best* dancer *ever* in the history of movement to music. I didn't even need a body double for my most difficult moves, unlike that useless cow in *Flashdance*. Not bad when you consider I normally get self-conscious tapping my foot and I had a full-blown anxiety attack the last time I had to dance – reception class, Christmas show, 'I'm a Little Snowflake'. I was slamming my body about for hours and would still be going now if Ant hadn't finally dragged me outside.

'*Wow*,' I gasped, blinking in the first glow of daylight. 'Dawn in Manhattan. It's so . . . Like . . . *Luminous*.'

'That's not the sun, Amy. It's a fucking street lamp. I think I'd better get you home.'

We're in a taxi now. It stops outside a big red-brick building. I have no idea where we are, but I know this isn't Ant's place.

'Where are we?' I ask.

'The Seminary.'

'I won't have to leave my boobs anywhere, will I?'

'Don't worry. They'll be closing up. I think it's safe.'

'There's something depressing about a club when it's empty,' I say. 'It's the people that make a place . . . And the DJ. The DJ is *sooo* crucial to the vibe.'

'Listen to you,' Ant says laughing. 'One tab of Ecstasy and you've turned into Manumission's Most Wanted.'

We're in the main bit of the Seminary, the part that was the church when it used to be full of young men in black cassocks rather than black leather. There are no longer any pews or crucifixes. Just a big dance floor and gantries supporting high-tech lights and speakers.

'I see you kept some of the original features,' I say, looking at the huge stained-glass window that towers over the spot where the altar would have stood.

'No, we didn't. Look closely and you'll see that the Virgin Mary is Ru Paul and the dying Christ is Rock Hudson – the pope would have a shitfit if he saw it. Come on, let's get a drink before they pull the grilles down.'

We walk the length of the room to the long bar at the far end. A man is cleaning the counter. He is shaved bald and wearing a tight black vest, and I can make out the glint of steel in his eyebrow.

'That's Christ,' Ant says. 'Well, Chris for short. He used to be a fireman.'

'Really?'

He's got the muscles, but he doesn't look like my idea of a fireman.

223

'Yeah, he was there when the Twin Towers went down. Couldn't hack it after that.'

'My God,' I whisper. 'A real *hero*.'

'Ant, baby, what're you doing here? It's your night off?' Chris yells.

'This is my friend Amy from England,' Ant replies. 'I wanted to show her where I work.'

'Work? *Ha*! Where you *plaaaaay*, sweetheart.'

He couldn't be more camp if he were dressed as a scout and sitting in a tent. I wonder if he kept this side of himself repressed when he was in the fire department? As he takes my hand and kisses it I look at the nipple rings stretching at the Lycra in his vest and wonder if they're allowed for firemen. Hey, perhaps it's somewhere to clip their hosepipes.

'It's lucky you didn't bring her by a coupla hours ago,' he says to Ant. 'Those awful homo bikers were up from Long Island. They'd've eaten her alive. You wanna drink?'

'Water, please,' I gasp.

I'm starting to have a mild panic attack. I've heard horror stories about teenagers taking Ecstasy and their brains dehydrating, so they drink loads of water and explode . . . Or something. Can't remember, but I am *parched*.

The water comes and I gulp it down.

Feel better now.

'So,' I say tentatively to Chris, 'you were actually *there*?'

'Where's that, babe?'

'Seven/Eleven,' I add earnestly.

He looks at me blankly.

'I think she means *Nine*/Eleven,' Ant explains.

Chris bursts into screaming laughter as I feel myself shrivel up – embarrassment rather than dehydration.

'Jesus, I thought she was accusing me of sticking up a convenience store,' Chris shrieks through the laughter.

Then he pulls himself together and says, 'Anyway, Nine/Eleven. Whaddabout it?'

'Ant said you were part of the rescue effort.'

'I fucking *wish*. All those dirty fire jocks. No, I was in Miami then.'

'But weren't you in the fire department?'

'Honey, the only time I've been in a fire truck was when I was fifteen and a two-hundred-pound fireman was giving me a facial . . .'

I don't think he's talking about the Clinique three-step programme.

'What the fuck has Ant been telling you?'

I turn to my best friend, who is snorting into his sleeve. 'You fucking *bastard*,' I hiss.

'I'm sorry,' he says, 'but I've really missed having someone so gullible around.'

I'm about to kill him when the phone rings. Chris ambles down the bar and picks it up.

'The Seminary,' he breezes. Then after a moment: 'I'm sorry, honey, we're kinda closing up . . . Father *who*? . . . We had a coupla cardinals in at the weekend, but I don't think they'd want us bragging about it . . . Uh-huh, this is the Seminary . . . Look, I think you got the wrong number . . . Don't worry, babe, shit like that happens.'

He puts the phone down and says, 'Crazy bitch wanted a fucking *priest*. Some dude called Father An*th*ony.'

But he didn't need to explain because the penny was dropping as he put the phone down. My mum must have worked out how to use international directory inquiries. I look at Ant, who has turned white. He obviously got there when I did.

'Shit,' he says.

The phone rings again.

'Shit, shit, *shit*!'

'What are we gonna do?' I say in a rush.

225

'I'd better get it,' Ant says, clambering over the bar and grabbing the phone before Chris has a chance.

'Hello, the Seminary,' he trills, his jolly tone belying the blanched, panicked look on his face. 'Hi, Mrs Bickerstaff, Anthony here . . . Yes, I'm fine. You? . . . Really? . . . *Really* . . . Oh dear . . .'

Oh dear? *Oh* fucking *dear*? What the hell is going on at home? She must have found out. I must be in the *Mail*. I look at Ant for a sign that she knows, but he's too immersed in the role of padre to notice me.

'. . . As it says in Matthew two, verse eight, *He that lieth with the camel shall* . . . Er . . . *Shall never passeth through the eye of the needle* . . . Well, maybe if you talked to your local priest . . . I'd love to fly over, really I would, but I've got . . . Um . . . My Jesus studies paper to revise for . . .'

Jesus studies? Who's he trying to kid?

'. . . And I've got my first big communion coming up . . . Yes, we get marks for style . . . Wow, Mrs Bickerstaff, that's a bit of a shocker . . .'

Fuck, she knows.

'. . . It's a very tricky one to give advice on over the phone . . . You must be aware of the Catholic teaching on divorce . . .'

Divorce! She *doesn't* know about me, then. Hang on. *Divorce*?

'. . . And I suspect that most convents frown on applications from married women . . .'

OhmyGod, she wants to be a nun?

'. . . Perhaps if you gathered your family around you and sought strength from them . . . I know, I know, they're all so busy, but have you tried to – . . . Amy? . . .'

Fucking hell, don't drag me into this. I signal frantically to Ant to cut this short.

'. . . Funnily enough she's with me now . . .'

226

Aaaaagggggggggggghhhhhhhhhhhhhh!

'. . . Oh, she didn't tell you? Well, the stresses of London life were getting to her. She needed some space to get back in touch with her spirituality and we offer a retreat here . . . Yes, even for non-Catholics . . . Well, I could see if we could fit you in . . .'

No, no, no, no, *noooooooooooooo*!

'. . . Amy, yes . . . She arrived a day or two ago . . . I'm sure she'd love to talk to you . . . I think she's in the chapel taking a moment with God. Let me put you on hold while I find her.'

He rests the phone on the bar and looks at me helplessly.

'What the fuck are you playing at?' I hiss.

'I'm sorry. I didn't know what else to say. You heard me. She's on the verge of losing the fucking plot and the fact that she's convinced I'm a priest is making things worse rather than better.'

Chris, who has not unreasonably been hanging on every word, now looks especially intrigued.

'Why's she losing it? What the hell's happened?'

'I'll tell you later . . . But you'd better talk to her now.'

'I can't. What am I going to say?'

'Why don't you tell her the truth?'

'The truth? She can't *handle* the truth,' I scream, wondering why that line sounds familiar.

'Perhaps she can. And from what I can see, most of your family's problems come from you not telling each other anything.'

'Ant, this is not the time for family bloody therapy.'

'Talk to her, Amy,' he says, picking up the receiver and proffering it to me. 'Or would you prefer I tell her?'

I grab the phone from him.

'Hi . . . Mum,' I say nervously.

'Amy! What on earth are you doing in New York? I've

227

been trying to reach you for days. No one knew where you were. Your office said you had chickenpox. I've been going out of my mind with worry.'

'I'm sorry, but I had to get away.'

'Well, I need you here,' she says, gulping back the sobs as she speaks. '*Everything* is falling apart with your father.'

Lisa must have shown her the photos. *Bugger.*

'Have you seen Lisa?' I ask.

'That sister of yours. She never returns my calls . . .'

So she *hasn't* seen the photos.

'. . . Anyway, what could be so terrible in your life that you need to get away?' She asks in her condescending voice, the one she uses to suggest that nothing could possibly go seriously wrong in my little world, that the only crises worth having are hers. Maybe Ant's right. Maybe I should tell her – I'll show her what a bloody crisis is.

And if I strain really hard I can still feel a tiny tingle of euphoria, the remains of the super-charged self-confidence supplied by the E – not much, but maybe just enough to get me through this.

Right. I can do this. Here goes.

'Mum, there's something I need to tell you . . .'

I look at Ant, who's giving me encouraging nods.

'. . . I should have told you ages ago. You won't believe it, actually . . .'

Where have I heard this speech before? That Sunday lunch at mum's house. But this time *I mean business*.

'. . . It's absolutely amazing,' I continue.

Ant's nods turn into *Go, girl!* air punches, as seen on *Springer*.

'. . . And once you get used to the idea I know you'll be thrilled . . .'

I think I'm giving it too much of a build-up – it's the E talking. Got to get to the punchline.

'. . . It's Ant . . .'

Ant's eyebrows shoot up his forehead as if they're rocket propelled.

'. . . He's gay.'

Oh yes, that went *brilliantly*. Like a dream.

With those two little words all of Mum's old prejudices about Catholic priests resurfaced, shattering her dreams of joining a convent and spending her remaining days in godly contemplation. No, she didn't take it well.

At least Ant is off the hook. He'll no longer have to rack his brains for Gospel references as he dispenses spiritual guidance to the one and only member of his flock. In fact, he's unlikely ever to see my mother again and if he does it'll only be for the briefest moment before he's set upon by the vicious attack dog she'll doubtless buy to keep him away.

'I ordered you eggs, bacon, pancakes, hash browns, all coated with a litre of maple syrup. I don't know if it'll help, but it can't do any harm,' he says, sitting down at our table by the window – we're in the diner opposite the Seminary.

'This is just getting worse and worse, Ant,' I wail. 'In less than three hours I've got to climb on a plane and face all that . . . *shit*.'

'It's tough, Amy, but I know you can do it,' he says taking my hand. 'You'll tell her . . . If only because you're running out of other secrets to hit her with. Pretty soon all you'll have left is Marsha Mellow. Then when it's out and she knows, well, nothing else will matter. That little shit will have nothing to blackmail you with, the *Mail* can write what they like –'

'Ant, I *can't* tell her. You heard me on the phone. When it comes to the crunch I just can't go through with it.'

'Let me tell you something. It'll probably upset you, but in a funny sort of way it might make things easier. I shouldn't be telling you at all because . . . You know, my holy vows and all that . . .'

The confession. I'd forgotten about that one.

'. . . Your mum had an affair.'

I nearly fall off the bench. *That is so not possible.* Even less possible than the total impossibility of my Dad having an affair. My mum's views on extramarital sex are so entrenched that she seriously considered turning republican when Di spilled the beans on Charles and Camilla. I remember the scene vividly: Mum repeating 'An adulterer shall never sit on the throne of Great Britain' (conveniently forgetting that several generations of adulterers already had) as she packed up her entire collection of royal memorabilia. She made Dad stow the three tea chests of commemorative plates, mugs and Queen Mum bog roll holders in the furthest corner of the attic. The glass-fronted mahogany dresser in the dining room stood empty for over *three* years, a potent symbol of the catastrophic collapse in standards at the very top of the establishment.

'That just isn't possible,' I say as I recover my breath.

And it *isn't*. I remember how she came within a hair's breadth of resigning her beloved Tory party membership when the papers splurged on John Major's fling with Ed—

Jesus bloody Christ and all the sodding saints, have I just had a moment of clarity *or what*? Edwina *Currie*. The makeover. That weird Tory harlot look that Mum went for, which I could make neither head nor tail of at the time, but which I suspected might have been to seduce Dad back into the marital bed . . . But which was, in fact, because she was being a wanton *hussy*.

'I'm sorry I had to tell you,' Ant says, reading my mind.

'Who was it?'

'No one you know. A guy called Pat. He's a gardener.'

'A *gardener*?'

'Don't worry. She didn't slum it with the lower classes.

230

He's one of those poncy ones who trim a few shrubs, install a water feature and call themselves landscape *archi-tects*. She met him at the Chelsea Flower Show – it was love over the begonias.'

'Never mind all that. Is it still going on?'

'No. It was already over when she came and confessed. She was totally eaten up with guilt – so much so that she was desperate to believe that your dad was at it too.'

'Well, he was . . . *Is*.'

'Yeah, but she didn't know that for sure then, and she still doesn't. She's just been so desperate to justify her own fling. She took a lot of persuading that God was definitely the forgiving type and she wouldn't necessarily burn in hell . . . I think she only slept with the bloke once, if that makes it any better.'

Hardly. Because even if it was just the once, I now have to file the mental image of my mother and *Pat* writhing around in the hardy perennials alongside the picture of my father getting a blowjob in a car park from *Sandra* the catering professional. *Fuck*, what is it with those two? Have they no bloody shame at all? They have no business having sex with each other, never mind anyone else.

'Fucking hell, Ant, I don't know how you can say this makes my situation easier,' I say as the full sordid truth about the Fabulous Bonking Bickerstaffs sinks in.

'Of course it does. Think about it. First off, your mum isn't the prim saint you've always thought she was. I mean, she *cheated* on your dad. Whatever you've done, you've never cheated on anyone. And secondly, if she's got any conscience at all, it'll make it much harder for her to condemn you for your book.'

Ant may well have a point, but I can't see it. I can't see anything for the squirming, sweaty heap of copulat-ing, fifty-something *parents*.

A tap on the window beside me lifts me out of my

mire. It's Chris. We left him at the club, his jaw still slack from the revelations he'd been party to. He's clearly ready for an encore. He bounds into the diner and slides onto the bench beside me.

'Father An*th*ony,' he breathes huskily, 'it's been six months since my last confession and, *Jesus*, have I been a sinning little *mutha*.'

'Any more of that and you're fired,' Ant snaps. I think he means it.

'Oh, don't be a spoilsport. Gimme six Hail Marys and spank my ass.'

'Please, Chris, this isn't a good moment,' Ant says.

'You two – *un*believable,' Chris continues, ignoring the gloom. 'I'd have to watch daytime TV for weeks to get the juice I got from you guys this morning.' He looks at our miserable faces and adds, 'And I bet there's even *more* where *that* came from.'

'Why don't you tell him, Amy?'

'Excuse me?' I splutter.

'Well, it'll be good practice for when you face your mum. Besides, I hardly think a queen like Chris is likely to bump into her at a Conservative Club bring-and-buy sale.'

He's right.

I turn to Chris and announce, 'I'm Marsha Mellow.'

'Ged*doutta* here!' he screams. Then: 'Who the fuck is she?'

'You *gotta* put me in your next book, baby,' Chris pleads when I've finished. '*Please* . . . I don't mind fucking some chicks, honest.'

'There won't be a next book if I can't tell my mum,' I mutter.

'Moms. Aren't they the worst?' Chris says. 'Actually, mine wasn't that bad. When I told her I was queer she said, "Go make me proud, son, 'cause only a real *man* can take a full *fist* up the ass."'

'She did not say that,' Ant says in disbelief.

'You're right. She didn't. But she didn't kill me either.'

'Good for you. Mine will bloody murder me.'

Visibly frustrated, Ant turns to me and says, 'Amy, I accept that statistically you're most likely to be murdered by a member of your own family. Even so, do you honestly believe that a woman as obsessed with stains as your mother would risk getting blood on her soft furnishings by slaughtering you?'

I don't reply . . . because, actually, I think she *would*.

'I've had an idea,' he says, suddenly excited.

What? I change my name and stay here, marrying an American so I can get my green card? Excellent plan! Where do I sign?

'Why don't I come back with you?'

Oh.

'Would you do that?' I whimper.

'Well, Alex will be fucking pissed when we pass in the doorway, but like I said last night, you and me have got twenty years on me and him. Let's go pack.'

Chapter 21

'We are cruising at an altitude of thirty-six thousand feet and we estimate that our flight time will be a little over six hours, so we'll arrive in hell slightly ahead of schedule. The weather there is blisteringly hot, so let's hope you all remembered to pack your sun block –'

'Hot towel, madam?' asks the flight attendant, rousing me from my half-sleep.

I take it from her and as I rub my face Ant turns to me and says, 'It'll be OK, you know. I promise.'

'Hey,' I say, experiencing a sudden surge of optimism, 'what if Colin Mount had a heart attack and died? I mean, he looks the sort to have dangerously high cholesterol. And what if the papers just get bored? They always do eventually and something else is bound to happen to make them forget about me. Posh and Becks might change their wallpaper next week – that should do it. Maybe I'll never have to tell Mum.'

'Go to sleep, Amy,' he says, pulling down his complimentary eye mask. 'You'll need your strength when we get there.'

Chapter 22

It's after midnight when I push open the door of my flat and hear the steady *beep-beep-beep* of my answering machine.

'I'll listen to it in the morning. I need to go to bed now,' I say.

But Ant is in no mood for denial. He dumps his bag by the machine and presses 'play'.

'You. Have. Eighteen. New. Messages . . .'

Beep.

'Amy, it's me. Where are you? Have you seen the picture of Mary in the *Mail*? You never told me she was *that* fat. Anyway, I have *got* to talk to you about Dan . . .'

Dan? . . . Oh, the boyfriend. Nerdy Tory. Forgotten about him.

'. . . Nightmare. And Dad. *Double* nightmare. Ring me.'

Beep.

'Amy, pardon the wolf whistles in the background, but I'm ringing from a call box by a building site – counter-surveillance measure, darling. Well, my dear, I've always wanted to see my ugly mug on the front page so I can hardly complain. Call me and we'll discuss next steps. The bastards are increasing the pressure.'

Beep.

'Hi, sis. Me again. *Desperate* to talk to you. Some snotty cow at your office said you had chickenpox. Please tell me it's a lie and you're bunking off. Bye.'

Beep.

'Hullo, Amy, it's Lewis here . . .'

Aaagghh! I feel my face heating up at the memory.

'. . . Um . . . Lewis at the office. Deedee tells me you've got chickenpox . . . But I suspect that maybe it isn't. I was . . . er . . . *concerned* when you ran off last –'

I cut him off by pressing '*delete*'. Can't deal with Lewis now . . . *Ever*, come to think of it.

Beep.

'Amy . . . Jake here. Hoping you might have cooled down enough to talk to me . . . You know . . . About our *misunderstanding* at the hotel –'

Misunder-bloody-*standing*? I may have been drunk and daft that night, but at which point did I say, 'You know, Jake, ever since we split up all I've dreamt about is walking out of a hotel bathroom and discovering you've hired us a hooker'?

Delete, delete, *delete*.

Beep.

'Amy, it's Julie. The witch told me you've got the pox. Poor thing. I was going to wear my nurse's uniform for Alan tonight but do you want me to come round and look after you instead? *Brilliant* time last night. Why did you disappear so early? Bye.'

Beep.

'Is that you or the blasted machine? . . . I detest these things. It's your mother, by the way . . .'

(Like I couldn't guess.)

'. . . I called you at work and they said you have chickenpox. I don't see how that's possible because you caught it when you were seven – you were sick as a kitten. Have you seen a doctor? As if I haven't enough to worry about. Wrap up, stay in bed and if it *is* chickenpox – *which I doubt* – *don't* scratch the spots. Do you want me to pop by with some soup? . . . On second thoughts I will stop

236

by because I desperately need to talk to you . . . It's your
. . . *father* . . . I've made a decision.'

Beep.

'Amy Bickerstaff, please tell me you are not hiding
under your bedcovers. Why in God's name did you not
tell me – your *agent* in case you were forgetting – that
you're being blackmailed? Yes, I've had a call from the
nasty little toe-rag. I'm meeting him in an hour to deal
with it. The things I bloody do for my fifteen per cent.
Just get in touch, will you?'

Beep.

'It's your mother again. I forgot to mention, *stop smoking*. Vile habit and I'm sure it does no good with the
chickenpox or whatever dreadful disease you've got.
Anyway, can't hang about talking to a machine all day.
I'm going to church now to light some candles for us all.'

Beep.

'Amy, is that your voice? . . . It's your dad . . .'

My *dad*? He hasn't phoned me *once* in twenty-five
years.

'. . . There's someone I want you to meet. It's quite
important. She's a lady I've been – Can't talk now. Your
mother's lurking. All a bit hush-hush. Call me when you
get a tick.'

Unbelievable. He wants me to meet his sodding –

Beep.

'Amy, it's Mary. I'm ringing from a call box in Piccadilly
station. Crawling with Jap tourists so I hope you can hear
me. Anyway, the good news first. I've handled the – Excuse
me, young man, I am using this phone. Bog off, will you?
. . . Now where was I? Oh yes, the *problem*. I've handled
him. Temporarily at least . . . Now, brace yourself for the
bad news. Tomorrow's *Mail* is running a story that
Marsha Mellow lives in north London. God knows where
they got that. I know for a fact that your smelly black-

237

mailer hasn't been blabbing to them and not even Jacobson knows where you live. Anyway, the good bit is that they don't have a name. They're determined to run the story, though. Trying to flush you out, I suppose. You must get –'

Beep.

'Bloody answering machines never give you enough time. I was about to say you *must* get in touch pronto because I suspect things are about to blow. *Call me*.'

Beep.

'Hello. This is David Dawkins from Dunston and Dawkins Family Funeral Service . . .'

Excuse me? Wrong number . . . I *hope*.

'. . . My apologies for pestering you at this *difficult* time, but there are some questions I have regarding the arrangements for your great-aunt's –'

Phew. Don't have one of those. 'Delete'. Too bloody surreal.

Beep.

'Aaaaagggggghhhhh! Have you seen the *Mail*? How the fuck did they find out where you live? No bloody wonder you're hiding. Mum'll go crazy bastard apeshit when she reads it. She always thought Crouch End was a bit suspect. Call me. *Soon*.'

Beep.

'And I still need to talk to you about Dad and Dan . . .'

Dan? Oh yeah, boyfriend.

Beep.

'Fuck, Amy, what's going on? I just phoned home and it's all going loopy-loo round there. Talked to Dad. He said Mum wasn't home but I could hear plates smashing. Have you told them about the book? And what's this about Ant being a paedophile priest? Fucking *call* me. I'm scared.'

Beep.

238

'Hello . . . David Dawkins again. My apologies, but I neglected to point out that the casket in the de Vere Millennium Eternity Deluxe package is made from selected teak grown in sustainable forests and the –'

Go *away*!

Beep.

'Amy, it's your father here . . .'

Again?

'. . . Now, try not to be too alarmed but . . . your mother has been arrested.'

Chapter 23

'Where is she, Lisa?' I ask.

'Still in the nick. Dad's down there trying to bail her out. Amy, where the *hell* have you been?'

'New York,' I reply. 'I got back half an hour ago.'

'What, you went there with chickenpox?'

'No, of course not.'

'You were bunking off? In New York? Did you see Ant?'

'He's here. He's just paying the minicab.'

'I think you'd better tell him to get the fuck back to America before mum comes home. I don't think she's very happy with him.'

At which point Ant walks into my mum's and dad's sitting room.

'So what's she done?' he asks breezily. 'Forgotten to pay for her TV licence?'

'I wish,' Lisa says. 'She was caught spraying graffiti on the door of Our Lady of Finchley.'

'Fucking hell,' I gasp. 'What was she writing?'

'*Burn in hell homo pree.*'

'What's that supposed to mean?'

'I think she was going to write *priests*, but the cops nabbed her before she'd finished . . . You two had better tell me what the hell's going on, because Dad and I can't make any sense of it.'

We tell her about Mum's phone call to the Seminary.

'Jesus, Amy, if you'd shown some guts at that Sunday lunch and told her the truth then, none of this might've happened,' Lisa spits angrily.

'No, Lisa, if I'd told her the truth I'd be dead now and you'd be waiting for the murder trial to start. I mean, look how she reacts when she finds out a little thing like a friend of mine happens to be gay.'

'A *little* thing? He also *happens* to be her personal bloody vicar thanks to you and your stupid bullshit.'

'Lisa, this isn't helping matters,' Ant says gently, trying to calm things down.

'Oh, fuck off, Ant,' Lisa screams. 'You're as bad as she is. Why the hell did you go along with the daft cow?'

'Hang on a bloody minute, Lisa,' I yell. 'Why the hell did *I* go along with *you*? If you'd never sent my book off in the first place –'

'You know what?' Lisa says, cutting me off. 'I don't care any more. I've had enough of this loony family. You two can sort out this mess.'

She spins around and flies from the room. Seconds later we hear the front door slam. We're on our own.

'That got things off to a good start,' Ant says. 'Now, how about I make us a nice cup of tea?'

I don't respond. I've spotted yesterday's *Mail* on the coffee table: 'QUEEN OF PORN TRACED TO LONDON SUBURB'. I pick it up and skim the story. As Mary's message assured me, they don't have my name, but they've got a description. I am, apparently, 'an unassuming, brown-haired woman in her mid-twenties' who lives in 'Crouch End, an otherwise respectable north London suburb'.

'They've got a bloody cheek, calling you unassuming,' Ant says as he reads over my shoulder.

I can't speak, because I'm experiencing an entirely new sensation. The Riverdancers, who took some well-earned time off while I went to New York, have returned. They're kicking back into action in my gut, but this time they're experiencing bad acid trips and they've replaced their tap shoes with running spikes.

'Where the fuck did they get this from?' I manage to gasp.

'Search me, Amy. What about your agent? Or Lisa? She seems pretty mad with you at the moment.'

I shake my head.

'Must be your blackmailer, then.'

'Mary said she'd taken care of him. And even if she hadn't, wouldn't he have gone to the paper with more than a physical description?'

'Your publisher?' Ant suggests.

'He doesn't even know my name, let alone where I live.'

I rack my brain to remember every word I said to him when we met. Maybe I let something slip. I come up with nothing, though.

'He wouldn't have done it. Why would he risk blowing his deal with you by giving you up?' Ant says. Then he puts his arm round me and hugs me because, of course, I'm crying.

'Can we go back to New York?' I blub.

I'm being serious. I don't care how many guns, random shootings and drive-by crack dens there are, I felt a damn sight safer over there.

'You can't run away any more,' Ant says softly.

And he's right. I can't. But only because I can hear the front door opening. Dad must be home with the prisoner.

'*Shit*, Ant, you shouldn't be here,' I hiss.

Neither of us moves, though. We're both rooted to the spot, glued in an embrace on the Axminster. Oh well, I suppose there must be worse ways to die than in the arms of your best friend.

The sitting room door opens.

But it's only Lisa and she doesn't look mad any longer.

'Sorry,' she says. 'I shouldn't have lost it.'

'It's OK,' I reply. 'Neither should I.'

I peel myself away from Ant and hug my baby sister.

'Dad just called me on my mobile,' she says. 'He's coming home.'

'You'd better go, Ant,' I say.

'No, we should be safe for now. He's on his own,' Lisa explains. 'They're keeping Mum in overnight . . . Apparently she put her handbag through a window in the police station. The desk sergeant needed three stitches.'

My mum, a martyr for the cause of decent family values, spending the night in a police cell with a bunch of drunks and joyriders. This just gets better and better.

'How about a nice cup of tea?' exclaims Ant.

He heads for the kitchen while Lisa and I sit down to wait. I should probably tell her now about Mum's little romp with Pat the gardener. She should know all the facts, shouldn't she? But I can't. Hasn't she got enough on her plate? More to the point, haven't I?

'We've got to have it out with Dad about Miss Strappy Heels, you know,' she says.

'Yes, but not tonight.'

'You're right. Let's try and sort out things with Mum first,' she agrees. 'We won't do Dad tonight . . . Definitely not.'

'Don't you think you owe us an explanation, Dad?' Lisa demands.

'How did you get these?' he asks as he looks at the spread of photos on the coffee table.

His face is a deathly white. It was pretty pallid when he arrived back from the police station, but now it has somehow managed to bleach even whiter and deathlier. I know he's a cheating bastard and all that, but I can't help feeling sorry for him. He must be going through exactly what I did when Colin Mount called me up with his black-mail threat.

Lisa's resolve to delay confronting him with Miss Strappy Heels lasted . . . Ooh, all of ten minutes. She snapped when Dad, who was understandably pretty frazzled by the day's events, turned on Ant and me and accused us of manufacturing Mum's breakdown. Lisa decided he shouldn't be allowed to forget his part in it and came to our rescue like Lara Croft in Versace. Ant made a strategic withdrawal at that point – he felt that more tea would definitely help the situation.

'Never mind how we got the pictures, Dad,' Lisa says now. 'What do you think you're playing at?'

'I was meeting her,' he mumbles quietly, seemingly at a loss for what else to say.

'That much is obvious. And don't try and tell us she's just some *work colleague*. We know *exactly* who she is. Sandra Phillips. *Sand* to her mates. She lives in Wood Green and she likes Southern Comfort and –'

'How on earth do you know all this?' Dad says, his eyes widening. 'Not even I know this much about her and I've been seeing her for weeks.'

'So you admit it, then,' Lisa says triumphantly as if she's cross-examining a key witness in the Old Bailey. 'Well, just in case you were curious for Valentine's, she's a thirty-four B.'

'Thirty-four what? And *what* am I supposed to be admitting to?' Dad splutters, though I think he's overdoing the confusion. We've pretty much got him bang to rights here. 'And how the hell did you get these pictures?' he goes on, indignant now. 'You've been spying on me . . .'

Well, *duh*.

'. . . My own children *spying* on me. Has this entire family gone stark raving mad?'

244

Oh, like, double *duh*.

'I don't know how you dare accuse us of anything, Dad,' I say – I've been silent until now, but his mock innocence is getting on my nerves. 'You're the one with the mistress.'

'Mistress? *Mistress*! . . .' His wide, scared eyes dart from Lisa to me and back again. '. . . She's not my bloody mistress. She's a caterer. A party planner for heaven's sake.'

'Yes, we know that, but what are you doing with a party planner?'

'I'm planning a bloody party, that's bloody what,' he explodes, a purple vein popping abruptly to throbbing life on his temple.

I have never seen that vein before. But then I have never seen my dad explode and I'm scared. I'm also beginning to get a faint, tingling sense that maybe, just maybe, we've got the wrong end of the stick.

'It's your mother's sixtieth next month in case you'd forgotten,' he continues at a bellow. 'I've never made much fuss of the poor woman and I thought I'd remedy things by planning a bloody party for her, if that's all right with you.'

'It looks like you're having a party of your own right there in the sodding car park, Dad,' Lisa shouts, not buying a word of his defence.

'What are you on about?'

'Look,' she says pointing accusingly at exhibit A, the picture showing him sitting on the van and Miss Strappy Heels on her knees. I'd forgotten about that one. *Bugger*. We got it right after all.

'What the hell am I supposed to be looking at?' Dad says, barely lowering the volume.

'Please, Dad, don't deny it,' I say, trying my best to sound soothing. 'It's pretty obvious what's going on.'

'I'm afraid it is not, young lady.'

'Come on, Dad,' shrieks Lisa, losing whatever reserves of cool she had left. 'She's giving you a sodding blowjob.'

Did I say that Dad exploded a moment ago? Well, that wasn't exploding. *This* is exploding: him snatching the photograph from the table, leaping to his feet and waving it angrily two inches beneath Lisa's nose.

'Look at this picture, would you? See this? See this lump here? The bulbous thingy?' he yells, jabbing his finger at . . .

My God, what lumpy bulbous *thingy* is he jabbing his finger at?

'It's a bloody *helium* bottle,' he continues. 'For the bloody balloons. For the bloody party. The joyous bloody celebration I was planning for my lunatic *bloody* family. The girl is on her knees showing me how to shut off the bloody valve.'

He throws the picture back on the coffee table and though I've recoiled against the wall I manage to steal a glance at it. Unmistakably there is a thingy – and it's far too lumpy and bulbous to be anything my dad or any other bloke could comfortably fit between his legs. Lisa must be reaching the same conclusion because she has slipped into a numb silence.

Dad paces across the floor, angrily running his fingers through the few remaining strips of hair that cover his scalp – a lot less than there was yesterday morning, I should imagine.

'Dad,' I say in a virtual whisper, 'we are so sorry . . . Aren't we, Lisa?'

'Jesus Christ,' he rages, ignoring my weedy little peace bid, 'why am I bothering to explain anything to you two . . . You two . . .'

Meddling kids?

Stupid prats?

Complete and utter morons?

'. . . You two fucking *idiots*?'

OhmyGod, total fucking shock. My father knows the fucking F-word.

'Look at the damage you've caused,' he continues, suddenly calmer. 'Your mother is in a police cell now. Nearly sixty years on the planet and what does she have to show for it? Two daughters who drive her to the brink of a nervous breakdown. And what about me? Frankly, I don't think I'm that far behind her.'

He looks at us for a response, but I for one have no idea what to say even though I don't think he's being entirely fair – I mean, it wasn't me who whipped out a spray can and attacked a church with it.

'I think you'd better leave,' he states flatly.

Lisa and I look at each other, both of us at a loss what to do.

'I said *go* . . .'

Ant appears at the door with a tray of tea and digestives.

'. . . And take the bloody homosexual *priest* with you!'

Chapter 24

'You have no idea how long I've wanted to do this,' Lewis whispers as he pushes up my top and touches my breast for the first time.

And you have no idea how long I've wanted you to, I think. My hand is resting on his leg and I inch it up his thigh until I reach his –

Not an Amy daydream.

It's actually happening.

How the hell did I get from a starring role in Finchley's most dysfunctional family to a bed scene with Lewis in less than twelve hours? *Un*believable. In fact, I do not believe it. It *must* be a daydream.

But it isn't.

It is actually happening.

I should explain. Rewind to . . .

2.02 a.m.: Lisa, Ant and I tip out of Mum's and Dad's house dragging our shame behind us. I try to persuade Lisa to come back to mine so we can wallow in misery together, but she *wants to be alone*. Bloody drama queen.

In the cab back to Crouch End I ask Ant if, despite the chaos and hysteria he has just witnessed, he still thinks I should tell my parents about Marsha Mellow.

'Abso-fucking-lutely, darling,' comes his unhesitating

reply. 'It's the lies that have dug you into this hole. You've got to put an end to it.'

Which is definitely the truest thing I've ever heard at gone two in the morning.

And the most depressing.

3.15 am: I can't sleep, so I force Ant to join me in sharing the only alcohol I can find in my flat – we were too stressed on the flight home to remember duty frees. I dig out two bottles of vile, lukewarm white wine. It doesn't help. I ask Ant if he thought to smuggle over any of that Ecstasy up his bum. He didn't. *Damn*.

3.33 am: the wine is beginning, at last, to numb me. As I slump into the sofa my mind drifts off . . . I picture a shop doorway on a cold, wet London street. There's a dirty, ripped sleeping bag with me inside it. I'm clutching a can of Tennents Super . . . *Hmm*, now there's a possibility.

4.10 am: back in bed. Still no sleep – too agitated. I nudge Ant: 'I'm phoning Mary.'

'Fuck, Amy, I was almost asleep then . . . You can't phone her now.'

'She calls me in the middle of the night all the time,' I say.

'Really?'

'She once rang at half past three to tell me there was a hanging participle on page sixty-seven of *Rings*.'

'A hanging *what*?'

'I have no idea, but apparently I'd written one. I'm calling her.'

'Just keep the noise down,' he says as I head for the front room.

She picks up on the third ring.

'It's gone four,' she mumbles, 'which means that could

only be you, Amy, or the police to tell me they've found your body.'

'It's me,' I say.

'Thank *God*. Where the hell have you been, girl?'

'I was in New York.'

'A word of advice for the future, my dear,' she lectures, suddenly wide a-bloody-wake. 'Holidays are best taken when things are a bit slack, not when the proverbial is hitting the whatsit by the metric bloody ton. Now, answer me this: why in all of our conversations did you not mention a certain blackmailer?'

God, is she *cross*?

'Sorry,' I mutter, 'I just . . . kind of . . . panicked.'

'Well, what do you think I'm here for? Mental note, darling: next time you panic, do it in the general direction of me, please. I'm a size-eighteen so you really can't miss me. Anyway, you'll be relieved to know he's been dealt with. For the time being.'

'Thank you, Mary . . . How did you manage it?'

'Animal cunning and an old-fashioned dangled carrot.'

'You paid him off?'

'Not as such. I met up with him and – crikey, where on earth did you come across him? He's positively unsanitary. Anyway, it didn't take me long to ascertain he knew pretty much everything about you short of your blood type. Obviously my first thought was to say sod the smelly oik and let him blow your cover, but I wasn't about to do that without your approval, so I –'

'Thank you, Mary, *thank* you.'

'Please let me finish. I'd like to get back to sleep. I switched to plan B. I told him that you'd gone away into secluded hiding, but that I'd spoken to you at length and that you'd agreed to grant him an exclusive interview and pictures –'

'*Mary!*'

'*Let me finish*. Material that would then be his to flog to the highest bidder. I knew this would appeal to him – rather than grub around as a seedy little extortionist, he'd become famous as well as rich. Anyway, to cut a long story short because I really am very, very tired, I jotted down an address and off he trotted with his notepad and Pentax. Flights are sporadic, but he should be in Malawi by now.'

'Where?'

'Darkest Africa. I have a cousin out there so I'm vaguely familiar with the terrain. Not to put too fine a point on it, it's a ruddy hellhole. Public transport is virtually non-existent, the telecommunications system amounts to two cans and a length of string and you can get arrested for picking your nose. Suffice it to say he might be some time.'

'He fell for it?'

'I have to tell you that he is spectacularly stupid, my dear. I really don't know where you found him. There is a small downside. He insisted I cover his ticket and expenses. Don't worry, I'll deduct it from your next royalty cheque. The way sales are going I suspect it'll barely make a dent.'

'I can't thank you enough.'

'Later. Now, if you don't mind I really would like to get some slee—'

'Mary, what happens when he comes back?'

'By then, precious, his knowledge will be worthless.'

'I'm not with you.'

'By then you will have told your mother and once she knows it surely doesn't matter who else does. Am I making myself perfectly clear?'

'But I'm still not sure if I'm –'

'*Enough*! Good night.'

Click.

*

4.54 am: the phone rings.

'For fuck's sake, Amy, what is it with this place?' Ant groans before burrowing his head beneath his pillow.

I climb out of bed to answer it.

'One thing I neglected to mention, my dear, and it happens to be quite pressing,' Mary announces without waiting for my hello. 'Jacobson grew quite twitchy while you were AWOL. He withdrew his final offer –'

'You're kidding.'

'– and replaced it with another one. So when your mother is beating you to a pulp comfort yourself with the fact that eight hundred and fifty grand should cover the reconstructive surgery. Anyway, he'd like an answer pronto. I think his patience is close to threadbare.'

'You know what he can do with his stinking money, Mary?' I say. 'He can shove it up his sleazy arse.'

At the mention of Jacobson's name, I had a blinding flashback to our meeting: him casually asking me if I came from London; me nodding moronically and almost spewing out the words '*Crouch*' and '*End*' before Mary kicked me sharply on the shin. That plus my physical description are the only things he has on me and, curiously, they were also the only facts that appeared in the *Mail*.

The *bastard*.

At this moment I really don't care whether I ever have another book published, but I'm certain that if I do, it won't have Smith Jacobson printed on the spine.

5.07 am: finally go to sleep dreaming, bizarrely, of Jacobson being clubbed to death by a baby seal.

8.51 am: wake up. My head is pounding and my mouth tastes like a bidet that has been giving some socks an overnight soak. I am feeling *rough*. Last night I drank barely a bottle of cheapo wine and now I've got the hang-over from hell. So un*fair*. I mean, the cheaper the booze, the worse the headache. Where's the justice in that? It should be the rich twits drinking priceless vintage champagne that get the killer hangovers, not the poor working class. OK, I'm not poor, but I'm still working class . . . Well, I *work*, OK? I'm feeling bitter this morning. Must be the fact that I've just remembered turning down Jacobson's eight hundred and something grand.

I leave Ant snoring in bed and stagger into the kitchen. I switch on the kettle, throw some instant into a mug and open the fridge. No milk.

Fuck, why is life so *shit*?

I've turned down the chance to be a nearly-millionaire, a national newspaper is calling me the Queen of bloody Porn and *they know where I live*, my mum's in jail, my dad hates me (and he hasn't even heard the worst of it) and now there's NO BASTARD MILK.

9.25 a.m.: sitting on my sofa trying to drink black coffee. I *hate* black coffee. Ant appears in the bedroom door. 'Not dressed?' he says.

Very bloody observant.

'I take it you're not going to work today, then,' he adds.

Work. *Jesus*. Forget I'm still working class. I don't want to think about it now. I don't want to think about Deedee or Julie and her bloody wedding bells or Lewis . . . God, *Lewis*.

Lately I've become rather good at making a prize prat of myself, but the occasion that makes me burn with embarrassment more than any other, the one that takes the Supreme Champion Prat trophy was definitely that night in the bar with Lewis. Just how many bloody times can a girl ram her foot into her mouth in a single evening?

And if I'd been wearing a sandwich board emblazoned with CERTIFIABLE NUTTER – KEEP WELL CLEAR he wouldn't have got the message more strongly. What must he be thinking?

Of course, in the grand scheme of things, in the context of my problems at nine thirty on this rotten, stinking Wednesday morning *What Lewis Thinks* really shouldn't matter. But it does. Because I still. Fancy. The pants off him.

'No, Ant, I'm not going to work today,' I say.

'Well, shouldn't you call in if you don't want unemployment added to your list of problems?'

'Good idea,' I say. 'I'll give them a call . . . I'm handing in my notice.'

'*Yikes*. It's new, improved Decisive Amy, now with added Assertiveness.'

'Ha-bloody-ha.'

'So, you're going to be a full-time author?'

'I doubt it.'

I tell him about turning down Jacobson's offer.

'Oh,' is all he says. Doesn't anything surprise him any more?

'You must think I'm an idiot,' I say.

'No, actually. I think it was the right thing to do.'

'Really?'

'Who'd want to be with someone they couldn't trust?' he says, speaking with experience (of being the one that can't be trusted). 'Anyway, you're a number one bestseller now. There must be loads of publishers out there who want to get their hands on you.'

Wow, I really am a number one bestseller. I have a sudden vision. I'm sitting at a table in a giant bookshop. In front of me is a huge stack of Marsha Mellows. A queue of eager fans stretches out of the shop. And round the block. And past several other blocks until it reaches some towering prison walls. Into which is set a small barred window. And through which stares my sad-eyed, hollow-cheeked mother.

'I can't think about publishers now, Ant,' I say as tears well up. 'I can't think about anything. My mum's in prison.'

'Call your dad. Find out what's happening.'

'I can't. He hates me.'

'Of course he doesn't. Call him. He'll have calmed down by now.'

'I'll call him,' says new, improved Decisive Amy. 'Later . . . I'll call work first.'

I pick up the phone and dial.

'Deedee Harris, please,' I say when the switchboard picks up.

As her line rings I *pray* for her voicemail – I *know* I can resign to a tape recorder.

'Hello, *Working Girl*, Deedee speaking.'

Bugger. That's twice in less than a week that she's condescended to answer her phone.

'Hi, Deedee, it's Amy.'

'Amy, how are the spots? . . .'

Spots? Oh, the chickenpox.

'. . . I hope you've not been scratching. The scarring can be frightful.'

'They're fine – clearing up really well, actually.'

'So when will you be in?'

'That's just it, Deedee, I'm not coming back.'

'Oh . . . Oh dear . . .'

Like she really gives a stuff.

'. . . What's happened?'

Damn. I knew I should have prepared myself for this question.

'It's . . . Um . . . I've . . . Er . . .' Oh, sod it. I might as well tell her the truth. It's not as if I have to see any of

255

them again, is it? 'It's my mum, Deedee. She's been arrested.'

'My God, what for?'

'Oh . . . It's very complicated . . . I don't even understand it myself . . . It's an insider trading sort of thing.'

Ant snorts coffee out of his nose. But when I decided to tell her the truth I didn't mean the *whole* truth. I can't possibly tell her that my mum is in prison for spraying homophobic graffiti on a church door, can I? That would just sound *insane*.

'Blimey, Amy, you poor thing,' Deedee says, managing to sound genuinely concerned for once. 'I entirely understand you wanting to leave. You need to be there for her. My God, what a shock for you, and while you're down with chickenpox . . . Look, don't worry about a thing here . . .'

Bloody hell, she's sounding like a truly caring human being now and it's making me feel guilty.

'. . . I'll sort things out with accounts and make sure they pay you till the end of the month . . .'

Really guilty.

'. . . and give you any holiday money that's owing. And don't worry about Lewis. I'll clear things with him. *Hey*, I've just had a brainwave. He knows loads of lawyers. Maybe he could help. Why don't you talk to –'

'It's OK, really, Deedee,' I gabble, 'but thank you. *Thank* you. Look, gotta go. I think the police are here.'

And I can't put the phone down fast enough.

Ant is doubled up on the floor having seizures.

'Insider trading,' he says through the giggles. 'That alone was worth the air fare back here. Well, I'm really glad you decided to take my advice and put an end to the lies.'

'Ha-*bloody*-ha. I'm going for a bath. Why don't you make yourself useful and buy some milk?'

*

10.12 a.m.: I wonder how wrinkly my skin would go if I stayed in the bath for ever? I wonder if I could drown myself by pushing my head under the water, maybe weighing it down with something heavy? . . . The lid of the toilet cistern? That might do it.

There's a tap on the door.

'I've made you a coffee,' Ant says. 'With milk.'

Milk! Maybe things are looking up. My hangover is fading, I can tick work off my list of nightmares and now I've got a milky coffee. Yes, *definitely* looking up. Only the minor matters of my mum, dad and a porny novel left to deal with.

I haul myself out of the water and wrap myself in my dressing gown. As I arrive in the front room the phone rings.

'You get it, Ant,' I hiss.

He picks it up.

'Hello . . . Yes . . . Yes, she's here,' he says despite the fact that I'm frantically shaking my head to the contrary. 'I'll just get her.'

He cups his hand over the mouthpiece and whispers, 'It's Lewis.'

'I can't speak to him.'

'Well, he really wants to talk to you . . . And I really want to hear this,' he says thrusting the phone towards me.

'You bastard,' I mouth, taking it from him.

'Amy, is that you?' Lewis asks.

Shit, I can feel my face reddening and he's only said four words.

'Hi, Lewis,' I say.

'Is it a bad time? Are the police still there? Was that one who picked up the phone?'

'No, they've . . . Um . . . Gone. That was just a *friend*,' I say, adding a glare in Ant's direction.

'Well, Deedee told me . . . Obviously. I am so sorry. I feel terrible for you, Amy.'

'Thanks,' I mumble, feeling terrible for myself. Why is this happening to me? Oh, yes, I know. It's happening because I am such a fucking *idiot*.

'This explains everything that happened the other night,' Lewis continues. 'I wish you'd told me about it then . . . But never mind. You weren't ready to talk about it, I guess. I can understand that.'

'No, I wasn't,' I say, desperately trying to think of a way to end this call before he starts to ask technical insider trading questions, a subject I'm even less well qualified to speak on than, say, tractor engine maintenance. 'Thanks for phoning, Lewis . . . Um . . . It's really kind of you . . . Anyway, you must be busy. I'll let you get –'

'I'd really like to help you out if I can,' he says a little desperately. 'I just want to help, OK?'

Why does he have to turn out to be so bloody *nice*? Everything was so much easier when I was convinced he was a total pig.

'I've got to go,' I say, an involuntary tremor entering my voice. 'Good –'

'Amy, *don't* hang up . . .'

Damn those tremors. I was nearly free then.

'. . . Can I come and see you?' he asks.

He can't do that. No *way*.

'You can't . . . The magazine . . . You're the editor . . . You can't just . . . Leave.'

'Like you say, I'm the editor. I can do pretty much what I want. And what I want is to see you . . . Because in case you hadn't fucking noticed I *like* you.'

He sounds angry. But he *likes* me. So why is he angry? I'm too confused and scared to say anything.

'I'm sorry,' he says, a touch calmer. 'I just don't want you disappearing on me again. Don't go anywhere. I'm coming round.'

I respond by putting the phone down.

'Well?' says Ant.

'He's coming round.'

'That's great . . . Hang on, why are you looking at me like it's the least great thing in the world?'

'I can't see him. Everything he knows about me is a bloody lie. I've got to get out of here . . . *now*.'

I realise that I'm running around in little circles. When did that start? Last night? Last week? For ever ago?

'Calm down for fuck's sake,' he shouts.

I stop running.

'OK, listen to me,' he says in a slow, steady voice, the special one he saves for dealing with hysterical lunatics. 'Lewis very obviously *likes* you. This is a *good thing* because you very obviously *like* him. And it is possibly the only *good thing* in your life at this exact moment in time. So here is what you are going to do. *One*: you are going to shave your legs and perform whatever other girly niceties you feel are necessary.'

'But –'

'No buts. *Two*: with my expert help you will pick out something fetching to wear. *Three*: you will send me out for a long and bracing walk to Priory Park. And finally, *four*: when the doorbell rings you will let him in, sit him down and tell him the *truth*. Do you know what that means? It means not lying, misrepresenting, bullshitting or otherwise saying things that are a complete fucking fabrication.'

'But he'll hate me, Ant.'

'This is the most amazing thing, Amy. He won't – not if he really *does* like you. You tell him the truth, he'll see you for the incredible, talented woman you are and – *bingo!* – he'll *like* you even more. He'll also think you're a bit bloody daft for not saying something sooner, but I suspect he'll let that go. . . . OK? Think you can do that?'

I nod because it sounds like a completely brilliant plan . . . In theory.

10.45 a.m.: 'Fuck, I can't wear this with this . . . What about my blue skirt? *Yes*! Blue skirt . . . *Bugger*. No buggering tights . . . OK, OK, think, think . . . *Got it*. Black trousers and grey silk shirt . . . Grey silk shirt, grey silk shirt, where the *fuck*'s my grey silk shirt? . . . Found it! . . . *Aaagh*! What's this fucking stain? Right on the fucking front as well . . .'

And so on.

But at least it's an improvement on my earlier hysterics. At least I'm only going mental over what to wear rather what to kill myself with.

Definitely making progress.

11.21 a.m.: The doorbell buzzes. I stand up and inspect myself in the mirror for the fiftieth time. In the end I settled on a tightish, rusty orange top and a pair of slightly flared jeans, both bought in New York. Too new and smart to look convincingly like slobbing-around-the-flat-on-my-own wear. More like slobbing-around-the-flat-on-the-off-chance-of-someone-fanciable-showing-up. Perfect, Ant reckoned. Any objectivity I possessed left me months ago, so I took his word for it.

I creep up to the window and peer out. He looks fantastic. Actually, he looks just as he has every day at work, but that *is* fantastic. I can't believe he's here. And I can't believe I'm about to do what I'm about to do . . . Which probably means that I'm not going to do it at all.

I wish Ant hadn't gone out. If he were still here, he could tell Lewis for me. Then he could go out, leaving us to have demented animal sex against the kitchen units.

I watch him reach forward and the buzzer goes again.

Shit, better let him in – Ant's brilliant plan is not going to move forward if Lewis freezes to death on the doorstep.

11.22 a.m.: I'm waiting by the door. Nervous? Only virtually wetting myself. I realise I'm also smirking like an idiot. I wipe away the stupid expression and will myself to look . . . What should I do with my face? I rapidly shuffle through an assortment of expressions that might be suitable for the All Important Greeting Moment on First (Kind of) Date with Potential New Boyfriend. Big smile or small pout? Small smile or big pout? Dry lips? Yes. . . . No, go for kissably moist. I'm still in mid-lip-lick when he reaches the top of the stairs and walks straight in . . .

No kiss.

Damn, shit, *damn*. Maybe I got it all wrong – it wouldn't be my first time with Lewis. OK, *think*, Amy. He definitely said he *liked* me. *Good*. But was it *like* as in 'I *like* you so much that I'm prepared to drop everything and neglect the wellbeing of my ailing magazine in the hope of getting a snog with you'? Or was it *like* as in 'I *like* you sufficiently as a co-worker to consider in-home employer/employee counselling in the event of a parent being arrested on a complex fraud charge'?

I have no idea. Better tread very carefully because, as I said, I have a history of getting it spectacularly wrong with Lewis.

'Coffee?' I ask as he stands stiffly in the middle of the front room. 'I've got milk,' I add stupidly, as if possessing dairy produce is some kind of bloody achievement.

'Later maybe. Let's talk first.'

He's still standing rigidly in the centre of the room and he's adopted a businesslike editor-cum-head-of-human-resources tone. This is not looking good, Ant.

I sit down on my sofa.

He stays standing.

Not looking good *at all*.

'For someone who's just getting over chickenpox, you look pretty good,' he says.

'I didn't have chickenpox,' I reply – one lie down, a few dozen to go.

'I know,' he says. 'Look, your mum . . . Do you want to talk about it?'

For the first time since he walked in he sounds warm . . . *-ish* – not exactly cooking on gas, but not stone cold either.

'Er . . . No . . .' I say, 'I mean yes . . . God . . . Um . . . My mother, eh?'

What is it with the mumbling? It's like a selective speech impediment that kicks in whenever Lewis is within ten feet of me. Could it be an allergy? Whatever. Must fight it.

'Yes, your mother, eh?' Lewis echoes. 'Do you want to tell me what she's been arrested for? My brother-in-law's a lawyer – does corporate, City type stuff. I'd be happy to have a word –'

'She . . . Er . . . Hasn't,' I interrupt in a stuttering attempt to get this truth plan off the ground.

'She hasn't what?' Lewis asks. 'Been arrested?'

'Yes, she has been arrested.'

'What *hasn't* she done, then?' Lewis prods, looking confused now. 'The crime she's accused of? Deedee said insider trading –'

'My mum has never bought a share in her life,' I say. *Yes*, an entire coherent sentence – an honest one as well. So why does he still look confused?

'Hang on, if she doesn't deal in shares, why has she been arrested for insider trading?' he says, his brow furrowing so much I'm getting a pretty clear idea of what he'll look like at seventy.

'She *hasn't*,' I say.

'But you said she *has* been arrested.'

262

He's raising his voice now. I'm trying desperately to stick to Ant's *brilliant* plan and all it's doing is to make him shout.

'She *has* been arrested,' I say, unintentionally raising my own volume. 'But she *hasn't* been arrested for insider trading.'

Suddenly his brow unfurrows and I realise where I've been going wrong. I was missing out that last crucial bit of the explanation.

'So what *has* she been arrested for?' he asks.

Shit. The hard part – the actual *truth* bit of the truth.

'Spraying graffiti,' I say quietly.

'Excuse me? How old is she?'

'Nearly sixty.'

'My God. Where? On a bus shelter? A tube train?'

'A church door,' I say, my voice growing quieter with each answer.

'Is she some kind of anarchist?'

'Not really . . . She's . . . um . . . vice-chairwoman of Finchley Conservatives.'

He seems completely thrown by this and sits down, at last, collapsing into the armchair facing me.

'It's a long story,' I say.

'Don't worry. Deedee cleared my diary.'

11.49 a.m.: 'So let me see if I've got this straight,' Lewis says. 'Your friend Ant – the guy who answered your phone, yes?'

I nod. He's spot on so far.

'He's a gay priest,' Lewis continues.

'No.'

'He's not gay? Oh, that's right, you said you caught him in bed with a woman. He's a *womanising* priest.'

'No, he's *not* a priest. He *is* gay. The thing with the woman was a one-off. I think.'

'And your mother thinks he isn't . . . A priest?'

I shake my head.

'Sorry, she thinks he isn't *gay* . . . No, no, no, she *knows* he's gay . . .'

I give him violent nods of encouragement.

'. . . but she doesn't know he isn't a priest.'

'*Yes*,' I say.

'And she doesn't like priests?'

'She doesn't mind priests . . . She hates gays.'

'So how did she find out he's gay?'

'I told her.'

'A brave move given her views. Why does she think he's a priest?'

'Because I told her he was.'

'*Ah*, I think we might be getting somewhere . . . Now help me out with this next bit . . .'

12.07 pm: '. . . I'm with you now. Your father is having an affair with a woman who does tricks with balloons and –'

'No.'

'*No*, he isn't having an affair or *no*, she doesn't do tricks with balloons?' Lewis asks carefully.

'Both those things. I *thought* he was having an affair but it turned out the photograph only showed her demonstrating how to blow up a balloon. It's my mum who had the affair.'

'With the priest?'

'No, with the gardener. The priest is gay,' I remind him.

'Except he isn't really a priest,' Lewis reminds me.

'That's right,' I say wearily. 'Anyway, back to my dad. Last night we confronted him and –'

'We? Who's *we*?'

'Lisa and I.'

'Who's Lisa?'

'My sister.'

'I thought your sister was called Mary . . .'

Where's he get *Mary* from?

'. . . You told me at work weeks ago . . .'

Ah, got it now. He caught me on the phone to Mary and I told him she was my sister – *Jesus*, the lies I've forgotten.

'. . . Remember? The day you lost your contact lens on the floor.' He pauses and gives me a look that suggests he has finally got the hang of me. Then he says, 'You don't wear contacts, do you?'

I shake my head dejectedly.

'You know what, Amy? I think I need that coffee now.'

12.10 p.m.: As I wait for the kettle to boil I think back to Ant's words of wisdom: 'You tell him the truth, he'll see you for the incredible, talented woman you are.' Well, I've been telling the truth, Ant, and all he's seeing is a dishonest pillock whose life is such a knotted tangle of lies that even she's beginning to lose the threads.

It's a miracle he hasn't cut his losses and gone back to work. But that's exactly what he should do. I'm going to take him his coffee and tell him to forget it. Tell him to get on with his life and leave me to carry on making a complete dog's dinner of mine.

Sorry, Ant, because it was a brilliant idea . . . In theory.

12.13 p.m.: I carry the mugs into the front room, set them down on the coffee table and take a deep breath. Then I say, 'Lewis, I shouldn't have let you come round here. Sorry . . . Perhaps it's best if you . . . um . . . go.'

'But it's just getting good,' he says, the tiniest crinkle of a smile appearing at the corners of his mouth. I feel my face redden. Now he sees me as some kind of freak show entertainment.

'Your life is like some experimental episode of

265

Neighbours,' he continues, grinning broadly now. 'One where the scriptwriters were on acid and they've shipped in half the cast of *Home and Away* just to throw the audience.'

The bastard is *laughing* at me. I feel tears sting my eyes.

'I'm sorry,' he says, still smiling. 'I don't mean to mock. But you've got to admit . . . What I'm trying to say is that I find you fascinating . . .'

Yeah, fascinating as in bearded lady or elephant man fascinating.

'. . . You're interesting and I feel as if I'm getting to know you at last . . . I *like* you, Amy.'

Really? After all the mad rubbish he's heard he *likes* me? It's not quite '*I'm finally seeing you for the incredible, talented woman you are*' but it's better than bloody nothing.

I reach for a tissue from the coffee table, dab at my eyes and flop onto the sofa. He looks at me and says, 'I should think you feel better now that you've told me everything.'

'Yes, I do,' I sniff.

Hang on. He doesn't know everything, does he?

Oh, fuck it. Why not just do it? Go for the burn, girl.

'Lewis . . . I'm being blackmailed.'

12.24 p.m.: 'So this bloke you and your sister – who *isn't* called Mary – hired as a private eye and who then started blackmailing you has been sent – *shit*, this just gets better and better – on a wild-goose chase to *Malawi*. By Mary. Who *isn't* your sister. Who is she, then?'

'My agent,' I snivel.

'So why is this nasty little prick blackmailing you? If you . . . Hang on. *Why* have you got an agent?'

We've finally got there. I feel as if I've hauled myself

all the way up Mount Everest and I'm only a couple of steps from the summit. Yet all I want to do is turn round and head for the bottom again because once I answer this one that's it . . . *All of it*. My chest is tightening and I can feel the saliva draining from my mouth – I can barely open it to speak. But. I. have. Got to. Finish. This . . .

'He's blackmailing me because he found out I'm Mmm . . .'

I can't finish the word.

'You're *married*?' he splutters. 'Shit. . . . Right, well, OK. . . . Um –'

'*No*, I'm Marsha Mellow.'

He stares at me bug-eyed.

'You know . . . The author . . .'

He's still staring.

'. . . Who wrote the book . . .'

Still staring.

'. . . That's in the papers.'

'Yes, I've heard of her, thanks,' he says at last. 'You're kidding me.'

'I'm not.'

'You're joking.'

'I *wish*.'

'I don't believe it.'

'Why not?' I demand, suddenly indignant. Does he think I'm stupid, that I couldn't possibly write? Or that I'm so unsexy I couldn't possibly write like *that*?

'Because it's amazing . . . Shit. Sorry . . . *Fuck* . . . I did not see that coming. You're Marsh . . . Amy, the Marsha Mellow thing has been the only decent news story this year. I'm a jaded hack, remember, but I've been getting totally wrapped up in it.'

Shit, he's a hack. Forgot about that. I've just given him an *exclusive*.

267

'You're a journalist,' I say – a statement of the glaringly obvious, but I am stunned. 'You're not going to – '

'Don't be stupid . . . Jesus, you're Marsha *Mellow*! This is the best, most *brilliant* thing I have ever, *ever* –'

'Lewis, do you mind if I –'

I don't finish, but he wouldn't have had a chance to answer because I'm squashing my lips onto his.

12.55 p.m.: 'Yes, uhh, yes, nnngg, Lewis, yes, yes, *yeeeessssssssssssssssssss*!'

It is actually bloody well happening!

Chapter 25

'How's work, Lewis?' I ask, taking a drag on my ciga-rette.

(By the way, why is it that the *best* fag is the one you have straight after sex? Apart from the one that you smoke after a meal. And the one you sneak in the toilet at your parents' house. And the one you light with shaky hands after eight hours strapped to a seat on a no smoking flight . . . Oh, stupid question. Forget I asked.)

'I'll tell you how work is,' Lewis replies. 'Ros started Monday.' He wafts my smoke away with his hand – *hmm*, potential problem here.

'Is she as good as you hoped?' I say, switching my fag to my other hand. So considerate of me – we are in *my* bed, after all.

'She's better, as it happens. . . . But I paid her off this morning.'

'Oh.'

'Publisher's orders. Cost cuts,' he says, swatting at another ribbon of smoke – *definite* problem here. 'The magazine is fucked, Amy. We'll be lucky to get the next three issues out.'

'Well, I resigned today. That might help a bit.'

'No disrespect, but it might save us enough to keep the coffee machine going. I can't believe the mess I've inher-ited – didn't say *that* on the packet . . .'

As he goes on about the problems at *Working Girl* I'm nodding earnestly, but I'm not listening. It's not that he's boring – *God*, no. Lewis is definitely the most interesting man I've been in bed with since . . . Rapid mental tot of all the men I've been in bed with, which, even including Lewis, uses up just four and a half fingers (the half is because I was never technically *in* bed with Jeremy Crane at Carol Lennon's party; more like pointlessly writhing around *on* it) . . . He's definitely the most interesting since for ever, but I'm not listening to him because I'm too wrapped up in thinking how wonderful this is. Lewis. *Here.* In my bed. Close enough for me to notice that one of his nipples seems slightly higher than the other, which was a bit spooky at first, but now that I've lived with it for an hour only makes him even *more* interesting. And he knows everything about me – even the deranged, embarrassing stuff – and yet he's *still here*. It seems perfect. No, it *is* perfect . . .

Just so long as we never have to step out of my flat and I don't have to read whatever the *Mail* is saying about me today or deal with Dad's disappointment or the prospect of visiting Mum in Holloway. And the thought of having to *tell* her (which might be preferable if she's in jail – at least I'll be separated from her by a sturdy grille). But however much Lewis likes me, I don't suppose he's up for barricading ourselves in and eking out the contents of my freezer (one Lean Cuisine Lasagne and something in Tupperware that has been in there for ever and might be bolognese sauce, but could equally well be Pedigree Chum) until we have nothing left to survive on but our love and we die in each other's arms blissfully happy and (in my case at least) gorgeously thin. No, I don't suppose he's up for that at all and, now I think about it, neither am I.

Which means that at some point in the not too distant

future I'm going to have to get dressed and *Face Things*. I'd rather not dwell on that now, so I go back to listening to him talk work.

'. . . Anyway, who said I'd accepted your resignation?' he says. 'Now I know you can write I'll be demanding three thousand-word features from you. About sex, of course – that shifts units. Just ask your publisher.'

'I . . . er . . . dumped him last night.'

'No shit. You turned your back on a million quid?'

'It wasn't quite that much.'

'Even so . . . Why blow him out?'

'He's the one who's been leaking all the stuff to the *Mail*.'

'He's only doing his job,' he says, going corporate all of a sudden. 'Keeping up public interest – maintaining sales.'

'I don't care. He promised me anonymity. He signed a bloody deal.'

'Why the secrecy?' he questions, deftly swinging the conversation onto the very subject I didn't want to think about. 'I meant to ask before, but I got kind of side-tracked.'

'Remember that woman I told you about? Votes Tory. Hates homos. In prison.'

'Your mum? She doesn't approve?'

'Well . . . she definitely . . . um . . . wouldn't approve if she . . . er . . .'

'You haven't told her?'

Why is he laughing? This is *so* not funny, so why the hell is he laughing? Is this what two years of agony boils down to? A naked bloke with one nipple slightly higher than the other sitting in my bed and laughing like a drain as if it's the most ridiculous thing he's ever heard? Well, maybe he's right. Maybe it is barmy, bonkers and so bloody nuts that I should just call a halt and *deal with it . . .*

Hang on, why am *I* laughing now?

Where's Ant when I need him? His walk has become awfully long and extremely bracing. Knowing him, he's probably discovered a hidden clearing among a tangle of bushes where he's busily establishing Priory Park's very first *Cruising Zone.*

I pick up my pen and write:

Ant - Gone to Mum and Dad's. It's got to be done. If not back by six, call that undertaker who left messages on machine. Where are you? Don't want you to come with me - that would be completely insane - but could do with some emboldening (is that the right word?) parting words. Love you - Amy xxx

PS - If not back by six, you and Lisa can split my CDs, but let her have my dresses.
   PPS - Told Lewis and he's still here! You're a genius!

I fold the note and prop it against the empty mugs on the coffee table.

'Do you want me to come with you?' Lewis asks.

'Thanks, but I don't think this is going to be the ideal Meet the Parents opportunity. "Mum, Dad, I'm that vile woman who writes dirty books and this is Lewis, my new boyfriend."'

Whoops. Where did *that* come from? Is he my boyfriend? I glance at him and he's not leaping for the window. Maybe he is, then.

'Surely it won't be that bad,' he says.

272

I flash him my trademark *You know nothing about the Bickerstaffs, do you?* look.

'Are you *sure* you don't want me to come?' he asks again. 'Tell you what. I'll give you a lift round there and wait for you at the end of the road – your getaway driver.'

I drift slowly through the hall in Mum's and Dad's house and wonder why my head feels wet. I stop by the mirror and look at myself. Pig's blood drenches my hair, streaks my face and stains my white satin . . . Is that a prom dress? I see something else as well. Something far more alarming. I've turned into Sissy Spacek. I hear screams from above and I climb the stairs towards them . . . Reach the top . . . Then head up the rungs of the extended loft ladder . . . Until I'm in the attic. I look at her. A sick, mad witch depraved by her love of God. My mother. She doesn't hear my arrival. She's too busy forcing a knife into the palm of Ant's limp hand. The finishing touch because the rest of her set of Kitchen Devils already pin his inert body to the roof joists where he has become an ironic crucifix.

His eyes flicker open and look at me over her shoulder. 'Forgive her,' he whispers, 'for she knows not what she does.'

She turns at last and sees me. 'You've come home, Carrie,' she says.

'My name isn't Carrie,' I reply.

'No,' she shrieks, 'it's Marsha *Mellow*.'

'You're really not up for this, are you?' Lewis says, mercifully stopping me before my *Carrie* fantasy merges seamlessly with *The Exorcist* and I spin my head, spew pea-green bile and call my mum an effing C-word in Latin.

'No, I'm not up for it at all,' I reply as I stare straight ahead at the traffic lights, willing them to stay red for, say, another week or two.

'How about this?' Lewis suggests. 'When you're telling her, picture her naked . . . With that gardener or whatever he was. She won't seem so smug and self-righteous then and you can –'

I don't hear the rest because my head is hanging out of the car window and I'm throwing up all over its metallic paintwork. Well, at least I'm not vomiting pea-green bile.

Hell must be a four-bedroom semi with a Rover in the drive and mature hydrangeas . . . Hang on, sudden overwhelming sense of déjà vu. When have I had that thought before? I know. Coming home a few weeks ago, preparing to give Mum and Dad some Big News. It's going to be even tougher today – back then Mum's wrists were free of handcuff marks that she could have rubbed at self-pityingly.

After a final glance to where Lewis is parked some hundred yards down the street I open the garden gate and step onto the path. When I get to the front door I reach into my pocket for my keys, but I stop. I'm not ready to go in yet. I crouch down, push open the letterbox and peer through the slot. No sign of life. Perhaps Dad is at court for Mum's bail hearing or something. Should have thought of that. Should have phoned first instead of just turning up. I could let myself in and wait . . . No, best just to leave . . . Try again later maybe . . . Maybe not.

'What do you think you're doing down there?'

I jump, startled. I turn and see a shadowy figure towering over me. He's clutching a hammer. And a long chisel. And a box of Polyfilla.

'Hi, Dad,' I say nervously.

274

'Spying on me again?' he asks. He's fresh from DIY therapy, but it hasn't worked. He sounds no friendlier than he did last night.

'No . . . Er . . . No. Just seeing if there's anyone home.'

'You might try the doorbell next time,' he suggests.

Irony? That's a new one for Dad. I've learnt a lot about him in the last twenty-four hours. Until last night I never knew he had a temper to lose. And he knows the F-word. Now the irony. All in all he has become a more interesting character, though I felt a lot more comfortable when he was boring. My angry, sweary, sarcy new dad pushes past me and goes into the house. I hold back, preferring the relative safety of the front step.

'Well, aren't you going to come in?' he says. 'You might as well join the happy family . . .'

There he goes with the irony again.

'. . . Your sister's here already . . .'

Lisa's here? Didn't think I'd see her for a while.

'. . . and your mother's asleep upstairs. She was pretty traumatised when I finally got her home. I called the doctor out and he gave her some sedatives. I'm going to make myself a sandwich. You want one?'

Well, it's a welcome. Of a sort.

'I'm OK, thanks,' I say, even though I'm famished.

He heads for the kitchen while I step into the hall and obsessively wipe my feet on the mat – don't want to add muddy carpets to my rap sheet. I poke my head round the living-room door and spot Lisa sitting primly on the sofa. Normally she sprawls on furniture, limbs akimbo like a centrefold's. Now she has her knees and ankles clamped together, her back ramrod straight and her hands resting demurely on her kneecaps. She looks as if she's here in answer to the ad for a governess. It's funny how guilt can transform a person. The TV is on and she's watching Ann Robinson insult some members of the public, but her mind is elsewhere. She doesn't even notice me step into the room.

'Hi,' I say quietly.

'*Shit*,' she yelps, jumping clear off the sofa. 'When did you come in?'

'Just now . . . How's Mum? Have you seen her?'

She shakes her head. 'Dad won't let me near her.'

'How's he been with you?'

'What do you think? I can't believe I stood in this room last night and accused him of getting a blowjob . . . I actually used that word,' she adds in a whisper, wincing at the memory.

'It was pretty bad, wasn't it?' I agree. 'Has Mum been charged?'

'Not yet. Apparently she's looking at two counts of criminal damage. But her lawyer reckons she won't do time.'

'Well, isn't that a bloody relief?' I say, catching the irony bug. I sit down next to her. We slip into silence and watch Ann Robinson cajole a bunch of perfect strangers into hating one another.

'Where've you been today?' Lisa asks after a few minutes. 'I tried to call you before I came here.'

'I took my phone off the hook . . . Lewis came round.'

'Oh, lovely. *Fan*tastic. *Mar*vellous. *Lewis* came round . . .'

Highly infectious, this irony.

'. . . While the rest of us were going out of our sodding minds, you and Lewis were bunking off work having *sex*.'

'Who said we had sex?' I say indignantly.

'Why else would you take your phone off the hook?'

I ignore her brilliant deduction and say, 'I told him.'

'You didn't,' she gasps. 'You barely know him.'

'It's time to put an end to the lies,' I say, stealing Ant's line – well, his strategy has worked so far.

'I'm glad you think so, because I reckon you haven't got long before your secret's blown anyway. Did you see the *Mail* today?'

She points at the folded newspaper on the coffee table. FIND HER demands the headline. Then she opens out the paper to reveal the picture covering the lower half of the page.

A staring, dead-eyed *me*.

'*Fuck*,' I say, but no sound comes from my mouth. A swirling nausea sweeps through me and if I hadn't just been sick over Lewis's car, I'd throw up on the carpet. The Riverdancers are back, this time with reinforcements – a squad of highly motivated Palestinian suicide bombers.

'Freaky, isn't it?' Lisa says.

I pick up the paper and examine the photofit. Freaky is not the fucking word for it. It may only be some expert's composite based on details supplied (presumably) by Jacobson, but she is *me*. She's got my hair, my nose, and even my mole that's too big to call a beauty spot on her right cheek. And something else. The picture has the quality that's visible in every photofit you ever see. Call it *evil*. I mean, who's ever looked at one and not immediately thought '*Guilty*'? The *Mail* couldn't have made me look more sinister if they'd given me three-day stubble and a four-inch knife scar. It makes the trial photo of peroxide Myra Hindley look like a portrait of Babysitter of the Year.

'Amy, calm down. You're hyperventilating,' Lisa says. 'It's not *really* you. It's only made up.'

I can't answer, but amidst the chaos in my head and gut one thing is singing out with crystal clarity: whatever it takes and whatever the consequences, I have *got* to tell them. *Today*.

'I have to tell them, Lisa,' I whisper.

'I know . . . Anyway, let's change the subject for a

minute,' she continues in a breezy voice that couldn't sound more forced if it had a gun pointed at it. 'Me and *Dan*.'

'Who?' I ask in a daze.

'Boyfriend. The one that definitely isn't a Triad.'

'*God*, sorry, Lisa, I've been totally –'

'Preoccupied? It's OK. You're allowed.'

'Dan,' I say. 'What's happening?'

'Total bloody disaster,' Lisa says.

'What's a total bloody disaster?' Dad interrupts, his mouth full of ginger nut.

'Nothing much,' Lisa says instinctively.

'Good . . . Good. "Nothing much" I can handle,' he says, sitting in his armchair. 'And would you mind switching this rubbish off? That bloody woman gets on my wick.'

Lisa kills the TV and then looks at me, shocked. I know what she's thinking. *The Weakest Link* is Mum's favourite programme. It's a basic Tory thing – she admires the way it pushes survival of the fittest with no safety net for the runts. Secretly she probably believes the NHS should be run along similar lines, with Nurse Robinson telling undeserving kidney patients, 'You are the weakest link. Goodbye,' before dispatching them through a trapdoor in the floor. I've always assumed it to be Dad's favourite TV show too. He's always joined Mum in watching it from the opening bar of the titles and commanding silence throughout. But, apparently, *bloody* Ann Robinson *gets on his wick*. Something has changed. I want to look at him, try to figure him out, but I can't. Instead I stare at my feet.

'I'm really, really sorry,' I mumble to the reflection in my shoes.

'What's that?' he asks.

'I'm . . . *We're* sorry. You know. For thinking . . .'

'Your sister's already told me,' he says. 'What on earth possessed you to imagine I was having an affair?'

'It was Mum, actually,' I reply. 'She was . . . er . . . *worried* about you.'

'Why does that not surprise me?' he says wearily and so quietly that I suspect it was intended only for him to hear.

'I'm sorry about Mum as well,' I say. 'You know, sending her off the deep end and everything.'

'What, did you give her the can and tell her to spray that stuff?'

'No, but –'

'So why the apology? Your mother did what she did all by herself.'

This throws me. Why isn't he blaming me? Is he forgetting how our family works? Because if he doesn't blame me, Mum will kill him as well.

'You can enlighten me on one thing, Amy,' he continues. 'Given your mother's *fragility* of late, why did you tell her that your friend is gay? I always thought you were the sensible one out of the pair of you. It's not like you to give a sleeping dog a mighty great kick in the ribs.'

What can I say to that? '*Well, Dad, I was trying to create a smokescreen so that she wouldn't notice I was corrupting public morals with my luridly dirty book*'? Actually, I should be saying exactly that, but . . . I . . . can't. Yet.

Dad doesn't wait for me to answer, though. He's off. 'Don't get me wrong. It's no skin off my nose what your friend is. He could be the Bishop of Limerick and wear ladies' frillies under his cassock for all I care . . .'

What's going on here? My father is sounding dangerously *liberal.*

' . . . If you ask me, I've always thought the priesthood a perfectly natural career choice for a homosexual . . .'

Hang on. I've just remembered the first report Lisa got from Colin Mount: Dad spotted in sandwich bar with *Guardian* under arm. I joked about it at the time, but now I understand. *It was a sign.*

'. . . What else can they do where there's no pressure on them to do the conventional thing and marry? And what about Jesus?'

'What about him?' I ask. I'm extremely nervous now. Alternative views on the Son of God are a definite no-no under Mum's roof.

'All those disciples? Didn't much care for the company of women, did he? And just say it turned out he was gay, wouldn't it cast a whole new light on all that wonderful stuff he said about tolerance and loving thy neighbour? No, I think there's far too much unpleasant claptrap preached about people like your friend, Amy. Let him get on with it and good luck to the man, I say. That's what upset me so much about the way your mother reacted.'

I glance at Lisa. Is she as flummoxed as I am?

'All she's worried about is losing her party membership,' Dad goes on, 'but it bothers me that she could do something so *hateful*. I'm going to tell her that when she's up and about again.'

He's going to tell her *that*? He's actually going to voice an opinion that he knows she won't like? This is the man who day after day has assured his wife that boiled to buggery for upwards of forty-five minutes is *exactly* how he likes his greens, even though it's always been obvious from the gagging noises that it isn't. I can't believe what I'm hearing. But maybe he will tell her. After all, he's already confessed that *bloody* Ann Robinson *gets on his wick*, which on Mum's scale of things is possibly slightly worse than suggesting that Jesus might've been a poof.

I'm grinning. Inside at least. Dad has given me a surge

of E-type confidence. He has to *live* with Mum and if he's finally decided that it's time to stand up and be counted, then so will I. I'm going to tell her *everything*. And I'm going to kick things off by telling Dad.

Because I *know* he'll understand.

Shit, from what I've been hearing over the last few minutes, he might even *approve*.

'Dad, there's something else about Ant,' I say.

'What's that? He wears frillies under his cassock?'

'Well, he might . . . if he wore a cassock. He's not a priest.'

'Bloody hell,' he splutters, spraying his lap with ginger nut crumbs. 'Whatever you do don't tell your mother . . .'

Oh, so the new outspoken Dad was a flash in the pan – that has just this moment finished flashing.

'. . . No, I'll do that myself when she's back on her fee—'

He's cut short by the door clicking open.

'You'll do *what* when I'm back on my feet, Brian?' demands my mum – who is unnervingly back on her feet.

'Nothing important, dear,' Dad says as he leaps up and moves towards her. 'You really shouldn't be out of bed. The doctor said –'

'Never mind the doctor,' she snaps as he arrives at her side. 'Why did you let him give me all those drugs? You know how I feel about them,' she adds, lumping mild sedatives in with crack and heroin.

I watch as Dad helps her to the other armchair. Her bare legs look wobbly beneath her dressing gown. There seems nothing wobbly about her mind though – that, apparently, is sedative-proof.

'Do you want a cup of tea?' Dad asks feebly, seeing hot beverages as his escape tunnel to the kitchen.

'No, I do not, thank you,' she replies. 'I'd like to talk to Amy.'

She fixes me with a glare, the one that I remember from when I was nine and was sent home from school for pulling Belinda Perry's pigtail so hard that she swallowed her brace. I cower on the sofa and watch Dad do likewise in his armchair. Depressing though it is to see him revert so quickly to being . . . well . . . *Dad*, I know where he's coming from. It must've been all too easy to talk the talk when she was supposedly comatose upstairs.

'The *truth* now, Amy,' Mum continues. 'How long have you known?'

'Known what?' I whisper.

'That your *friend* was a *homo*?'

I could now do what I'd normally do in this situation: lie through my teeth and say something like '*God, Mum, I only just found out and I was as shocked as you were. I mean, I didn't rush out and spray Manhattan with homophobic filth, but I can so understand your reaction.*'

But I don't do that.

Instead I say, 'I've known for about twelve years.'

Despite my raging terror I tell her the *truth* and it shocks me as much as it stuns her. For a moment neither of us can speak. Then she says, '*Twelve* years. You've known all this time and you've brought him into *my* house, let him sit at *my* table?'

'My house too, Charlotte,' Dad says very tentatively, trying his new opinionated hat on for size and not getting a very good fit.

'Shush, Brian,' she snaps. 'I can't believe you'd do that to me, Amy.'

She couldn't look more wounded if I'd run her through with a rusty sword. This should make me angry. I mean, the sheer *hypocrisy*. This is the woman who painted pure hate on a church door and who – *let's not bloody forget* – romped around the rhododendrons with a sodding gardener she'd met at the Chelsea Flower Show. The one who then had the gall to suggest that Dad was the one having the affair. And now she's blaming *me*? It *should* make me boil over with anger, but it doesn't. Instead I feel myself doing the usual and imploding with guilt. I *pray* for rage to well up inside me because I know that only something like blinding fury (or drugs) will get me through this, but it won't come and I'm left staring abjectly at my shoes again.

'And knowing what you did, how could you let him simply *waltz* off and be a *priest*?' Mum adds, making it clear that I've hurt God's feelings as well as her own. 'As if there isn't enough wickedness in the world without *them* making a mockery of –'

'There's something else you should know,' I mumble. I'm terrified of what I'm about to say, but I can't listen to her launch into another frenzy about gay vicars. I take a deep breath and announce, 'Ant's not a priest.'

I ignore her gasp and Dad's violent choking because I have just seen Ant at the bay window. He's standing directly behind mum and he's peering at me through the net curtains. Comic timing was always his strong point in school productions. So good to see he hasn't lost it. But what in *God*'s name is he playing at? Doesn't he realise that coming round here is a sure-fire recipe for a bloodbath? How can he possibly imagine that this is going to help? I gesture frantically at him to go, but that only makes him squash his nose up even harder against the glass and, of course, it makes Mum and Dad swivel round and look outside. Ant gets the message in the nick of time and drops below the windowsill.

'What's going on?' Mum asks.

I don't know how to answer, but luckily Lisa does it for me. 'Just some bloke. Looked like a double glazing salesman.'

'Never mind that,' Mum snaps. It's back to business. 'Why did you tell me he was a priest? How could you let me think such a thing?'

'Because she was terrified of telling you the truth, Mum,' says Lisa, thankfully stepping in for me again.

'What are you talking about?' Mum asks.

'Well, how would you have reacted if she'd told you he was emigrating to work in a gay nightclub called the Seminary?'

'Well, I'd have been upset, but I'd have –'

'Come off it,' Lisa says. 'You'd have done what you did yesterday and gone ape. So Amy decided to avoid the aggro and . . . Well, she lied.'

Mum looks dazed. Like she never knew she was scary. Like spray-painting church doors is all in a day's work for a respectable pillar of the community and not at all loopy. Then in a pitiful little voice she says, 'But I always brought you up to be *honest* . . . How many other lies have you told me?' She fixes me with the biggest, saddest puppy dog eyes that I've seen outside of an RSPCA appeal. She's going for the sympathy vote and boy, is it working because I feel *terrible*. Lisa nudges me – my cue to hit her with the Big One . . .

I don't take it. I can't do anything.

For Mum my silence is as good an admission of guilt as she needs and she sets off on a self-pitying ramble that I've heard a thousand times before and that gets me every single bloody time.

'I always tried to do the right thing, to instil you with *values*, but look what it got me. One daughter who wants to flit off to Hong Kong with a Chinese gangster that she's too ashamed to bring home and another who can't even speak the truth to her own –'

She stops because a phone is ringing.

In my pocket.

My mobile.

I fish it out and stare at it dumbly as it vibrates in my palm.

'Well, aren't you going to answer it?' Mum chivvies. 'It's probably that queer friend of yours.'

I put it to my ear.

'Got to the good bit yet?' asks my queer friend.

Why is he bothering to phone? Why the fuck doesn't he just yell from the hydrangea bush?

'It's . . . not . . . a . . . good time,' I answer – like I'm *really* going to tell him how it's going.

'Look, it's OK. Don't say anything,' he says. 'But if she pulls a gun or anything here's three words to shut her up: *Chelsea Flower Show*.'

The line clicks dead.

'Double glazing salesman,' I say. '*Ha . . .*'

Dad smiles weakly, but Mum isn't listening. She's spotted the *Mail* on the coffee table. She picks it up and looks at the picture, at the truth literally staring her in the face.

Fuck, I'm not going to have to tell her because she's going to see it for herself. My breath stops as I wait for the penny to drop . . . But it doesn't and after a moment she says, 'It's a sad world we live in. What sort of people buy this woman's . . .'

As Mum trails off, lost for a suitably disgusted word for what *I* write, Lisa nudges me again – hard. This is *definitely* my cue – this one has been scripted by God.

But I still can't do it and I don't know where to look now. I can't look at Mum and I can't stare past her out of the window because Ant has re-emerged from the bushes and now Lewis has joined him. That's all I bloody need – my brand-new boyfriend taking a ringside seat at *Fucked-Up Families 'R' Us*.

This. Is. Hell. And I can't stand it.

I'm not the only one because Lisa interrupts my torment

and says, 'Look, Amy, this is stupid. Are you going to tell them or am I?'

She gives me a look that I think is supposed to be encouraging, but which comes across as '*Please put us all out of our fucking misery and get this over with*'.

'Tell us what?' My dad says timidly, finally coming out of his knitwear bunker.

'Amy wants to tell you that –'

'I'll do it, Lisa,' I say, recovering my voice at last. Lisa's right. I have to end this. 'Look,' I begin tremulously, 'you probably won't believe this. I don't believe it myself sometimes. I know you won't like it but you're my parents and you need to know . . .'

Shit, I am *sooo* waffling, but I don't know where to start. I fix my eyes on Mum and try to do as Lewis suggested. I force a mental picture of her rolling around in a floral border with Pat the gardener, but he comes out looking like a ruddy-cheeked Old McDonald. This is not helpful. *Focus*, Amy. *Tell her*.

'You're right, Mum,' I continue, adding a bit more padding, as if it might cushion the blow when it finally arrives. 'I should have been honest with you about Ant . . .'

Ant's brilliant new plan! That's it.

'. . . We should be straight with each other, shouldn't we?' I continue, uncertain how I'm going to work Ant's three magic words into this, but determined to try. 'I mean, *all* of us . . . Take . . . um . . . Dad . . .'

Mum looks baffled. Dad looks panic-stricken – *take me where*?

'. . . Imagine he told you he was going . . . um . . . off on business somewhere, but really he was sneaking off on a *jaunt* . . .'

Mum looks intrigued now. Like she's finally going to get the dirt on Dad as well as on me.

'. . . to the . . . um . . . *Chelsea Flower Show*.'

Mum's turn for panic-stricken.

'Why would I do that? It's your mum who loves gardening,' Dad says, his face crinkled with confusion.

Mum doesn't speak. For the first time in my life she looks cowed. I can do this now. *Thank you, Ant.*

'It's just hypothetical, Dad,' I say. 'I'm just trying to say we should be more open with each other . . . Like I'm about to be with you now . . . Because I'm going to tell you something that –'

'What? What are you going to tell him?' Mum's almost up on her feet, frantic with panic. What can she do to me? She's terrified. I am so nearly there. I can do it.

'I'm Mmm—'

'Married?' Dad pipes up – what is it with everyone and the married thing?

'No, Dad! Let me finish. I was just going to say –'

'Stop! Whatever it is, you don't know the first thing about the Chelsea Flower Show. I didn't even go this year. I was –'

'Let her finish, Charlotte. What is it, Amy?'

'I just wanted to say . . .'

Nothing else will come out. My voice has ceased to work. For the first time in my entire life, I've got the upper hand with my mother, but I *still* can't fucking do it. What sort of wimp am I? The Chelsea Flower Show has got me this far, but it's not going to get me over the finish line. The trauma is too much and my body has decided that this would be a perfectly good moment to shut down. I feel my knees weaken – obviously they'll be the next to go. I look helplessly at Lisa who seems strangely calm.

'It's OK, Amy,' she says, standing up and turning to face Mum and Dad. 'What she's trying to say is that she's Marsha Mellow's sister.'

287

'What on earth are you talking about?' Mum exclaims.

'Mum, Dad,' Lisa announces serenely, 'I'm Marsha Mellow.'

Chapter 26

'Could have been worse,' Lisa says as Lewis ferries the two of us to the North Middlesex Hospital. 'We could be on our way to the morgue. All's well that ends well, eh?'

Personally, I wouldn't have characterised Mum throwing her bone china shepherdess through the front-room window (hitting Ant full on the forehead), before barricading herself in the garage where she downed the contents of a Toilet Duck bottle as being a happy ending.

While Dad tried to force open the up-and-over door at the front, Lewis took his shoulder to the one that connects garage to kitchen. It was like watching Tom Cruise in *Mission: Impossible* and I was quietly thrilled (while simultaneously cringing that he had to demonstrate his manliness surrounded by my family behaving like chimps with serious personality disorders). The door gave way before Lewis's shoulder did and inside he found Mum collapsed on the floor. While he tended her I dialled 999. Then I found the empty Toilet Duck bottle. I searched it frantically for the warning: *If consumed, drink water and seek immediate medical assistance.* 'Quick, give her some water,' I yelled.

'No need,' Dad said calmly as he swung open the big garage door and walked in to join us. 'That's exactly what she tried to kill herself with.'

Mum wasn't to know that Dad had taken the empty lavatory cleaner bottle and refilled it with distilled water

289

– he found that its cleverly angled neck was ideal for topping up his car battery. She's spent her entire marriage complaining about his obsessive DIY and now it's saved her life. I guess her collapse was the result of shock and not because her insides were receiving a toxic blast of pine forest freshness.

When the paramedics arrived they wheeled my still swoony mother off on a stretcher. Then they went to take care of Ant, who was bleeding on the lawn and being nursed by Lisa.

We're following the ambulance containing Mum and Dad now. The most ironic thing is that Ant is in there with them. I would laugh if I weren't genuinely worried for him.

'She's going to be OK, isn't she?' Lisa guiltily asks the doctor as we stand at a safe distance and look at Mum lying peacefully on a trolley.

'She's suffering from shock, but she'll be fine,' he says in his I'm-a-doctor-and-you-should-feel-reassured voice. Then he adds, 'Though she still has some stubborn traces of lime scale in her trachea.'

Clearly the Toilet Duck story is going to keep them entertained on those long nights in Casualty.

A nurse taps me on the shoulder. 'Excuse me, miss. Your friend would like to see you. He's behind the curtain over there.'

I head for the cubicle and find Ant being stitched by a young doctor who looks as if she hasn't had a night's sleep in several months. I sit down and wait for her to finish/nod off and sew Ant's eyelids together.

'Are you OK?' I ask as she finally ties the knot.

'I suspect there're still some slithers of that fucking shepherdess in there . . . But, yeah, I'm dandy – I've always wanted a scar. What about you?'

'I'm fine, I suppose. Still reeling, but fine.'

'I take it from the mayhem that she knows,' he concludes.

'Kind of . . . She thinks Lisa did it.'

He starts to laugh. 'Don't explain yet . . . I want to enjoy the sheer madness of this for a while.'

'Talking of madness,' I say, 'what were you doing back there?'

'I thought I could help. Stupid, huh?'

'What were you thinking?'

'I wanted to draw some of the fire, soak up some of the blame. I figured I'd be her ideal target. I was bloody right as well,' he says, fingering the messy two-inch cut on his forehead.

'That's really noble of you, Ant . . . Thank you.'

'Your Lewis seems nice,' he says.

'I'm surprised you were able to form an opinion with Armageddon going off.'

'Well, it's only first impressions. We kind of managed the introductions while we were crawling around the shrubbery – he looks good on his hands and knees.'

'Thanks for making me go through with seeing him,' I say. 'I didn't think your plan was going to work for a while, but –'

'You should always have faith in me, Amy. Where is he now?'

'He had to make some calls – he'd forgotten it's press day today.'

'What's that?'

'You know, when they print the mag. If he hadn't phoned in, there'd be nothing in it on Monday.'

The doctor stands up and peels off her gloves.

'Thanks,' Ant says gratefully. 'You must think this is all a bit weird.'

'Oh, this is fairly normal,' she replies nonchalantly. 'I've got to go and find a transvestite's missing nail extension now. You don't want to know where he lost it.'

Lisa, Ant and I sit on the edge of the ambulance bay while I have a fag.

'You know, I've always thought it's pretty unreasonable that they don't let you smoke in hospitals,' Lisa says.

'How do you figure that?' Ant asks.

'Well, everyone's already sick. What harm is a bit of secondary smoke going to do? . . . Amy, I've been meaning to ask. What was all that rubbish about the Chelsea Flower Show?'

Ant laughs and I'd like to tell her now, but a far bigger question has been pending since we arrived here.

'Later,' I say. 'Why did you do it, Lisa?'

'Well, someone had to get the bloody words out – you were taking too long,' she says.

'Go on, seriously.'

'I couldn't bear watching you go through hell a minute longer,' she explains. 'Apart from anything else, I felt really guilty. The last few days must have been a nightmare for you and all I've been doing is worrying about Dan.'

'God, *Dan*,' I gasp. I knew there was something completely unrelated to gay priests or porny books that we had to talk about. 'What's going on? You're not pregnant, are you?'

'You don't half sound like Mum sometimes. No, I'm not. He asked me to marry him.'

'Lisa, that's *fantastic* . . .' I watch her face contort. '. . . Isn't it?'

'Well, no one's ever asked me that before,' she says after a moment. 'And the ring he'd bought was big enough to choke a horse . . . But he's a *Tory*.'

'You've put up with that for two years. You've got to get over being hung up on the thought of Mum liking him.

Anyway, right now I reckon she could do with a straw to clutch at. You should do us all a favour and say yes.'

'I've already said no,' she whispers.

'You haven't . . .'

I look at her face, her mournful eyes.

'It's really over?' I ask.

'He left for Hong Kong this morning, so I guess so,' she says sadly.

'God, I'm so sorry, Lisa.'

'I'll be OK,' she says bravely. 'I've already . . . Kind of . . . Met someone.'

'*Lisa*!'

'He's in Goa at the moment. He's fantastic. I can't wait for you to meet him.'

'Don't tell me,' Ant says. 'He's an international gun runner.'

'How could you say that?' Lisa splutters indignantly. 'He pays his taxes and everything. He's got his own business.'

'What is it?' I ask.

'A lap dancing club in Bethnal Green.'

Phew. After the nightmare prospect of her going legit with Tory Dan, it's good to see her life back on track.

There's a moment's silence before I say, 'You still haven't really answered my question. Why did you take the rap?'

'Because being preoccupied with Dan wasn't the only reason I felt guilty. You've always said that I got you into this mess in the first place, and you're right, I did. It only seemed fair that I should get you out of it.'

'You didn't have to, you know,' I say.

'I know I didn't, but I'm just an angel like that. Anyway, I've always been the black sheep, haven't I? It's just another crime Mum can stick down on my record, and as far as she's concerned, she'll still have one daughter who'll join her in heaven one day.'

'Yes, but what the fuck do we do now?'

She doesn't get a chance to answer because Dad walks out of the hospital. Out of habit I furtively stub out my fag on the wall. He spots us and makes his way across the forecourt, a black look on his face.

'How is she?' I ask nervously when he arrives.

'Asleep . . . Comatose, actually. The doctor gave her enough sedatives to knock out an elephant . . . Did you know that it's the only animal with four knees?'

'We're really sorry about what happened . . . Aren't we, Lisa?' I say.

'Yes, Dad, we are,' my sister says, sounding more apologetic than she ever has about anything.

'It's your bloody mother who should be sorry,' he snarls. 'It'll cost a fortune to fix the bay window, not to mention the garage doors. And the time I'm having to take off work. I'm supposed to be getting out my first big order of colour-coded hangers today. No, she should be *damn* sorry.'

He looks down at the ground and shakes his head. Then he snaps to attention and we both flinch.

'As for you,' he says, glaring at Lisa, 'well, I'm lost for words. You've written a *book* . . . *That* book. I can't believe I'm saying this . . . Today of all days . . . But this is the proudest moment of my life.'

Chapter 27

Once we're all gathered, Lewis stands on a desk and clears his throat.

'I know how worried everyone has been by the rumours of the magazine's closure,' he begins. 'Frankly, they've been more than rumours and I've spent the last few weeks trying to get us a stay of execution. I was ready to give up, but then something remarkable happened – something that I believe will guarantee a future for *Working Girl*.'

He reaches into his pocket and, with a slightly theatrical flourish, produces a cassette.

'On this tape is something that every newspaper, magazine and TV station in the country would very probably commit serious crime to get their hands on.'

He pauses to allow the tension to build – I have to admit he's rather good at this.

'I know editors are guilty of abusing the word "exclusive", but this is the real thing – a genuine, twenty-four-carat world exclusive. The first ever interview with Marsha Mellow.'

No one (well, almost no one) has seen that one coming and the room explodes. When Lewis called the staff meeting, everybody (well, almost everybody) assumed they knew what it was about and had been speculating how many more issues we'd be allowed to put out before we collected our P45s. Marsha Mellow was not on the agenda.

Lewis jumps off the desk and is immediately besieged by a backslapping throng. I look on and beam because for once something has turned out just as I daydreamed it would. If we only get one Hollywood moment in our lives, then this must be mine.

Julie, who has been standing next to me, hugs me, 'That is *so* amazing,' she squeals. 'Do you think we'll get to meet her?'

'I've no idea,' I reply. 'Anyway, I won't be around if you do.'

'I forgot, it's your last week,' she pouts. 'Why are you going just when it might be getting half decent around here?'

'Er . . . I guess my work is done,' I say. I've always wanted to use that line – shame it went straight over my audience's head.

Deedee sidles up to us and says, 'It's *such* a shame you won't be around when the mag goes mega, Amy. Still, you've seemed a little lost for a while. I suppose not everyone can hack working on a *proper* glossy. '

So good to see her back at her catty best.

'It's such a relief that the secret's out at last,' she continues.

'You knew about the interview?' Julie squeaks. 'God, how could you keep it quiet?'

'I wouldn't expect you to understand,' she says, giving Julie a crushingly superior look, 'but discretion is *key* when working for the *editor*.'

'Did you talk to her? You know, to help set it up or whatever?' Julie gabbles excitedly.

'Yes, a couple of times,' she replies.

'What's she like?' I ask – well, I just can't resist.

'Oh . . . you know,' she squirms. 'It's so hard to tell over the phone.'

'Isn't she a bit snooty,' I continue, 'you know, after all her success?'

'Um . . . a little, I suppose.'

'Where's she from, then? Does she have an accent?'

'Er . . . not really.'

'There must be a trace of something. Northern? Brummy? Irish?'

'Um . . . Er . . .'

'Welsh?'

As Deedee picks awkwardly at her nails, I realise how much I'm enjoying her pain. The sadistic streak is a new one – I guess you can't write as much as I have about S&M without something rubbing off.

'I know – the *Mail* said she's a Londoner,' I continue. 'Does she talk like me?'

'Er, no, not really. She actually sounds quite . . .' She pauses as she searches for the right word. '. . . Unassuming? Yes, that's it. Unassuming.'

I look over her shoulder at Lewis struggling through the mob. When he reaches us Julie gives him no chance to relax. 'Tell us, Lewis, tell us – what's she like?'

'Wait and see,' he says with a cool smile that masks how he's really feeling – if he had a tail, it would be wagging furiously.

'Aw, *pleeease?*' she begs.

'I'll tell you one thing.' He grins. 'She's anything but unassuming.'

'That's not what Deedee said.'

'How would she know? I never told her about it.'

As I watch Deedee climb into the grave she's just dug for herself, I'm thinking, you wait your whole life for a Hollywood moment, then two come along at once.

Chapter 28

The fly posters have been up for a week. Under the *Working Girl* masthead the headline blared WORLD EXCLU-SIVE – MARSHA MELLOW'S FIRST EVER INTERVIEW – not very clever, but it did the trick. The normal print run was trebled, but when the magazine hit the tube stations this morning, every copy was gone by eight thirty – 'I reckon we could have charged a tenner each and they'd still have disappeared,' Lewis observed.

He's done a great job with the interview. It's intelligent, balanced and extremely revealing, though not so revealing that any reader would be able to tell that he has seen his subject with her clothes off. Personally, though, I think the best thing is the photograph that goes with it. With hair by Nicky Clark and in an outfit from Donna Karan, Lisa has never looked so stunning.

Later

Day one: I sprawl like a satisfied cat on my towel, take a lazy sip of my daiquiri and, through half-closed eyes, watch the sun sink spectacularly into the Andaman Sea. The soporific afterglow of the afternoon's Thai massage is still with me, and I have all the time in the world to reflect that life is just about perfect. Further down the beach Lisa and her new boyfriend cuddle beneath a palm tree. Lisa looks how I feel – carefree, happy and madly in love. I watch a tanned figure emerge from the warm crystal water and head towards me. As he draws near, I congratulate myself on my choice of birthday present – getting Lewis the personal trainer has had unimagined benefits. He bends down to give me a lingering, salty kiss, and sits beside me on the soft white sand. 'This is just about the most idyllic place I have ever seen,' he says. 'I feel so blissed-out.'

'Me too,' I agree dreamily. 'I have never been so –'

– fucking sick in my entire life. My hand is clamped over my mouth, and I'm sprinting to the loo. For the past twenty-four hours this – dashing for the bathroom, wondering from which end it's going to spray – has been my life. The sewage system of Phuket must be close to overload by now.

Yes, I am in Phuket, Thailand's hedonistic playground. Lewis is with me, as are Lisa and New Boyfriend. It should be a dream, as per the above with knobs on.

In reality it's a bloody nightmare.

For a start, I've been sick as a dog – if I *were* a dog, the vet would've put me out of my misery hours ago. Ironically, on our first night I decided my stomach needed to acclimatise to the shock of Thai cuisine. While Lewis, Lisa and Kurt (New Boyfriend) were noisily sucking chilli-drenched lobster claws I stuck with the safe choice of a big plate of chips and a couple of tomatoes.

Ha!

I think I've finished throwing up – for now. As I rinse out my mouth, the phone rings in the bedroom. I go through to answer it. It's Deedee. Fantastic – I fly six thousand miles and I still can't escape her.

'Amy,' she trills. 'So sorry to bother you on your hols, but is Lewis around?'

'He's out snorkelling. Can I give him a message?'

'Just tell him the shots of Brad and Jen are in . . .'

Brad and *Jen* – like they live next door and she feeds their goldfish when they're away.

'. . . Ask him if he wants me to e-mail them to his laptop.'

'OK, I'll let him know. I've got to go now – I'm having my first diving lesson in a minute.'

A lie, of course, though I do have to get off the phone. I'm feeling nauseous again. The effects of the bug or of talking to Deedee? Anyone's guess really. I hang up and lie back on the bed. Lewis's laptop lies closed beside me. He didn't want to come on this holiday and he insisted I let him bring his portable office with him. All he's done since we got here is think about the job. *Working Girl* has taken over his life. The Marsha Mellow exclusive really started something. Since then celebs have spurned the usual outlets and they've been forming an orderly queue to break their stories to Lewis. Among others, Liz Hurley, Kate Winslet and two of the Kittens have been prepared to slum it alongside the job ads. Now it's *Brad* and *Jen*.

As I wait for him to return I close my eyes and drift off. Maybe I'll have an as-seen-in-a-Bounty-ad-type dream. I hope so, because I think it's the closest I'm going to get to my perfect holiday.

No chance. The phone rings again.

'Green chicken curry,' Mary recommends, once I've explained how I'm feeling. 'It'll go through you like a dose of drain cleaner, but once it's over, it is *over*. Anyway, to business. The powers at Arrow are itching for your book, my dear, and I'm running short of excuses.'

My book is the main reason I insisted we all come away. I was supposed to deliver it a month ago, but I'm stuck for an ending. I thought a change of scene might help, but I haven't been getting much inspiration from the inside of the toilet.

'Tell them I'm working on it right now and it'll be ready as soon as I get home,' I say, still in fibbing mode after Deedee.

'I hope so, my dear, I truly hope so,' Mary sighs. 'And don't you dare tell me this is writer's block because that is the lamest excuse since "Sorry, Miss, I left my gym kit at home". Anyway, here's a snippet to jolly you up. I had the strangest call yesterday. The operator asked me if I'd accept the charges from a caller in Lilongwe Prison.'

'Where?'

'It's in Malawi, precious.'

'*Jesus*. Did you speak to him?'

'Of course not. Believe me, I'm doing him a favour. A few more months on the locust and crushed root diet will do the power of good for his beer belly.'

After I've hung up I feel guilty. No, not about Colin Mount. About my new publisher. I really like Arrow. Well, I really like my editor there. She's the only one I've met, and she's sworn to keeping my identity a secret – some things never change.

Once Mary had got over the shock of me turning down Jacobson (it took her all of five minutes), she threw herself into finding another publisher. In the end, four of them were bidding for me. Mary was in her element. 'I wish you'd told that slimy scum sucker to bog off ages ago,' she said. 'I *adore* a juicy auction.' Arrow won, paying £1·5 million for my next three books.

One point five million!

I'm a fucking millionaire!

Unbelievable, amazing and staggering.

The only problem is that I now feel unbelievably, amazingly and staggeringly guilty because I'm stuck. I'm going to be sick again. Is it the bug or the pressure? No time to think about it – *here it comes.*

Day three: I'm feeling well enough to venture out of our hotel. We're on the main drag and this is not what any of us expected. Last night the US Navy arrived. So too, it seems, did every hooker in Thailand. We can't move for strapping American sailors and their new companions – two each, one for each arm.

'Yanks love to bloody show off,' snarls Kurt.

'It wasn't like this in the brochure,' moans Lewis.

'Well, I think it's fantastic,' exclaims Lisa. 'All these hookers – they're great research material.'

'But you don't even –' Lewis protests, but cuts himself off because Kurt isn't in on the secret.

'I have to immerse myself in the whole scene, Lewis,' she says. 'You wouldn't understand. You're not an author.'

She takes Kurt by the hand and drags him off to the nearest heaving bar.

Poor Kurt.

What am I saying?

He's been doing plenty of his own immersing-himself-in-the-scene these past few days. We've barely seen him. It wouldn't surprise me if he's been doing some buying of . . . er . . . *local produce*. (Mental memo: check suitcases thoroughly for unusual items before departure.) Kurt isn't, by the way, the owner of the lap dancing club. That one only lasted ten minutes. Lisa being Lisa, she had plenty of offers when he bit the dust. The weirdest was from Jake Bedford. He called her up and suggested dinner, saying along the way 'It's sad about Amy, but it wasn't going to work – not being a writer she couldn't connect with me on the . . . *ah* . . . *creative* level.' Lisa said she couldn't hear the rest for laughing.

In the end she settled on Kurt. Not sure what he does. He claims he's trying to get off the ground as a DJ, but he won't look you in the eye when he says it so it could mean anything. This is the first full day that Lisa has spent with him, but she doesn't appear to mind. He's shifty, disreputable and completely charming when he wants something – basically, her type to a T.

Anyway, she's been far too busy to notice his absence. She takes her duties as the public face of the Marsha Mellow Corporation very seriously and they don't stop simply because she's on holiday.

Since *Working Girl*, she's done countless magazine interviews. She's also appeared on *Parkinson*, *Friday Night with Jonathan Ross* and *V Graham Norton*. And then there have been the meetings in Hollywood. I sold the film rights to *Rings on Her Fingers*. (I can't say how much – it's embarrassing.) The producers were talking about Sarah Michelle Gellar and J-Lo for the part of Donna, but when they met Lisa one of them had a brainwave.

'Babe, can you act as well as write?' he asked.

Nothing's certain, of course, but who knows? She flies

off for a screen test next month and, well, stranger things have happened lately.

Poor Mum. She hasn't even begun to come to terms with Lisa writing *That Book*. What if she has to deal with her daughter taking off her clothes and simulating deviant sex for the camera? Somehow I don't think the old the-integrity-of-the-script-demands-it argument will cut much ice. But Lisa is Marsha Mellow now and one way or another Mum will have to learn to live with it.

It honestly doesn't bother me to admit that she makes a far better Marsha than I ever would. We're well and truly in this together – the fact is that we were from the moment she took it upon herself to send my first type-script off to Mary. I couldn't do half the things she does in the name of publicity and she's the first to admit she struggles to write a postcard. We're a pretty good team. She gets to strut her stunning stuff and I get what I've always wanted – a quiet life.

Day six: Lewis and I are relaxing in a bar by the beach. No Kurt. Again. Lisa came with us, but she disappeared to the shop across the street to buy postcards (that I'll probably have to ghost-write for her). On the way back she was accosted by a bunch of sailors who recognised her. She's entertaining them with tales of how she researched the daisy chain chapter in *Rings*. Not surpris-ingly for men who've spent several weeks at sea, they're hanging on her every word.

Lisa tears herself away from her fans and rejoins us. She sits down and hands me a postcard. 'Do you want to send this one to Mum and Dad?' she asks. I look at the picture of a pair of pendulous naked breasts above the words *Having Phun in Phuket*.

Yeah, right.

Possibly the day will come when the Bickerstaffs are

once again a happy-ish semi-dysfunctional family, but it's way, way off. Mum won't speak to Lisa and she's hardly any warmer with me. And I can only deal with her because whenever she steps out of line I have three plant-related words to keep her in her box.

The new, improved Dad is managing to keep a lid on her worst excesses – no fresh acts of mindless vandalism to report. The whole saga seems to have given him the courage to stand up to her. There are a lot more rows at their house these days, but he seems determined to drag her round or die in the attempt. I think much of his bravery comes from his pride in his author daughter. He can't stop talking about her – I was with him in Finchley High Road and he dragged me into Waterstone's so he could hang around the display and say 'I'm her father, you know' to anyone who picked up the book. He can't bring himself to actually *read* it, but that doesn't stop him arguing forcefully that it's a major literary achievement. Mum, though, still thinks it should be pulped, probably along with its writer.

Hey, maybe if we'd brought them on this holiday it would've helped the healing process.

Joking!

The sight of so many prostitutes and pole-dancing bars would've sent Mum permanently over the edge. Anyway, she couldn't have come even if she'd wanted to. She's not allowed to travel abroad until she's finished her sentence. She was charged with criminal damage and the magistrate gave her a fine and a hundred hours' community service. He was quite imaginative about it as well. She has to help out at a gay counselling centre. Right now I should think she's stuffing envelopes with safe sex leaflets.

When I phoned Ant and told him I could hear the laughter clear across the Atlantic. He and Alex are back on track now. Not exactly love's young dream by the sound of it, but Ant *has* reformed. A bit. At least he's sworn to keep his affairs (a) strictly male and (b) under double figures in any one calendar month.

Day seven: Lisa has returned from a shopping trip. We're in her bedroom going through her purchases.

'Look at this,' she says, holding up a pretty beige handbag. 'It'd cost a fortune at home, but it was only seven hundred baht – that's like . . .' she pauses to do the arithmetic. '. . . a tenner.'

She opens it and scrutinises the label.

'Hang on. One or two Ns in Chanel?'

I burst out laughing. Maybe there's hope for this holiday after all.

Day nine: Lewis is in our room – his turn for the tummy bug. Lisa is out schmoozing her public. Kurt has decided to take a day off from whatever it is he gets up to and is tagging along behind. Every Westerner in Phuket seems to have recognised her and she hasn't had to buy a drink all week.

I'm sitting alone at the hotel bar. I'm quite happy, though. I've nicked Lewis's laptop and I'm furiously writing the final chapter of the new Marsha Mellow. The American sailors and busloads of hookers couldn't help but inspire me. It's going to be the best Mellow yet – OK, it's only the second. It'll be the filthiest, anyway.

I'd have finished it ages ago if it weren't for the constant interruptions. Here comes another one now – an Aussie backpacker who was hanging around Lisa earlier.

'Excuse me,' she says timidly, 'aren't you Marsha Mellow's sister?'

'Yes,' I answer proudly, 'I am.'

*

Day twelve: I sprawl like a satisfied cat on my towel, take a lazy sip of my daiquiri and, through half-closed eyes, watch the sun sink spectacularly into the Andaman Sea. The soporific afterglow of the afternoon's Thai massage is still with me, and I have all the time in the world to reflect that life is just about perfect. Further down the beach Lisa and Kurt frolic beneath a palm tree. They look so happy – though did she really have to hit him that hard? I watch a tanned figure emerge from the warm crystal water and head towards me. I look at his body and wonder if he'd like a personal trainer for his birthday or would he see it as a cheap shot at revenge after the quit-smoking hypnotherapy he signed me up with for mine? He bends down to give me a lingering, salty kiss and sits beside me on the soft white sand. 'You looked miles away,' he says. 'Daydreaming again?'

'Not this time,' I reply.